A
Christmas
Wedding

ANDREW M. GREELEY

A Christmas Wedding

A TOM DOHERTY ASSOCIATES BOOK

New York

A CHRISTMAS WEDDING

This book is printed on acid-free paper.

A Forge Book
Published by Tom Doherty Associates, LLC
175 Fifth Avenue
New York, NY 10010

www.tor.com

Forge® is a registered trademark of Tom Doherty
Associates, LLC.

Library of Congress Cataloging-in-Publication Data

Greeley, Andrew M.
    A Christmas wedding / Andrew M. Greeley.—1st ed.
        p. cm.
    "A Tom Doherty Associates book."
    ISBN 0-312-87224-0
    1. Irish American families—Fiction. 2. College students—Fiction. 3. Chicago
(Ill.)—Fiction. 4. Young men—Fiction. I. Title.

PS3557.R358 C47 2000
813'.54—dc21

                                                                                00-031652

First Edition: October 2000

Printed in the United States of America

0 9 8 7 6 5 4 3 2 1

For those who grew up in St. Angela
during the Depression and the War

CLANCY (Powers), Clarice Marie. Beloved wife of James Patrick, mother of Rosemarie, daughter of the late Helen (McArdle) and Joseph Powers, M.D. Suddenly. Visitation Wednesday and Thursday at Conroy's Funeral Home 420 North Austin. Funeral Mass at 9:30 Friday to St. Ursula's. Internment at Mount Carmel Cemetery. Please omit flowers.

❦

WOMAN'S DEATH RULED AN ACCIDENT

The Cook County Coroner's office ruled late yesterday that the death of Clarice Powers Clancy, 40, last Tuesday was an accident. Mrs. Clancy, wife of investor James P. Clancy, died as a result of injuries incurred in a fall at her home at 1105 North Menard. Assistant Coroner Joel Starr said that Mrs. Clancy apparently tripped on the hem of her dressing gown and fell down the steps, hitting her head on the concrete floor of the basement. Death resulted from a fractured skull and brain injuries. "There is no evidence of any foul play," Mr. Starr said.

Police are known to have questioned Mr. Clancy and the couple's daughter, Rosemarie Helen Clancy. Rosemarie, a student at Trinity High School in River Forest, and a friend discovered Mrs. Clancy's body.

"It was a tragic and unnecessary accident," Mr. Starr told the *Tribune*.

Prologue

"This marriage is a mistake," the shivering woman said to me. "You should cancel it while you still have a chance."

Surrounded by banks of newly shoveled snow, we were huddled in the dark at the entrance of the new white stone St. Ursula Church, which loomed above us like a doubtfully brooding angel. The rest of the wedding party had left with cheerful promises that the warmth of Nuptial Mass and the banquet at Butterfield Country Club and the subsequent marriage bed would exorcise the subzero cold.

The rehearsal itself had been a giddy slapstick comedy, with bride and groom both—the groom more than the bride—nervous about the change that was about to occur in our lives. I assumed responsibility for making everyone laugh, a familiar enough task.

"Father Raven," I had said at the beginning of the rehearsal to our wise and handsome assistant pastor, "weren't you the one that said that it would be a cold day in hell when I married this woman?"

General laughter, despite a gentle reproof from my mother.

"You will sleep in a warm bed tomorrow night," my younger sister had whispered, a suggestive comment that was most unlike her. Never one to miss a chance to reply, I had observed that a couple of extra blankets would serve just as well.

Now the woman wanted to call it off. Or rather she wanted me to call it off. I might have to resort to those extra blankets. On the whole, I preferred a woman to blankets—though not necessarily tomorrow night.

"What do you mean, I should cancel the wedding?" I demanded through chattering teeth. "If you want to call it off, go ahead."

One part of me did want to call it off. I was much too young to marry. We both were too young, weren't we? I would wake up in that warm bed the next morning a husband, with a wife in bed next to me. Wasn't I too young to have a wife?

I had some small knowledge of the physiology of a woman, much less of the psychology. I was no more ignorant than other men my age who were rushing into youthful marriages. Unfortunately for me, perhaps, I was aware of my ignorance. I had enough problems in life without adding a wife to my list of worries. Why couldn't I just settle down and be an Irish bachelor, a crotchety old Irish bachelor?

Across Massasoit Avenue, Christmas tree lights glowed faintly in several of the bungalow windows, a reassurance that goodness flourished somewhere in our neighborhood, if I wanted such reassurance.

"I'll be nothing but trouble," the woman insisted. "You know that. My father is a monster, my mother died in dubious circumstances. I drink too much. You're marrying into sickness."

That was a vivid way of putting it. I was about to marry into a stench of vomit and alcohol, a cacophony of curses and sobbing, a sloppy emotional mess like a women's washroom in a madhouse.

She had also finally admitted that there was a mystery about her mother's death. Did I want to marry into a police investigation, a ticking bomb that might explode when I least expected it?

Nonetheless I said, lamely, I admit, "That overstates the problem."

Her head averted, her body wracked with shuddering, she continued her argument. "You go around saving people in trouble. You're very good at it. Don't waste your time on me. I'm doomed. I'm not worth saving."

"I don't think so," I said, with an attempt at manliness.

"I don't want your help," she said bitterly. "Anyway, I seduced you into this marriage. You should get out of it while you still can."

Had I been seduced? If I had, I had been a willing victim.

She was not weeping yet. Rather she spoke with the icy detachment of a woman who thought she was damned.

My family would be embarrassed. Or would they? During the weeks of wedding preparation they had seemed uneasy, as if a stealthy germ had infected their joy over a marriage they had long anticipated. Besides, my mother was convinced that anything her firstborn son did was wise and good. Well, almost anything. Would they sigh with relief if I went home and told them that my bride-to-be and I had decided to cancel the whole thing?

We were much too young to marry, were we not?

Yes, we certainly were.

"I appreciate what you're doing," she continued, her face a dim blur in the faint street light. "It just won't work. Besides, we're too young to marry."

"If you don't want to marry me," I said, trying to sound reasonable, "then just tell me that and we'll call it all off."

"But I do want to marry you!" she cried. "I just don't want to ruin your life!"

Life was a long time.

"You know me," she continued, "I have a vile temper and I cling to my rages and I have a terrible tongue."

"Vile," I corrected her. " 'Terrible' is too generic."

We laughed together. Some of our friends said that we were at ease with each other like a man and a woman who had lived together for years. "One of the advantages of incest," I had replied brightly, "is that you know the bride pretty well before you bed her."

She had been a kind of foster sister for as long as I could remember. We knew a lot about each other—enough to understand how little we actually knew. Still, we could put on a good act, harmonizing our dialogue as we did our duets, she the soprano and I the Irish whiskey tenor who didn't drink whiskey.

"I love you too much to marry you," she said, sniffling. "But if you are dumb enough to want me, then you can have me. Only please don't."

The argument was typical of her. Did she really want to cancel our wedding or was she trying to calm her conscience? Or both?

"Please don't do what I want? Many a husband would love to hear those words!"

She didn't laugh this time, harmony off-key.

"I'm serious!" she snapped.

She was certainly afraid of hurting me. That was typical too. Beneath her rage was a paralyzing tenderness, so sweet as to break your heart with pleasure if you were fortunate enough to be its target.

All I had to say was, "Let's postpone it for a while. Give ourselves time to mature and understand a little bit more about life."

How much time? Twenty years maybe?

"More time," would have been the perfect answer. We would go back to the house on East Avenue in Oak Park and tell my family that we had made a sensible, rational, adult decision.

The only problem was lust. Or desire. Or maybe love. Maybe. At twenty-two, do you know the difference?

She had used the magic word—"want." Did I want her? When had I not wanted her? Even when we both were too young to know what wanting another human being meant I had wanted her, though I did my best to pretend that she was just an obnoxious pest, which she often was. I hadn't known in those days what wanting was, save that it was a need to possess. Now I would add "the need to be possessed," as an elderly Jesuit had put it at a dinner party up in Lake Forest. That night in the passionless ivory shadow of the new St. Ursula's, I wanted desperately to possess this woman for whom I had yearned so long. I was uneasy about the need to perform in the marriage bed the following night, but I wanted with more hunger than I had ever known to make that lovely body my own.

Love?

Did that enter into the calculation at all?

Maybe it did. In the frigid wind that attacked the gothic pile of St. Ursula's and then bounced back to hit us a second time, fear dominated the equation.

I was a careful and circumspect young man, a prudent accountant in the making. My prospective bride was perhaps correct. Beautiful young woman that she was, she could easily ruin my life. That was the long run. In the short run she would be a luscious bedmate.

No insurance for long-run failure? Was I going long, as they said at the Board of Trade, in what might be a buyer's market?

There was not the slightest doubt what a careful investor ought to do.

1950

— 1 —

"What about the Buddhists, Father Danielou?" Rosemarie asked.

The short French Jesuit in the black turtleneck sweater blinked through his thick glasses like a cheerful rabbit and then sped off in a whirlwind of barely intelligible English.

I was in my final year at the University of Chicago. Rosemarie Helen Clancy, my quasi–foster sister, was in her second year. She expected me to listen to a lecture by this intense and slightly mysterious young priest. My attention wavered. I stole another look at our hostess, attentive and professional in her light gray sweater and dark blue skirt. Looking at Rosemarie, as I had told John Raven, was a proximate occasion of sin. He had dismissed this observation with a laugh. I thereupon added that I had reached such an advanced stage of carnality that I could not prevent my imagination from taking off her clothes.

"Good for you," he had said, "so long as you do it respectfully."

"My life would be in danger if I did it any other way."

So, more than a little bored by the French Jesuit, I permitted myself to undress her mentally, albeit respectfully—whatever that meant. To honor respect I forced my lascivious imagination to appreciate her fully clothed before it embarked on its exploration.

"She has the look of the little people about her, poor sweet little thing," my mother had once said. "Even if there are no little people. She's the sort of faerie sprite you might see dancing over the bog of a spring night under a quarter moon."

"She is indeed," my father had agreed, as he usually did.

"When has either of you been out dancing on the bog of a spring night under a quarter moon?" I had demanded.

"Why must you always be so literal, Chucky darling?" my mom asked, exasperated as she always was when the issue was my (feigned) indifference to Rosemarie.

The image was apt, however. Rosemarie combined fragility, delicacy, and beauty in a fashion that might be appropriate for a faerie sprite—so long as that sprite was tough enough to play a mean and wicked game of tennis.

"Maybe what you mean," I said, with the sigh of one much put-upon, "is that, in her better moments, Rosemarie appears light and graceful, delicate and strong, not unlike Peter Pan's Wendy perhaps."

"Isn't that what I said, dear?"

She was slim and slender, maybe five feet six inches tall (dangerously close to my generously estimated five eight), with trim and elegant breasts that caught every male eye (my own obviously included) and shapely legs that the said male eye noticed immediately after her breasts. Her long black hair framed a pale face that tended to flush red in moments of excitement or enthusiasm or anger. That face compelled your attention if your hormones let you get that far; it was the kind of face that might have emerged from the Pre-Raphaelites if any of them had painted from an Irish model. The flush was usually accompanied by the flashing of her blue eyes that signaled danger. A sprite surely, but one with a fierce temper and deep passions and also one whose fragility could break your heart. You wanted to kiss and caress her and at the same time protect her.

As the Jesuit droned on I pursued my exploration of the faerie sprite, slowly and with appreciation and, I hope in retrospect, some measure of reverence. First the sweater, then the blouse under it, button by button, then the skirt, zipped down in the back, then the slip, and then, with infinite gentleness, the bra. I paused at the girdle and its attached nylons. It would not be respectful, I told myself, to go any farther in a Catholic student meeting. Maybe tonight in my dreams.

Nonetheless, I paused to admire my work and then noticed that she was frowning at me. My glazed eyes might have suggested that I was not paying any attention to the speaker. Did she know what my imagination had been doing? Since she never protested my wantonness, she either did not know or did not mind.

I tried once again to focus on Père Danielou.

There were lines of fatigue around Rosemarie's eyes, the result of a hangover, which in turn had been the result of a another one of her wild drinking bouts the night before. The second one that I knew about since she'd been a student at the University.

She had seemed relaxed and peaceful as she filled up the glasses and passed the potato chips to her guests; whatever demons had possessed her the night before had been temporarily exorcised.

"I'm sorry," she had whispered in my ear earlier in the evening as we left Calvert House, the University Catholic center, to walk through the blizzard to her apartment on Kenwood just south of Fifty-fifth Street. "I goofed up again. Thank you for dragging me home."

A kid who was in my econ class had phoned me the night before.

"O'Malley? I knew you lived in Oak Park. Hey, that woman with the gorgeous teats you study with in Harper? Well, I was in Knight's bar until a few minutes ago. She's drinking a lot. Shouting and arguing with people. That's not safe for a woman in that bar, know what I mean?"

"Thanks, Howard, I'll be right out."

There were no expressways in Chicago in those days, so the ride from Oak Park to Hyde Park required forty-five minutes.

Rosemarie, sound asleep and smelling like a brewery, was behind the bar. Her clothes were disheveled.

"I didn't know what to do with her," the soft-spoken bartender told me. "A guy said he was going to call her boyfriend, a tough little redhead, he said. That you?"

"My twin brother."

He paused and then laughed. "She's a real looker. You shouldn't let her come in this place alone."

"Ever try to argue with an Irishwoman?"

He laughed again.

I woke her up, found her coat, pushed her arms into it, and dragged her back to her apartment. I helped her to remove her dress, dumped her into bed, and pulled the blanket over her.

"Chucky, you're an asshole," she murmured as I turned out the lights.

"At least you know who it was that took off your dress."

"A real asshole." Her voice was slurred. "Why didn't you leave me in the bar?"

"That's a very good question."

When she thanked me the following night, she was properly contrite. I'm sure she didn't remember the use of language that was strictly forbidden in the O'Malley house.

"I'm glad I was there," I said fervently. If I hadn't found her in the bar on Fifty-fifth, she might have been there all night or collapsed in the snow on the way home. Rosemarie needed a keeper all right, only it shouldn't be me.

"You didn't take my slip off this time." She nudged my arm.

It was the first reference she had ever made to the incident at Lake Geneva when I had pulled her in her prom dress out of the water.

"Dress and shoes seemed to be enough for the occasion. I'll admit that the possibility of a more thorough investigation did occur to me."

"You're wonderful, Chucky." This time she squeezed my arm. "Simply wonderful."

"Why, Rosemarie?"

"Why do I do things like last night?"

"Yes."

"I'm not sure. I become discouraged and I don't care . . . but I won't do it again. I promise."

I didn't quite believe her, but I didn't know what to say.

So the next night I tried to focus my imagination away from the delightful difficulties of trying to unzip and remove a dress from an inebriated young woman and to concentrate on Father Jean Danielou, of the Institut Catholique de Paris, and the question of the relationship between Jesus and Buddha. On the whole, the former images were much more appealing.

Jesus and Buddha, the priest seemed to be saying, were both allies and enemies. The reconciliation between the two could never be pursued so long as the Catholic tradition was tied to the Thomistic paradigm. But in the study of ancient Church fathers, there could be found much material for conversation with Buddhists. The New Theology, La Théologie Nouvelle, which had emerged in Europe since the war, would make possible conversation not only with Buddhism but with all the world religions and the non-religions like Marxism too.

He referred to one of his papers, "La Theologie Nouvelle, où vat elle?"

I remembered one of the members of the Greenwood Community telling me earlier in the evening that Père Danielou's brother René Danielou was a convert from Catholicism to Buddhism. All this was very heady stuff for a reject of the University of Notre Dame who had left the Catholic Church—to hear him tell it anyway.

Ironically, Père Danielou was teaching at Notre Dame—where I had never heard of him. (My buddy, Christopher Kurtz, insisted that he had mentioned him often but that I did not listen because I was prejudiced against anyone without an Irish name.)

Catholic intellectual ferment had exploded at the University of Chicago after the war, as the first generation of post war Catholic graduate students had appeared—indeed the first generation of Catholics to seek academic careers in substantial numbers. The Church was not ready for an intelligentsia where there had hitherto been none. But the Catholic chaplains at the University were clever enough to give the young intellectuals and would-be intellectuals enough room to do what would later be called "their own thing."

And occasionally to invite one of their heroes to lecture.

Père Danielou didn't look like a hero, but he wasn't gratuitously rude and insulting to Americans, as a matter of principle, as some of the French "religious sociologists" of that era were—men profoundly shocked and affronted by the religious devotion of American Catholics. "Sacrilege!" one had exploded after describing the hordes of men receiving Communion at

Holy Souls parish just south of the University on Holy Name Sunday. In the presence of such men, I shut up and indulged myself in snide thoughts, which Rosemarie had briskly dismissed: "Irish Catholic anti-intellectualism, Charles. You know better than that."

"But I am an Irish Catholic anti-intellectual!"

"No, you're not! You're the smartest one in the group. You just have to pretend that you're a dumb accountant."

I hung around the intellectuals and their arrogant French friends because Rosemarie did, and because I thought their pretensions were funny. I also objected—though to myself—that they seemed immune to her beauty.

Père Danielou, however, even smiled at Rosemarie, having noticed, unlike the religious sociologists, that she was a) a woman, and b) a beautiful woman. He could not, I figured, be all bad.

Our concerns in the gatherings, either at the apartment of the Greenwood Community (on Greenwood, of course) or at Rosemarie's apartment, were vague, intense, disorganized, and, from the viewpoint of later years, shallow. We had written to Cardinal Stritch asking for Mass on Saturday afternoon so that "workers" could attend. The workers' cause was our cause, whoever the workers might be—in this case policemen, firemen, hospital workers, public transportation employees. The Cardinal had replied, somewhat haughtily, that since the time of Pliny the Younger mass had taken place in the morning. The response, my angry friends had sputtered, was both inaccurate and irrelevant.

We worried about evolution: not whether it had occurred, but how the Church's teaching on original sin could be reconciled with the conviction of archaeologists that the race could not have descended from a single pair.

We damned Thomism on the grounds that Aristotelian philosophy was not compatible with modern science.

We were furious that Monsignor Fulton Sheen had denounced Freud. I kind of liked the good Monsignor, who had preached at St. Ursula's once.

We feared that many young people would be lost to the Church unless Catholic scripture teaching was modified to take into account what Bultmann had taught about the process of "demythologizing." I didn't know from either Bultmann or "demythologizing" but they both sounded dreadful.

We quoted the great men like Tillich and Barth as though they were personal friends, though I doubt that any of us had read them—or Bultmann either, for that matter.

We were all profoundly concerned, so concerned in fact, that we forgot to comb our hair or do the dishes or take out the garbage. We were all vehemently anticlerical but most of us went to Mass every week and some every day.

(I didn't go at all. Our hostess, on the other hand, still not sure about God, was to be found in the Calvert House chapel every morning. Still, as she told me with her contagious laugh, "to whom it may concern.")

We denied the importance of authority and did our best to win the local priests, the Cardinal, and the Vatican to our point of view.

We were all committed Catholics; we had made the decision that our Catholic heritage was compatible with our intellectual concerns. (I exclude myself from "we" because I was still furious at the Catholic Church. Some of the most wide-eyed of the intellectual radicals urged me to forget about my hurt feelings and "join the team.")

There were lots of ironies in the fire.

Driving back and forth between Oak Park and Hyde Park every day in my 1942 Ford, I would never have stumbled on this group of intense young intellectuals if it had not been for Rosemarie, who during our first quarter at Chicago had dragged me off to the Calvert House lectures.

The lectures were a brief respite from study. I had never studied so hard in all my life and never been so pushed to the limits of my capabilities. I was also working part-time downtown in the accounting office of O'Hanlon and O'Halloran at the Conway Building across from City Hall.

"Have you ever just not done anything?" Rosemarie demanded. She was offended by my midafternoon rush to the Loop on the Illinois Central (a ten-minute trip from Fifty-ninth Street).

"I wouldn't know how."

"You ought to."

There were many other "ought tos." I ought to work more with my camera. I ought to go to church again, because I would do that eventually anyway. I ought to join her at her voice lessons. I ought to rent an apartment instead of commuting in my "funny little car" or, on days I worked, riding on the El and the I.C.

I paid no attention. Indeed, if Rosemarie said I ought to do something, her suggestion in itself seemed enough reason not to do it.

How did she become involved with the young Catholic intellectuals? It was a most improbable alliance. She was a well-groomed, flawlessly dressed rich girl among a group who resented wealth and tried to affect a Bohemian style of life.

She'd met them at the Calvert Club and simply hung around. Her good looks probably would not have made much difference to the Greenwood Group, and they would have been reluctant to use her apartment and her money, but she was also very smart, so bright in fact that many people on the fringes of the group thought she was a graduate student in "the humanities."

You couldn't quite figure out where she stood politically, or religiously, or intellectually by her questions, but you could tell that she had a first-class mind.

"Père Danielou, what do you think the Church in Europe might learn from the Church in America?"

It was a heretical question. We were to learn from Europe, especially from France, instead of vice versa.

The Jesuit smiled gently. "A number of important things. But what, mademoiselle, would you suggest we might learn?"

"Enthusiasm, maybe, and pragmatism, and closeness between priests and people?"

"Excellent," he applauded her. "And your wonderful openness and hope for the future."

Rosemarie blushed happily. Some of the others in the room beamed. They thought she was special, obviously, and were proud of her.

Just like my mother.

"She is such a darling, sweet little thing, Chucky. You're a perfect match. She's so simple and you're so complicated."

Me, complicated? Nonsense!

There was a final question for Père Danielou: What will happen if Rome condemns La Théologie Nouvelle?

"We must have the integrity to continue to do our work no matter what happens," he said with a grim little smile, "otherwise nothing will ever change in the Church."

In 1950 the Vatican condemned the New Theology. Although no names were mentioned, Père Danielou and several others were transferred and forced out of the classroom. Later the New Theologians were rehabilitated and became influential at the Second Vatican Council. Danielou, however, learned the lesson of ecclesiastical politics and managed to ally himself with the conservatives in the Church. He ended up a cardinal, though a conservative, not to say reactionary one. He died outside a disorderly house, and rumors said he had actually been inside. His friends argued that he preached to the poor unfortunate prostitutes of Paris. Yet I could not forget that cold winter night in 1950 when he had smiled at Rosemarie.

About eleven-thirty, the session ended. The French Jesuit was escorted back to Calvert House, and the members of the Greenwood Community trudged off in the falling snow toward their apartment building.

No one offered to help Rosemarie clean up. As usual, I stayed after the others to help remove the glasses and the empty bags of potato chips, and to vacuum the carpet. Her apartment was small and frequently chaotic, but it was expensively furnished and carpeted. I knew that if I didn't designate myself as the clean-up brigade, Rosemarie would let the job go till the morning and possibly the morning after that.

"Chucky," she would say to me, "unlike you, I can sleep at night if the apartment is a mess. I'll clean it up eventually."

"I learned my housekeeping habits from the good April."

We would both laugh because my mother was, to put it mildly, relaxed in her approach to housekeeping.

We were perhaps potential lovers, though both of us would vigorously deny it. We were friends, a much more relaxed and, I told myself, safer alliance. Rosemarie dated others, often Ed Murray, my old-time football rival from Mount Carmel, and I of course dated no one.

Sometimes Rosemarie dragged me back to her apartment for hamburgers or sandwiches and an occasional fruit salad. "You'll die if you eat that University food or Jimmy's hamburgers all the time."

"It's no worse than what they fed us at the Dome."

"And look what happen to you there, storing beer under the bed, of all things."

I had been thrown out on that charge, though I didn't drink beer or anything else, and had been framed.

Sometimes we were very serious, even personal. She more than I.

"Daddy put all that property and money in Mommy's name so that if he was ever in trouble at the Exchange they wouldn't be able to take it away from him."

"Unable to meet his margin calls."

"Whatever. Anyway, she hated him so much before she died that she made a will and left it all to me in such a way that he couldn't touch any of the property. Or the bank accounts. He's furious. Mr. O'Laughlin, Daddy's lawyer, is after me all the time about it."

Since shortly before the Flood, I think, Joe O'Laughlin had enjoyed the reputation of being the most dishonest lawyer on the West Side, a perfect legal adviser for Jim Clancy.

"Will you sign it all over to him, then?" We were talking in whispers since we were in a library reading room. I couldn't remember how we had entered this strange conversation.

"I'm not sure. What do you think I ought to do? Mommy wanted me to have it all."

"Was it hers to give? I mean, he really owned all those buildings, didn't he? It was just a legal fiction."

"Was it, Chuck?" she tapped a pencil against her lips. "Dad used her money to begin his investments at the Exchange after his mother died. She said that was the only reason he married her."

Small wonder that the young woman was a little crazy.

"Do you hate your father?"

She stared up at the ceiling of Harper Library. "He's so lonely and unhappy."

"You don't live at home because of the fight over your mother's will?"

"It's not a fight exactly. I mean, we're not enemies because of it. I think he did love her and didn't know how to express it. Wouldn't that be terrible?"

I agreed that it would. And hoped that she would change the subject. I did, however, manage to touch her hand sympathetically.

"Stop distracting me," she said, grinning, "and get back to your Pascal."

I hated Jim Clancy. When I was a kid, he took me out in a sailboat on Lake Geneva and deliberately got me seasick. Then, after I had vomited over the side of the boat at the Clancy pier, he shoved a chocolate ice-cream bar at my face. I vomited again, unfortunately missing him.

"He has always liked his little practical jokes," my mom sighed, "poor man. First one, then, your guard is down, another."

"Once, at Twin Lakes," my father added, "he set off the fire alarm. Then when the firemen had gone back to Walworth, he threw stink bombs into two of the washrooms and started real fires."

"Very funny," I commented.

I had hated him because he was rich. Now I had another reason to hate him.

I returned to the agonized, contorted, ecstatic reflections of that great, God-haunted man. Out of the corner of my eye I noted that Rosemarie was still staring at the ceiling. Still wrestling with a puzzle, I thought.

And I don't want to know what it is.

I was troubled by the mystery surrounding her mother's death when I was away in the Army, in Europe. My parents and sisters, normally immune to secrecy, refused to discuss the matter when I asked direct questions, and they avoided any hints when I tried to approach it indirectly.

"Mrs. Clancy's death must have been a terrible shock to Rosemarie?"

"Rosie is a pretty tough young woman," my dad would answer, not even looking up from his copy of the Chicago *Sun*.

There had been, I learned from press clippings, a police investigation and a coroner's report that Mrs. Clancy had died an "accidental" death from an unfortunate fall down the stairs into the basement of the Clancy home at 1105 North Menard.

Pushed down the stairs? By her husband? By Rosemarie? Drunk?

It was none of my business. Yet I remembered hearing her sob in St. Ursula's late one night. Life in that family would drive anyone to drink.

Whatever had happened, she was still admired—no, adored—in the O'Malley family. Yet despite my mother's blunt if clichéd comment about felines and curiosity, I wanted more details. I never asked Rosemarie about the accident. That would have been gratuitously cruel.

We joked that we would be incompatible marriage partners. Rosemarie was a morning person. She bounded out of bed with full-steam energy. The eight-thirty class was her favorite of the day. I on the other hand did not join the human race (her words) till ten-fifteen.

I flourished at midday, when Rosemarie began to think of a nap. And I crashed early in the evening, when she had acquired her second wind.

"It wouldn't work, Chuck. Our schedules would be so different that we'd never produce children."

"You're absolutely right."

But even in my groggy, early-morning daze, she still seemed gorgeous, a potential bed partner who would be attractive at all hours of the day.

And if Mom's snapshots of Rosemarie's grandmother were any basis for judgment, at all the times of her life.

"Rosie has such fine facial bones, Chucky dear, and a naturally splendid figure. If she takes care of herself, she'll be lovely all her life."

"Did her grandmother drink too much?"

"Not at all," Mom replied, ignoring the implication of my question, as she frequently did. "Neither did her mother until after she married."

Then the good April added one of her non sequitur comments that only seemed irrelevant. "Most women would die to have a waist that slim."

"Skinny, emaciated," I replied.

Mom and Dad both chuckled. I had indeed protested too much and thus admitted my interest in Rosemarie's body. I'd have to be more careful.

"Well, the poor little thing could use five or six more pounds."

"More like ten."

"And maybe that would slow her down on the tennis court, huh, Chucky?" my father asked, with no respect for his son's mediocre athletic ability.

"Well," I said, deliberately trying to shock, "she sure has great teats!"

The good April, whom I had expected to reprove me for my language, only sighed and said, "I'm surprised you noticed, dear."

Would Rosemarie be as attractive in her middle forties as the good April? And as sexually appealing as the good April was to my father?

Such questions, I warned myself sternly, were not appropriate. You'll mess up something good if you even think about them. Naturally, I thought about them all the time. In Bamberg I'd had a lover, a young woman I had planned to bring home as my wife. She disappeared after I had saved her and her mother and sister from the Ruskies, who would have raped them to death. I had never found her. I had learned from her, however, the pleasures of sexual love. A least I thought it was love. It was certainly pleasurable. Trudi had been a straightforward young woman, fighting to stay alive. Our affair, if it could be called that, was straightforward, uncomplicated. Rosemarie was much more problematic.

What would happen if they ever met? Thank God there wasn't much chance of that ever happening.

Rosemarie was a good friend, loyal and helpful. I enjoyed being with her and she seemed to enjoy mothering me. We were not suited to be lovers, I insisted mentally, but we might well be lifelong friends.

We even went to an occasional film in the early evening, and during the seasons to the opera and the symphony. We did not hold hands. People do that on dates, you see, but we were two friends watching a movie or an opera together, not a couple on a date.

Was I kidding myself? Of course.

Did I realize I was kidding myself?

To tell the truth, I can't remember. Not that it mattered.

We saw Eliot's *Murder in the Cathedral* and agreed that the last temptation was indeed the greatest treason, to do the right thing for the wrong reason.

Neither of us thought that we might ever do that in our lives.

And we saw Christopher Fry's *The Lady's Not for Burning* and argued about whether Rosemarie was like the heroine, I taking the affirmative position and she the negative.

"I'm not that smart."

"You are too."

"Or that good."

"Better."

(Storm clouds gathering). "Don't say dumb things, Chucky, when you don't know what you're talking about."

We listened in awe to Fry's *A Sleep of Prisoners* on tape and agreed that we thanked God that our time was now, when the enterprise was exploration into God.

We didn't know what that meant.

There were no romantic exchanges between me and Rosemarie at that point. In fact, we avoided touching as though it would transmit an infectious disease. Both of us were satisfied with our friendship and did not want to risk endangering it with romance.

At least that's how I reasoned, though it's clear from the way I write about her today that she had become an obsession, a delightful and mysterious obsession. I had no idea how Rosemarie viewed the matter. Could not a man and a woman spend a couple of hours every day with each other, take care of each other, listen to each other's hopes and ideas, and occasionally sit next to each other in a theater without having to worry about love or sex?

The answer obviously is no. Not at our stage in life anyway. And not with a woman as spectacularly attractive as Rosemarie.

"Do you go to bed with her?" one of my classmates asked as we left the library and Rosemarie slipped away in the direction of her next class.

"Oh, no, we're just friends. We were practically raised together."

"I'd say she was a distracting friend."

"After awhile you hardly notice."

Lie.

"Thank you for the help," she said when we had put away the last glass on the night of the session with Père Danielou. "You make a great kitchen maid."

"Faithful servant."

She hesitated, made a face, and then said, "Chucky, you shouldn't look at me that way during talks."

"What way?" I asked, feigning innocence.

"Ogling me, like you did during poor Père Danielou's talk."

When an Irishwoman uses the adjective "poor," it invariably serves as a warning that the person in question is temporarily immune from criticism.

"You don't like it when a man ogles you?"

"It depends on the man." A rose tint appeared on her face.

"Ah?"

"I don't mind it from you because you look at me so sweetly, but you shouldn't do it during a lecture."

"People notice?"

"Certainly not! I notice! You should pay attention to great men like Père Danielou."

For my own good.

Did she know what was the content of my sweet reveries? I almost asked her, and then realized that the ice beneath me was getting very thin. "As your faithful servant, I hear and obey."

"A little mouthy, but basically all right . . . Charles C. O'Malley, look at that snow! Eight inches already. I'm not going to let you drive home in that funny little car. You can stay in my guest room."

Gulp.

"It's not that bad."

"It is too." She reached for the phone. "I absolutely forbid you to go out in it."

"But I have to—"

She waved me to silence. "April? Rosemarie. Sorry to call so late but I am not going to let your older son drive all the way back to the West Side in this weather. . . . I'm glad you agree. You know how much he likes to play the hero. . . . Oh, I'll lock him in the guest room. And, anyway, you know how he is. He doesn't go in for that sort of thing."

Triumphantly she handed the phone to me.

"Rosemarie is perfectly right, dear," Mom said, trying to sound severe. "You can't drive home tonight. You stay there till the streets are cleaned."

"Yes, ma'am."

"And be good."

"Mom! You know me. I wouldn't even think of not being good."

"That's what I'm afraid of, dear."

Rosemarie promptly ushered me to the guest room, pointed to the bathroom, and waved good night. I inspected the room. Very neat. Nothing out of place. I took off my khaki sweatshirt and hung it up neatly. I folded my fatigue trousers so that the creases were perfectly in line and hung them up too. Then, in my old but serviceable GI shorts, I knelt down for my nightly prayers, a custom I had begun in Germany when there was no one else in the room and then resumed after my expulsion from Notre Dame to reassure the Deity that my problem was not with Him, but with the Catholic Church and especially the Congregation of the Holy Cross.

I am sorry, I informed Him, if I took excessive delight in imagining Rosemarie without her clothes. I tried to be respectful. She even thinks that I ogle her sweetly. I wonder what she means by that and what she thinks I'm doing. However, I hold you partially to blame because you made her so attractive and me so horny. You know that I would never do anything to hurt her. I am in somewhat unusual circumstances tonight, compromising, one might say. Like a lot of bad movie plots. If You ask me, and You rarely do, I think the good April went along a little too easily with this situation. Besides, I'm too tired tonight for romance. If it is all the same with You, however, I'd just as soon fall asleep instantly so my imagination won't run wild. I could do without the dreams too.

God apparently heard my final prayer. Clad in my shorts, and having dispossessed one of Rosemarie's teddy bears, I fell asleep as soon as my head hit the pillow. If she did indeed lock the door, I thought in the last few seconds of consciousness, she did it very quietly.

"Are you awake and decent?" I heard her voice from a great distance.

"Yes to the latter"—I rolled over and buried my head in the pillow—"and no to the former."

She propelled herself through the door, a tray laden with bacon, eggs, toast, raspberry jam, and tea in her hands, a newspaper under her arm.

"My hotel provides these services erratically," she announced briskly. "Guests are advised to take advantage of them while they can."

She put the tray on the bed next to me, bustled over to the window, and pulled open the drapes, illuminating the little bedroom with glittering winter sunlight reflected in a thousand icicles, a ballroom in a fairy wonderland.

Rosemarie was a tidal wave of fresh energy, a robust, well-scrubbed erotic presence, a clean and healthy promise of coming springtime. You realized that she was also a well calculated and discreet temptation only when you had been lured into her glowingly wholesome trap.

In other words, that morning she had designed herself to be an interesting hint of what it might be like to wake up next to her every morning.

Much too energetic for my tastes, but it might be pleasurable to be swept up in that energy.

She was wearing a tightly belted white satin robe. Her freshly brushed hair hung neatly to her shoulders, her face glowed from a recent shower, and she smelled of soap and inviting scent.

A carefully arranged entry.

"The maid service in this hotel," I observed, rubbing my eyes, "is loud, pushy, and extremely attractive."

"Thank you, sir." She bowed. "And a good morning to you too."

"The door wasn't locked?"

"Really, Chucky"—she waved her hand—"I have a lot of more serious worries than defending myself from your amorous intentions."

"You don't think you could seduce me?"

"I didn't say that and you know it. I said I wasn't afraid of your seducing me."

"Ah."

I would doubtless make a mess of it.

"Chuck," John Raven had told me, "your tragic flaw with women is that you help them when they're vulnerable. So naturally they fall in love with you. You can't resist a vulnerable woman who is in love with you."

"I've resisted a couple of them."

"Just barely."

Rosemarie waved her hand again. "Not that it wouldn't be interesting to see you try."

"High comedy."

The wave was becoming a familiar gesture. It was a little flick, upward and outward, of her right hand. It said that I was perhaps an amusing little boy, but wasn't it time, after all, that I began to grow up? However, the implication was always of patient, maternal affection.

The wave almost always melted my heart. It offered me warmth and comfort and a secure spot on the desert island she brought with her. Secure, but not necessarily restful.

"Anyway"—she sat on the edge of my bed—"your wife, whoever she's going to be, poor woman, will have to resign herself to love between eleven and noon, because that is the only time you'll be wide enough awake to have sex on your mind."

Her robe slipped away, to reveal a touch of ivory thigh.

"I suppose you're right." I sighed. "I mean you can't make love with raspberry jam on your fingers."

"*You* couldn't anyway. . . . So what do you think?"

"About love with raspberry jam?"

"About last night, silly. And the whole business."

"I'm a lot happier here than I was at Notre Dame," I began.

She nodded. "That's obvious."

"I've studied harder than I thought I possibly could. My head reels sometimes from all the ideas. I've learned more about Catholicism from your friends than I did in sixteen years of Catholic schools. It's exciting. What more can I say?"

"Better than Notre Dame in everyway?"

"No." I thought about the rest of my answer. "You and I share some basic values with the guys at Notre Dame that we don't with many of the people here. Notre Dame is less arrogant, and heaven knows it has reason to be less arrogant than this place; and loyalty—what we'd think of as loyalty anyway—is almost invisible here. But universities are about ideas and there are a lot more ideas in a day here than in a semester at Notre Dame."

"The people last night?" she drew the robe over her thigh.

"They're not St. Ursula people, Rosemarie. Not that everyone has to be. But they're something new in the Church and I think there will be a lot more of them."

"And what they stand for will eventually affect St. Ursula's and every-thing else in the Church. Our children"—she blushed deeply and tightened the belt on her robe but did not completely cover her delicious thigh—"in separate families, will live differently because of their ideas."

"Maybe," I admitted.

Which turned out to be an understatement. But then no one, not even someone as perspicacious as Rosemarie, could have anticipated the Vatican Council.

"And you?" she persisted.

"Early morning catechism?"

"Why else did you think I kept you here all night?" Her grim lips indicated that she was not joking. "I wanted to catch you off guard."

"With me in my GI shorts and you in that lovely robe?"

"Shut up"—she poked at my naked ribs with a quick, sharp finger—"and answer my question."

"Yes, Mommy." I ducked away from her tickling jab.

"Well, someone like you needs at least two mommies."

"I ask myself sometimes what a would-be accountant and an occasional photographer—"

"Too occasional, but go on."

"—needs with so much heavy thought and so many tantalizing ideas."

She rose from the bed and walked over to the sun-filled window. I squinted to watch the satin-covered back. Yes indeed, a perfectly acceptable rear end too. Maybe I would shock the good April with that comment. ("I've just noticed, April Mae, that Rosemarie has a lovely ass.")

"Accountants are members of the human race too, Chuck. They need ideas and vision as much as anyone else. Besides, you're a lot more than just a potential accountant with a camera."

"What am I then?"

She turned to face me, a living statue bathed in wonderful backlight that turned her long dark hair to black fire. "I'm not sure," she said slowly and carefully, choosing every word, "but I know you're someone with the mark of greatness."

"Come on, Rosemarie, that's a romantic daydream."

"No it isn't. But hurry up and get dressed or you'll miss your first class."

— 2 —

There was trouble back in St. Ursula's, trouble I didn't need.

Leo Kelly, my classmate from St. Ursula's, who was a senior at Loyola and trainee in Navy ROTC, called me on the phone and proposed that we meet at Petersen's ice cream palace on Chicago Avenue just east of Harlem to discuss a couple of problems that had arisen in the neighborhood.

"Seven-thirty tomorrow night all right?"

"Okay . . . Will Jane be there?"

"Of course Jane will be there, Chuck."

"You're too young to marry."

"Aren't we all. Jane and I are not engaged yet. We haven't even talked about it. Maybe after my four years in the Marines . . ."

He didn't ask me about Rosemarie. The common opinion in the neighborhood was that I'd eventually succumb, but that we were a long way from that. Hence it was unwise to ask either of us about our relationship. I would have denied that there was a relationship. Rosemarie? She would probably just laugh.

Technically, the crazy O'Malleys no longer lived in the parish. Our new home was several blocks into Oak Park and beyond the boundaries of St. Ursula's. However, my father claimed extraterritorial rights because he was the architect of the new church there. Rosemarie's voting residence was at her father's house at the corner of Menard and Thomas, though she spent most of her time either in her apartment in Hyde Park near the University, or in one of our guest bedrooms, called, by everyone but me, "Rosie's room." (I called it, when I called it anything, "Rosemarie's room," because that was her name. The name Rosie, I argued—uselessly—was vulgar.) It was at the other end of our second floor from my hideout.

Peg and I, deeply attached to St. Ursula's, refused to identify with St. Arthur's our proper parish in Oak Park. St. Ursula's problems were our problems.

I phoned Rosemarie at her Hyde Park apartment.

"Would you feel secure enough in the shower to spend tomorrow night at the crazy O'Malley's?"

"The door is always open there too, Chucky Ducky."

"I'll try to remember that."

"Any special reason—in addition to your lascivious fantasies?"

"Leo called. Some kind of problem in the parish."

"With Jane?"

"I don't think so."

"Why do you need me? I'm not a fixer like you are. I have enough problems of my own without intruding into other people's problems."

"Since I don't engage in vulgarities with the gentle sex, I won't say what I think of that statement. We're both born fixers."

She laughed. "I'll be there."

Leo Kelly had been my opposite number at St. Ursula's grammar school. Just as I was a noisy, obnoxious, contentious show-off (to use some of the milder words the nuns used), Leo was quiet and unassuming to the point of invisibility, a simple fellow, with a simple face and a simple air about him. Or so it was thought. Peg, who at one time had a distant crush on him, thought he'd make a great precinct captain because, unlike her brother, he knew when to keep his mouth shut, which was most of the time. He had gone to Quigley to study for the priesthood, though as my mother said in a rare moment of uncharity, the vocation was more his mother's than his own. He left the seminary after third year and went to college at Loyola University. He majored in political science and planned, after his hitch in the Marines, to seek a Ph.D. at Harvard.

"He wants to get away from that terrible woman," the good April commented, continuing her violation of charity though hardly of truth. When Leo had left the seminary, his father, at his mother's instigation, refused to pay his Loyola tuition. Leo joined the Navy ROTC to earn the money he needed.

Jane was in our class too, the only civilized human being in a family of black Irish savages, the male members of which were alleged to be crooks. She was the acknowledged leader of the class, smart, pretty (black curls clustered around milk white skin), and dynamic. She hardly noticed Leo and she tolerated me as someone whom she might allow occasionally to steal the show from her. Not too often, however. Peg and Rosemarie at that time thought she was "stuck-up" but later revised their opinion to "sweet."

Packy Keenan, whose family lived in St. Arthur's and were thus dismissed as rich snobs by us St. Ursula kids, attended Quigley with Leo and brought him up to their summer place at Lake Geneva, where somehow he and Jane discovered each other.

Since I had returned from Germany, Leo and I had joined forces as problem solvers for the young people in the parish: he found the problems and I solved them. Well, he found the problems I didn't find.

So we met at Petersen's and did our usual orders of sundaes and malts, two malts for me and two for Rosemarie.

"Are you trying to match Chucky?" Jane asked with her usual dazzling smile, which enabled her to say almost anything and get away with it.

Rosemarie waved her hand. "I may just have to order a third. My doctor says I should put on at least ten pounds."

"You look great!" Jane said, now solicitous.

"Great but skinny," I observed.

"Chuck!" Jane exploded. "You're terrible! Rosie is gorgeous."

"I bet she doesn't drink three malts!"

"Five dollars," Jane said extending the little finger of her left hand and hooking it with mine—a Sicilian sign of a bet.

"She can't get sick, however." I insisted.

"Only outside!"

"All right!"

"Which one gives me the bigger cut?" Rosemarie demanded as she knocked off the first malt quicker than I did.

"No fair!" Jane insisted.

Gluttonous, but we were not dancing at the edge of sickness with alcohol. Not tonight anyway.

We sang with the jukebox: "Mona Lisa," and "Ghost Riders in the Sky."

Jane was too open ever to be a Mona Lisa. Rosemarie, on the other hand . . .

Then, to the applause of Peterson's patrons, Rosemarie and I did our theme song, "Younger than Springtime."

In my imagination it applied to Rosemarie.

More applause.

"One more!" begged a waitress.

"Which one?"

"You know!"

I knew all right. Jane and Leo didn't. It would be most embarrassing.

"Rosemarie," I temporized, "even if she is skinny, is prettier than Jeanette MacDonald."

"And you're no Nelson Eddy," Jane replied, "so it evens out."

So it did. We'd sung "Rose-Marie, I Love You," often at home since the film in 1936 (when I was eight and Rosemarie was five!), and once or twice at Peterson's. But neither of us liked doing that. The lyrics said things we weren't quite ready to admit, even to ourselves, in public.

Both of us, however, were crazy O'Malleys, I by birth and she by association. We loved a stage and an audience.

"You gotta picture Chucky Ducky in a bright red Mountie jacket with one of those lanyard things around his neck," Rosemarie warned the impromptu audience. "Make him taller and stronger. And I'm the one with the red hair."

> *Oh sweet Rose-Marie,*
> *It's easy to see*
> *Why all who learn to know you love you.*
> *You're gentle and kind,*
> *Divinely designed,*
> *As graceful as the pines above you.*
> *There's an angel's breath beneath your sigh,*
> *There's a little devil in your eye.*
>
> *O, Rose-Marie, I love you!*
> *I'm always dreaming of you.*
> *No matter what I do, I can't forget you;*
> *Sometimes I wish that I had never met you!*
> *And yet if I should lose you,*
> *'Twould mean my very life to me.*
> *Of all the queens that ever lived I'd choose you*
> *To rule me, my Rose-Marie!*

I must admit that the real Rosemarie and I hammed it up a bit. However, the Petersen's gang loved it. The applause was thunderous, as they say. The two singers were embarrassed and refused to look at each other. Jane watched us very carefully, opened her mouth to say something, and then shut it again.

Then, out of loyalty to Rudolf Friml, I began the first bars of "Indian Love Call." That gave us both a great chance to show off.

Naturally there was more applause. The manager came over to shake our hands and say, half fun and full earnest (as the good April would have put it), that he'd like to schedule us for regular nights.

"Romantic musical theater," Leo observed pedantically, "reached its height in Europe before the war with the work of Franz Lehár of *Merry Widow* fame and then came to this country after the war with Sigmund Romberg, who wrote *The Desert Song* and *The Student Prince*, and Rudolf Friml, who was responsible for that theme song of yours. Both were

"But we don't know the address."

"Didn't your dad have an Irish girlfriend, Chucky?"

"The virtuous Vangie?"

"Vangie" was a corruption—which Mom loved—of Dad's middle name, "Evangelist, as in John Evangelist O'Malley."

"You never listen, Chucky! The good April kids him about her all the time. Her name was Siobhan."

"So?"

"Maybe we could have her check on Timmy for us."

With a loud sigh she finished her third malt, and then she gobbled down the last two of the butter cookies that always accompanied malted milks in those happier days.

"Not a bad idea," Leo agreed.

"Chuck," Jane said, "you owe me five dollars."

I gave her a five-dollar bill, the last one in my wallet, with a great show of reluctance.

"If she gets sick, I get it back."

"If she gets sick before we leave."

"I do not plan on getting sick."

Given Rosemarie's willpower, she would not.

"You'll follow through on it, Chuck?"

"Sure, we'll see what we can find out. I'll be in touch."

"What do you think of them?" I asked Rosemarie as she drove me home.

"We shouldn't talk about them," she said primly.

"They'll talk about us."

"They'll never figure us out."

"Can we figure them out?"

She took a deep breath. "*Well*, I think they'd be very happily married, but I don't think they'll ever get that far."

"Why?"

"They're both afraid of love."

"Aren't we?"

"Not the same way."

That was that.

The next morning at breakfast I raised the question about Siobhan.

"The Clancy brat is defaming you, Dad."

That got all their attention.

"I wouldn't doubt it," he replied. "Just like her."

Dad was the only one in the family who enjoyed my games.

"She's saying that you had a girlfriend in Ireland."

"I'll have to talk to a lawyer," he said, turning crimson. "I've never been in Ireland."

"Now, dear," Mom corrected him, "you did have an Irish girlfriend when you were in Rome. Certainly you haven't forgotten about Siobhan, the one who married the little Irish lawyer with the red hair."

Aha.

Having read my father's memoirs, I knew all about Siobhan.

"Oh, yes," he said, returning to the Chicago *Sun*, "Siobhan McKenna."

"Siobhan Moriarity, as she is now. We really must go over to Ireland and visit them when our work slows down."

The work would never slow down unless Peggy and Rosemarie and I intervened again.

"You're in touch with her and her husband?"

"Ronan is her husband's name," Mom added helpfully. "We exchange Christmas cards. She's a very lovely woman. A good loser."

"Mom!" Peg exclaimed.

"Well, dear, she did lose, you know."

"Dad could write to Siobhan or Ronan," I said, "and ask them if they can locate the address of the pub on Eyre Square in Galway where an American named Tim Boylan works. Also answer some questions about his behavior."

"You've found Timmy!" Peg's eyes lit up. Young women found Tim cute, for totally different reasons, I suspected than they found me cute.

"We think so."

"What will you do if they find him?" Dad asked, looking at me shrewdly.

"Depends on what you find. Send him a note wishing him well."

"And tell the poor dear that we all still love him."

"And that Jenny will never stop loving him."

"Depends," I said.

"I'll get the letter off today," Dad promised.

3

"We'll double for the St. Patrick's Day dance, of course," my sister Peg, the other pea in the pod occupied by Rosemarie, said at the breakfast table.

I continued to eat my second helping of buttermilk pancakes without comment.

Breakfast was an important family ritual for the remnants of the crazy O'Malleys, as we were often called by fellow parishioners at St. Ursula's. My younger brother, Michael, was off in the seminary. My older sister, Jane McCormac, now happily pregnant, lived with her husband. So there was only four of us around the breakfast table. Soon Dad would bury himself in the blueprints in his office at the back of the house and Mom would take over as office manager. Peg would dash over to Rosary College in River Forest, where she was a sophomore majoring in music education. I would be the last to leave the breakfast table. Before departing for the University I would naturally wash the breakfast dishes and clean up the kitchen so that the family would not look like slobs to the cleaning lady when she arrived.

"I was talking to you, Chucky," Peg insisted.

"I think I've heard this argument before," my father said, as he savored the second of the two cups of coffee we permitted him at breakfast.

"Now, dear, don't be difficult," my mother insisted.

"I was not planning to go to the St. Patrick's Day dance at St. Ursula's," I said. "While I can claim to be a veteran, I am not a war veteran. I'm therefore not eligible. Besides, at the moment I am not dating anyone."

I knew it was a lost cause. However, the traditional rituals must be observed.

"The dance is for everyone. The Catholic War Vets is only the sponsor."

Outside our house on East Avenue, the Chicago region was reverting to its primal swamp as, under the fiercely bright sun, an early February thaw—a false promise of the coming of spring—melted a couple of feet of snow. It would be a slushy drive to the University. There would, however, be many opportunities for my photographic archival activity, perhaps a shot of Rosemarie as the ice maiden of Russian folklore melting into slush. It would be an interesting trick, if I could pull it off.

Yes, I was taking pictures again, mostly of her.

"That does not deal with my second problem," I said, soaking the pancakes with more maple syrup.

"You can be so exasperating, Chucky," my sister said impatiently. "It would be Vince and me and you and Rosie."

Rosemarie and Peg don't really look like twins. My sister is taller and somewhat more statuesque. Her hair is short and curly, her face round and freckled. One thinks of them as twins, however, because they always seem to be together and to read each other's thoughts without talking. Especially, I had reason to believe, if I was the subject matter of their thoughts. Their personalities were different too. I had once compared Peg to a mountain lion and Rosemarie to a timber wolf—metaphors that had pleased both of them.

"Rosemarie and I are not dating," I said firmly.

Peg and I adored each other. We merely had to play out our usual scenario.

"The four of us saw *All the King's Men* when Vince was in from Notre Dame."

"A film," I said, "is not a date, a dance is. Besides, the virtuous Rosemarie is dating my old enemy Ed Murray."

"He is not an enemy. Won't you ever forget that terrible football game?"

"I've been trying to forget it."

"You're close friends and you know it. Besides, Rosie and Ed broke up over Christmas."

That I did not know.

"Did they?"

"And do you know why?"

"Why?"

"Because, just like your buddy Christopher, Ed got tired of all their conversations being about you."

I felt my face turn red.

"They must not have talked very much."

"And you spent a night at her apartment too!" Peg accused me.

"Locked behind a door."

"She didn't lock the door!"

"That's because she knew, dear, that she could trust poor Chucky," Mom said.

"I'll grant you, Peg, that she looks quite attractive after her morning shower."

That stopped them all.

"Tell you what"—Peg grinned shrewdly—"the guy and I will be there on a date and you and Rosie can tag along with us on a non-date."

"I see no reasonable objection to that."

Dad put down his copy of the *Sun*, Mom paused as she prepared to pour me another cup of tea, Peg's grin faded. I had raised the white flag much earlier than usual.

"You want to go to the dance with Rosie!"

"I told you, I was quite impressed with her after her morning shower." I lifted the tea cup toward my mother.

Peg frowned. It was unlikely that I had actually seen Rosemarie coming out of the shower. If I had, she would have certainly reported such an encounter to Peg. On the other hand . . .

"Now, dear," Mom intervened, "I'm sure nothing like that happened."

Dad, quicker than the others to catch on to my word games, chuckled.

"Ask her," I said as I polished off the last remnant of the pancakes.

"I certainly will!"

"After you tell her that I agree to tag along to the St. Patrick's Day dance."

That evening Dad showed me a letter from the Moriaritys.

Dear John,

Your son must be a very interesting young man. We'll really have to meet him soon. Next year you must come see us. It's only twelve hours in those new DC-7s from St. John's in Newfoundland to Shannon. We could meet you there. We have a summer home near Rory's birthplace out beyond Dingle. He's Irish-speaking, you know.

There surely is a young man named Timothy O'Boylan working in Brandon's Pub right across the street from the Railroad Hotel in Galway. He's a quiet boy, very good looking and very respectful. The publican told us that he works very hard and doesn't drink and had terrible war experiences. He does look a little haunted.

All our love,
Siobhan

Aha!

I drafted a card and called Rosemarie for approval.

"Be sure you send it air mail, Chuck."

"That's expensive!"

I then checked with Leo.

"I knew you'd find him, Chuck."

"We Mounties always get our man."

Dear Tim,

    As I'm sure you expected, I found out where you are. Don't worry that we'll come swarming across the ocean to drag you back. We miss you and await your return. Everyone still loves you, especially the wondrous Jenny Collins. You'd better answer this.

Charles Cronin O'Malley

Perhaps there would be a trip to Ireland soon. Mom and Dad were taking their afternoon nap almost every day as they had when we lived in the cramped two-flat on Menard Avenue. Maybe they realized that they couldn't keep on living the way they had in the boom years immediately after the war. Peg and Rosemarie and I knew about the naps, of course, but we didn't talk about it to each other.

That spring of 1950 was a glorious time. The weather was wonderful, the songs and films were memorable, and we were all young and full of hope. Maybe I was in love. The country was more prosperous than it had ever been (though not everyone—especially Negroes, as we called them then—was benefiting from the prosperity). By the end of June it would be all over. On the last Sunday of the month the headlines reported an invasion of South Korea by North Korea. The war would shape and sober our generation. I would lose several friends, one of them forever. I had seen tragedy in Bamberg with the Constabulary. Young men I knew had died in the Second World War, but no one of my generation. I left my youth behind in 1950. Maybe I even grew up a little, though there are those who would dispute that.

Later that morning, with no sense of impending doom, I struggled to escape Rosemarie's laughing revenge as she buried me in a pile of melting snow and washed my face, not the first time she had worked that indignity on me.

"You saw me coming out of the shower!" she shouted as she pushed another mittful of snow into my mouth.

"Peg did not listen to what I said," I pleaded. "I said you were attractive after your shower, which was certainly true. She chose to put a salacious interpretation on it."

"Because you wanted her to!"

She released me and stood up, proudly surveying the damage to person and my clothes.

"A man is permitted his fantasies. Besides, the door was locked."

She extended her hand to help me up.

"You knew it wasn't, Chucky Ducky."

"I overslept."

"Anyway, I'm glad you're going to the dance. It should be a lot of fun."

"We'll see," I said grudgingly.

"You'd better act right," she warned me.

"What choice do I have, trapped between a mountain lion and a timber wolf?"

"Shall we go up to the reading room and get to work?" she asked, flushing as she so often did.

"The chairman of the economics department wants to see me."

"Are you in trouble?" she asked nervously.

"Probably. I think they may have caught up with me."

"They're smart around here," she snorted, "real smart. But they're not *that* smart."

As I ambled up the stairs of the social science building to the fourth floor offices of the economics department, I remembered hearing my mother say in our apartment on Menard Avenue, when I was supposed to be asleep on the porch that adjoined our parlor, that Peg and Rosemarie had their first periods on the same day. Could they be planning to have their marriages on the same day and perhaps give birth to their first child each on the same day?

You're slipping into their trap, I told myself.

Maybe I'd always been in it.

Palmer Tennant, the departmental chairman, kept me waiting for fifteen minutes, less than students were normally left fretting in his outer office.

"Come in, Mr., uh, O'Malley," he said with a massive scowl. "Sit down."

Mr. Tennant always scowled.

(At the University everyone was Mr., not Doctor or Professor. There were not enough women faculty in those days to worry about whether they were Miss or Mrs.)

"The department has been watching you closely, Mr., uh, O'Malley."

Palmer Tennant was a squat, bald man with expressionless gray eyes behind thick horned-rimmed glasses. He had held an upper-level job at the Treasury Department during the war. It was said that if there had been a Nobel Prize in economics, he would have won it.

"The red hair is pretty hard to hide, sir."

He squinted, not quite getting my point. Then his lips parted slightly in what might have been a smile.

"You would stand out in the classroom even if you were silent, which, of course, you're not."

Peggy had said that I had a fast mind and a faster tongue. That had generally worked to my advantage at the University. Maybe they had indeed caught up with me.

"Genetic weakness, sir."

He didn't try to figure that one out.

"However, papers like this"—he waved my paper at me like it was a lethal weapon—"in which you compare the Negro neighborhoods of Chicago to Germany after the war, would attract our attention anyway."

"I ride through them every day on the El, Mr. Tennant. It was hard not to notice the similarity between them and Bamberg when I first arrived there in 1946."

"Germany is struggling out of it now," he observed.

"The Marshall Plan made a big difference, sir."

He smiled. As well he might. He'd been one of those who had sold Dean Acheson on the plan, which Acheson had then sold to George Marshall.

"It wasn't all that much money, Mr., uh, O'Malley."

"Enough to prevent starvation, enough to start the wheels turning again."

"You quote General Lucius Clay in this paper. Did you know him?"

"I met him once, sir, when he was visiting the Constabulary headquarters with the Herr Oberburgomeister of Cologne."

I was not above name-dropping when it suited my purpose. I would have told him the whole story if he had asked. Naturally he didn't.

"A great man . . . You cannot, however, seriously compare the Negro population of Chicago with the population of Germany. Whatever we may think of the latter, those that survived the war had the work habits and motivation necessary to rebuild their country. We don't see much of that in the ghetto."

"As I said in the paper, sir, I don't mean the comparison to fit perfectly. However, if one could increase the purchasing power of Negroes it would go a long way to sustain the present prosperity of this country."

I had by 1950 abandoned my notion that the Great Depression would inevitably return. I still believed in the Business Cycle, however. I was terrified of it.

"We may be going into a bit of a recession," he said, scowling more deeply, "but we now know a lot more than we did twenty years ago about containing such events."

"Yes, sir."

"In any case, you are quite right that improving the quality of education among the Negroes is absolutely essential. . . . All in all this is a very intelligent and creative paper. The department is pleased with your work. You do not use your patent creativity as a substitute for rigorous analysis."

The hell I didn't, but I let that go.

"Thank you, Mr. Tennant."

"What are your, uh, plans upon graduation, Mr., uh, O'Malley?"

"I already have a position, sir, with a downtown accounting firm. I will continue to work for them."

"Accounting?" His thick eyebrows rose in disbelief.

"Yes, sir."

"Young man, you have enormous talent and the discipline necessary to harness that talent. While accounting is not without its creative aspects, I must tell you in all candor that it is the opinion of this department that your abilities would be wasted in such a profession."

"Oh."

"Moreover, I have been authorized to offer you a full-tuition scholarship and, uh, some kind of financial aid for the pursuit of a doctorate at this University. I should think, on the basis of this paper," he brandished it again, "that you might like to study the economic revival in West Germany."

"Oh."

"Do you find that offer attractive?" he demanded.

Frightening.

"Yes, sir."

How could I tell this man that because I was a Depression child I didn't believe in taking chances in any aspect of my life?

"It surprises you?"

"Yes, indeed."

He paused, then said, "Perhaps this department should have made clearer to you its, uh, interest in your work. In any event, I'm sure you will want time to think before you make a decision. The offer is not exactly open-ended, but it will be on the table," he dropped my paper on his desk, "for another couple of years."

It was time for my quick tongue to operate again.

"I am not only surprised, Mr. Tennant, I am very grateful for the department's vote of confidence. I would be very interested indeed in studying the situation in Germany. However, as you say, I will have to think about it and discuss it with my family."

I knew what they'd say, so I really wouldn't tell them about it. Nor Rosemarie. I'd take time to appear to think so as not to offend the department unnecessarily. The Chicago Irish never burn bridges.

"Excellent, Mr. O'Malley." He rose and actually extended his hand. "We'll be expecting to hear from you."

I left his office dazed. I was no academic. I didn't want to be an academic. Certainly not an intellectual. I wanted a secure controlled life, didn't I? Why should I be flattered because a bunch of ivory tower intellectuals thought I would fit into their world?

I remembered a conversation I'd had a few months before with my father.

"Dad, what was it like when the Depression hit you and Mom?"

He had looked up from blueprints over which he had been puzzling. "Uhm? What was it like?" he mused. "Well, like a combination of a tornado and an earthquake, I guess. Everything was swept away and the ground collapsed beneath us."

"How could you go on?"

He put aside the blueprints and glanced up at me. "How could we not, Chuck? We had each other, we had Jane and you. We were a lot poorer but still happy. It wasn't like the famine hitting Ireland in 1847."

"Did you think it would ever end? Did you really believe that your ship would come in?"

He had laughed—the big hearty laugh for which all of us O'Malleys loved him.

"Certainly not! Then it did, a whole convoy of ships. They're still coming in. A lot of men my age attribute it all to their ability and intelligence. Truth is that it was pure luck. We happened to be alive at the right time."

"Do you think something like that will happen again, the tornado and the earthquake together?"

"We journey with our fingers crossed, Chucky. If it happens it will happen. We'll still have each other and the four of you and a bunch of grandchildren probably and our friends and our music. If it does happen again it will be different. We understand now that life can be tragic and that we can absorb tragedy. . . . We lost all our money. Family is more important than money."

I had wanted to argue further and then thought better of it.

As I entered the reading room of Harper Library, I resolved that I would certainly not tell Rosemarie about the interview.

She looked up at me as I joined her at our usual study table and frowned.

"You look like it was bad news," she whispered.

"Not bad really," I replied.

"Then why do you look unhappy? Let's get out of this mausoleum and go someplace where we can talk."

There weren't many places to talk either in Harper Library or in the adjoining social science building. We ended up on the first floor looking out the pseudogothic windows on the torrent of melted snow rushing down Fifty-ninth Street in a desperate effort to get to Lake Michigan.

"Every word," Rosemarie ordered, jabbing her finger at me. "I want to hear every single word."

So naturally I told her every single word.

"Chucky! How wonderful! I told you all along that you are a genius."

"I'm not," I insisted. "All I want is a simple, quiet life."

"You should know by now," she said sternly, "that God has other plans for you."

"He didn't ask me what I thought."

"You could be an academic and famous photographer at the same time."

"You know me well enough, Rosemarie, to know that I'm not an adventurer. All I want is to be a modestly successful accountant."

She laughed at me.

I shrugged my shoulders.

"Let's get back to our books."

She laughed all the way back to the Harper reading room. An unfair form of argument, I thought, but effective nonetheless.

4

On St. Patrick's night, I kissed Rosemarie passionately for the first time. Or maybe she kissed me. It was hard to tell. Suddenly and without warning we were in each other's arms. We clung to one another for dear life. Our lips locked together in joyous fury.

"Oh," she gasped when I finally released her. "You didn't really do that, did you, Chucky Ducky?"

"Nope," I said hoarsely. "Not at all. It was someone else."

Someone else recaptured her in his arms and kissed her again, even more vehemently this time.

It was her turn to ease away from me.

"I always knew you'd be a good kisser," she sighed. "I didn't think you'd be that good."

Twice before I had engaged in my first passionate embrace with a woman, my lost Trudi in Germany and my equally lost Cordelia at Notre Dame. As I fought to regain control of my breathing, I realized that this encounter was utterly different. A forest fire was blazing in my soul. I did not want to put it out.

"I'm sorry," I said.

"About what?"

"I assaulted you?"

"Maybe I assaulted you."

"Let's fight over it."

"We've had enough fighting for one evening, Chucky Ducky."

"Maybe if we fight again, we will kiss like that again."

"We don't need a fight to do that!"

This time she definitely assaulted me.

For weal or woe, the whole direction of my life changed that night.

Moreover, the question of who assaulted whom first is irrelevant. I started the whole process when I decided I would play the role of the perfect gentleman that night. Since I'm sure that was God's idea, He is to blame for what happened.

"You are going to wear a suit and tie tonight, aren't you?" Rosemarie had demanded as we left Mass at the Calvert House that morning.

"Certainly not!" I insisted.

Bad enough that she had dragged me back to church. Worse still that she thought she could force me to become both a photographer and an academic. She would not turn me into a gentleman with a suit and tie.

Then I decided that perhaps it was time for me to wear a new mask. I was after all now twenty-two years old. Maybe it was time to stop acting like Henry Aldrich, the stereotypical adolescent on the radio when we were in grammar school. Maybe a new, suave Chucky would be as intolerable as the old diamond-in-the-rough Chucky. I smiled to myself. That would disarm Rosemarie and everyone else. A Cary Grant Chucky might soon become more unbearable than a Humphrey Bogart Chucky.

That's how I rationalized it to myself anyway. As for the comparison with the two actors, remember I was only twenty-two.

So that night I greeted Vince Antonelli in a charcoal gray suit (purchased several months earlier by the good April), a white shirt, and a conservative red-and-blue tie. I had even done my best to slick down my wire-brush red hair.

Vince recoiled in surprise.

"Do we have a wake to go to first?"

Excellent!

He, of course, also wore a suit and tie. Peg would tolerate my being a slob but not Vince's.

"The Catholic War Vets' St. Patrick's Day dance," I said piously, "is a very important social event."

"It's only a party in the old parish hall." Vince continued to look very puzzled. "A bunch of vets and their girls or their wives and some other people."

"Chuck," my father said, "is undergoing a metanoia."

"Now, dear," Mom remonstrated, "I think he looks cute. Rosie is such a good influence on him, poor little thing."

It was not immediately clear whether "poor" applied to Rosemarie or to me.

"Well, maybe she'll straighten him out, like someone tried to straighten me out."

The good April giggled complacently.

My parents were waiting for the apparition of the mountain lion and the timber wolf in their full St. Patrick's Day array, an epiphany of gracefulness.

They walked down the stairs together, hesitantly, as if they were not quite sure of the impression they would create, my sister in white with green trim, Rosemarie in dark green. The former wore a diamond pendant (borrowed from the good April) around her neck, the latter a flashing emerald. Though they usually condemned makeup, both had permitted themselves light touches.

"Do you think, Vince, I would get in trouble if I whistled?" I asked.

"I think you might get in trouble if you didn't?"

"But I can't whistle!"

My parents applauded.

Peg's gown was formfitting and reached to mid calf. Rosemarie was impossibly beautiful in a dress that fell freely like a shift to her knees. Peg's shoulders were bare, Rosemarie's supported thin green strips without which her garment would surely have fallen to the floor. Both had piled their hair up on their heads.

Archduchesses at least.

"Would you two young women mind holding that pose while I take a picture?"

They didn't mind.

"Just one more," I begged.

They didn't mind several more.

"I had thought of bringing this gift from the charming beauty in the green dress along to the dance, if there is no objection?"

"Are you feeling well, Chucky?" my sister asked suspiciously.

"It's just a new act," Rosemarie said, hitting very close to the truth.

I kissed her cheek. "I've never seen you look so beautiful."

She blushed, the rose tint creeping down to her throat.

"I think he is sick, Peg," she said, but her eyes glowed.

We drove over to St. Ursula's in Rosemarie's Buick. The four of us took the dance by storm, the newly burnished Chucky almost as much of an attraction as the two lovelies.

"Shall we dance, my dear?" I asked my date almost as soon as we entered the hot, crowded room which was already permeated by the smell of gallons of beer.

"You don't dance," she said dubiously.

Lieutenant Nan, a young woman with whom I'd half dated before I found her a man she would marry, had taught me to dance. I had told no one of this accomplishment.

I put my arm around Rosemarie and led her to the dance floor.

"Not bad, Chucky Ducky. In fact, pretty good."

I held her close, but not too close. That's what gentlemen do, isn't it? Early in the evening I discovered how little there was to her: hardly a bag of bones, but so slender that you might think she'd break in two if you squeezed too hard. There was no need for the armored corset under her dress.

The bare skin of her back seat electric currents racing through my body. I must keep that under control if I was to continue in my Cary Grant role. I kept my eyes on her eyes, swimming in happiness, and restrained myself from looking down at the top of her breasts.

Well, most of the time.

Intermittently she would consider me quizzically, trying to figure out who this new Chucky really was. I enjoyed every minute of it.

We danced and we sang and we danced some more. Then the Rosie-Chucky duet was called upon to lead the songs. We went through our whole Irish repertoire (including "Clancy Lowered the Boom") and then, for some odd reason, turned to Victor Herbert, who was also Irish, and then sang our songs from *Rose Marie*. I rejoiced in Peggy's wide-eyed astonishment as I sang this romantic love song like it was intended for the Rosemarie standing next to me, which maybe it was just a little.

"You'd better dance with poor little Jenny," Rosemarie instructed me.

"Yes, ma'am."

Let her think it was her idea.

Jenny enfolded me in her sweet smile when I asked. "Rosie won't mind?"

"Does she look like it?"

"No."

We danced quietly for a few moments.

"To answer your questions, Chuck. I have not heard from him. I know he will return. I will wait for him. Is that enough?"

"I wasn't going to ask."

"He's worth waiting for. He will be all right eventually, you know."

"He's a good man," I agreed cautiously.

Naturally Rosemarie wanted to know what Jenny said.

"Poor little Jenny."

The party continued. Rosemarie continued radiant. Then suddenly the magic vanished.

"I want to go home," Rosemarie insisted angrily. "Now. Immediately."

It was a warning sign I had seen before. I'd better get her out of the hall before she started to drink. I told Vince and Peggy that we had to leave. My sister seemed to know why. They assured me that they would have no trouble getting a ride home.

We rode back to East Avenue in stony silence.

Inside the house she blew up at me.

"What the hell are you up to, you creepy little runt!"

"Uhm . . ."

"You're not fooling me with that disgusting little act you put on over there. You're playing one of your sick little games! Why?"

"I was merely trying to act like a gentleman should act," I stammered, "when he is on a date with a lovely young woman."

Her face, crimson in anger, twisted in disgust. "You couldn't act like a gentleman if your life depended on it. I hate you! I hate you! I hate you!"

Thereupon she began to pound my chest with hammer blows from tightly clenched fists.

I retreated a few feet. She pursued me and resumed her attack.

Then she stopped, looked at her fists, looked at me, and began to sob. "I'm sorry, Chucky! I didn't mean it!"

Then we fell into each other's arms and the passionate kissing began.

"Can we sit down and talk?" she gasped.

"Sure."

We sat on one of the couches the good April had brought from her family home on South Emerald. I put my arm around Rosemarie and we huddled together while she dabbed at her eyes with a tissue and then rearranged her makeup.

"I don't even know why I was angry," she said, fighting back another outburst of tears. "You were wonderful, like I always knew you'd be someday. I couldn't figure out why . . ."

"Well, maybe because it was that vision of you coming out of the shower."

"Chucky Ducky, you are still impossible." She sniffed, touching my arm gently.

I began to massage her neck and her back, very gently and slowly. She relaxed herself into my care. "Regardless"—she waved her hand weakly—"I'm sorry."

"I will hold it against you for the rest of your life."

She giggled.

"I promise I won't ever hit you again."

"Except when I deserve it."

"Of course!"

We laughed together.

"How long is this 1950 model of Chucky Ducky going to be around?" She turned her face and looked at me cautiously.

The haunted beauty of that face silenced me for a moment.

"I don't know. Not all the time. Some of the time anyway. I think Sir

Charles, *le parfait gentilhomme*, would be unbearable if you had to put up with him all the time."

I kissed her bare shoulder. She sighed. I drew her closer and kissed the front of her neck.

"I like him a lot," she said. "Especially when he turns into a gentle lover."

Oh, boy. You're in deep water, Chucky.

"It's time I grew up."

"Don't ever grow up completely, please."

"Yes, Wendy."

We laughed together again. Two young lovers.

We cuddled for a while. Time stood still. We kissed passionately a couple of times more. Then we heard a car outside.

"The good Margaret Mary returns."

"How long have we been doing this?"

"I don't know. It seems like no more than eternity."

"Silly!"

She drew away from me, rearranged herself, and moved to an easy chair some distance away.

"What if April had seen us?" she said piously.

"She would have thought it was about time."

She giggled again.

Then Vince and Peg came in. They paused to take in what must have seemed a strange picture—the two of us sitting in the parlor like an old married couple having a casual conversation.

"What's going on?" Peg demanded. "Are you all right, Rosie?"

"I'm fine," Rosemarie responded brightly. "I think the heat in the hall affected me. Chucky has been amusing me with stories of his romantic conquests in Germany."

I gulped. That would be the day.

"What did he talk about after the first minute?" Vince demanded.

"The Marshall Plan," she said innocently.

"It won't last," Peg said uncertainly, still trying to get a reading of the situation. She would have to wait till she and Rosemarie were alone.

"It might. . . . Wasn't that a great party! I really felt sorry for poor Alice. She's still carrying the torch for that creep. . . ."

So we talked about the gossip and the old pairings and the new pairings and who was pregnant and who was dating.

"I'm tired," Rosemarie said finally. "I'm going to bed."

The 1950-model Chucky waited a few discreet moments and then said,

"I guess I better leave you two lovebirds alone. I've had a hard day. See you in the morning, Peg."

My sister and her date were too astonished to reply.

In my room I hung up my suit and put a robe on over my shorts.

It's all Your fault, I told God. You were the one who sent the snow that kept me in her apartment that night. I've never been the same since. Now you've got me just where you want me. I'm in love, damn it. Sorry. . . . I don't want to be in love with Rosemarie or anyone else. I'm too young to be in love. I don't have time to be in love. I don't have the money to think about being in love.

Now what am I supposed to do? It's all Your fault. You want me to take care of her. You sent those other women into my life to give me some practice. It's not fair.

You're trying to tell me that I've been in love with her for a long time? Well, that's true, but it's irrelevant!

She is wonderful!

I didn't mean that. Well, I did mean it. But it's irrelevant. Am I supposed to marry her?

I shivered at the thought, partly perhaps with delight at the prospect.

"Anyway," I said aloud. "She's Your problem as well as mine. Take good care of her for me."

I unfastened the belt on my robe, thought a moment, fastened it again, and then slipped out of my room and hurried softly to the other end of the corridor.

What if Mom or Dad or Peg found me?

Well, that would be too bad!

A trail of light escaped from beneath the door of "Rosie's room." I pushed the door open without knocking.

She was sitting in front of a vanity mirror clad in the black, strapless corset which had been the armor under her dress. She was brushing her long hair, disconsolately, I thought.

"Chucky!" she exclaimed.

She cowered, surprised and frightened and delectable.

I took her chin into my hand and tilted her face up so I could look into her eyes. "I forgot to say something."

She gulped.

I touched her lips lightly with my own and touched her bare shoulder with my free hand. "I forgot to say that I love you, I have always loved you and always will love you."

I kissed her a second time, with equal gentleness, and tightened my grip on her shoulder. "I don't intend ever to let you go."

Her eyes were wide and confused.

And wonderful.

"Now go to bed and get a good night's sleep and don't worry about anything." I turned and walked to the door. Luck or providence kept me from falling flat on my face.

I turned at the door. My love was still sitting on the vanity bench with the hairbrush frozen in her hand, a wonderfully erotic statue.

Why had I not brought my camera? Next time.

"Good night, Rosemarie. Pleasant dreams." I closed the door before she could answer.

Just as I reached the door to my room, I heard Peg drifting up the stairs. I managed to make it into my room in time. Just barely.

I leaned against the door and realized my heart was pounding furiously. Why had I taken such a foolish chance?

Because I was in love?

Why else?

And she did look lovely in that black corset, didn't she?

You win, I informed the Deity as I collapsed into instant, satisfied, and peaceful sleep.

I woke before the rest of the house and rushed to the darkroom. Before I began on the previous night's work, I opened my Rosemarie file, extracted the best of my shots, and pinned them, in neat order of course, on the walls—a little private Rosemarie showing.

When I developed the new rolls of film, I found a dozen shots from the Vets dance that were worth printing. Great archival work of Peg and Rosemarie!

And, I sighed to myself, such beautiful women!

Their beauty would fade, I told myself. They would age and die. So would I. Morose thoughts on a morning when I had admitted to myself that I was in love, indeed hopelessly in love. Yet I knew dimly, in ways I could not understand or articulate, that the beauty of these two beloved young women would triumph even over death. What I had caught in my camera the night before could never disappear.

"Women of the house," I shouted as I burst into the breakfast room, "I want me breakfast!"

"Chucky!" the good April, Peg, and Rosemarie exclaimed together.

They were sitting around the table in pajamas and robes chattering over their tea and coffee, doubtless about me and how cute I had been at the dance.

"We thought you were still in bed, dear!"

"I've been working since sunup." I laid the prints on the table and piled bacon and waffles on my plate.

"I'll make you some fresh ones, dear. . . . Oh, what cute pictures! You are clever with your cute little camera!"

I swallowed a large glass of orange juice as they looked over the pictures.

"No men in them," Peg protested with a frown.

"Women are more interesting."

"Only two women," Rosemarie murmured. "You should have taken a picture of Jenny to send to that idiot in Galway."

Naturally I had.

"Such beautiful young women," Mom said as she poured batter into the waffle iron.

"They don't look like us, not really," Peg said slowly. "Too perfect."

"She looks like you." Rosemarie gestured at one figure. "The other one isn't me at all."

I shoved a syrup-drenched quarter waffle into my mouth.

"Ingrate!" I tried to say.

"Don't talk with food in your mouth, dear."

"They're wonderful, Chuck," Peg said. "They really are. You see us all too clearly—shrewd, scheming fishwives all dressed up for a party, but conniving every moment."

"I don't see anything," I said, sticking to my historic position that I was merely doing archives and not interpreting. "The camera is the only one that sees."

"It's embarrassing to be seen the way we really are." Rosemarie shook her head. "Kind of spiritually naked. You shouldn't see us that way, Chuck."

"Rosie darling," the good April came to my defense as she replaced my vanished waffle, "you don't understand what Chucky has done. He sees two strong, beautiful, and tender young women and celebrates them. He's really very clever with that little camera."

"And very determined," I added.

My sister and foster sister looked up at me, still frowning.

"What did you say?" Peg asked.

"I agreed with the good April that the two grand duchesses were strong, beautiful, and tender young women—which is obvious—and added that they are also very determined."

The glanced at each other, exchanging signals, and then laughed together.

"You win, Chuck," Peg said. "Very determined indeed. And they're wonderful pictures. You must make some prints for Vince."

"I always said you were a genius, Chucky!" Rosemarie hugged me. Both of them then kissed me, interfering with my consumption of waffles.

"Of course," the good April concluded as she placed a new stack of waffles on my plate, "he'd love to take pictures of you with your clothes off. That's why he's going to be a photographer."

"Curses, I'm found out!" I mumbled as my face burned.

I dared not look at my two young models.

Later, when I was in the darkroom making more prints, Rosemarie knocked on the door.

"May I come in, Chuck?" she asked meekly.

I had never admitted her into my sanctum before.

"Okay."

"At least I knocked," she said as she entered and gently closed the door. She was still wearing her pajamas and robe.

"That you did."

She glanced around the walls.

"Is this a Rosie exhibition or something?"

"A Rosemarie exhibition," I corrected her.

"Doesn't it distract you from your work?"

"A lot less than the real person when she enters my darkroom."

"I knocked."

"You did."

"You didn't knock last night."

"I didn't."

Enough of this conversation, I told myself. I embraced her and kissed her. She didn't fight me off.

"I'm glad you're not wearing that armor this morning."

She giggled. "I hate it too."

"Now the real Rosemarie is in my arms."

"Not too much to her."

We locked in an ardent embrace.

I pushed aside her robe, opened the top buttons of her pajamas, and caressed her breasts, warm, firm, delicious.

"Chucky . . ."

"I've wanted to do this since your breasts first appeared."

She leaned against me. I touched both nipples gently, then carefully redid the buttons and rearranged her robe.

"You don't own me," she said, struggling for breath. "You have no right to think you can do whatever you want to me."

"I certainly don't own you, Rosemarie my love, but still you're mine and always have been and always will be."

"I could say the same thing to you."

"I hope you do."

"All right, Chucky Ducky," she said, laughing. "I will. You're mine and always have been and always will be."

In such exchanges are lives predestined.

She slipped out of my arms. "Which is why I came. You didn't give me a chance last night to say I love you. I do, Charles Cronin O'Malley. I do love you and I'll always love you. Now I'm getting out of this room before the aphrodisiac smells destroy me completely."

I let her go and leaned against my worktable.

Conquest.

Whose?

Just then I was in love and it didn't matter.

She opened the door again and poked her head into the darkroom, her face crimson. "I'm more embarrassed by what your camera sees than by what you might have seen if you were hiding outside my shower."

She disappeared again before I could respond.

I am embarrassed as I tell this story of St. Patrick's Day, 1950. We were so young and innocent. We knew so little of life and its tragedies. Two young people fell in love, married, and they all lived happily ever after. Wasn't that what it was all about?

We were too young. In our defense, in those times, shaped by the war and the postwar prosperity, people married young. Twenty-two and nineteen did not seem unreasonable ages to make lifelong decisions.

5

Peg was pounding on the door of my room.

"Wake up, Chuck! Rosemarie had an accident."

It was a Saturday morning in late May. Mom and Dad were at Long Beach, opening the house for the summer and enjoying a rare respite from the obligations of the firm. The new staff members had eased their work, but not their need to be obsessive about it.

However, they felt they were entitled to at least one weekend off, mostly because Rosemarie virtually ordered them to take it.

"You should celebrate the first grandchild with two weeks' vacation, not two days'," that imperious matriarch-in-the-making had announced.

For Charles John McCormack had made a somewhat early appearance and shortly thereafter had been inducted into the Mystical Body, as we used to call it, and now the People of God.

Both of which were dumb names for the Church.

That's right: Charles McCormack. And so that there would be no doubt that Uncle Chucky (not, as I would have thought, the far more promising "Uncle Charley") was the one being honored, that worthy was pressed into service to be godfather when Monsignor Mugsy poured the waters of Baptism over the child's sleeping head. Rosemarie, radiant at the tiny kid in her arms, was of course the godmother.

"She's entitled to it," Peg whispered in my ear. "If she hadn't bawled Ted out, he would have never broken with Doctor."

News to me.

Perhaps the child's name was suggested by the fact that the new Mc-Cormack was tiny and had red hair, which even then showed signs of turning kinky.

Doctor had not come to the Baptism. He had taken one look at Charles John in the nursery at St. Anne's Hospital and announced, "Sickly child. Must take after his mother's family," and departed.

As I understood the hints and allusions, Doctor's "allowance" had been terminated and replaced by a "loan" from my parents, to use Rosemarie's vocabulary. Ted, I suspected, was going through the torments of the damned as he struggled to break away from Doctor's domination. Perhaps he was learning, as he prepared to begin his own psychiatric practice, that there are some parents whom a child can never please, no matter how hard they try.

Then there were the crazy O'Malleys, who were pleased with almost anything. Or almost nothing.

They were, heaven knows, pleased with my budding "romance"—as they saw it—with Rosemarie.

And especially delighted when the two of us walked down the aisle of St. Ursula's gym to receive Communion together at eleven-fifteen Mass.

Despite my liberal interpretation of sin when I had romanced Cordelia, I debated, only half seriously, with Rosemarie about receiving Communion. I argued that the "necking and petting" in which we were engaged had to be confessed on Saturday night if we were to receive Communion. Moreover, I insisted, the most that was to be tolerated between Confession and Communion the next morning were very chaste pecks on the cheek.

Rosemarie thought that was funny.

"We don't intend to stop, Chucky, so why pretend?"

"Absolution is valid so long as we intend to try to stop."

"We don't even intend to *try* to stop. Anyway, do you think God is going to send us to hell for a little gentle loving? Isn't that the way he made young people? Isn't that how He prepares us for marriage?"

It didn't seem very gentle to me.

"I think God probably understands," I admitted, "but the Church doesn't."

"I'll bet on God," she said,

I would let the marriage remark pass completely unnoticed.

Our foreplay was in retrospect pretty mild. We both enjoyed it enormously. Unlike many young women of her generation, Rosemarie was not given to drawing lines. Rather she trusted me completely. She was a gift to which I could do whatever I wanted. Such a strategy guaranteed that I would be both restrained and gentle.

"You trust me too much," I told her after one particularly joyous romp in the front seat of her convertible.

"No," she said, rearranging her hair. "If it was some other boy, I would be trusting him too much, but not you."

"You have me all figured out?" I grumbled.

"You're an intriguing mystery, Chucky." She pinched my cheek. "I could spend a lifetime trying to figure you out and not succeed. But I do know that you won't exploit a woman. Probably you couldn't if you wanted to."

Rosemarie was not pushing me toward the altar, not even toward the kind of commitment that seemed to exist between Peg and Vince. She seemed quite content to trust me in this as in all other matters.

"You're ogling me, young woman," I said as we sat on a bench at Skelton Park after I had beaten her 2–1 in a tennis match. "That's why you lost."

She laughed happily. "You are a terrible distraction, Chucky Ducky. Put your shirt back on before the Oak Park cops come and arrest you."

I did as I was told.

"Besides, you ogle me too."

"Do you know what I do when I ogle you?"

"Certainly! You imagine that you're taking off my clothes!"

"You don't object to that?"

"If it were some other men, I would."

"You do the same thing?"

"Not exactly." She pushed me flat on the bench and covered my face with kisses. "Don't ask personal questions like that."

I had a hard time picturing myself as sexually attractive. "Cute," maybe, but little more.

I was about to graduate from the University. I had figured out the system—or rather I had finally accepted Rosemarie's definition of it. Glib talk in class counted for nothing, although many of the verbal young people in the undergraduate college thought that it did. Flair was more important in tests and term papers than rote repetition of lectures and notes, the exact opposite of the Notre Dame standards. Since, heaven knows, I was not devoid of flair, I did pretty well, though not as well as Rosemarie.

I had not replied to Palmer Tennant's invitation. All I wanted to be was an accountant. Still, I might earn more money in the accounting market if I had a doctorate.

Doctor Chucky?

No. Charles Cronin O'Malley, Ph.D. It had a nice ring to it. Well, why not? That would show them all, though I wasn't sure who it would show, save for Notre Dame—and they wouldn't notice.

Maybe I could continue as I had—school and work and GI Bill and living at home. Why not?

No way to support a wife and family?

Well, who was expecting a wife and family?

Having won her argument about my taking my camera out of mothballs, Rosemarie had returned to her voice lessons. I had never seen her so happy.

The "postwar" world was going strong, despite increasing signs of a serious recession. GM had developed a one-piece windshield, RCA had developed a color TV tube, educators were complaining that TV was getting in the way of homework, Kurt Weill and Nijinsky had died, the Vietminh had started a war against the French, Joe McCarthy had launched his anticommunist crusade. Everyone at the University was fighting about George Orwell's *1984*. Elizabeth Taylor married Nicky Hilton, we were singing "Mona Lisa" and "C'est si bon," and Rosemarie and I had loved *King Solomon's Mines*.

"You only liked it"—she poked me—"because Deborah Kerr was naked in it."

"Not naked enough," I responded, earning yet another poke.

"Chucky, you are obsessed with women's bodies."

"Would you rather have me uninterested in them?" I asked, squeezing her thigh.

"*Well*, I'd never swim naked in a pool like that."

"I bet you would."

"Only with a man I loved."

"Fair enough."

Only a few of us knew where Korea was.

I heard whispers around the house that Vince and Peg would be married in two years, after he had finished two years of law school and she three years at Rosary.

"So young," Mom had whispered to Dad—a remark that has been on the lips of every mom in human history.

"Older than you were."

"That's different. Times were different then."

That has been the rejoinder of moms for the whole of human existence.

Since the war, Catholic women who attended college had been almost expected to be engaged at graduation, and it was not uncommon for them to leave college after two years to work for a year, so that they would be married before their twenty-first birthday. Moreover, the experience of the vets who combined education and marriage and parenthood had demolished the notion that a man should postpone marriage until his education was finished, at least.

My commitment to such a doctrine was becoming increasingly theoretical, although I would not have admitted it.

We didn't know it then, but we were in the midst of the baby boom.

— 6 —

"An accident?" I said to Peg that morning in May when she woke me up. I shook my head, trying to shake sleep out of it, still convinced that I was dreaming.

"Her father is away someplace. The housekeeper never answers the phone at night. Mom and Dad are down at the lake. She's in Jackson Park Hospital. Where's that?"

"On Stony Island, I think."

"Is that a city or something?"

"No, it's a street, sixteen hundred east. Is she hurt?"

"I don't know," Peg wailed. "Can we drive out there and find out?"

"Sure," I said. "Why not?"

The sun was just beginning to peek over the roof of Jackson Park Hospital when we arrived. Peg charged into the lobby and up to the reception desk.

"We're members of Miss Clancy's family," she said smoothly. "She was raised with us. Everyone else is out of town. May we go up to her floor and talk to the nurses?"

A modest enough request, no? And in those days it was much easier to get by a hospital reception desk.

On the third floor, Peg searched out a wispy young intern who might not be immune to her charms.

He was putty in her hands.

"Miss Clancy is all right," he said. "Lucky to be alive I'd say. A slight concussion. Some stitches on the top of her head which that wonderful black hair will hide. Two spectacular shiners. She's resting quietly now."

"May we see her, Doctor?" there was a pathetic plea in the title. "We were raised together and the rest of the family is out of town."

"Well . . . ," he hesitated.

"It would reassure her to know that someone cares."

The young man nodded sagely. "You're right. It has been a long night for her. She's in 310. Try to be quiet. Other people on the floor are still asleep. I'll tell the nurses it's okay."

"Impressive," I said when we were alone.

"A snap," Peg replied.

Rosemarie was sitting up in bed, looking battered and confused. A bandage around her head and two ugly black eyes. Her hair fell in disorder against a white hospital gown. She looked as gorgeous as ever. Not quite indestructible, perhaps, but just then maybe the next best thing to it.

"Rosie!"

"Peg!"

Embraces, hugs, tears.

"Hi, Rosemarie."

"Hi, Chuck."

"What happened?"

"I'm ashamed of myself," she murmured. "I wasn't even all that drunk."

"Down on yourself again?" Peg sighed.

"I guess I must have been. I'm glad no one was in the car with me. I could have killed them."

Tears spilled out of her eyes and down the big black blotches.

"Poor Rosie!"

"I don't remember what happened. The doctor—cute little blond guy—"

"We saw him."

"He said I hit a stoplight. Knocked it down. Pretty near totaled the car. Thank God I didn't hit anyone else."

"You just can't get down on yourself that way."

"I know that, Peg. It was something one of my professors said, I guess . . . I'm terribly sorry, Chuck. I promise it will never happen again."

"Sure, Rosemarie." I patted her hand.

"Are you planning on marrying her, Chuck?" Peg demanded as soon as we began the long ride back to Oak Park.

It was a straight question and deserved a straight answer. So I offered one that for me was pretty straight.

"Probably."

Silence.

"The two of you are in love?"

"Possibly."

"I've never seen her so happy as she has been since St. Patrick's Day. She's put on five of the fifteen pounds her doctor says she needs. Her hard edges have softened. She sings a lot. . . . Then something like this happens."

"She's had a hard life."

"Now you're making excuses for her instead of my doing it."

"You don't think I should marry her?"

That startled Peg.

"That's a very direct question, Chuck. I've never known you to be so direct."

"Is a direct answer possible?"

"No . . . yes . . . I don't know. Goof that I am, I thought love would straighten her out."

"No advice, then?"

"I love her very much. But you're my brother. I love you too. . . ."

It was sufficient warning.

She was out of the hospital in a couple of days, with only a few headaches and traces of double vision. The white convertible turned out to be repairable. Rosemarie was charged with driving too fast for conditions. Dad told us that there were only small amounts of alcohol in her bloodstream. I suppose her father had the ticket fixed.

Coming home from my Saturday morning efforts at O'Hanlon and O'Halloran later in the day, I told myself that I was cured of Rosemarie Helen Clancy. Permanently and forever.

If I need a powerful reminder of the dark side of her character, I had been given it. Stay away from the girl. She's pretty, she's smart, she's willing.

And she's poison.

That night there was a card—surface mail—from Tim Boylan.

> Charles C.
>
> Conas ta tu!
>
> That's Irish. It means "How are you?"
>
> I figured you'd find me eventually.
>
> I like it here. It's poor, but peaceful, and the people are wonderful. They leave me alone. Right now that's all I want. Thank you for writing. Maybe we'll see each other again someday. I'm off the sauce. For good.
>
> Slan go foil!
>
> Tim
>
> P.S. Give my best to your Rosemarie. Besides Jenny she's the most beautiful woman I know. You'll never get away from her, Charles C.

I reread it, pondered it, and decided that it was a tiny bit more hopeful than not. I'd reply, but not like I was in a rush.

For a little less than two weeks I stuck to my resolution to stay away from Rosemarie. We drove down to the Notre Dame graduation with Peg on a hot and humid June day. By the time we had reached South Bend I was as captivated by Rosemarie as I had ever been. She certainly would, I told myself, stop drinking soon.

College graduations are anticlimactic. Parents, relatives, romantic partners, even the graduates themselves understand that real life still waits. At Notre Dame, under the oppressive sun and surrounded by fresh green grass and bright flowers, with the Golden Dome looming baroque and ponderous above us, happiness seemed to me to be edgy and forced, the cheerfulness and the joyous hugs not quite authentic, bright eyes and quick grins somehow haunted. Perhaps I'm reading back into it what was to happen in Korea before the month was over. Maybe all graduations are that way.

I had expected I would be angry and bitter. I still hated the Holy Cross priests for what they had done to me, but I realized that I had not belonged there and they had unintentionally done me a favor.

"What are you doing now, O'Malley?" one of them asked me as we were milling around outside after the ceremony.

"I'm surprised that you recognized me, Father."

"You're the kind of person that's hard to forget. I hope you're planning to go back to college."

Rosemarie cheated me of my line.

"Charles is graduating from the University of Chicago in two weeks, Father. Then he has a fellowship at the University to go on for his doctorate in economics."

"Well, don't lose your faith there, O'Malley."

"If he didn't lose it here, Father, he won't lose it anywhere."

The priest drifted away.

"My lines."

"More effective from me, Chucky."

We went through the same little act with many of my former classmates, especially those who thought that the University of Chicago was a hotbed of Marxist paganism. Then we came upon Christopher, splendid in his Marines uniform with its shiny gold second lieutenant's bars. Cordelia was chatting with him.

"Been telling everyone about your own graduation?" Christopher asked with a wicked grin, before I could congratulate him.

"Rosemarie is saving me the trouble."

"And I'm telling everyone that he has a fellowship to study for a Ph.D. in economics at the University," she added.

It was not quite the truth, but it was adequate as a shorthand.

We all congratulated one another. Rosemarie, with a winner's good sportsmanship, was especially nice to Cordelia.

Actually she wasn't the winner. I was kind of a recovered fumble.

"I'm leaving for Paris next week," Cordelia told us joyously. "Two years at the Conservatory."

We congratulated her again. Rosemarie hugged her. She slipped away to talk to others.

"Nice girl," said Rosemarie.

"You're kind to your rivals," Christopher said with a wink.

"She never was a rival, not really. Are you still convinced that she has no talent, Chuck?"

"Lots of skills, no talent."

"Poor kid. Someone will have to pick up the pieces someday."

I had yet to learn that when my foster sister said that sort of thing she meant that she would eventually pick up the pieces if no one else did.

"Maybe she'll meet a nice Frenchman," Christopher said.

"There are no nice Frenchmen," I informed him.

We all laughed. Chucky was reformed but still outrageous.

Christopher had his orders to leave for the Western Pacific the following week. We wished him well.

"You two are being civilized to each other," he said, his brown eyes darting back and forth between Rosemarie and myself.

"I've always been civilized," she replied. "Chucky Ducky is learning."

We found Vince and Peggy and Ed Murray and his current date, whose name I don't remember, and their friends. We congratulated them all, Rosemarie hugged everyone in sight. Peg raised an eyebrow in approval.

"She seems fine."

"Why wouldn't she?" Vince asked.

We didn't answer.

Peg would stay with the crowd and join us later at Long Beach. Rosemarie and I slipped away.

"Odd experience for you, wasn't it Chucky?" Rosemarie asked as she drove her convertible down U.S. 20 toward La Porte.

"Not as odd as I thought it would be."

"They're all nice boys, but you're not like them, are you?"

"Old man."

"The years in Germany?"

"Probably."

"And a feeling that you're going in a different direction?"

"Maybe."

She chuckled to herself.

I was still planning on being an accountant, right? Okay, an accountant with a Ph.D., but still an accountant. How was that any different from the plans for law and medicine and business of my Golden Dome contemporaries?

Yet I did sense that I was different from them, even from Christopher with his plans for Republican politics on the North Side of Chicago. Did I have other, as yet unspecified, games to play? Had my years at the University made me different, perhaps given me illusions? Or was it Rosemarie who had filled my head with nonsense? If it was nonsense.

I banished such foolish thoughts.

On that warm Saturday evening of the Memorial Day weekend, Rosemarie and I, in our swimsuits, lay in each other's arms on the dark beach, content that night merely to embrace.

"I absolutely promise that I'll never do it again," she said, for perhaps the tenth time.

If it had required only willpower, I'm sure she would have kept that promise.

I nibbled at her bare breasts. She moaned with pleasure.

Either I had to end our relationship, or we were headed toward the altar and the marriage bed.

Later I paused at the top of the stairs leading from our house to the beach, took one step down, and then made the rest of them in a flying leap. Pleased with this accomplishment, I trotted down the beach and took the one leap to the top of the house next door. I turned at the top and floated back to the beach and soared briefly over the lake. Then I raced down the stairs to the cafeteria at Fenwick High School and made the last half of the trip in another quick soar. The white-robed Dominican priest at the bottom of the stairs whirled on me and pointed a warning finger. Only it was Rosemarie, naked underneath the robes, who was screaming at me. I discovered that I had lost my clothes.

Then I experienced a terrible agony of pleasure.

I woke up with a jump. It took me several moments to realize that it had been only a dream. I had flown at Fenwick, hadn't I? After thinking about it for a couple of minutes, I realized I hadn't done that either.

What was that all about? I asked God. Never mind, I don't want to know.

Mostly because Rosemarie insisted, I continued to work at O'H and O'H during June and began my graduate work at the University. I told Palmer

Tennant that it was an experiment and I could make no promises. He must have decided that it was a rational economic choice to settle for that.

I was distracted at both the lectures and at my job downtown by obsessive and delectable fantasies about Rosemarie. I would like to be able to say that I tried to think out, clearly and sensibly, what I ought to do. I didn't do that, however. I'm not sure that any young male would have. I drifted, postponing both thought and decision.

7

Rosemarie made the decision for me, as the woman usually does.

"Would you stop the car in front of that big Dutch Colonial house, Chucky Ducky?"

We were driving north on East Avenue, returning from the Lake Theater on a hot June night. We had seen *Twelve O'Clock High* and stopped at Petersen's for our two malted milks each.

Rosemarie was wearing white shorts and a blue blouse that matched her eyes. The shorts made it possible for me to caress her thigh in the theater. She had, however, arranged our seating at Petersen's so she was out of reach.

"I'll have to stop this soon," she had told me with a wink. "I have put on twelve pounds in the last five months. My doctor says fifteen is about right. . . . Do you think I'm getting fat?"

"You'll never get fat, Rosemarie."

"That's what my doctor says too. He says the real danger is that I'll end up a beanpole. Still, some of my clothes don't fit me anymore. Do you notice the change, Chuck?"

"I notice that you are happy most of the time."

"Yeah, I know. That's because I'm in love. But I mean do you notice that I've put on weight?"

I was naïve about women, but not so naïve as to think that would be an easy question to answer.

"You're more shapely," I said cautiously. "There's more of you to cuddle. Either way, you're beautiful."

She blushed and beamed.

"Same old Chucky Ducky. Always clever with words"—she touched my hand affectionately—"especially when the woman asks a loaded question."

I kissed her hand. She giggled.

"I'm glad you weren't flying in one of those B-17s."

"I'm sorry I ever wasted time in the Army."

"If there's another war, they won't be able to take you."

"There's not going to be another war."

We sang "Good Night, Irene" as we drove north. I was to drop her off at her father's house. He was away in Las Vegas. Then I would pick her up the next morning and drive to Long Beach and join the rest of the family. Neither of us was willing to risk my staying.

Then she told me to drive over to Euclid and stop in front of the big Dutch Colonial.

"They're doing some work here," I said.

"Remodeling it completely."

"Nice place . . . whose is it?"

"Mine."

"Yours?"

"Uh-huh. My guardian had no objection to my buying it. . . . I'm putting in a really big darkroom. All modern equipment."

Gulp.

Double gulp.

"You're going to take up photography?" Slap on the arm. "When are you planning to move in?"

"Probably January."

"A Christmas wedding?"

"Maybe."

"Who's the lucky man?"

"Haven't made up my mind yet!"

I realized that the decision had been made long ago, long before the St. Patrick's Day dance, long before the night at her apartment, long before I had been thrown out of Notre Dame. Probably when we had started corresponding during my time in Bamberg.

"Well, if you don't find anyone else, I might be available."

I thought of Trudi, my lost love from Germany. I had tried to find her, had I not? She probably had found someone else.

"I'll consider that possibility."

We laughed and hugged fiercely and assured each other of our enduring love.

"I've made some other arrangements too."

"Oh?"

Why did I feel a trap closing on me?

Doubtless because one had.

"I've bought a seat on the Board of Trade!"

"What!"

"Not for myself."

"I don't want it," I said firmly, knowing that I would have to take it. "I'm no good at exciting situations!"

My hand, working entirely on its own, found its way to her breast. She held it and pushed it harder against herself, unbuttoning her blouse with her other hand.

"Yes, you are. I don't know what you did in Germany, but they would not have given you that medal unless you did something exciting."

"I want to be an accountant," I said stubbornly, as my fingers probed beneath her bra.

"Accounting is boring."

"It is not."

"It is too. This way you can go to school and take your pictures in the afternoon."

"I don't want my wife to support me."

"I'm not supporting you, I'm loaning you the money. Some capital to trade with too."

"Absolutely not!"

She considered my refusal.

"I don't want to live in your house either," I said.

"If you want to live with me, you'll have to live in my house."

I found her nipple, already hard, and caressed it gently.

"Chucky," she gasped.

"You want me to stop?"

"Certainly not!"

"All right, I'll live in your house till I can afford to buy one, but I won't take your money."

"Fair enough compromise," she said. "Now you'd better take me home . . . to my other home, that is."

I slipped her bra back into place, buttoned up her blouse, and kissed her solidly.

Even as she trotted up the steps of the house at 1105 North Menard and turned to wave back at me, I knew that she would find an indirect way to put me on the floor of the Board of Trade.

Fair exchange? A risky job in exchange for her body?

It certainly seemed so that night.

Back at the O'Malley residence on East Avenue, I realized that our engagement would become common knowledge at Long Beach the next day. Doubtless she had requested Father John Raven to reserve the day at St. Ursula's. No escape, not that I wanted to escape. Exactly.

Yet I was scared, terrified, if truth be told. How had I managed to slip into the trap so easily?

I would be expected to provide a ring for her. I chuckled to myself. Fortunately I had bought a ring with a presentably large stone at a sale I had seen in a small jewelry store on State Street. Just in case I should need it.

The next morning I put the ring on her finger as she sat next to me in the car in front of her father's house at 1105 North Menard.

"Chucky!" she exclaimed. "Did you go shopping this morning? Oh, what an idiot I am! You've had it all along!"

"I learned in the Army that a good solider has to be prepared for everything."

She kissed me enthusiastically.

"It's such a big stone, Chuck darling, you shouldn't . . ."

"Yes?"

"Strike that last comment," she said grimly. "I'm an ass."

I laughed. "Don't use such terrible language about my fiancée!"

"Yes, sir."

She stared at the ring in fascination as we drove through the city.

On Sunday morning of that weekend the headline in the *Tribune* reported that North Korean troops had invaded South Korea.

8

"Are you sure they can't take you, Chuck? Aren't they calling up the re-serves?

"Only after the women and the children." I sighed, contemplating my first malted milk with distaste. "It's the active reserves they've called up. I was inactive and my term expired in June."

We were sitting in Peterson's on a drab September evening. Rosemarie, having added twelve of her intended fifteen pounds, was now limiting her-self to but one malt. I didn't feel like a second, but for the sake of my reputation I would have to drink it.

The jukebox reminded us that "diamonds are a girl's best friend."

Rosemarie brushed her ring possessively.

"Do you feel bad that you're not over there fighting?"

"No. I did my time. I feel bad that Christopher and Leo are over there and that, if this foolish thing doesn't stop, Vince and Ed and all my friends will be over there too."

The American public was supporting the war, as it always did when the war was new and the casualties were light. If the war stretched on and more and more young men were killed, then the people would turn against it.

Chris had been in the Western Pacific before the invasion. Leo was there now too. Since the First Marine Division had not been in combat yet, there was obviously something afoot. I prayed every night for both of them.

I accepted the conventional wisdom that we had to draw a line beyond which Stalin could not go. But I hated the war and had begun my pilgrimage toward opposition to war—at least to long overseas wars fought by draft armies. My hatred for the war was based on the fact that my generation had to fight it—my friends, my classmates at St. Ursula's and Fenwick and Notre Dame and Chicago. I was very happy that I would not have to join them.

Coward?

Never said I wasn't.

Christopher had sent me one brief note.

Can't say where I am or what's up. Action soon I think. I'm scared. Pray for me. Love to Rosie.

Chris.

I called Jane Devlin to ask whether she had heard from Leo.

"Lunkhead called our house at Lake Geneva before he left. I wasn't home. He left a message. It was a week before anyone told me that he'd called. I don't know what the message was."

She sounded so sad, almost like she had lost him already.

"Any letter?"

"No . . . it was kind of a strange relationship, Chuck. We loved each other, I think. Mostly at the Lake in the summer. We weren't close when we were in Chicago."

That was weird, but who was I to talk about a weird relationship with a woman?

"You didn't break up or anything like that?"

"I don't think so. We were very close and not that close at all. He didn't invite me to his graduation from Loyola. I guess they didn't give him time in June before they sent him to camp somewhere. . . . I'm worried sick about him."

I promised her my prayers.

"I hear that you and Rosemarie are engaged. Congratulations!"

"A lot of people are saying that. She has a diamond and she claims I gave it to her. So I guess we're engaged."

"Same old Chucky."

Her laugh was sad and lonely. My heart ached for her.

It had been a bad summer. The Catholic War Veterans' softball league had dried up. The vets were now for the most part responsible husbands and fathers. Some of them were back in service. They had stayed in the active reserves to make a few extra dollars and now would be in harm's way again. None of my crowd were at the Magic Tap anymore. The Greenwood Community had collapsed, as communes do. Some of the members had been called back into the service; others were threatened with the draft. They were fighting one another over ideology; the Pope's condemnation of the New Theology had disillusioned them. Many of them never finished their dissertations and were teaching at small Catholic colleges. Of those who did finish, only one or two had distinguished careers. There would be many more young Catholics at the University in later years, some of them destined to be brilliant scholars. But the enthusiasm of that first wave was never matched.

I had taken my classes at the University and worked at O'H and O'H.

My parents had proposed to provide me with the money for a seat on the Board of Trade—the last refuge for a young Irish Catholic male who didn't seem to be qualified for anything else. Rosemarie was behind it, of course. I had procrastinated. Wait till after the wedding, I had argued.

"Chucky, dear, you don't seem like a young man who is engaged to be married at a Christmas wedding."

"I'm worried, Mom."

"Poor dear, you always worry too much. You laugh a lot and cut up, but deep down inside you're a worrier. That's a shame because you'll be happy with Rosemarie . . . eventually."

That settled that.

Nevertheless, I continued to worry.

About marriage, about the war, about my friends, about Peg and Vince, about the future. I didn't hang out anywhere, except one or two nights a week with Rosemarie at Petersen's.

The North Korean army was far better trained and equipped than Americans had anticipated. They had wiped out the Twenty-fourth Division, the first American outfit to arrive in Korea, and pushed us back into a small enclave around the port of Pusan at the bottom end of Korea. However, we had held them there and there were rumors of a counterattack.

That meant the First Marines and Leo and Christopher.

The Twenty-fourth had been part of the Army of Occupation in Japan, no more prepared for battle then we had been in Bamberg. No wonder that our infantry broke and ran—"bugged out," as they called it—at the first sign of an enemy.

"You're worried about them, aren't you, Chucky?" Rosemarie asked me that night at Petersen's.

She touched my hand with her fingers and sent a shot of warm electricity through my body. Would her touch always do that to me?

"I guess so."

"There's nothing you can do."

"Do you remember when Dad was at Fort Leonard Wood in 1941 and likely to go to New Guinea or some other terrible place?"

"Sure! You said he would be a menace to all the troops, including himself."

"And a certain obnoxious little ten-year-old said that if I knew so much why didn't I do something about it."

She colored and lowered her eyes. "I can't imagine who that would have been."

"You don't remember saying that?"

"It sounds like me, Chuck, but I don't remember."

A remark that changed my life and she doesn't even remember!

"Then you don't know what I did?"

She shook her head.

"I went over to see the Congressman and got Dad transferred to Fort Sheridan where he belonged."

"You did? Chuck, how wonderful! And you were only thirteen!"

"Yeah, so the Congressman asked me if I played football and I said I did, which was true. I didn't say I was fourth string quarterback on a team with three strings, and that's how I got into that comedy of errors when we beat Mount Carmel for the Catholic league championship in 1945."

"You beat Carmel, Chucky, all by yourself!"

There was no longer any point in arguing. Even Rosemarie, who knew the facts better than anyone, had reinterpreted them. The facts were that I was a mascot and the holder for kicks. When the real quarterbacks were wiped out by injuries and the flu, they sent me in with orders not to call my own play, of which there was no danger in any event. The team moved down the field toward the Mount Carmel goal line by dint of my skillfully keeping out of their way. On the last play the Carmel defenders broke through our line. In sheer terror, I threw a pass in the direction of no one. Some idiot blocked it and it fell on my head and then into my unwilling hands. I saw this ten-foot monster—Ed Murray, as it later turned out—coming toward me and I ran for my life. He hit me like a locomotive. I flew into the air and the ball flew out of my hands, according to the ref only after I broke the plane of the goal line.

Somewhere there must be movies that show the truth.

"You're sure you don't remember telling me that if I was so smart I would do something about it?"

"I don't. But I was a terrible little bitch in those days. . . . Oh, you think you should do something about Vince and Leo and Christopher and Ed!"

I shrugged and slurped up the rest of my first malt. The young waitress, knowing the game, promptly replaced it.

"That's ridiculous, Chuck. You can't assume responsibility for everyone."

I shrugged again.

The jukebox played "C'est la Vie," which didn't help my mood.

"I sent Timmy Boylan an airmail invitation to our wedding," I said. "I put in a note saying that we would expect him."

"Do you think he'll come?"

"No. But he'll know we haven't forgotten him."

"Are you marrying me to save me, Chuck?"

Bad question. Wrong time. Maybe I was.

"I'm marrying you because I think you'll be a good lay!"

"Chucky Ducky!" She turned purple. "What would the good April say if she heard you!"

"Something like 'Well, darling, that is one of the things men, poor dears, want from their wives, isn't it!' "

We both laughed.

I was pleased with myself. I had avoided the question.

"Well, Chucky Ducky?"

"Well what?"

"Do you think I will be a good lay?"

The music changed to "Younger Than Springtime," our song. We began to sing it, an obligation we always honored. Like everyone else who witnessed our little act, a musical comedy come to life, the Petersen's people applauded.

"Well . . . ?" she persisted after the applause died.

"Certainly you will. The point is, Rosemarie, I'm marrying you because I love you."

I wasn't so sure that I had the faintest idea what love meant.

It was an evening like the whole summer. I felt miserable after Rosemarie dropped me off at the O'Malley house on East Avenue and drove off to "our" place on Euclid, where she was living some of the time so she could supervise the construction.

I knelt by my bed. The words would not come. All I could say to God was "Help!"

Three days later the X Corps, which included the First Marines, landed at Inchon in the most brilliant American military tactic in history. They recaptured Seoul, the capital of Korea, and joined with the Eighth Army, which was driving up from a breakout at Pusan. The North Korean army was destroyed. We had won the war. There was nothing to worry about.

I could not have been more wrong. Without asking anyone's permission, General Douglas MacArthur crossed into North Korea and drove toward the Yalu River border with China—the worst mistake in American military history. The Chinese repeated their warnings to stay away from their border. MacArthur did not listen. He was so popular in America that no one dared to try to stop him. The First Marines landed at Wonsan on the east coast of Korea and marched toward the Yalu. Then, in the snow and the wind and the bitter cold, a hundred thousand Chinese troops attacked. Despite plenty of warnings, MacArthur was caught by surprise.

The First Marines were trapped in mountains at the Chosun reservoir and buried in snow and cold.

9

I guess I don't have to say that Rosemarie and I were utterly unprepared for marriage.

We were not even smart enough to know that we were unprepared. Thus, when Father John Raven suggested we make one of the new pre-Cana conferences, we agreed, more to humor John than because we thought we needed to plan our married life together.

Pre-Cana was a cautious Catholic attempt at marriage education, progressive by the standards of the Church then, simple-minded and chauvinist by the standards of today, and inadequate in terms of the problems our generation of husband and wives was going to face.

The Church once again was doing too little, too late, for its laity.

Our pre-Cana was scheduled for the week before Halloween, the first anniversary of my first tennis triumph over Rosemarie at Skelton Park. We still played at least once a week, despite the activity of trying to finish school and prepare for the wedding, mostly at Rosemarie's insistence.

"I'm not letting my husband get out of shape," she asserted.

I won an occasional set, but not on the anniversary Saturday. The angel Gabriel could not have beaten Rosemarie that day.

The next day, after I turned off the broadcast of the Chicago Cardinals game, Rosemarie and I walked over to St. Ursula's for the first part of the three-day conference.

When the priest began his talk at the Sunday afternoon session, he said, "The mark of success of a good pre-Cana is the number of men and women who cancel their marriage after the conference." The participants laughed, some nervously. Rosemarie and I joined in the laughter.

My laugh might have been a little nervous because I knew it was too late to cancel anything.

We were both too young to marry. If any of my children had told me that they planned marriage at our ages, I would have been profoundly offended. Fortunately none of them did. We understood nothing about the strains of the common life. We never discussed money, though it was obvious that we had very different attitudes toward it and would bitterly disagree about whether any of Rosemarie's money could be used for our family needs.

We had been raised together. We had spent many hours together in the year since I had been expelled from Notre Dame. We had argued about Plato and Goethe, Augustine and Freud, William James and Thomas Aquinas. Rosemarie had won most of the arguments, I had won a few. But neither of us understood much about the meaning of life. Or about one another. Despite our long acquaintance and our intimate friendship we hardly knew each other at all.

Nor had we discussed sex. We knew we wanted it. We knew we would like it. We were convinced that we would never tire of it. Unlike most devout Catholic young women of her age, Rosemarie did not seem to be afraid of sex or inhibited in her sexual feelings. What else did we need?

She wanted five children, which seemed to me a nice number.

And we certainly did not and would not and probably could not discuss her drinking problem—if that's what it was.

That Sunday afternoon, in the stuffy, tile-lined parish hall in the basement of St. Ursula's school, the handsome young priest explained to us that the man was the head of the family and the wife the heart of it.

"Many Catholic couples feel," he said, "that the wife should quit working at the time of the marriage. It is not good for the head of the house to have to depend even for a few months on his wife's income to support the family, especially if, God forbid, she should make more money than he does. That would be a disastrous beginning for a marriage. You're going to quit as soon as you're pregnant anyway, and that'll be only a few months after your marriage, maybe even when you come home from your honeymoon. So why not quit before you're married and avoid the conflicts of two-income families, of families where the wife thinks that because she has some money, she is also head of the family.

"That would be a terrible embarrassment to the husband and, worse still, would make it hard for the wife to play her God-given role as the warm, tender, affectionate member of the partnership.

"Some women think that they are doomed to second-class citizenship because they are the heart of the family and not the head. But doesn't everyone know that the heart is more important than the head? Most men will admit that it is the love of their wives that keeps them going. If anyone is second-class in a family, it is the head, not the heart."

The last is true enough, God knows, if your wife is Irish.

I didn't and couldn't, given my own background, accept the passive description of women implicit in the theory; it offended me.

Rosemarie merely giggled, hand over her mouth so as not to offend the others, especially the young women, who were feverishly writing in their notebooks, just as they had in their high school and college classrooms.

The "head and heart" theory was carried throughout his whole presentation and used to account for the "differences" between men and women.

Men were more rational, women more emotional.

An affronted snort from my future bride.

Women forgave more easily then men and were less likely to hold grudges.

Vigorous nod and a poke in my ribs.

Men tended to be insensitive, women oversensitive.

A derisive grunt.

Men like to argue about differences. Women like to seek compromises.

A rare poke from my elbow.

Women are more affectionate, men more guarded emotionally.

A triumphant poke in return.

Time was allotted for questions after the priest's talk—written questions.

Rosemarie scratched on the sheet that had been provided, "What if you're smarter than your husband and he won't admit it?"

I wrote, "What if your wife is oversexed?"

Neither question was read aloud by the priest.

He did, however, answer a lot of questions about birth control.

Sample: "Is oral intercourse permitted after marriage?"

We both gasped at that suggestion.

"Anything is permitted so long as the marriage act is completed in the proper fashion. But no man would want to impose on his wife something she finds repulsive. Often, of course, that kind of intercourse is simply another form of mutual masturbation—birth control, in other words."

"What if," Rosemarie whispered in my ear, "the wife wants it?"

"Then the husband is lucky," I replied uneasily.

Birth control was the big issue. The priest's answers were blunt: it perverted the purpose of marriage. The Church would never change on the issue. "Rhythm" was always a possibility for Catholics, though it was usually a sign of a lack of self-control, especially on the part of the husband. If married couples did not want to have as many children as God would give them, then they ought to sleep in different bedrooms.

The group stirred uneasily. They didn't buy it.

"I should think five is enough, don't you?" Rosie asked me as we were walking by the new church, now almost finished. "Do you think God really expects more?"

I hadn't thought about it.

"It's a full house."

"And I bet He doesn't like it when husband and wife sleep in separate bedrooms. He made them to sleep together, didn't he?"

I could only agree.

"I don't think the priests or the nuns know what they're talking about. Sex is for holding husband and wife together as well as having kids, isn't it?"

"Seems reasonable to me."

Which is as far as we went on that one.

Indeed it was the only discussion we had the first day of our pre-Cana conference.

Monday night we were back in the parish hall to hear the talk by the married couple, a sleek-looking lawyer and his worn-out wife. Small wonder that she was worn out: she had born thirteen children, all of them alive and well.

Much of their presentation was devoted to jokes about having that many kids around the house. They were good speakers and the jokes were funny and it was patent that they loved each other very much. It was also patent, however, that most of the group could not identify with them.

One question: "It's all right for you to have thirteen children because you're a professional man and make a lot of money. But what about those who don't?"

Answer: No one has that much money, but God will provide for those who trust him.

Another question (from Rosemarie): "Suppose that the wife has inherited some money. Would it be wrong for the family to use it?"

Answer: It would threaten the husband's position as head of the home. Much better that the money be saved for the college education of the children.

An angry snort from Rosemarie and a "See!" from me.

"Do you want to live in an apartment instead of my house?"

"You win."

That was our only discussion about the second part of the pre-Cana. To be fair, the speakers were wise and witty and had many sensible things to say about dealing with each other's moods, about sex as a renewal of love, and about financial problems.

Neither of us listened.

And we were, I think, the green wood. Most of what was said went in one ear and out the other. I think now that such wisdom would have been much better received in the second year of marriage. The problem, however, then as now, would be to get husband and wife to come.

Wednesday night was devoted to talks on SEX! by two M.D.s, one for the men and one for the women. I mean, you can't have a man and his future wife hear about sex and even discuss it in the same room, can you?

My doctor knew all the technical terms for the relevant organs. But he didn't seem to know anything about women. Nor, to judge by the questions, did most of the other grooms-to-be know anything about them. The session scared the hell out of me.

I was grateful to Trudi for what I had learned from her. Again I wondered what had happened to her. It was an academic question by then, almost as if Trudi had been a person I met in a storybook and not in real life.

"Learn anything?" I asked Rosemarie as we walked through the dark streets of Austin back to Oak Park and our house (she was living at our place almost all the time now).

"Men are horny beasts."

"You knew that."

"And women's job is to keep them in line."

"Which you do by . . . ?"

"Manipulating them. Give them something but not everything. They're insatiable."

"Do you believe that?"

"Not about my future husband." She put her arm around me.

"I'm probably insatiable."

"The way you're insatiable I won't mind."

Thus for our marriage preparation.

Like everyone else, we stumbled toward consummation with our eyes closed.

10

Rosemarie offered me an escape hatch from marriage.

I desired her. I admired her. I wanted her, I guess. She still drank too much and had a crazy father. And she was only nineteen. I had lots of second thoughts—and third and fourth and fifth thoughts too. But I went along with the drift, driven by a mix of lust and inertia.

Maybe a little bit of love too.

She opened the hatch the same week we attended the funeral Masses for Christopher Kurtz and Leo Kelly.

The phone had rung at our house on Thanksgiving afternoon. As always I was the only one to hear it. It was Mrs. Kurtz.

"Charles, I knew you would want to hear the news." Her voice was calm, controlled, but I knew the news before she spoke it. "We just heard from the Defense Department. Christopher was killed during the retreat from the Chosun reservoir."

"Dead?" I said in disbelief. "He can't be!"

"I feel that way too, Charles. But I'm afraid it's true. The memorial Mass will be at St. Gertrude's next Monday."

"I'll be there. We'll pray for you and the family, Mrs. Kurtz."

"Thank you, Charles, I'm sure we'll need those prayers."

So simple. So quick. So devastating. I would never have a friend like him again.

He had been promoted to captain in the field, I would learn later, and had died covering the retreat of his outfit in the face of the Chinese attack that Douglas MacArthur had foolishly brought on.

They awarded him the Navy Cross. That did not bring him back for any of us.

Even today I miss him. Even today I feel the numb shock of his loss. We will not see his like again.

At least I won't.

Sometimes at night even now, I wake up from a dream in which he is still alive and we are both laughing together as we did in the spring of 1949.

And, in truth, even today I feel that he is not absent from my life.

I must have looked like a zombie when I returned to the dining room.

"Chuck!" Rosemarie screamed. "What's wrong?"

"Christopher is dead," I slumped into my chair and spoke automatically. "Killed in action at the reservoir. The funeral is Monday at St. Gertrude's."

Rosemarie sobbed in my arms. "I loved him almost as much as you did," she cried.

"He loved you too, Rosemarie."

"He'll watch over our marriage, won't he?"

Tears in my eyes, I could only nod. He'd have his work cut out for him.

"Maybe we should stop the Thanksgiving dinner," Dad said tentatively.

"Christopher would be the last to want that," I said.

"We should be grateful"—Rosemarie's voice was muffled by my chest—"that we had him with us as long as we did."

There were few dry eyes in the crowded church on Monday morning. Christopher had more close friends than any of us had realized. He was a magic young man.

He should have been a priest, I thought again. And that way he'd still be alive.

Cordelia had flown in from Paris for the Mass and stood next to Rosemarie in St. Gertrude's church. My friends from Notre Dame were all there, sad over the death of someone they all had liked and worried about their own fates.

When the final prayers were over we walked slowly back to our cars.

"How is Paris?" Rosemarie asked Cordelia.

"All I could have hoped for. I work very hard and I'm still trying to get used to living in a strange country, but I'm doing quite well. . . . You've settled on a Christmas wedding?"

"I think we have. . . . Rosemarie?"

"You know very well, Charles Cronin O'Malley, that it will be the Saturday after Christmas!"

"That's right! Why do I keep forgetting?"

We needed to laugh. But we were unable to do so.

"Congratulations to both of you," Cordelia said. "I know you'll both be very happy."

"I'm sure Christopher will take care of us," Rosemarie said fervently.

Before we separated, I probed Cordelia about her concert career.

"I'm working with Madame Boulanger. She's very nice but very demanding. Today makes it all seem a little absurd. None of us have much time, do we?"

"We all live under death sentences," Rosemarie agreed grimly.

*   *   *

"What do you think?" I asked my bride-to-be.

"I think she's having a very hard time."

"You were sweet to her."

"I can be sweet on occasion, Chucky Ducky."

We were hardly in the house on East Avenue when the phone rang.

"It's for you, Chuck!"

Jane Devlin.

"I heard today, Chuck, that Leo was killed in Korea. His family didn't bother to tell me. Mass at St. Ursula's tomorrow."

"Dear God, Jane!"

"I'll be all right, Chuck. I'll be fine. Don't worry about me."

Her hollow voice made me worry all the more.

"They're giving him the Medal of Honor."

Mild, soft-spoken, serious Leo Kelly a war hero!

"That's nice," I said lamely.

"It doesn't bring him back. I would never have had him anyway."

"Why not?"

"There was a terrible accident at the lake last Memorial Day. Four of us in a car ran into a tree. Leo was nearby. He pulled me out and tried to save the others. He burned his hands trying to open the door. Then the car blew up. The parents of the dead kids looked for someone to blame. The sheriff arrested Leo and beat him. Then Jerry Keenan—you know, Packy Keenan's father—made them stop because Leo was not responsible. He went off the next day for the Marines"—she gasped to overcome a sob— "and he never called me after that."

I mumbled something. What could I say?

"Thank you, Chuck, he admired you very much."

"Leo?" Rosemarie said as I joined the others.

"Another funeral tomorrow . . . at St. Ursula's."

Everyone in the room wept. Poor Peg sobbed hysterically. Rosemarie and the good April hugged her.

I wanted to swear.

I muttered only to myself, "Goddamn war!"

We all went to the Mass the next morning, the womenfolk in black. The mourners filled every pew in St. Ursula's most of them weeping. Monsignor Mugsy struggled to contain his tears. John Raven preached. I'm sure he was wonderful, but I don't think I heard a word of it.

Leo Kelly would never have thought that he had meant so much to so many people.

After Mass, Rosemarie and I tried to find Jane.

"I wonder if she came."

"I don't think so, Rosemarie. She sounded so hollow yesterday."

"Hollow?"

"Someone deprived even of the right to grieve."

"How terrible. . . . If you don't mind, I'll spend the rest of the day with Peggy."

"Good idea."

On the Thursday following Thanksgiving, the last week of our semester at Chicago, she cornered me after my late afternoon class.

"Come to my apartment for supper?" Her expression was somber and grim, her color the same as the gray of her jersey dress. "I have something to discuss with you."

"Sure." I felt my stomach do a tentative half turn. "Anything serious?"

"Probably. You'll have to decide that for yourself."

Sounded like Clancy was about to lower a boom.

I went to the library to study for an hour, accomplished nothing, and then walked in the chill rain to her apartment.

The last time she had summoned me to such a conversation, the subject was her demand that I quit my job or at least take a leave of absence till March. "If you're studying full-time and working full-time, what time will you have for your bride? I'm working every day to fix the house and all you'll do is sleep in it. I won't tolerate that."

I acquiesced, not really having any choice. She was not certain yet about her own academic future. She would ride out to the University with me every day for the winter quarter after our honeymoon. It didn't make much difference to her whether she would finish the five remaining quarters for her degree. "It's important for me to learn," she contended. "And I intend to do that for the rest of my life. Degrees don't make any difference."

Not if you had as much money as she did—and as strong a dedication to reading. She had lost most of the weight she had put on during the spring and the summer.

"Too much on my mind to worry about eating," she said, waving her hand dismissively.

She often didn't show up for class during the autumn quarter because she was busy supervising the remodeling of our honeymoon house and trying to calm Peg.

"I'll pass the exams anyway." She waved off my concerns. "I'm learning more from redoing the house." She returned to the interior design book she had been studying.

I looked around at the still empty living room of the old place. "It's an awfully big house."

"We'll fill it up."

I didn't want to argue that point. I had already moved my photographic records into a spectacularly appointed darkroom Rosemarie had prepared in the basement of the house. I was sure, however, that she didn't mean with photographs.

Peg was smiling gamely, even though she was worried sick about Vince. Like most of my classmates from Fenwick, he had been drafted for the Korean War. He hoped to get the weekend off for our wedding. If it looked like he was going to be sent overseas, he and Peg would be married before his departure, even if it meant moving the wedding up from its early June schedule.

Although MacArthur had squandered his victory at Inchon by invading North Korea, American leadership (including President Truman) was loath to bring the general to heel. The Chinese had entered the war, as they had promised they would if we pressed on to their borders at the Yalu River; and, despite his anguished pleas to start a war with China, MacArthur was forced to fall back to the "waist" of Korea. Only brilliant field leadership, particularly by General Almond of the X Corps, prevented the American retreat ("advance to the rear," the Marines called it) from becoming a debacle. It looked like a long war.

The war had ended the five years of peace and prosperity after the end of the big war. My generation was devastated by the wholesale draft when we least expected it. You cannot expect the same generation to fight two wars.

I did not think that I was in much danger. I would be called up only if there was general mobilization. Even with the defeat at the Yalu River, I doubted that there would be a general mobilization.

As I approached Rosemarie's apartment on Kenwood that day in December in the cold rain, which was beginning to turn to snow, I devoutly thanked God that I had done my time in the military. Nothing could be quite as bad as the situation in which poor Vince found himself.

I took Rosemarie in my arms when she opened the door, intending . . . intending what, I don't quite know.

"Please." She squirmed away. "Later, if at all."

Was she going to beg out of the marriage? My spirits soared. I really wanted out.

Then I felt depressed. Part of me, the demonic part, I suppose, didn't want out at all.

She was beautiful and fragile and needed my help and my protection. If I was strong enough and resourceful enough and courageous enough, I could save her. I would save her.

I was mostly self-deceptive, not facing the truth that most of the time I was either a coward or a fool, especially with women.

I had to think, I had to take out my idea notebook and write down my master plan. My instincts, particularly when dealing with women, were almost nonexistent. To the extent that they did exist, they were untrustworthy.

That's too harsh.

"We'll work it out, Rosemarie," I said, trying to sound reassuring.

"Will we?" she fired back at me. "Typical of your naïve Lockean optimism."

Not bad for a put-down, huh?

I mean, how many of you can say you've been written off by your bride as a naïve Lockean optimist.

"I'm sorry," I said, intimidated as always by her temper.

"Later," she repeated. "After supper."

She had been decorating a small Christmas tree in the corner of her front room. "Why decorate a tree when you're not going to be here for Christmas?" I asked.

"Because I like to decorate trees."

We had decided to keep the apartment in Hyde Park for the winter quarter anyway. Well, Rosemarie had decided.

"We might not want to take the long ride back to Euclid Avenue every night," she announced on the day she informed me that we were going to keep the apartment, "especially if it's snowing. And we might want it for other purposes."

"We might. A man gets breakfast in bed in this place, as I remember."

"Depends on what else happens in bed."

I figured that perhaps this pre-Christmas command performance would be about our future sex life.

We ate ravioli and meatballs and talked about school and about my still-uncertain plan to continue graduate school.

"All right," I said as I helped her to clear the table. "What's up?"

"In the front room," she said, "with our coffee."

So I sat on her beige couch, Irish Belleek cup in front of me on the coffee table, next to a book about Vermeer.

"So?"

"So—" she stirred her coffee vigorously—"I think you ought not to marry me."

"Why not?" I tried to keep my voice steady, neutral.

"I'm damaged goods, Chuck." She was icy calm. There would be no tears tonight.

"Damaged goods?"

"You assume I'm a virgin, don't you?"

"Not necessarily—" I began.

"Well, I'm not. I've had intercourse, oh, I suppose at least eight or nine times."

"With different men?" Dear God, I didn't want to sound like a prosecuting attorney.

"No. One man."

"Who?"

"My father."

"I'll kill the bastard! I'll cut off his balls and stuff them down his throat!" I ranted, clenching my fists and pacing the floor.

Big deal, huh? But what else do you say? Anyway, at the time I meant it. Or thought I did.

"No, you won't," she said sadly. "The question is whether you want to cancel the marriage."

I stopped pacing long enough to look out the front window and watch the snowflakes melt on the pavement of Kenwood Avenue. Why were there always snowstorms?

"Of course not." The words rushed from my lips before I had a chance to think about them. Words didn't matter anyway. Now there was no chance at all to escape the marriage.

"Are you sure, Chuck? It would be much better for you—"

"I'll judge what will be better for me."

She did not respond. I turned away from the window. She was sitting quietly on the couch, head bowed, arms folded across her chest, a prisoner waiting for sentence. My anger, still free-floating, unfocused, surged to escape. I shut it down. Mostly.

"Do *you* want to cancel it?"

"No, Chuck." Her eyes flickered at me and then away. "Dear God, no."

"Well then, shall we dismiss that alternative?"

"If you say so."

"Why did you wait so long to tell me?"

"I was afraid."

"Of what?" Why was I sounding like a district attorney? I was no virgin either. But that was different. . . .

"I don't know. Of you. Of everything. You're the only one I've told. And Father Raven. Last week. In Confession. He probably had no trouble figuring out who I was."

"What did he say?" I slumped into the easy chair.

"He said that I didn't commit any sins and that I shouldn't worry about the bad confessions I thought I'd made when I didn't confess . . . what happened."

"Certainly, you didn't sin," I barked at her. "What else did John say?"

I wasn't coping very well with her shattering announcement. In my defense I plead that I was twenty-two and it was 1950. Paternal abuse of girls and women was a crime of which we were unaware. Or that we tried to pretend was impossible. Even Freud had not believed his patients. Or had not wanted to believe them. Now it is a recognized "problem." One woman out of every twenty is a victim of assault by a father or stepfather, though not all of them are assaulted as often or as destructively as Rosemarie.

"He said I was an innocent victim and that I needed sympathy and help, not punishment. I don't know whether that's true. I asked him whether I should tell my fiancé. He said that it was up to me, but I didn't have to. And I said I felt obliged to because it would explain why I am crazy some of the time. And he asked what you would say."

"And you told him what?" I snarled.

"I said I wasn't sure."

"Why weren't you sure?" I shouted.

"I don't know, Chuck. I just wasn't."

I took a deep breath. And then another.

"I may not be saying the right things, Rosemarie." I lowered my voice several octaves. "Forgive me if I sound harsh. I don't mean to. I want to be sympathetic and helpful."

"Oh, Chuck—" her voice caught.

"Why don't you tell me whatever you want to tell me."

"You're so wonderful." She still wouldn't look at me.

"I doubt it."

For some reason we both laughed.

"All right, I'll try to repeat what I told Father Raven." She paused, gathering her resources. "I can't remember a time when Daddy wasn't very affectionate with me. I think way back when I was little I enjoyed it. Then, in seventh grade maybe, what he did didn't seem quite right. Too . . . too intimate. I suppose it gradually crossed the line without either of us realizing that he was going too far. I didn't know what to do. I tried to stay away from him. Mom didn't seem to notice or to want to notice."

She stopped. Then her head slowly came up. "Oh, Chucky . . ."

"Do I look like I'm judging you? I don't mean to."

"No, not at all. Just the opposite. You look so kind." I didn't feel kind. "Should I go on?"

"It's up to you."

"I guess I have to. I mean, what bothers me is that I did love him and I did enjoy his affection and I liked to make him happy. At first . . . I don't know . . . I might have encouraged him without thinking that it was wrong. Or maybe without knowing how wrong it was."

"John Raven told you that you can't do serious wrong without knowing fully what you're doing?"

She smiled wanly. "Sure. He said that I should stop tormenting myself by worrying about the degree of my responsibility. He said that I was innocent. And I asked whether that meant mostly innocent or completely innocent."

"And he said that no one is completely innocent?"

"You're wonderful, Chucky. You really are. I'm so ashamed of myself for not trusting you before."

"You're innocent of that too, mostly innocent anyway. Maybe you'd better tell me whatever you think you should tell me and take yourself off the stove."

"All right. I'll try to be as brief as I can." She choked back a sob and continued. "In fifth, sixth grade he was definitely, well, petting me. A lot. He was so pathetic, so hangdog, I felt sorry for him. I didn't like what he was doing but I wanted to make him happy. You can't imagine what a weak, despondent little man he is. Then in seventh grade . . . well, I suppose you could say he began to rape me. I didn't understand what was happening, not very often. I didn't know anything about sex. I didn't even know that what we were doing was sex. I was frightened and there was no one to talk to. I still felt sorry for him and wanted to make him happy. But"—her tone turned to a fervent plea—"I never took pleasure in it, Chuck. Never. I mean there was never any . . ." She paused, flustered.

"Orgasm is the clinical word, Rosemarie."

"Thanks. It was never like that, never."

"I'm sure it wasn't. You don't think I would hold it against you if it were, do you?" An impulse, way down in a hidden basement of my soul, urged me to put my arm around her thin, dejected shoulders. I couldn't embrace her, not yet. She seemed spoiled, spoiled for the rest of her life. I was bound to her now by ties that could never be ended, chains that could never be broken.

"I know that. I guess I'm saying what I have to say." She paused for me to respond and then went on. "Anyway . . . it went on for three years, not very often, as I said, but still too often. Finally, when I was a freshman and had figured out what was happening, I made him stop. It almost broke his poor heart. He said he thought we were going to be good friends forever—"

"My God!"

"I know. It was crazy, but somehow he thought . . . I don't know what he thought. Anyway, he tried again, often, but I managed to stop him with a feel or a hug or a kiss. It was so . . . I don't know, so cheap and slimy. Remember that time when you saved my life at Geneva and then kissed me in front of the fireplace?"

"I'm not likely ever to forget it"—I found myself grinning—"Rosemarie, not ever."

She blushed at the memory, the happy memory. "I knew that was the way it should be when a man and woman love one another and that what had happened between Daddy and me must never happen again. So you really saved me twice that day."

"I'm glad I did."

Savior, hero, knight, fool, clown, comedian.

"So I fended him off, more or less, till I was a junior. Then when Mom died he became determined again. I told him that either he left the house or I would. He said that he wouldn't permit me ever to be separated from him. I said that if he touched me again I would kill him. I can be very angry when I want. Never at you." She smiled shyly. "He believed me. I think I might have killed him too. I mean, I heard him talking to his friends one night about professional killers. I thought I had the right to defend myself."

"I'm sure you did."

"I guess that's all."

"How did you manage to live with it, Rosemarie? How did you . . . keep it all inside yourself?"

"I pretended, Chuck. I'm very good at pretending. I walled it up in a corner of my life. After it stopped I told myself that it had not really happened. I tried to forget about it. It was over. I had stopped it. My confessions were not really sacrilegious. God still loved me."

"And John Raven agreed."

"I had to tell you. Are you displeased that I did?"

I considered that question carefully. I wished she had kept her dirty secret to herself. Now it was my burden as well as hers. At least I knew what it was that I was carrying.

"I'm glad you trusted me enough to tell me."

She rose from her couch, walked across the room, curled up at my feet, and wrapped her arms around my knees. "What are you feeling now, Chuck?"

"Anger."

"At me?"

"Certainly not. At him."

The sick little bastard had destroyed the life of a beautiful woman.

"Don't be. If you only knew how sad and miserable he is. . . . Any other feelings?"

"Pain."

"I'm sure it hurts you."

"Not my pain," I said roughly, still trying to focus and understand my emotions.

"Whose, then?"

My hand found her long, smooth black hair. "Yours. Hurt. Fear. Shame. Humiliation. I wish I could make it all go away."

"Thank you, Chuck." Finally she was able to weep. "You've healed a lot of it already." She pressed my hand to her lips and kissed my fingers.

Charles Cronin O'Malley as substitute for Jesus.

Bottom-of-the-barrel substitute. Forth-string substitute on a team with only three strings.

I bent over and kissed her smooth, cool forehead. She smelled of evergreen. The tree in the corner of her tiny living room glowed hopefully.

"I absolutely refuse to let this interfere with your happiness, Chuck . . . if you still want me?"

"Let me be as clear as I can." I tried to make my tenor voice sound firm and resolute. "I do still want you and that is that."

"Then I will be a good wife and a good mother and a good bride." Her lips tightened and her shoulders squared. "I won't let the past interfere with the present or the future. Definitely. Nothing that has happened will prevent me from being a good . . . lover. Nothing."

If raw willpower could make it so, then it would be so.

"You shouldn't feel that you have to try too hard." I touched her cheek. "Anyway"—a brilliant idea hit, brilliant for me that is—"no one who has any sense of how passionate a person you are Rosemarie, could doubt that eventually you'll be a wonderful lover. Give yourself time. You don't have to be instantly perfect"—another smashing notion—"because I know I won't be."

"If"—she sighed sadly—"you'll just be a little patient with me."

"Certainly not"—I was on a roll—"unless you promise that you'll be more than a little patient with me."

She smiled through her tears. "Fair enough."

That was the extent of our premarital conversation about marital sex.

"Okay?" My fingers remained on her cheek. My emotions were still a tangled mess, more fury than anything else.

"What are you thinking now, Chuck?"

"It's kind of strange."

"I won't mind."

"There was a time last winter when we had started to go to concerts and occasionally to the College Inn at the Sherman House . . ."

"When you started to dance with me . . ."

"In spite of myself. Anyway, just before that and a little after too, I thought we were good friends and nothing more. We studied together, we joked together, we had fun together. I told myself that I wanted you as a friend for the rest of my life. Being friends was so calm and uncomplicated."

"And it would have worked fine if we didn't both have bodies that got in the way."

"How odd of God to have made us with bodies, huh? So, now don't be hurt, what I'm thinking now is that I feel like something terrible has happened to a friend. Does that make any sense?"

"A lot of sense." She squeezed my hand. "I love you, friend, I'll always love you. Let's be friends and lovers forever."

Later that afternoon I found Jim Clancy in his office at the Board of Trade, his tie askew, his face unshaven, a glass of whiskey in his hand.

I yanked him out of his chair by the tie and clamped my hands around his thick little neck.

"I know what you've been doing," I whispered softly. "If you try it again, I'll kill you. Stay away from her. Stay away from us. I don't want to see you ever again. If you come to our wedding, you're a dead man, understand?"

"I don't know what you're talking about," he stammered, his face turning purple.

"Yes, you do." I kept my voice deadly calm. "And don't think I'll kill you in such a way as to get caught. No one will know who did it."

"I just want to be friends with you," he begged. "Can't we forget about the past and just be friends?"

Tears began to stream down the pathetic little man's face.

"Try to be friends once"—I threw him back into his chair—"and you're a corpse. Understand?"

He bent his head over the desk and sobbed.

I walked out of the office and closed the door gently behind me. I knew I had not seen the last of Jim Clancy.

— 11 —

On Christmas Eve, before Midnight Mass at St. Ursula's, the crazy O'Malleys gathered around Mom's harp in our house at East and Green-field, a harp now the center of attention in her "music room." We were all there, Jane proudly pregnant for the second time and Ted even more proudly protective; Peg and Vince, who was home on leave; Michael, a tall, quiet priest-to-be; and my shy, distant bride. Michael could not be best man at the wedding because the seminary forbade that (might give bad thoughts!), but he would be the altar server at Mass.

Vince was in uniform, confident and smiling. Peg, more a young April than ever, refused even to think about the possibility of his being sent to Korea. I envied them their seemingly simple, uncomplicated love—though not so much, antihero that I was, that I would have gone back into the service on a trade.

I wrapped my arm around Rosemarie's shoulders as we sang "O Holy Night"; she was a supple gift, a live teddy bear who felt warm and good in your arms, but not a desirable woman into whose body I would shortly have to enter.

I was now not only worried. I was frightened. I had agreed with her that it would look bad if her father didn't give her away. How could we ever explain to my parents if he were excluded from the wedding party. I clenched my fist every time I thought of him.

I must have hid it well.

"They blend beautifully, don't they?" Mom plucked some strings of the harp. "Just like they always did."

"Let's see how well they blend next year," Peg said with a broad grin.

Jane joined the fun. "I'm surprised that Chuck doesn't look scared. Ted certainly did before our marriage."

"What's there to be frightened of?" Michael demanded, "Would sweet little Rosie scare anyone?"

"Brides are always scary," Dad observed wisely, "especially when they are sweet and beautiful."

"Me, scary? Quiet, self-effacing Rosemarie?"

General laughter in which I joined, though I didn't think the conversation funny.

"Now, dears, you should all drink your eggnog while there's still time so you won't break your fast for Holy Communion."

"To Chuck and Rosemarie." Dad raised the Waterford tumbler. "May they always be as happy as his mom and dad."

We drank the toast and Rosemarie, flushed and teary, kissed them both. I shook hands, rather formally I fear, with Dad and kissed Mom.

Our marriage had been their dream for years. "Poor little Rosie" would now officially be a member of our family. Strange, mouthy little Chucky would have a wife who would take care of him and love him despite his alleged complexities.

All would live happily ever after.

Eventually we would disappoint them. There would come a Christmas when . . . but I banished that picture from my head.

Rosemarie drank too much eggnog and could barely walk a straight line to the Communion rail at the first Midnight Mass in my father's prize-winning church. No one seemed to notice. But she was led off to one of our many guest rooms after Mass.

"No point in her sleeping alone in that drafty old house on Euclid Avenue," Mom remarked soothingly.

"Only a few more nights without someone else there," Peg said with a laugh. "I mean if you count Chucky as someone."

Rosemarie was being married from our home, not from the apartment in Hyde Park nor from the house on Menard. No one discussed the reason for these arrangements. I wondered if, at some level in their serene souls, my family knew about what Jim Clancy had done to their foster daughter.

If they did, they'd never admit it even to themselves.

John Raven was no help when I cornered him in his rectory study on Saint Stephen's Day. (Under Monsignor Mugsy, the second floor of the rectory was no longer off-limits to laity.)

"Terrified, Chuck? I don't blame you." He rocked back and forth with laughter. "The girl will drive you out of your mind. One surprise after another all the days of your life."

"I'm not exactly terrified, Father."

"No, but you feel that if you could, you'd call the whole thing off?"

"Maybe only delay it a few months."

"Too late, my friend, too late!"

"I know that—" I spoke irritably—"but I don't think it's very funny."

"You will eventually." He stopped laughing long enough to light his pipe. "Most people marry strangers, Chuck; after the wedding come the surprises. Sometimes they're quite unpleasant surprises. Sometimes . . . well, they go in the opposite direction."

"I've known her all my life, Father." I shrugged. "How could I know her any better?"

"Because Rosie's been around all your life, you can deceive yourself into thinking you know her. She's a very special girl, Chuck. Larger than life. Magic."

This was a new theme: Magic Chuck and Magic Rosemarie.

"Beautiful and smart," I said hesitantly, "and sometimes mysterious and sometimes hilariously funny . . ."

"That doesn't even begin to describe her. Take my word for it, young man, it's going to be a roller coaster, a very pleasant roller coaster, I might add."

A priest's-eye view of my bride. Priests, I knew, found women appealing, just like every other normal, healthy man. Since they knew so many women more than just superficially, I presumed that they had a better perspective than most men. So John Raven's delight in Rosemarie seemed, well, strange. Almost as though he knew that, given different circumstances, he could love her too. I didn't begrudge him that fantasy. Quite the contrary, he was entitled to it.

He knew about her father, did he not? It was under the seal of Confession, so he couldn't talk about it; but did he have to pretend to an optimism about us that he couldn't feel?

"Well, thanks for the reassurance, Father."

I rose to leave, zipped up my jacket, pulled on my gloves.

He grinned, enormously pleased with the prospects of my downfall. "You think too much, Chuck, you spend too much time analyzing and examining your motives, you try to make the world fit your own outlines."

"Sounds pretty bad."

"Not at all. You're a fine young man," he said as he led me down the steps to the first floor of the rectory. "Intelligent, ambitious, generous, responsible. Maybe a little bit too conventional in reaction to your flamboyant parents . . ."

"Dull?" I pulled off my right glove to shake hands with him at the rectory door.

"And probably more gifted than any of you"—he ignored my self-deprecating comment—"in ways you don't begin to understand yet. Your wife will challenge you to your limits. The surprises may rock you, but they'll be good for you."

"My larger-than-life, magic wife?" I shook his firm hand.

"Much larger than life and very magic."

I left St. Ursula's rectory more confused than ever. But happier.

After the rehearsal, on Friday night Rosemarie once again offered me a chance to leave the sinking ship. We huddled together at the door of the church, shivering in the bitter wind as she told me I was making a terrible mistake.

It would be so easy to postpone the marriage till spring, perhaps a double wedding with Vince and Peg.

I opened my mouth to accept her offer.

Instead I said, "No."

Could I possibly have refused to run for cover?

"No, what?" she said softly.

"NO!"

"You want to tell everyone that we've agreed to postpone the wedding?"

"NO means NO!"

I took her into my arms roughly.

"We will be married tomorrow morning, Rosemarie Helen McArdle Clancy. That is that. Till death do us part. Moreover, it's not a terrible mistake at all. You're a very special girl, Rosemarie. Larger than life. Magic. You will be a challenge and a delight for the rest of my life. I'm the luckiest man in the world!"

Who said that? I couldn't possibly have said that! Could I? Like Peg says my mouth is faster than my mind.

It's all your fault, I told God as I held my almost-wife to my chest. She leaned against me, breathing deeply, struggling to recover her composure.

Then someone told me something else brilliant to say. "I'm glad you gave me the final chance, Rosemarie, my love. Now I have no doubt what I want. And what I want is you. I want everything that you are, body and soul, hopes and fears, sorrows and joys. Tomorrow night I'm taking on the first taste of a mysterious and glorious meal."

She giggled. "With chocolate ice cream for dessert?"

"And for salad too."

So that was that.

I ran through the neighborhood that night, down the streets, through stores and bungalows, dodging in and out of doors and windows, scurrying behind curtains, hiding in empty rooms, racing across Austin Boulevard to Oak

Park and then back to Chicago. I didn't know who was chasing me but they were right behind. Wherever I went they followed after. Finally, at Austin and Division, a streetcar waited for me. As I drew near, it changed its warning bell and then lurched away. I reached for the handrail to pull myself up on the running board and missed. I fell into a snowbank.

Who is chasing me? I demanded. Then I looked around my room and realized that I had been dreaming. I sat up and quivered with the cold of the snow into which I had fallen. It was real, it wasn't a dream. I had run for hours. Otherwise, why was I cold?

Then I realized that I had left the window open. I jumped out of bed and slammed it shut.

Tomorrow night there would be someone to keep me warm.

12

The next morning, the morning of my marriage, my Christmas wedding, I was as morose as a mourner at a wake. It was one of those clear, brutally cold days in which the Middle West specializes between Christmas and New Years. Inside the soaring arches of St. Ursula Church the air was warm—Dad's heating system worked—and the big, impressionistic stained-glass windows bathed the nave in magical colors. Christmas wonderland inside and out. A slightly kinky mixture of Impressionism and the Gothic that somehow worked.

The perfect setting, it seemed, for my magic bride.

"You don't look quite as happy as a lucky groom should look, fella," Vince chided me.

Michael was to be the altar server, Vince the best man, Peg the maid of honor. No one else. Rosemarie did not want, and God knows did not need, a large wedding party.

"I am tired," I complained testily, "of being told how lucky I am."

Vince found that very funny. "Well"—he shrugged his massive shoulders—"maybe Rosie is a little lucky too."

"There's an Irish saying that fits," I continued to complain. " 'The Lord made 'em and the divil matched 'em.' "

He found that amusing too. Then he became deadly serious. "I don't have any premonitions, except that I'll be back here in law school in eighteen months, but if anything happens—"

"You'll be back all right—" I gripped his arm—"and we'll take good care of Peg while she's waiting."

"Not many guys"—he blinked a couple of times—"have friends like you, Chuck."

Wedding-day sentimentality, I told myself, and then prayed for Vince and Ed Murray and all the rest of my generation who had not been as fortunate as I. And for eternal peace for the souls of Christopher Kurtz and Leo Kelly.

We started fifteen minutes late. Mom was striking in maroon and white—University of Chicago colors, we all insisted. I suspected that she and Dad were more concerned about the appearance of the bride than of the groom. In fact, I doubt that anyone looked at me all through the Mass.

After Mom was seated and had found the tissue required to dab at her nose, Peg, also in maroon and white, proceeded down the aisle and joined arms with her own intended groom. She seemed quite satisfied with herself—as well she might be. Her plot to marry me off to Rosemarie had succeeded.

Then Rosemarie herself, waxen and yet radiant, drifted toward the front of the church, seemingly borne on waves of light. Her bridal gown was simple and unadorned, the sleeves reaching to her wrists and the collar enclosing her neck: pure, virginal, ethereal. She glided along on my father's arm as though he were a guiding seraph.

Morose and worried and reluctant groom that I was, I still felt a catch in my throat. The first bride in the new church would be the most beautiful it would ever see.

I looked up at Father Raven and Monsignor Branigan. The ineffable Mugsy winked at me.

I looked back and Rosie and Dad were already at the head of the aisle.

Jim Clancy had believed my warning. His housekeeper had called Mom the day before: Mr. Clancy had a high fever. The doctor said he must stay in bed for a week. He was so sorry to miss his daughter's wedding. Would Mr. O'Malley do the honors for him?

Rosemarie seemed neither surprised nor disappointed.

Dad kissed her and shook my hand as he placed hers in mine.

"You're a lucky man, Chuck."

"I know I am, Dad," I croaked.

Now I had to say something to Rosemarie. "I'm awed, Rosemarie, blinded."

"Thank you, Charles," she murmured, not looking at me. Was she scared? Or worried? Did she have last-second doubts about me?

"You really want to marry this galoot?" Monsignor Mugsy peered over his trifocals. "Sawed-off redhead?"

The Monsignor gave away at least an inch and a half to me.

Rosemarie turned toward me, as if considering her options. Then she lit up the whole sanctuary with a dazzling smile. "I think I'll take him, Monsignor." She may even have winked. "He'll do. And he has nice parents."

It was the last time I saw her eyes until after the Mass.

My vows were spoken in a loud, clear—and arguably obnoxious—voice. Rosie, now visibly quivering, spoke in a frightened whisper. The hand that held mind was not about to let go.

Not ever.

My fears, my doubts, my worries about the night ahead of us (in the house at Long Beach where Rosemarie insisted we should consummate our marriage) were temporarily erased by the bewitching aura of my bride—now, after the words had been spoken, my wife.

"Mrs. Charles Cronin O'Malley," Monsignor Branigan announced happily.

A sound came from behind her veil, which had somehow fallen back into place.

Gasp? Sob? Laugh?

Surely the last.

Our kiss in the back of church, with the cold air rushing in through the open doors, was perfunctory. Neither of us was ready for passion.

"Anyone tell you that it'd be a cold day in hell when you found a wife, Chucky?" Perhaps a hundred people insisted on that tasteless remark.

Cold weather or not, there was a maroon-and-white canopy ("for OUR university") at the entrance to the church. And there were forty Irish pipers.

"Did someone die?" I demanded as they began to wail. "That noise would chase all the banshees back into hell."

"Only"—she tightened her grip on my arm—"an Irish bachelor."

At Butterfield, after a seemingly endless receiving line, we finally marched into the dining room with Wagner's march (portraying, in the opera, a march to the bedroom) drowned out by the cheering guests. They must have thought this was a special wedding. Special bride, yes? But didn't many of them wonder why she had not found a better husband for herself?

Dull little redhead. Thinks too much. Talks too much. No accounting for a woman's taste, I suppose.

"I'll always love you, Chuck," she whispered as I drew back her chair, carefully so as not to entangle her train.

Still the reply froze on my lips.

Vince proposed the toast to the new Mr. and Mrs. O'Malley. It was now my turn to toast my wife.

Dear God, she isn't my wife, is she?

Yes, she is.

And I forgot the literate and carefully nuanced toast I had prepared.

"Ladies and gentlemen," I am alleged to have said, "I had a toast appropriate for a graduate student from the University of Chicago: elegant, literate, probably obscure, a trifle arrogant. Someday, perhaps, I will remember that toast. But right now it is as lost as are the Chicago Cardinals' hopes for a football championship. All I can say is that a man who can remember a toast, or anything else, on the day that he has, astonishingly, acquired a wife so beautiful, so intelligent, so charming, so good, and, to quote Father Raven, so magical, probably doesn't deserve her."

Mom and Dad were grinning. I was doing okay. Now what?

"So what can I do but give you Rosemarie, *my* Rosemarie"—then the daimon took over—"my wild Irish Rosemarie!"

I began to sing, not in the whiskey tenor with which this sentimental Irish-American kitch is usually sung, but—what shall I call it, clear as it is in my memory after all these years?—a romantic tenor.

I sang it unaccompanied for only one verse. My wife rose next to me, encircled me with her arm, and joined the song.

We must have been pretty good, because the rest of them kept silent till the final chorus.

"Dazzling, Chuck," she whispered. "And *so* typical, my love."

What, I wondered, as I sipped the champagne, was typical?

"Hey, this stuff is good," I announced between swallows. "Great!"

"Easy does it, husband mine."

Rosemarie was beginning to enjoy herself. I thought I might as well do the same. You are, after all, married only once. I drained my glass and gratefully accepted a refill from the ever-present waiter. Why had no one told me champagne was so splendid?

We cut the cake and fed little bites to one another—the only food I was able to force into my mouth all day. We danced with each other.

"Not bad, husband mine," she smiled shyly, "for someone who pretends to be a stumblebum. I think I'll keep you for a little while anyway."

"I'm merely floating on your cloud."

She laughed and kissed me, delicately, affectionately, proudly.

I danced with Mom. Rosemarie danced with her dad, who had shown up looking not sick but sheepish. He watched me uneasily. I should have put my foot down about inviting him. I couldn't think of a good explanation that would not have betrayed Rosemarie's secret.

"I'm so happy," Mom said through her tears. "God made the two of you for one another."

"I'm glad you're not unhappy about losing me."

"Lose you?" She was genuinely astonished. "To Rosie?"

"You haven't lost a foster daughter, you've merely locked up a son!"

"Chucky!" She thought it was pretty funny too.

"What did you say to my father?" Rosemarie asked anxiously when I reclaimed her for the next dance.

"I more or less told him to leave you alone from now on."

"Thanks, Chuck." She squeezed my shoulder, "I appreciate that."

I'd thought she might be angry at me for banishing him from the wedding. Was everything I did fated to be defined as good, wonderful, perfect from now on?

Well, that might not be all bad.

I must not be a complete failure tonight. She had been badly hurt by sex before. I didn't want to make it worse.

I thought about it over another glass of champagne. Wonderful stuff. Maybe it was time, now that I had become a married man, to learn to enjoy wine—sherry and port and champagne.

I was not, I insisted to myself, drunk when the time came to leave Butterfield for our marriage bower.

Just not quite sober.

I changed into a brown suit, chosen by my mother and sisters, and met my wife, in a navy blue suit and white blouse, at the door of the club.

"Let me help you with your coat." I held her mink, somewhat unsteadily.

"Is that the courteous Chucky Ducky speaking or the Dom Pérignon?"

"I beg your pardon?" I bowed elaborately.

"Just a minute, dear." She patted my arm. "I have to throw this bouquet so Peg can catch it."

Peg didn't leave the catch to either the skill of her quarterback or the chances of the wind. She dove for Rosemarie's pass like she was Don Hutson of the Green Bay Packers (who still holds many of the NFL pass-catching records—but I digress).

"You look darling in that brown suit, Chucky. Heavenly."

"Your co-conspirators picked it out for me. I suppose the same for your suit, which"—I choked with tipsy sentimentality—"my wild Irish Rosemarie, clings to your lovely self in such a way"—I searched for a way out of the sentence into which I had plunged—"as to confirm my conviction that you are in all probability the most beautiful woman in the world."

She dragged me out the door into the bitter cold. "Button your coat, dear," she warned. "We can't have you catching cold before Acapulco, can we?"

"Where's that?" I stumbled toward the waiting limo.

I now realized that I was drunk, very drunk. On my wedding night.

"Steady, lover, the walks are still slippery."

I was the one who was supposed to protect the innocent and the vulnerable, wasn't I?

In the limousine, which had been assigned to drive us to a garage on South Boulevard in Oak Park, the new Mrs. O'Malley held out her hand.

"The keys, husband mine."

"I beg pardon?"

"The keys to my . . . 'cuse, *our* Buick."

"We're driving to Long Beach."

"I'm driving to Long Beach."

"Are you implying that I am inebriated?"

"No, dearest one, only that you ought not drive. You might not be as lucky as I was on Stony Island Avenue. Now give them to me."

"Yes, ma'am."

I searched for the keys in my overcoat and dropped them into her imperiously extended hand.

"Thank you, husband mine. And don't think I'll hold your first bout with champagne against you for the rest of the marriage. I may forget it"— she chuckled—"in forty years." Then she huddled against my arm. "You're so adorable, Chucky Ducky, so wonderfully adorable."

"Even if I am not permitted to drive your . . . 'cuse, *our* Buick."

She dismissed me with her favorite hand-wave. "Just for today, dear. And, to tell the truth—as you'd say—you're even more adorable when you're so solemnly funny."

Isn't that nice?

Well, John Raven said I was in for some surprises in my marriage. I suppose this is the first one.

There would be others before our wedding day was over. And our honeymoon.

13

Dear April,

I'm so glad that you invited us to the wedding and that we were able to come. It was one of the most beautiful weddings I've ever attended.

You had so much to be proud about that day. Chucky. What a fine, witty, handsome young man he has grown up to be, so much like his mother and father.

You have even more reason to be proud of Rosemarie. You had faith in her when everyone else had written her off as an insufferable brat. Now she's so sweet and gentle. And so, so beautiful.

"I haven't had one of those terrible temper tantrums in years, Mrs. Cleary," she says to me. "I know you hated them. So I thought I'd tell you I gave them up. And not just for Lent."

"I sometimes thought, dear, that you did them just to make me mad."

She kissed me and said, "You know me too well, Mrs. Cleary. Don't tell my husband, you know, that cute redhead next to me, any more of my secrets."

I saw Jim Clancy on Michigan Avenue before we left Chicago. I thought he looked terrible, a withered little hulk of what he used to be. Still beady-eyed and mean, but now old and like he was on drugs or drunk all the time. My Steve says that the people in the Mob, who own those hotels with him, had better be careful or he'll rob them like he's robbed everyone else.

How did he father a daughter as beautiful as your son's bride?

I hope that Rosemarie and Chucky keep away from him. He ruined her mother's life and he'd ruin Rosemarie's if he could.

Martha

14

I rolled over in the bed and buried my head in a pillow to escape from the blinding light.

"I'm sick," I announced to whoever might be listening.

"Three times on the way up and once after we got here."

"Who are you?" I demanded, rolling over again and opening my eyes. A woman, backlighted by the sun reflecting off a sheet of ice, towered over me.

"Your wife."

"I don't have a wife," I said, closing my eyes.

"You do now, Chucky Ducky."

Rosemarie! Were we really married yesterday or was it another one of my bad dreams? Why was I naked under the covers?

"Here's a glass of water and some aspirin."

I opened my eyes again and accepted the medication. The woman who offered it, the one who claimed to be my wife, was wearing a lacy negligee that revealed a promising body. If she was my wife, maybe I was very fortunate.

"Did we . . . ?"

"No, Chucky Ducky." Her smile washed me in amused affection. "We didn't. You were too sick."

I swallowed my pills like a good little boy. I had traded one gentle mother for another.

"Are you hungry?"

"If you really are my wife, you know that I'm always hungry."

"Good! I'll get you some toast and tea."

She slipped away.

Sick on your wedding night because you drank too much champagne! You might be married to the woman with that delicious rear end for fifty years and she'll never let you forget it!

I felt sick again.

She returned, sat on the bed next to me, and offered me a tray with a cup of tea and two pieces of toast. Her robe slipped partly open.

I swallowed the toast in one bite.

"You'll never let me forget it," I said.

"No," she laughed, kissing my forehead, "never! But I won't tell anyone else!"

I would have to make love with her soon. How could a man bed his bride when he was hungover?

"Please may I have some more toast?"

"Maybe a waffle?"

"Drenched with maple syrup?"

"Just the way you like it."

She gathered her robe together and flounced off to the kitchen. I sipped the tea. We'd have to get it over with soon.

I disposed of the waffles almost as quickly as the toast. She sat on the side of the bed again, looking at me worshipfully. How could she adore a goof who was drunk—for the first time in his life—on his wedding night and couldn't make love to her?

"Am I disturbing you?" Her fingernails skimmed my thigh and flank. "Do you mind if I do this? I'm"—giddy laugh—"kind of new at caressing men."

I gulped. There was not the slightest possibility of my asking for another cup of tea.

"You are ticklish, aren't you?" She jabbed at my ribs.

"Stop it!"

"I won't!"

"Cut it out." I tried to squirm away.

"Have a mint." She jammed it between my teeth.

"Prepared for everything," I muttered.

"More breakfast?"

"No . . . well, yes!"

She bounded off the bed, drew the flimsy peignoir around her shoulders, and rushed toward the stairs. "I'll be back in a jiffy with grapefruit juice and pancakes and pork sausages and coffee and the Sunday papers."

"Rosemarie?"

"Yes?" she stopped in midflight.

"You don't have to—"

"Enjoy it while you can, husband mine." And off she went, a comet in full array, trailing the flimsy gown behind her pale legs in a burst of winter sunlight.

"Hold the papers!" I shouted after her.

I ate the breakfast rapidly, now knowing that the time for love was at hand. I would, however, have eaten it rapidly anyway.

"Did you take my clothes off last night?"

"I had to, Chucky Ducky, they were covered with vomit. I put them in the washing machine while you were sleeping. . . . You know, you're kind of cute without any clothes."

I ignored that remark. "I suppose you think that it's time we consummate our marriage?"

"I wouldn't mind."

"Well," I sighed in mock protest, "the first thing you have to do is take off that robe and let me look at you—legitimately this time."

She bounced off the bed, tossed aside her negligee in a single move, and eyes averted, hands behind her back, permitted me to look at her. I felt like the Burlington Zephyr had rolled over me at seventy miles an hour.

Despite my headache and my hangover, I was ready for love. I had to say something. Where was my quick tongue?

"Do you like me, Chucky Ducky?" She looked up at me.

"Have you ever seen me speechless in all the years you have known me?" I said, stroking her belly with one hand and her hip with the other.

"As a matter of fact, no!"

"I'm speechless now," I said, pulling her gently into bed with me.

What followed was comedy—delightful, rapturous comedy. I had been an idiot to think it would be anything else. My new wife was a richly sensuous woman, a partner who reveled joyously in every touch and kiss and caress. Perhaps she had willed herself to be that way.

The daimon couldn't get enough of my bride and I felt constrained to cooperate with his wild and violent excesses. But what I thought was shameless and untamed use of a shy and frightened bride turned out to enchant and entertain her. I was proclaimed several times to be the best bridegroom in all the world.

I doubted the praise. Her satisfaction did not seem physical, no spasms of joy or piercing cries of delight such as Trudi had given, even the first time with me. Still there was no denying Rosemarie's enthusiasm. For the moment it was enough that she give me pleasure and then rest peacefully in my arms. If I was satisfied, she felt that it was proper for her to be ecstatic.

Poor child must have been terrified that she would never be able to please a man.

Well, we had exorcised that demon. There would be many others, but this morning I would not think of them.

Then she broke the rules again. It is the man who is supposed to fall into exhausted sleep. Instead Rosemarie, her black hair a halo on the pillow, was dead to the world and to me beside her.

I gathered up the remains of breakfast, carried them into the kitchen, washed the dishes and put them away. I realized half way through this process that I was naked and so was the woman who waited for me in bed.

She was still sleeping when I returned.

"Rosemarie," I said gently.

"Uhm . . . you want something, Chucky Ducky?"

"You!" I shouted, and fell upon her.

Later, when she returned with lunch, her robe was tied, her hair brushed and tied with a ribbon, her lips touched with lipstick, and her body liberally splashed with an enticing scent.

Wedding nights were not supposed to be like this at all. On the morning after, the bride was supposed to be disappointed and teary, not a shooting star of energy and diligence.

And the man was supposed to be frustrated at how little pleasure he had felt and not a complacent satyr.

"More fighting in Korea," she announced. "New Communist attack. We're supposed to be in orderly retreat to previously prepared positions. Not much else. . . . Mind if I share your lunch, lord and master?" She nestled into the bed next to me.

"I'm no one's lord or master. Only an exhausted new husband."

"You are to my lord and master. On approval, needless to say. Open to brusque dismissal if you don't measure up in the role."

We both dug into our hamburgers—smothered with onions, ketchup, and mustard, they were prepared just to my taste. Rosemarie must have been watching my eating habits for years.

When we were finished with the chocolate ice-cream dessert, she put the tray on the bed table.

"You should bring that into the kitchen," I said.

"Look, Charles, we'll compromise on cleaning things up. You like to do it immediately. I like to do it at the end of the day."

"So, what's the compromise?"

"We'll do it at the end of the day!"

"Oh."

She snuggled in next to me.

"Now, who were those two women?"

"What two women?"

"The cornflower blonde from Kansas and that gorgeous giant from Boston."

"Oh, them! They were General Radford Meade's assistants in the First Constabulary when I was in Bamberg."

"Uh-huh! They still think my husband is pretty cute."

"Most women do."

"Regardless!" She waved her hand. "They adore you."

"Most women do."

"They told me how fortunate I am."

"I can only agree."

"Did you date either of them?"

"No . . . well, I took Nan to the movies once or twice. She's sweet, but not my kind. So I found her a husband."

"The man she was with?"

"Right. And Polly was married to John Nettleton—the big mick she was with. I didn't sleep with either of them."

"I know *that*! I want to know why they both told me you're a hero."

"I'm *not* a hero," I exclaimed.

"They said you were. What did you do? I'm your wife and I have the right to the whole story."

So I told her about our comic-opera trip up to the border of the Russian zone, where my inept command almost started World War III, and how we arrested the Russian kids who were trying to smuggle caviar, and how I bought the caviar from them and sent them back to their zone."

She had laughed at all the appropriate places.

"That's where you got the caviar you sent me. Why did you buy it from them?"

"I figured that they had taken a terrible chance and that they probably deserved a few extra Yankee dollars."

"Oh," she said softly. "You really are so sweet!"

"That's what I always say."

"Now why did they give you that medal you never wear?"

So I told her the second comic-opera story, of how I had spied on the black marketers, banged up my knee, organized their capture, and would have been shot had it not been for a quick-thinking shavetail fresh out of the Point, and how the black market was back in business in a couple of weeks.

"You really are the craziest of all the O'Malleys! Why did you do all those things?"

"I told myself someone had to."

I hoped she'd didn't ask for a third story.

"I love you, Chucky Ducky."

"Cut that out, woman!"

"You're so much fun, Chucky Ducky. I like being your wife."

I began another delirious ride up the mountain of pleasure to the sparkling waterfalls of rapture that waited at the top.

And so it went for all the day.

"Shower or bath?" She pulled me out of bed in midafternoon.

"Rosemarie, I don't think—"

"Now who's the prude?" She continued to drag. "Come on, a wife has her rights, you know. I think a bath will be better. And didn't dear Vangie put in a double-size bathtub just for that?"

The thought had not occurred to me. The dirty man. He and April . . . shame on them.

"Come on!" I was pushed toward the tub into which steamy water was already pouring. "I will *not* tolerate you hiding behind silly male modesty, not after all I've done for you." Shame seemed absurd under the circumstances. "In you go, husband mine. Just keep telling yourself that I like you naked as much as you like me."

"I doubt that." I settled back in the comforting warmth, "But I take your point."

"That's not all you'll take." She plopped in next to me. "Here's the soap and sponge, now get to work."

I did. She groaned sedately. "That's better, *much* better."

"I'm not hurting you, am I?" I stopped the sponge in its brisk progress across a shimmering breast.

"You don't have to be *that* careful with breasts, Chucky Ducky. You can push much harder and it won't hurt. And I'll like it more."

"I don't mean now . . . I mean in bed."

Her eyes widened in surprise. "Chuck"—she turned serious and solemn; her hand squeezed my fingers and sponge against her breast—"you would never hurt a woman. You're the most tender man in the world."

Hardly that.

"Yeah, but—"

She guided my other hand to a submerged thigh. "It *is* vigorous exercise"—she chuckled—"*very* vigorous. I know that I've had a very ardent man inside of me. But I like that, even more than I thought I would. I'm fine. Really."

"If I ever . . ."

"I'll let you know. Now, clumsy slave, get on with your task of bathing the empress."

"I thought I was the lord and master."

"That was a lifetime ago. . . . *Well*, slave, that is a little bit better. You do improve with age. . . . Oh my God, Chucky Ducky . . . what are you going to do NOW? . . . Don't stop, damn it, just because I shout!"

So I didn't stop.

I wondered in my less tumescent moments (which were few and short) how much of her manic vitality was playacting, a pretense that the ecstatic dream was really ecstatic. But the daimon gave me no choice but to go along with the dream. She had assigned herself a role, donned a mask, acquired a persona, and she was now improvising around it. Brilliantly.

Was it all an act?

Foolish question. We become that which we portray.

Enjoy her while you can.

Because my bride insisted, we said our prayers on our knees before we went to bed for our night's sleep.

I have kind of been out of contact the last couple of days, I told Himself. All I can say right now is thank you. I'll do my best to take care of her.

It would be a long, long time before I realized the Deity had a much more complicated plan in mind.

"I'll drive," she announced on Monday morning when we ducked out into the subzero cold for our drive to Midway airport and the flight to Mexico.

"I'm sober."

"As to drink, yes."

"You don't think I can drive and admire you at the same time?"

"Right."

"I agree." I again dropped the keys in her outstretched hand. "And this way I can amuse myself in various ways during the drive."

"Drumming your fingers against the dashboard." She kissed me and hopped into the car.

"That was nice."

"What was nice, husband mine?"

I jumped in the other side and closed the door. "Turn on the heat, it's cold."

"Not for long, I bet." She flicked the switch. "What was nice?"

"Our weekend."

"I'm glad you liked it." She smiled, quite satisfied with herself. "Chuck, not until we get off the ice. Then within limits you can pursue your, er, amusements."

"You know what Dad said to me?"

"No, what did the poor dear man say to you?"

"That women were fun."

"*Well*, I'm sure April is fun in bed, though since you're her son you shouldn't think about that." Then, with a tentativeness that tore at my heart: "Was I fun?"

"What do you think?"

"Chuck! I said within limits. . . . Yes, I think I might have been a modest amount of fun. I hope I was . . ." She paused uncertainly.

"Let's go back to Long Beach," I said as we turned down Ninety-fifth Street.

"Why?"

"It was nice."

"Mexico will be much warmer."

"I never noticed the cold."

"We have our reservations."

"I don't care."

"You're afraid of the airplane ride!"

Caught. I'd better get used to it. "I've never flown before."

"Better get used to it!"

"What if I get sick!"

"We're flying in one of those new DC-6 things. You won't get sick."

"What if I do?"

"I'll take care of you. I'm getting used to it."

Despite the newness of the DC-6, I did get sick. Even more so in the old Dakota that took us to Acapulco. When my wife finally tucked me into bed in our cottage near the sea, I murmured, "I'm certainly happy that we're husband and wife, Rosemarie. Now I can take care of you for the rest of our lives."

She thought that was very funny.

15

"What is that thing?" I demanded of my naked wife as she held two small pieces of cloth in her hand.

"This?" she said innocently.

"Right! Those two pieces of fabric."

"It's a bikini," she said as she put it on. "You've certainly seen pictures of them."

"I didn't know women actually wore them."

"Sure they do. Do you object?"

"No . . . but you might be attacked even more."

She grinned. "How could that be possible?"

The surprises would continue through our honeymoon.

As I try to recollect those sweaty, hot-blooded days, it seems that I was learning a number of interesting truths about my woman.

First: By definition, as solemn and as irrefutable as a papal pronouncement ex cathedra, I was a sensational lover. Doubts, hesitation, discussion on that subject were instantly ruled out of court. In bed I was the boss, truly the lord and master. What I wanted and when I wanted it were mine not only by husband's right but also because I was such a spectacular bedmate. I entertained considerable personal doubt about this praise—not, mind you, about Rosemarie's honesty, but rather about her objectivity. She was determined that the honeymoon would be good for me and thus for her too. If I was happy with our two weeks in the sun, she would be happy too. Such determined goals are admirable, but when you have willpower like hers, wishing can make it seem so.

And maybe help make it so too. Her solemn high definition that I was superb in bed probably did make me better at the game.

She was much less troubled by intimacy than I was. Modesty and privacy were whatever she defined them to be. Occasionally, in bed, she would snatch a garment from the floor to cover herself, but she would not tolerate my doing the same thing.

One night, toward the end of our first week in Mexico, as I worked my way into our "good night" romp, there was a subtle change in her response. Ice floes were cracking up inside her, mountain streams beginning their race to the sea; her passive submission subtly changed to active cooperation. Delicately at first, then fiercely, she grunted and groaned, twisted and ground, heaved and struggled, climbing for the first time her own mountain.

I shifted my strategy so that I might help her on the climb and then soar with her. She smiled briefly, knowing that I was with her, and returned to her now frantic effort.

She was a long-distance runner, rushing with desperation toward the end of the course, her face contorted with effort and anticipation, her efforts more violent as the end came into sight.

Her moans grew louder, her efforts more abandoned, her acquiescence in our joint movements more vehement. Then we were two wild creatures of the forest caught up in a common paroxysm that was beyond pleasure and pain, a desperate, glorious, finally triumphant quest for deliverance.

Her sharp cry of pleasure was like a song of joy and her face was transfixed with elation. Elation and pride.

Now she was completely mine. My conquest was absolute.

And so was hers.

We both plunged from our mountaintop toward exhausted sleep.

"It'll get better," she whispered philosophically. "But not bad for a beginning."

The second thing I learned: While I was the lord and master in bed, I barely rated as an equal partner in all other activities. My suggestions about where we should eat supper were usually accepted, but in a manner that said that my bride was reserving the right to reject these recommendations if I started making mistakes.

I was also presented with a long list of "ought tos." As in, you ought to put more suntan oil on your back, you ought to take more pictures, you ought to work on your swimming, you ought to learn to water-ski, you ought to practice tennis, you ought to try to relax, you ought to stop budgeting your time, you ought to buy a new swimsuit, you ought to stop staring at that shameless girl, after all, you're a married man.

I was not being nagged. Rosemarie's oughts were merely suggestions, something between objective advice and imperial commands.

She only enforced the commands that were within her immediate power. If I did not apply the suntan oil, she did. If I did not swim in the pool in our private yard, she would push me in. And then throw off her robe and dive in naked after me. (You can imagine what that would lead to.) If I continued to look at the shameless girl, she would simply shift her position on the sand so that I couldn't see the girl. If I wouldn't buy a new swimsuit, she'd buy one for me at the same time she purchased the bikini for herself that made that shameless girl look like a paragon of modesty.

(All swimsuits were banned in our private pool. If I tried to wear trunks, they were promptly pulled off with grumbles about "silly male modesty.")

I did try on my own to water-ski—lest I have no peace at all—and with some small, very small success. Which success was greeted with loud shouts of encouragement and pride.

She was big, not physically but in presence. You could not help but notice her. When she sauntered down the beach in her new bikini imported from France, she was hard to miss. Similarly, when she strolled into a dining room in a white strapless dress, you knew that she was there, unless you were blind. Even if you didn't see her but only heard her voice in the hotel lobby or on the street, you became very conscious of the presence of a confident, strong-willed woman.

Yet she would wake up at night sobbing.

"What's wrong, Rosemarie?"

"I'm crying for my mother. Her life was so sad. She was pretty and nice and everyone liked her and she had to ruin her life and die before her time."

I cuddled her in my arms.

"She loved you, Rosemarie. She's proud of you and who and what you are."

She sniffled. "Do you really think so?"

"I know so."

She rested her head on my chest and drifted back to sleep. There was no one to protect poor Clarice. I promise You, God, that I will protect Rosemarie. Do you understand that?

I think God must have laughed. He had another scenario in mind.

My new wife was an exuberant filly who never walked when she could gallop. She would charge out of her hotel, turn in one direction and proceed at full tilt as though she were utterly confident that it was the right direction, which it often was not. She was a steam engine pulling out of I.C. Station, picking up speed as she went and trailing behind a cloud of dust and noise.

Rosemarie did not enter a room, she swept into it, often knocking objects over with a fearsome clatter. She did not close doors, she slammed them. She did not open doors, she rammed into them. She did not laugh, she hooted. She did not put down a coffee cup, she crashed it into the saucer, one morning even breaking both cup and saucer.

My aptly named wild Irish Rosemarie came in two tones: loud and louder.

I told myself I would have to face a life in which there would be moments of quiet only when she was not around.

Since she had known nothing but a room of her own, she was delighted to have a companion to chatter at and occasionally to torment. When there was nothing else to do, she was quite capable of deliberately driving me up the wall.

"Chucky Ducky, are you napping?"

"Yes."

"Do you mind if I ask you where you want to eat supper."

"Yes."

"Yes, you don't mind?"

"Yes, I do mind."

"Good, where shall we eat?"

"I'm TRYING to sleep."

"Oh, is little Chucky Ducky mad that his poor little bride-ums woke him up?" Luscious kiss for little Chucky Ducky.

"All right, where have you decided that we should go?"

"Would I wake you up if I had?" She turned from kissing to tickling.

"Yes."

I couldn't keep up with her but there wasn't much choice. She ran. I followed.

Her vigor did not extend to keeping our suite clean save at the end of the day. Clothes, towels, robes, American newspapers, postcards, gifts, bottles of Coca-Cola were scattered about in utter disregard of the proprieties. At the end of the day she would diligently rearrange the mess, while murmuring that it was just her bad luck to marry a fastidious man.

When we returned home, I reflected, there would always be help. Poor, dumb Charles C. O'Malley had gone through life thinking that if you wanted an orderly house you married a neat wife. It had never occurred to him that it was just as easy to marry a rich one who could pay someone else to keep the premises clean and respectable.

I did not know, in fact, how much money Rosemarie possessed. We had no more talked about money than about sex. I had resolved that I would support my wife and family with my own money. But it would be proper for her to provide the upkeep on the house since the house was hers.

Male chauvinist?

What can I tell you?

I raised the issue of accounting for the costs of the honeymoon (she had made all the arrangements with a travel agent.) It was proper, I said, that I pay for it, since I was the husband.

"Ha!" She continued to rub cream on my back.

"We could split it, since we're both wage earners."

"This empress will not discuss money at the present." She tossed aside the tube and performed one of her cartwheel stunts to the water's edge.

Literally. Among the many things she had "taken" in grammar school was gymnastics. Proud of her athletic skills and barely able to hide her dismay at my lack thereof, she would frequently walk down the beach toward the ocean on her hands or cartwheel into the water.

My Rosemarie cartwheeling into the water in a bikini attracted lots of attention, as she fully intended to. The lifeguards were particularly interested, even when I was introduced as her husband, the welterweight boxer.

So I spent much of my time on our honeymoon simply watching her, admiring her, trying to figure her out, studying the responses of her body to my assaults and the response of her person to the world around her.

She knew what was happening and reveled in my curiosity. I'm sure she went out of her way to be outrageous merely to befuddle me the more.

Late one afternoon, the sun already reaching toward the cobalt waters of the bay, she sat at her vanity in bra and girdle, brushing her long, shiny hair.

A Coke in hand, I sat relaxed on a chair across the room admiring the grace in her motions and the tiny sprinkle of freckles across the tops of her breasts.

"You ought to take pictures, Chucky Ducky, instead of just staring."

"Pardon?" I stirred out of my fantasies.

"I don't mind being sized up by a cameraman's eye, but I'd like it better if he recorded what seems to interest him so much."

"You wouldn't mind?"

"Mind?" She put down her brush. "If you don't realize by now that I'm a bit of an exhibitionist, what can I do to persuade you?"

"Take off your bra—but only after I get some shots just the way you are."

"Well"—she went back to brushing—"finally."

So I used all the film I had brought with me and a lot more besides.

She didn't seem to mind the constant eye of the camera. "After all," she sighed philosophically, "if you finally have a nude woman to shoot, Chuck, you should take advantage of it before she becomes big and fat and pregnant."

"You'll be beautiful when you're pregnant too."

Enjoy her while you can.

My third discovery: She was even brighter than I realized in our study sessions at the University. She had somehow picked up enough Spanish to flatter the help and the other natives with her knowledge of their language.

She knew all about the history of Mexico. She knew that the crime rate in Guerrero, the state in which Acapulco is located, was the highest in Mexico. She knew that Our Lady of Guadalupe had originally been a pagan goddess in Spain before she migrated to Mexico.

"You wonder where Jesus is in the painting?" she asked me as we considered the statue in the local church.

"I hadn't, but now that you raise the point, where is he?"

"Inside her. The Mexicans will tell you she's pregnant."

"She doesn't look pregnant."

"How would you know?"

"A point well taken."

"You'll know soon, Chucky Ducky," she warned. "Then you'll be sorry when you have to share me with your son."

"Why would I be sorry?"

"Because"—she clapped her hands—"there'll be another man in my life."

Smart, quick, intelligent—and she knew practically everything. I was no match for her and in the fervor of my passions I didn't care whether I was or not.

Finally, for all her beauty and charm and vigor and intelligence and her increasing sexual experience, she still seemed to me to be a doomed young woman. For most of the first week of our honeymoon I was able to put aside my foreboding of doom. I did not worry about what her father might have done to her psyche. I refused to be troubled by memories of the self-destructive incidents in the past. I would not permit myself to agonize over what the dangers might be for our children.

I might have been able to get away with these denial mechanisms (as I would learn to call such behavior later) if it had not been for what happened the night after she had joined me in a romp up the mountain of physical love.

Before supper I walked to a photo shop a couple of blocks from our hotel to buy some more panchromatic film. (I was using the Leica for black-and-white and the Kodak for color.) Rosemarie was already in the hotel dining room waiting for me when I returned.

"Got hungry." She frowned at me. "Hurry up. Let's have an early dinner and get a good night's sleep."

Such an untypical concern should have alerted me. But I was riding high on the wave of pleasure with my masculine success. I even brought the Leica to the supper table.

"No pictures," she snapped. "I'm not in the mood to be a fantasy model tonight."

"All right." I put the camera on the chair next to me.

"Where did you ever get that ugly little camera?"

"It used to be a funny little camera."

"Well, it's ugly now. And I want to know where you got it."

"In Germany."

"From whom?"

"A friend?"

"A woman?"

"Yes."

"Why did she give it to you?"

I knew now that she had been drinking while she waited for me. If we split the bottle of wine that was already on the table, she would be thoroughly drunk.

"She thought I saved her life."

"Hmf . . . a trollop. A whore."

"No, Rosemarie, that's not true."

"I don't want to talk about her."

"Fine, we won't talk about her."

"Good." She splashed wine into her glass. "I hate her."

"That's not fair. You never met her."

"I still hate her. I hate all your other women."

She couldn't finish the fish dinner. I guided her to our suite and eased her into bed.

"I'll sleep it off, Chucky. Sorry. Won't let it happen again. Not your fault."

The next morning she was ready to cartwheel on the beach as if nothing had happened. We did not discuss the incident. I cooperated in pretending that it had never occurred and hoped the problem would quietly go away.

"You know, Chucky Ducky"—she clung to me the last night of our honeymoon after we made love—"you're a strange one, not completely normal." I extended my arm down her back to her delicious rear end and drew her even closer. "That's nice. I'll know you're still here when I wake up afraid that I've lost you."

"And I'm not normal."

"No, you're really not," she continued, as if she were trying to figure out a puzzle. "I mean, you pretend to be a dull bean counter and you're actually a wildly passionate lover. You'd like people to believe you're mediocre and dull, and you're actually a genius—"

"Rosemarie"—I patted her derriere—"you're being absurd."

"No, I'm not. I don't know what kind of a genius you are, but I know you have the mark of greatness on you. I smell it."

"You smell your own sexy perfume."

"And you're going to be famous as a great man whether you want to or not, if I have anything to say about it."

"That sounds like a threat."

"Maybe it is."

Then she seemed to sleep. The only sound was the Pacific surf thumping against the beach, like a gentle and soothing metronome. I felt serene and content, sad only that the days of relaxation and pleasure were coming to an end. The ride through snow and cold to the "Gray City" on the Midway was hardly an appealing alternative to a honeymoon in the sun with a cartwheeling wife.

It was a great university doubtless, but I was still a neighborhood boy from the West Side of Chicago. I would never quite be part of that world. Did I really want a doctorate from there? Did I really want to work in the madness of the pit at the Board of Trade?

Then the troops swarmed ashore. They wore bandoleers and sombreros and carried bayonets. They were killing people on the beach. I faced them with a BAR, a Browning Automatic Rifle. They kept charging. My bullets had no effect on them. One of them was running at me with a bayonet.

Then I half woke up. I had to go back to the dream to drive them off. This time they were wearing North Korean army uniforms and the beach was covered with snow. My BAR worked this time. I killed them by the hundreds. Finally they withdrew in their rubber boats.

When I woke up and realized it was a nightmare, I reflected I had never touched a BAR in my military career. So why did I know how to operate one?

I fell asleep again. I woke up, flaming with passion.

What had I been dreaming about? Who? Trudi?

Dear God, Trudi. I had forgotten about her. A different love, simple, straightforward, guileless—till the end anyway. I was older now, and I had known this woman most of my life, which only made the love more intricate. Maybe it was better with Trudi.

In my dream, she had been weeping. Why, had I been hurting her? Is that what aroused me?

No, not Trudi. It was Rosemarie who was crying.

Groggy and confused, I tightened my arm around her.

"What ails you, woman?" I mumbled.

"I'm such a little shit."

"No, you're not. I don't want to hear you say such things."

"You could have found yourself a sane and sensible wife instead of a crazy freak."

"Is it my fault I like freaks?"

"It's not funny. I'll ruin your life."

"An hour ago you were going to make me a great man."

"No, I wasn't. Why do you always misquote me? I said you were going to be famous as a great man whether you wanted to or not. That's different. But I'll still ruin your life, I just know it."

I turned on the light and was shocked at how much grief had blotched her face. She must have been weeping for hours.

My fair bride was now a wounded, frightened little girl. All the hurt of her life was branded on her face and her shrunken frame.

That bastard, I thought. He deserves to die.

"I'm no good, Chuck, no good at all."

I wrapped my arms around her and pulled her against my body, breast to breast, loin to loin. I was weeping too, with fury, hatred, determination— and something else.

"Chucky, darling, you're crying! Don't cry for me, I'm not worth it."

"Yes you are, and I'll cry whenever I want."

She managed to chuckle despite her tears. "See, only great men can cry. I'm so proud of you, husband mine."

"Will you shut up and listen for just once?"

"Yes, lord and master." Mercurial little wench, she jabbed at my ribs. "I will now, as of this second, shut up and listen."

I didn't know what it was that I wanted to say. Something important, no doubt, if only I could remember it.

Then the daimon took over. I SAW.

What?

Everything?

It was as if someone had turned bright stage lights on a set that had been immersed in total darkness. On the stage I saw my new wife and myself and the roles we had played all our lives—the masks and the costumes around which we had improvised our parts.

In the first decade of our marriage I made two terrible mistakes. At the end of the honeymoon I finally saw the first of them. It would take a long time before I discovered the second.

Still, that night and the next morning were a moment of truth. The words formed on my lips:

I love you, Rosemarie Helen, I love you with all the power of my not-normal soul. I've always loved you, since you were a pushy little brat driving me out of my mind with your noisy babble—which you are still doing, incidentally, not that I mind anymore. Or minded even then. I will always love you. Now stop crying and go back to sleep.

I didn't speak then. Rather I drifted back to sleep. The next morning I realized that I'd had an important illumination, but I didn't quite remember what it was.

~ *16* ~

In the airport at Mexico City the next day, changing planes for the flight back to Midway Airport, I watched her bound back from the newsstand with two copies of the *New York Times* under her arm, and I realized how gallant she was. Running on the enormous energy generated by determination and willpower, she had turned what could have been a disastrous honeymoon into a happy one. My wild Rosemarie charged right through obstacles.

Even obstacles like me.

"Something wrong?" She shoved one of the newspapers into my hand. "You know what, Chucky? I think I've lost our baggage tickets."

I was not permitted to touch these tickets, since it was assumed, almost by definition, I would lose them.

"I was watching this beautiful woman—"

"Fine, but that doesn't find the tickets." She was poking around in her purse, with increasing concern.

"I love you, Rosemarie. I've always loved you."

"Yes, of course, dear." She sounded just like her mother-in-law. "I know that, but I have to find our baggage tickets. You must have them."

"I don't."

I was hurt because she didn't seem to think that my protestation of love, a cliché in words but entirely new in meaning, was important.

"Ah, here they are! See I did find them without your help!"

I took her into my arms and recited the lines I had just prepared about her gallantry and about how she had made the honeymoon so special.

"You're not going to make love to me right here in the airport, are you?"

"I'd like to, but I can wait till we're home."

We continued our embrace for the next moment or two.

"Am I glad"—she slipped away from me—"that I found these tickets! We'd have a terrible time at Midway without them. . . . And, oh, Chucky what you just said was beautiful"—she winked at me—"but I'm sure I've heard it from you before. Still, it's nice to hear it again."

Thus for my great reform.

Except that when I opened my eyes briefly during my nap on the flight to Chicago, I saw tears of joy flowing down her face.

Now there was one more bond tying me to my mysterious, appealing, vulnerable, and probably doomed bride. When we left Butterfield Country Club to drive to Long Beach I was tied to her by the bonds of church and of society, by the obligation we all have to protect the innocent and the persecuted, and by the loyalties of long and affectionate friendship.

Now I was bound to her by something much more terrible in its power. Passionate love.

1951

"Can I come into that terrible, smelly room?"

"When the red light is not on, it means you can come in."

"It does *not*. It merely means that I won't ruin your film if I come in. It doesn't mean that you *want* me to come in."

I opened the door for her. "You're irritable enough to be pregnant."

"No such luck," she said forlornly.

"Really?"

She nodded. "A couple of days ago. I didn't want to disappoint you. And I hoped that this time would be it."

She was wearing the same white robe she'd worn the night I was entrapped in her apartment on Kenwood.

"I'm not disappointed. We've been married how long?"

"Six weeks."

I had learned much about my wife in six weeks. Her favorite musician was Bach, though she "adored" Coltrane.

She "had" to exercise, in some way every day if only to run off her filly energy. She set up an exercise room in the basement near my darkroom where she jumped rope and rode an exercycle, with the Brandenburg Concertos playing over and over again on a phonograph.

Her favorite color was maroon; hence our bedroom was decorated in maroon and white, colors that I would not have thought erotic but that somehow became very tempting when I entered the room. She luxuriated in maroon lingerie, but would wear white to please me. "I absolutely hate black. I won't wear it even if you like it. And the maroon has nothing to do with *your* university, either."

In vain did I tell her that a) I liked her in maroon too, b) she never had to don black lace as far as I was concerned, and c) it was her university before it was mine.

She had not tried to preserve the Victorian arrangements of our house. "I hate *small* rooms." So walls had been torn down with ruthless vigor. But the bright and airy results of her destructiveness were not decorated in airy colors, because "I *hate* pastels."

The house was stylish but in an elegant and formal way—royal blues and deep grays and rich mahoganies and maroons, as though Rosemarie was nodding politely at the house's refined shape and history.

It was a dramatic change from the cramped apartment on Menard. Recently I visited a young married couple in a similar apartment in a gentrified yuppie neighborhood. I was astonished at how small it was. So quickly do you forget what you have left behind.

It was expected and demanded that I approve of all arrangements in "our" house, but heaven help poor old Chucky if he ventured a dissent, much less a suggestion of his own.

"Chuck" was my usual name. "Chucky" was affectionately maternal. "Chucky Ducky" was an erotic invitation. "Charles" meant I was in trouble. "Charles Cronin O'Malley" meant I was in deep, deep trouble.

Her swings of mood were sudden, erratic, and often profound, but I could usually bring her out of the bad ones simply by touching her hand. I understood neither the moods nor my influence over them.—

"When I'm glum"—she pointed a book at me—"I read history. It's better than fighting, right?"

"Right." Who was I to disagree?

She had spent a lot of money on the house, but ordinarily she spent little on her clothes. Her dresses were the imitations of fashion you could buy at Marshall Field, or even more likely, at Wieboldt's.

She did volunteer work every week at Marillac House and did not want to talk about it. "I just do it, that's all. Any objections?"

"I'm impressed."

"Don't be."

She was also careful with food, warning me, in Mom's words, "Waste not, want not," and adding as Irishwomen do a reference to the group that was currently supposed to make us feel guilty—"the poor starving people in Pakistan."

"It has never been clear to me," I remonstrated in a fashion I would have never dared with Mom, "what impact my eating has on people in other countries. Arguably, if I ate less, there would be—"

"EAT!" Grinning, she pointed a carving knife at me. "Don't argue."

I was threatened by her anger even when she was joking. So I twisted more spaghetti around my fork and ate—as I had been told.

She loved me passionately the way I was, but had nonetheless determined to improve me around the edges.

And had fiercely, furiously determined to be a mother.

"And because you're not pregnant yet," I said that night in the darkroom, "you are afraid you're not going to have babies."

"We've done a lot of screwing, Chuck."

"I hadn't noticed."

"Beast." She poked at my arm. "I suppose I'm being silly. Probably when I am pregnant I'll hate it. . . . Can I come into your secret room and see what it's like?"

"See what it's like? You outfitted the whole thing—brilliantly, I might add."

Somewhere in a magazine she had found a design for a perfect dark-room, all the equipment, every possible convenience, an ingeniously con-trived layout, flawless electrical connections—everything the amateur would need so that he could mess around to his heart's content.

"But you must have found something in here to distract you from your fair bride. I thought I'd check out the competition."

"Just the night to do that. I'm working on the fair bride."

"Really?"

"Really."

"Then I can come in?"

I bowed reverently. "Please do, your Majesty."

"Thank you, Sir Charles. Hey, it's hot in here!"

"It has to be seventy-two degrees to keep the chemicals from spoiling." I returned to the prints that I was soaking and then drying on the big dryer she had provided, the first one I had ever owned, if I could be said to own this one.

"So hot that I have to take off this robe."

"I figured we were going in that direction. It looks like my art suffers again tonight."

She flicked the robe away. It fell to the floor. I picked it up and hung it on a hook behind the door. Beneath the robe she was wearing a short white lace gown that was better than nothing, but not much.

"You said you liked white," she explained.

The casual little seduction was an attempt at reconciliation. We had not quarreled. I did not know to quarrel constructively with a woman, having had no experience of such activity in my family. Hence my only response to trouble with Rosemarie was to sulk. Such conduct was no help: it hurt me, it hurt my wife, and it did not help me face the problem between us.

You do what you can do. So I sulked. And felt like a fool, and like a small, pouting child.

The conflict started with her father.

We came down from the clouds of our honeymoon with an uncomfortable thud. The city was paralyzed by a January thaw that had frozen overnight and made all the side streets as slippery as skating rinks. Then, just as we landed, yet another winter storm roared out of Canada and covered the ice with deceptively innocent snow. The rhythm of storm and subzero weather had frayed the nerves of Chicagoans, who in such winters come to believe that they are under attack by a mean-spirited lunatic and the only recourse is to act like mean-spirited lunatics themselves.

The drive back and forth between Hyde Park and home was a long, wearing struggle with ice, snow, and dangerous ill-tempered traffic. The sidewalks at the University were slippery, faculty members sullen, students suspicious of one another, and the staff prickly and dour.

Catching up on the first ten days of graduate school classes, an easy-seeming task when we planned it, now was absurdly difficult, especially since no one wanted to share notes.

To aggravate my own depression, Montezuma's revenge, having held off until I returned home, smote me the second day of class.

"You ought to have been more careful of the water" was the only consolation available from Rosemarie, who was having reentry problems of her own. About which I didn't want to hear. She definitely was not returning to school this quarter. We were not yet properly settled in our new home. She didn't feel like sitting in a dull old classroom. She was not obsessed by the need for a degree the way I had been, anyway. And besides, she had to prepare for Peg's wedding, didn't she?

Peg and Vince were to be married the first week in March, after which he was going overseas, presumably to Korea. The Chinese had recaptured Seoul (the third time it had changed hands) but had been stopped cold by American artillery when the Eighth Army, now commanded by the brilliant Matthew Ridgeway, had fallen behind its prepared defenses—the talk about "prepared defenses" for once in military history had been true. There were rumors of an American counteroffensive.

It also seemed that everyone was fighting with his woman.

"Jane hasn't spoken to Ted for three days," Rosemarie announced to me one night. "I suppose"—she laughed—"you'd find it a blessing if your wife shut up for that long."

"Is it serious?"

"The fight? Sure, all fights between lovers are serious. They'll get over it."

"What's it about?"

"Who knows? Something dumb. Doctor again. He wants to give Ted office space in his own medical office building. The man never quits. . . . Most fights between lovers are dumb. Even between April and Vangie."

"They don't fight."

"Sure they do, husband mine, but so subtly that only an outsider can notice it. They do it constructively."

Aha.

Peg blew up at Vince, home for a weekend leave, the next night at supper at their house.

"Look, lover," Peg said coolly, "I don't expect to lose you. But if I do, I'll never forget you and you'll watch over me from heaven. But I absolutely refuse to permit you to ruin this happy time in our life. No morose stuff, understand?"

"You're not the one who will be going into combat," he snapped back at her.

"And you're not the one who will be home alone, worrying every day. It'll be hard for both of us. Let's not have a contest to see who suffers more."

"You want to call it all off?" His eyes flashed with anger at this outspoken lover of his.

"Just try it."

"You don't talk respectfully to me." He frowned.

"Wrong nationality if you want a dutiful wife."

"I'm sorry." Vince looked sheepish. "I've been an ass."

"I love you." She embraced him.

The quarrel melted away.

"She was tough, wasn't she?" I said to my wife in bed later.

"That's Peg. She was right too."

"Far be it for me to disagree."

Why did men and women who loved one another have to fight that way? Wouldn't it be better if they could work out their problems calmly and rationally?

Like archangels.

I was deeply troubled by all the conflicts, but there was nothing I could do about them.

So with unstable stomach and leaden spirits and anxious heart, I fought the maniac drivers alone every morning and evening without the consolation of my wife in the front seat next to me, offering irritable advice about how I "ought to" cope with the traffic.

"You'd probably murder me by the time we arrived at Chicago Avenue."

"I might at that."

By the beginning of February we had hit rock bottom and, as young lovers do, begun our slow rebound. We were very much in love, she eager still to please me and I penitent (in my own mind) for not recognizing that I had always loved her.

"*Well*"—her fingernails ran down my back—"it's about time we did something like that. I was afraid we'd forgotten how."

"My fault." I wanted to collapse into sleep, already dreading the morning ride.

"Let's have a fight over whose fault it is."

"Why?"

"Then we can make love again."

"Tonight?"

"Why not?"

"Why bother with the fight?" I turned the light back on, pushed the covers off her, and enfolded her passionately. "I love you, Rosemarie. I'll never be able to love you enough."

"Oh, Chuck . . ." She was especially sweet that night, subtle, numinous.

The next morning, my eyes barely open enough to peer through the thick snow flurries, I regretted our indulgences. We ought not to do those kinds of things when I had an early-morning class.

I did not regret it so much that I was innocent of lust when I arrived home late that afternoon. Rosemarie was in her "study," dressed in an Aran Islands sweater and matching slacks.

"Whatcha doing?"

Her "study" (as opposed to my "office"—the names were hers and both nonnegotiable), like the rest of the house, displayed little evidence of what one might think of as typical femininity. It rather reminded one of the "study" of an English rural aristocrat—oak and mahogany (more of the latter), thick carpet and drapes (maroons and beiges), leather chairs (including the massive judge's chair behind her desk), prints of horses on the walls, large bookcases. There were also Early American antiques, placed in strategic positions. The rather frail Sheraton table that served as her desk looked a little overwhelmed by the maroon leather chair, but somehow it all fit together—elegant, tasteful, and strong. Dear God, how strong!

The sumptuous leather easy chair facing the desk had obviously been placed there for use by the consort. I would not have dared not to use it.

"Going over checklists for the wedding." She looked up at me, frowned, and then smiled. "It looks like you have rape on your mind."

"Me?"

"You . . . my God, Chuck, you're crazy. Let me go. We *do* have a bedroom you know. Hey, stop that—"

"Who needs a bedroom?"

"Are you trying to set a record"—she twisted in a pretended attempt at escape—"for stripping me?"

"Twenty-five seconds," I exaggerated as I yanked off her panties and pushed her back on her big, luxurious chair. "Have you ever been ravished on this chair?"

"Chuck . . . don't! I have work to do."

"Indeed you do, now start working."

"All *right*, since you put it *that* way." Her voice diminished to a satisfied moan. "A woman isn't safe anywhere in her own house."

Later, the sweater tied provocatively at her waist, she made us both hot chocolate and cuddled with me on the chair. "I should keep a blanket here for these events."

"I may not strike here the next time."

"Anytime." She stroked my chest. "Any place."

I had promised to start to work at The Exchange (called that in the same way that the University of Chicago was The University). I did my best not to think of the confusion and chaos of the wheat pit. My fear was not helped when Jim Clancy called me to offer me some advice. He was quite drunk.

"Who was that, dear?" Rosemarie asked.

"Your father."

She turned pale. "What did he want?"

"He offered to show me the ropes."

"Listen to him, Chuck, but don't trust him. Ever."

Rosemarie did not try to defend her father on those rare occasions when we discussed him. He was a poor, sad little man, she would say, but such pity did not blind her to his evil.

The next night, when I came home from the University, she was drunk. I heard the key turn in the lock of her study when I came in the house. She spent the night there, leaving me alone in our marriage bed.

Which, without her, was appallingly empty. Privacy I had again and I didn't want it.

The next night was a repeat performance. I was wakened about three by a stirring besides me. The nuptial bed was no longer empty. I went back to sleep.

And left the next morning without waking her.

That night she was prepared to pretend that nothing happened.

So I punished her by sulking.

We slept as far apart as we could and still be in the same king-size bed. By day, her dull, dejected, guilty eyes tore at my heart. Finally I resolved that whatever I did the next time she went on one of her binges, I would not sulk. It didn't help her and it made me feel terrible.

So now in her diaphanous frills she had invaded my darkroom.

As she was poking around in my inner sanctum, I figured out the immediate causes of the latest tailspin. My conversation with her father, followed almost immediately by her period, had devastated her. If she didn't produce a child, she must have thought, she was worthless.

How could a callow twenty-three-year-old boy cope with that sort of mentality?

"What are you working on?"

"My wife, like I said."

"No, I mean in your pictures."

"I mean my wife in pictures. The honeymoon shots you complained that I hadn't developed."

"May I look?"

"You're the model."

The darkroom was the inner corner of my soul into which no one had ever penetrated, a part of myself I had shared with no one.

I wanted to share it with her and I wanted to keep it private. If she had not been draped in alluring wisps of lace, I might have sent her away. My life was about to be changed forever because of her blatant womanly appeal. The same womanly appeal was patent on the Kodak photographic paper. I was ripe to be changed.

"Oh, Chuck!"

"You don't like?"

"How utterly beautiful! You're a genius, really you are!"

"Good model."

"You took this the first afternoon, when I was brushing my hair?" She held the print against her breasts.

"When you practically demanded that I take it."

"What I said was that if you were going to look at me that way, you might as well take pictures." She peeked at the print. "Dear God, it's perfect."

"So are you."

"I don't mean that. I mean the light and the composition and the expression. You really ought to take lessons. I have some folders from the Art Institute—"

"Look at the other prints."

She went through them, slowly and carefully, with the solemnity of a child in her First Holy Communion procession. When she was finished she put them back on the worktable where I had stacked them, facedown. She stood by the table, as if frozen in time, one hand still on the pictures, another clutched at her breast. She was breathing rapidly and deeply, but not crying.

I dried my hands and encircled her waist. I pressed the firm muscles of her stomach.

"What do you think?"

"I wish I was that beautiful."

"The camera only records reality. It does not interpret." I kissed the back of her neck.

"That's not true, Chuck, and you know it. The photographer catches a single second of the passing parade on a woman's face and explains who she is with that instant of illumination."

"Fine." I kissed her again. My fingers touched a fresh young breast. "If you want to explain it that way. I see the real Rosemarie and capture her in that instant when she is most who she is."

She slipped away from me and donned her robe again.

"Can I sit and watch?"

"I suspect that you installed that comfortable couch for sitting and watching."

"Minimally. Will you teach me how to develop pictures?"

"No."

"Please!"

"No."

"Why not?"

"You'll be better than I am."

"If I promise not to be better than you?"

"Well . . ."

"Goody!"

My Rosemarie in those days was not very good at sitting and doing nothing. Give her a book to read and she would wait patiently till Judgment Day and indeed protest when called upon to put it down. But without a distraction she would shortly pop up and bound around a room, sniffing and snooping like a high-spirited Irish wolfhound.

"What do you have here in your secret cabinet, Chucky? Can I look? Are there any pictures of other naked women?"

There weren't. My picture of Trudi and the roll of shots that had produced it were locked in a bank vault.

"Hey, that's private!"

"We're *married*!"

"Stay out of there!" I charged across the room.

She slipped away from my rush and opened the neat brown folder on top of my secret portfolios.

"Give it back."

She retreated across the room, folder in both hands.

"No."

"You have no right to look at those pictures."

"Maybe you're right." She considered my claim carefully. "But I don't thinks so. And, *Chucky*, you look just like you did when I started to take off your swim trunks at the pool in Mexico."

"I feel the same way." Should I tear the folder—it was one about Germany I had titled "The Conquered"—out of her hands, surely the only way I would recover it?

While I was deciding, she opened the folder, glanced at the first few prints, and then collapsed into the couch.

"I'm sorry, Chuck. I really am." She closed the folder. "I apologize. I had no idea. I really didn't. I don't know what I expected, but I didn't expect anything like . . ."

I was disappointed. I had wanted her to see them and hoped desperately that she would be impressed.

"You're apologizing for looking at my pictures?"

"Certainly not." She dismissed that possibility with her brisk hand gesture. "I'm apologizing for being dumb."

"Dumb?"

"Suggesting that you go to the silly old Art Institute." She opened the folder again and examined the prints with respectful caution. "Busybody little housewife trying to make her husband into a good picture taker when he's already a genius."

"I'm not a genius, Rosemarie." I was enormously pleased with myself.

"I mean, these poor people, so much suffering, so much hope, and a lot of arrogance too."

"And you feel so ambivalent about them."

"Right. Is this the girl who gave you the Leica?" She turned the picture of Trudi, in front of the food store, in my direction.

"Yes."

"Poor little kid. Did she make it?"

"I think so. She disappeared, but I believe she's all right."

"I'm glad."

"She's not a trollop, Rosemarie."

"Only an idiot would think she was."

So she didn't remember what she had said the night she was drunk in Mexico. Or maybe she did and was apologizing.

I still dreamed that she and Mom and Peg would meet Trudi somewhere and disown me as a coward and a liar. But in my realistic moments I knew they would never meet. And if they did, Trudi would never tell. And, finally, so what? I wasn't perfect. Who was?

Those rationalizations did not assuage my guilt or my fears.

"Definitely a genius." She continued to page through my prints.

"I'm not a genius," I said irritably.

"Yes, you are." She examined me shrewdly. "And I think you suspect it too."

"I just take pictures."

"I say you're gifted." She closed the folder abruptly and pointed a sharp index finger at me. "And I am a woman of enormous taste. In men too." She grinned impishly. "You know, you want a man, and he never does propose. So one night you show him the house in which the two of you will live after you're married and you've got him. Good taste."

"Good political skills."

"Regardless." She waved her hand again. "Grant that I have good taste? I mean seriously."

Her invasion of my darkroom and my secrets was an experience very like the wedding night when she reveled in undressing me. I had to yield my modesty again and make a gift of myself. I was delighted with the experience but also embarrassed and disconcerted.

The image of the wedding night repeated sent torrents of hormones rushing into my bloodstream.

"All right"—desire for her, imperious, violent desire, surged in my body—"seriously, I do grant that you have good taste."

"Then you agree that you are a great artists because I say so?"

"I don't know, but if you say so—"

"Oh, Chuck, this poor old woman at the railroad station—"

"She's not old, Rosemarie. She's in her early thirties. I call it 'Fidelity.' She waited at that station every afternoon for the train from Leipzig. Her husband was a Panzer commander who was captured at the battle of Krusk, the biggest tank battle in history. Occasionally Stalin sent a few of his prisoners home. They always came down on the Leipzig train."

"And he never came?"

"Oddly enough he did. Here, let me find a picture of the two of them."

I pulled out the shot of Kurt and Brigitta and their two children, Henry and Cunnegunda.

"It's not the same woman!"

"It is. She's expecting their third child."

Thank goodness she didn't ask me the child's name. It was Karl, out of gratitude for the job I had found for Brigitta at our headquarters at the Residence. Nor was there any point in telling Rosemarie that I had met Kurt at the train because Brig was translating for Herr Oberburgermeister Konrad Adenauer and General Lucius Clay, and the future Herr Reichkanzler and I had it off well.

Rosemarie closed the portfolio.

"Fine . . . what other portfolios do you have for me to see?"

"I'll show them all to you, Rosemarie. Every one of them."

"Great! Let's start right now."

"Later."

"Why later?"

"Take off that robe, woman," I demanded.

"Don't look at me that way, Chuck." She meant it. "You frighten me."

"I intend to. Take it off, I said."

"But—"

"Damn it, woman, you come in here and stir me up and then hesitate. Do what I say and do it now!"

"All right." Timidly she let the robe fall to the floor. "Please don't look at me that way. You never have . . . acted that way before."

"And the . . . whatever you call it."

"Chemise. Chuck, you're going to hurt me."

"I thought that was impossible. Take it off before I rip it off."

"All *right* . . . I'm afraid of you." She pulled the tasty bit of lingerie over her head and, holding it protectively against her breasts, backed up against the wall.

What a wonderful picture it would have made. Threatened woman? Ah, no. Wife egging on her husband, challenging him, testing him to see how he could improvise this role in their commedia *dell'arte all'improvviso*.

Very effective challenge at that.

"Drop it."

"You're trying to prove you're a man after I invaded your privacy and found out about your pictures."

"Right." I gripped her wrist. "And I propose to prove it spectacularly. Now drop it."

The chemise joined the robe on the floor. She cowered against the wall. "You're . . . scary. Can't we go upstairs? All these terrible smells."

She was a little scared, and delighted in herself being a little scared.

Being assaulted by her funny little husband was like riding the Bobs at Riverview.

"They're an aphrodisiac." I pinned her against the wall.

"Chuck . . . don't . . . oh my God . . . what are you trying to do . . . ? Stop it . . . don't drop me . . . PLEASE. . . ."

Do I have to say that it was a game, that she knew it was a game, and that I didn't hurt her? We were improvising around our roles. We romped in the most abandoned coupling thus far in our marriage. Then we looked at all my prints and romped again.

Whatever problems we would later have in our marriage, we could never argue that they were caused by sexual maladjustment during our early days. We improvised spectacularly in our first months together.

Many turning points were reached that night, not enough maybe but still a lot. Among other things, as improbable as it may seem given the calendar of Rosemarie's physiology, we conceived our daughter that night.

⁓ 18 ⁊

"Just sign your name on that cute little dotted line"—my wife sounded like a wandering catch-basin cleaner—"and you get a check for two thousand dollars."

Hector Berlioz was playing on her stereo, at a sufficient volume to wake up those peacefully sleeping in distant Mount Carmel Cemetery.

"I lost that much last week at the Exchange." I was in no mood for Rosemarie's daffy little games. It had been another brutal day at the Board of Trade. I was convinced now that Jim Clancy and a ring of his cronies were making sport of me, jerking me up and down—in the slang of the trader. I had yet to figure out how the game was being played and how I might defend myself against them. I did not want to be a trader. I ought to sell my seat and return to being an accountant—concentrate on my doctorate.

"This is the first of many contracts that will make you a lot more famous than the silly old Board of Trade, husband mine." She jabbed a ballpoint pen at me. "Just sign here, please."

I shook my head, blinked my eyes, and tried to focus on the long document in front of me. What mischief was she up to now?

"I'm afraid I don't understand." My stomach knotted and unknotted as it had done all day every day for the last two months.

"You don't *have to* understand." She tapped the antique desk in her study with the top of her pen. "I'll do the understanding, you do the signing."

Pregnancy, even more than marriage, had lured out the natural goblin in Rosemarie. She was sick in the morning for exactly two days, which she took to be a sign that God had excused her from all purgatory in this life and in the next because she had to put up with me. She bounded more enthusiastically, laughed more boisterously, fought with me more cheerfully, and spent money more wildly. Before I knew it she had a closetful of maternity clothes, albeit inexpensive maternity clothes. She changed dresses three or four times a day just so she could examine her pregnancy in different colors and perspectives. She enrolled in Rosary College and returned to her voice lessons, the former (despite her dislike for nuns) to keep Peg company, the latter so she would sing pretty lullabies to "little April"—that our child would be a girl and would be named after her grandmother was a foregone conclusion I dared not dispute.

"No parading on the sand at Long Beach this summer." I had looked up from my *Daily News*, in which I was searching (vainly) for some understanding of the day's grain prices.

"I *will too*." She lifted her nose into the air. "I want everyone to know that I'm not practicing birth control."

In those days, to have a large family was to reaffirm your Catholicism. Big families were in fashion after the war, especially among Catholics. The children of such families almost always opted for much smaller families and chose to display their Catholicism in other ways. The country was making up for the low birth rates of the Depression, and Catholics, having finally climbed out of poverty, were doing so with special vigor.

I don't think the birth control teaching was all that important even then. Most of the women who were bearing five or six children before they were thirty began to disregard the Church's teaching around 1960.

Our marriage at that time was happy enough. The only problem was that Columbine was larger than life and Pierrot smaller than life. In Columbine's world there were, for example, two volume levels for the radio and phonograph: loud and louder. Come to think of it, there were two styles in her life: forceful and more forceful.

I would ask her politely if she might possibly turn the radio down a little bit. She would promptly comply, with a faint nudge to the knob that created no difference in the volume that I could discern. "That doesn't seem to make much difference, darling."

"Maybe you ought"—she'd frown, as if worried about me—"to see a doctor about your hearing. You seem to have lost your ability to discriminate in volume."

"Maybe I never had it."

I liked to watch Ed Sullivan on our four-inch TV screen. She thought he was a jerk. So I didn't watch him. She liked the news broadcasts because she thought there might be good news from Korea. I didn't want to think about Korea. So we watched the news.

In a proper marriage, we would have had it out then and there and negotiated (a term my kids use routinely) compromises. I had no idea how to push back.

She was so vulnerable, despite her vigor, and so deeply in love with me—to my endless astonishment—that I thought noise, admittedly Bach or Mozart noise, was not important.

So I repressed my anger. It festered beneath the surface, as did a lot of other repressed complaints.

Loud music was a minor irritant compared to her occasional drinking bouts. It was impossible to reason with her when she was drunk; she'd scream obscenities and throw whatever object might be at hand—never hitting me. Rosemarie on a binge was a disgusting sight—foulmouthed, untidy, violent, spit drooling from her mouth, body odor filling the room, drunken laughter echoing through our vast house.

After the binge she was so fragile and penitent that I was afraid to hurt her by argument.

"I won't do it again, Chuck, I promise. That was positively the last time."

"I don't like to see you hurting yourself."

"I don't matter. You do."

"If I could help—"

"I have to do it myself." Quiet and firm. "If only I didn't have such a weak will."

"How can you do it alone?"

"How else can I stop drinking?" Some asperity, thunderclouds gathering. "I guess I'll have to pray harder for more character. Please don't make it harder for me."

"I'd like to help."

"I SAID I had to do it alone." More tears.

Pierrot retreats in confusion. Blew it again. The results of his cowardice would haunt him in the years to come.

In that spring of 1951 Vince was in Korea, in combat at Heartbreak Ridge, as a bloody battle in that forgotten war was called. Peg needed someone on whose shoulder she could cry.

Ridgeway had counterattacked in late March and inflicted a massive defeat on the Chinese. He recaptured Seoul and drove the enemy back across most of their prewar border. There was talk of stalemate and negotiations, but it was still a dangerous war for Vince in the frontline foxholes.

That was the year of the film *Quo Vadis* ("Deborah Kerr in a negligee," Rosemarie tittered, "no wonder you like it), of "In the Cool, Cool, Cool of the Evening," and of the first hydrogen bomb test. It was the time of the national orgy of support for General MacArthur, whom Truman had fired. The millions who cheered for MacArthur in the streets didn't seem to realize that he was the one who had prolonged the war.

The Board of Trade seemed at first to be pure terror, a mistake that would have no silver (even somewhat tarnished) linings. I felt that I did not belong there. I had neither the physiology nor the psychology for the daily gambling pool that was the wheat pit. I hesitated, I doubted, I thought, I worried. The good traders acted. They won some, they lost some, but—if they survived the first couple of years—they won more than they lost.

Cautious, careful, orderly man that I was (and am, despite what you may have read elsewhere), I did not belong in the tumultuous battles on which the successful traders seemed to thrive. I belonged rather in the quiet, reflective, subdued precincts of O'Hanlon and O'Halloran (the Double O's, as the two little gnomes who were the senior partners in the firm had been dubbed by my fellow traders, who entrusted all their complicated tax problems—as they thought then—to the whispering gnomes).

I was there at the Board of Trade because I had promised my wife that I would give it a try. A curious attempt at a distant reconciliation with her father? Or did she want me to defeat him in the pit as I had in love?

The nuances of her ambivalence toward her father were beyond my understanding.

"How did Daddy seem today?" she would occasionally ask at the supper table.

"A little tired. He had a good day, I think. There's talk around the Exchange of him investing in a hotel in Las Vegas."

"Different kind of gambling, poor man."

When the doctor confirmed her pregnancy, I suggested she call him and tell him.

"I don't want to do that. You tell him tomorrow at work."

His only comment was, "Well, I suppose that was inevitable."

I lost heavily that day, unable to keep pace with a grain market that first slumped and then rebounded with unnatural vigor.

"What did Daddy say?"

I lied. "He beamed proudly and said I should congratulate you."

She smiled happily. "I'm so glad he's pleased."

"He certainly seemed to be."

Then, after a moment's reflection, she looked at me strangely. "You *are* telling the truth?"

"About what?"

"About Daddy's reaction."

"He seemed very proud to be a grandfather."

Maybe I should have told her the truth. Maybe I should also have told her that he was systematically taking away my capital, or to be more precise, her capital. Perhaps he was merely reclaiming that which he thought by right was his—the money out of which his wife had tricked him in her final revenge. Perhaps he thought I would be so addicted to the pit that I would commit all of Rosemarie's money and even our elegant old home, of which she was so proud, in a last roll of the dice.

In that hope he was kidding himself. I was not a plunger, not a go-for-broke person. When the hundred thousand dollars Rosemarie had put in her investment account (to supplement the money my parents allegedly paid for my seat on the Exchange) was exhausted, I would wend my way back up LaSalle Street to the Double Os and the quiet life. And perhaps leave the economics department to enroll in the graduate school of business at the University. Or maybe, just maybe, continue in the economics Ph.D. program.

There are, broadly speaking, three ways of earning your keep in the commodity markets. The most extraordinary way is to see a long-term trend developing, say in oil between the early seventies and the middle eighties, and put your money behind your faith in that trend—with a considerable amount of laying off and hedging, against the possibility that you might be wrong (at least you do it that way if you have any sense). The second method is spotting a powerful short-run trend just before it happens, like the soybean price explosion in 1972 or the expansion of the grain markets at the start of the Korean War. The third technique is to ride up and down, a little bit ahead of the trends, in the daily and weekly fluctuation of the markets. If you sign on for either of the first two styles and have enough sense to know when to get out, you can become very wealthy indeed. But big surprises of substantial duration are in the nature of things infrequent, so most traders make their money on the minute daily fluctuations in which nerve, instinct, and gut feel were critically important in the early fifties. They still are even today, despite all the computer programs that are loaded into the PC that your serious trader keeps by his bedside so he can trade on the Singapore Exchange at 2 A.M. (Chicago time).

Every mature capitalist economy must have a commodity exchange so that farmers (and now businessmen and bankers) can hedge against the random ups and downs of their markets. Even the socialist economies, I argued in an article some fifteen years ago, have them to hedge in their black markets. The traders and their clients (politely called investors and not riverboat gamblers) absorb the risk from producers in return for the chance to speculate on their guesses/hunches/instincts/voices in the night (to which today one would add *computer programs*). There are a lot of things wrong with the way this works out in practice, as many things today, when we speculate not only on grain or animals or butter and eggs but on such ephemeral pieces of paper as eurodollars and T-bills and "derivatives," as there were when I rode home on the Lake Street El a nauseated wreck, oblivious to the spring lace appearing along the streets of Oak Park. But despite the mistakes, the corruption, the injustices, the occasional downright dishonesty, you can't do without commodity exchanges.

And while, God knows, they need to be regulated, there doesn't seem to be a government in the world that has enough sense and intelligence to know how to regulate them.

In principle, you can make money by being a bull or a bear. In the former case you buy futures, betting that the market will go up and you can sell them for more than you have contracted to buy them for (with a very small part of the actual costs, a "margin"). In the latter case you sell futures on the hope that the market will decline and you will be able to purchase grain more cheaply than you have sold it and thus make a profit. Rarely does a trader hold on to a contract till delivery time. You might buy October wheat today and sell it tomorrow because the cost of a contract has gone up overnight and you will make a nice profit. If you hang on to the contract too long, the market might fall and you'd lose your profit and your investment and might have to find more money to cover the losses that exceed the original margin you have invested. That way you can make a lot and lose a lot. In a hurry.

I spoke of contracts being sold on the next day. In fact, it is quite normal to sell and buy and then sell again, all on the same day or in the same hour, as you bet, not on what a bushel of wheat will cost in October, but on what a contract for that bushel of wheat will cost in half an hour.

I was convinced that I lacked the temperament for such quick and potentially costly decisions. There was no time to reach for my idea notebook (which amused my wife immensely) or to order my thoughts on a pad of yellow paper. I was therefore a sitting duck for the vultures who hover around the pits, looking for newcomers whose flesh they can pick off their bones.

Jim Clancy, I would learn quickly, was a prime vulture, and the leader of the other vultures.

While those who live off the daily fluctuations of the market have to be bears and bulls alternately—and often at the same time as they hedge against their own hedging—the long-term propensity is to be, you should excuse the quote, bullish on America. Over the long haul, the American, even the trader—especially the trader—believes in expansion. With each year that the Great Depression (out of which the truly shrewd bears like Joseph Kennedy had made huge fortunes) receded into the past, fears of another monumental contraction faded. Generally this long-run bullishness has paid dividends, and rich ones at that, in the last half century. Occasionally even the wise traders, or those who think they are wise, ride the market up even when there is excellent reason to think that it is too inflated. Thus in the notorious Hunt family attempt to corner the silver market in the late nineteen seventies, anyone with common sense knew that a silver contract was worth between five and ten dollars at the most and not almost forty dollars. They also knew that, if it became necessary to change the rules of the exchanges in midstream to protect themselves from the Hunts, the men in power would do just that.

Yet a lot of traders were badly hurt in the run-up—sophisticated traders and not just the poor suckers who grab the coattails of every exciting trend with a sure instinct for their own self-destruction.

The really shrewd traders and investors got out of silver early and made millions on the collapsing markets. But to sell against a trend that powerful requires not only shrewdness and sophistication but a naturally bearish personality.

Like mine.

If I had managed to bet in some systematic way in favor of the continued expansion of world grain demand occasioned by the Korean War, I could have survived my daily losses as the vultures manipulated prices up and down to amuse themselves while doing me in.

"This Korean 'police action,' as that dumb hat salesman from Missouri called it, is almost as good as war," I heard one of them say after the closing bell had hushed the madness and he and his cronies were leaving for the bars just off LaSalle Street. "It has kept the Depression away for five more years."

I reacted with the emotions of a brother-in-law and not of a trader. "The kids dying at Heartbreak Ridge might think differently."

"Tough shit. I don't notice you fighting the gooks."

My instincts, notoriously inaccurate in most respects, said that the grain market was overvalued.

But what did I know about it?

Rosemarie was insistent about the contract she wanted me to sign "*Please* just sign this contract and then we can eat supper. April and I are both terribly hungry."

"What kind of contract is it?" I stirred myself out of my lethargic fog. "Wheat or corn?"

"Pork bellies." She jammed the pen into my hand.

I lifted my pen to sign, hesitated, and began to read the long, obscure, tedious document more carefully.

"It's a book contract!" I rose from my consort's easy chair in righteous anger.

"Regardless." She smiled demurely. "That's what I've been trying to tell you. This nice man from New York will publish your book for nothing and give you two thousand dollars, plus whatever royalties the book earns. I've had my new lawyer, Dan Murray, Ed's father, look it over and he says it's a good contract." (Ed was flying a Phantom jet off a carrier on the Korean coast.)

"That's nice." I scratched my jaw dubiously.

"So all you have to do is sit back and collect the royalties—well, maybe write a teeny-weeny introduction."

"I'm not a writer." I tried to read the contract again.

"You're a photographer, a great one, the man from New York says, so he must be right."

"How did you get to know this man in New York?"

"Oh, *that*. Well"—she talked very rapidly—"a woman on the board at Marillac is married to a publisher and he knew this agent, Mr. Close, and Mr. Close knew this publisher and I sent him your German pictures and—"

"My German pictures!"

"Well, I thought I would begin with them." She followed me as I paced up and down with anxious eyes. "There's a lot more downstairs if this one is a success, which it certainly will be."

"I do not intend to sell my pictures."

"Why not?"

"They're personal, a personal vision."

"Not just archives?" She was mocking me now.

"Personal archives."

"It's the personal vision, the man from New York said, that makes the book so moving."

"No."

"Yes." She didn't sound too confident, however.

"I won't do it, Rosemarie." I slumped back into the leather chair and tossed the contract back on her desk. "I don't want any part of the professional artist's world. It's worse than the Board of Trade."

"How do you know?"

"From my father."

"He's a success, now isn't he?"

"At designing buildings, not at painting. There's not enough money in it to support a family, Rosemarie. It would be crazy."

"Can't you do it in the afternoons when you come home from the Exchange and after you've been to class? It's better than drink or women. I have enough money to support a family."

"I won't live off your money."

"Why not?" Her lips were tightening into an angry line.

I must be careful. There had not been a drinking episode since she suspected she was pregnant. I did not want to induce another.

"It's just not right, Rosemarie, it wouldn't be manly."

A male chauvinist? What can I tell you? It was 1951, remember.

"Just one book," she begged. "How would one book hurt?"

"I'd make a fool out of myself."

"Which is it?" Her eyes flashed dangerously. "Making a fool out of yourself or living off your wife?"

"I appreciate what you're trying to do, Rosemarie. I really do. But it's only a hobby. I'm just not cut out for that kind of life."

She looked like she was about to ask me what kind of life it was for which I was cut out. Instead she sighed and said, "Definitely no?"

"Definitely."

"You're the boss." She folded up the contract. "They're your pictures, not mine."

"Thank you for understanding."

"I don't exactly," she wavered, ready to launch another attack, and then thought better of it. "I don't want to be a nagging wife."

"You'll never be that."

Which was both true and not true. Rosemarie's "ought tos" would never drive me up the wall. Not quite. She always knew when to stop a fraction of an inch short of being a scold.

"Let's eat." She led the way to the kitchen in which, to judge by the smell, we were going to eat spaghetti, our usual fare on the day our cook/maid was not around. (An extravagance I accepted because I had no choice: "Chuck, the poor woman needs the job.") Rosemarie's Italian food was excellent. Alas, it was all that she could produce. Well, you can get used to spaghetti once a week.

If you have to.

"By the way"—she heaped my plate with three times as much pasta as I could possibly consume—"Peg's pregnant too. Honeymoon baby. They beat us in—what do you call it in the sailboat races?—elapsed time."

How did she know about sailboat races?

She read the sports pages too. She read everything.

"How is she?"

"Sick, poor kid. And worried too. She had to leave Mass this morning before Communion. Father Raven told her she could eat bread when she gets up without breaking her fast because then it's medicine. She didn't want to." Rosemarie made a wryly funny face. "Afraid that Father Raven might not have cleared it with God."

I put down my fork. "Does Vince know?"

"She wrote him."

We both were silent.

"It doesn't seem fair."

Rosemarie put her hand on mine. "He'll be all right, I just know he will."

"It's a dumb war."

"All wars are dumb."

"Why is he there when I'm not?"

She squeezed my hand. "Maybe because I'm not nearly as strong a woman as your sister."

"It doesn't make sense."

I toyed with my fork. The Board of Trade was a jungle, but not as bad as Heartbreak Ridge.

"Eat," she said, "you're getting thin. People will say that terrible woman doesn't feed you."

"Plenty of good pasta." I picked up the fork.

"I'm reading a book about French cooking; pretty soon we'll have pasta only every other week."

She could have said that she was asking me to risk less with my pictures than Vince was risking in Korea.

She didn't. Maybe she knew that I would think it without her telling me.

The next day I actually made some money in the wheat pit. I had begun to figure out the signals Jim Clancy was using with his buddies and I crossed them up at the last second jumping off one of their artificial surges before they could pull the bottom out from under me.

"Got the bastards today," John Kane, silver-haired Irishman with a handsome red face—he could have been a cop or an undertaker as well as a trader—said to me, "didn't you, son?"

"Figured out their strategy." I could hardly walk off the floor. "They'll have another one tomorrow."

"Some of them lost a little of their precious capital. Beat them a few more times and they'll leave you alone. It's hazing, you know, like those college fraternities. They don't mean nothing by it. They do it to all the young fellows."

"To see if you're a man?" I asked bitterly.

"Well, that's what Old Jim might say, and himself such an impressive specimen, if you take my meaning."

"He'll be back again tomorrow."

"It's a little bit more vicious than usual, I'll admit that." He clapped me on the shoulder. "But I like the cut of your jib, son. You know how to fight back."

"I hope so."

"You've got good eyes. Watch their faces. See the fear when they think they're going to lose."

"They make great pictures," I agreed, "Old Jim more than most."

"He'd break the camera."

For the first time that year I noticed the early May signs of spring as I walked down East Avenue from the Ridgeland El station—ten blocks, but I needed the exercise. What a dope you are, Charles Cronin O'Malley, to permit a clique of evil old men to prevent you from enjoying spring and the springtime of your life.

"Made some money today, dearest," I chirped as I strutted into her office.

If I had been smart, I would have noticed that the stereo was silent: a trap was being baited.

She was, as promised, poring over a French cookbook—in French, mind you—with a notebook on her lap.

"Two thousand dollars?" She cocked a critical blue eye at me. "Like you could have made yesterday."

The contract was resting dead center on her desk, a pen next to it.

If the red-faced mick hadn't spoken his few words of praise, I might not have been tempted.

As it was, I hesitated. "And after it fails, where does the next two thousand come from?"

"We wouldn't even consider"—she turned up her pretty Irish nose in disgust—"two thousand the next time. There's a wonderful little thing in the contract called an option. Your second collection will earn a five-thousand-dollar advance."

"That's crazy." I shifted uneasily in her leather chair, purchased and positioned precisely for a weary husband coming from work to render an account of his stewardship.

"The man from New York, Mr. Close, says that your 'Football Weekend' portfolio would make a fine book."

"Have you taken all my prints out of the cabinet downstairs?"

"Not the early ones."

"Hey . . . come to think of it, how did you get into them in the first place. I lock the cabinet after every time I use the darkroom."

"You don't think, do you, husband mine"—she favored me with the wicked, crooked grin of which I was seeing a lot lately—"that I'd have a cabinet like that made without a spare key? I mean, what if you lost your key, with your disorderly habits and all?"

"How dare you!" I was now, belatedly, furious.

"I'm your wife. It comes with the body."

"The bad with the good!" I was working myself into a rage.

"Suit yourself."

"How many times do I have to say no before you understand that I mean no?"

"Three times." She glared at me defiantly. "No more. So, O'Malley, you have one more shot and then I leave you alone."

I leaped out of the leather chair, bent over the desk, and furiously scrawled my name on the bottom of the final page.

I was so angry that I didn't think to put in "Cronin" or "C."

"Satisfied?" I growled at her.

"Astonished." She looked at the signature carefully. "I guess it's valid. I'll just sign my name, much prettier in both sound and appearance, and we'll be two thousand dollars richer. There."

"You didn't think I'd do it?" Unaccountably, I was breathing heavily as though I were sexually aroused. In fact, I was not; that, I imagined, would come later.

"No, I didn't," she admitted, hugging me. "I'm so proud of you."

"You have every intention"—I still was simmering—"of changing my life?"

"Isn't that what wives are for?"

"Now let me ask you some questions about money."

"Anything you want to know, husband dear." She lowered her eyes modestly.

She had a surprisingly precise knowledge of her own financial affairs—money, property, investments. Her fortune was substantial, but not unlimited. "Satisfied?" she asked me when she'd finished.

"I have an accurate picture. I guess that finishes the agenda for this afternoon."

"Not quite." She rose from her judge's chair and crossed to me, sitting on the edge of my assigned consort's chair. "I'm not finished with you yet."

"What else?" I had missed the wicked gleam in her eye.

"What do you think?" She unbuckled my belt.

"Rosemarie, do you want everything?"

"Exactly." Her hand probed my loins. "Your pictures and your career and your body. Now don't squirm while I undress you."

"Gravy for the gander—"

"Is gravy for the goose. Precisely. I *said* hold still."

"How can I when you're teasing me that way?"

So I was appropriately rewarded for my twin acts of courage, signing the contract and asking about her money. I'm sure she viewed only the first as courageous. At the most.

Over supper she said, "I almost forgot. I had a letter from Polly Nettleton today."

"Who?!"

"Your good friend Captain Polly."

"What did she want?"

"To answer my letter."

"What did you write to her for?"

"To find out the details of why you were a hero in Bamberg."

"I wasn't a hero, damn it!"

"The good April would disapprove of that language. You told me the truth all right, Chuck, about the black market, but not the whole truth. Polly told me the whole truth. I could hardly believe you'd be so reckless."

"Controlled recklessness. I didn't take any chances that I didn't have to take."

"She also told me that you like caviar."

I felt my face turn hot as I remembered the party at the Nettleton's apartment where I made a fool of myself by eating a pound of caviar.

"Woman has a big mouth. Why did you want to know all the details?"

"I kind of figured what you'd do in such a situation. And you did. So I wonder why you don't do the same thing at the Exchange?"

"Oh," I murmured. "You want me to act like I did in Bamberg?"

"I'm sure you could and you'd beat my daddy and those other terrible men and make a lot of money."

"Maybe," I admitted.

Somehow the possibility appealed to me.

The next morning on the Lake Street El, I calculated how much my potential capital (including Rosemarie's money), against margin calls, would be if I protected the house and enough money for the education of three or four children. I had no intention of doing anything reckless, no conscious intention at any rate.

If I were to pursue the photography game, I could not continue working at the Board of Trade. The two occupations were quite incompatible, I told myself. Obviously I couldn't earn a living with a camera. However, the Double O's still liked my neat ledger sheets. (If my handwriting wasn't as pretty as my wife's, it was notably more legible.) Their offer of half-time work was always open.

I might well try that for a while. Until I proved to the damned beautiful, sexy bitch with whom I slept that I was not a great artist.

Right?

After I had failed at the career she was forcing on me, I could work full-time at the firm and maybe continue my education in night school. Fine. Everything neat and orderly?

The young redhead doth protest too much, you say?

Didn't he sign that contract in an awful hurry?

Tell me about it.

On the front page of the *Tribune* that morning there was a story that General Eisenhower, then president of Columbia University, was considering a presidential race on the Republican ticket. Already Henry Cabot Lodge (whom the *Trib* despised) was reported to gathering a staff which would help the General deny (the *Trib*'s word) the nomination to Senator Robert Taft, who, most Washington Republicans were saying, was "entitled" to it.

The war was settling down to a stalemate and there were rumors of peace negotiations. They could drag on for a long time. But I thought that Eisenhower might end the war more quickly than Harry Truman, if only because he might be in a position to threaten to use the bomb against the North Koreans and the Chinese.

Vince's year would be up before the presidential election, so it wouldn't make any difference to him.

It might make a difference to other young men, however.

Those were my only reactions to the possibility of Ike's running. The Republicans, I thought, can't win with one of their own, not even against Truman. So they're about to nominate a man who has been a Democrat most of his life.

Maybe Colonel McCormick of the *Trib* had a right to be angry.

I had not thought of the possible impact of the story on the grain market.

Everyone else had. Peace, even a ceasefire or negotiations, would depress the price of wheat. The market in October wheat took a nosedive that morning, which is what I'd figured it would, especially because I was convinced that it was overvalued and had been for weeks. I stood by watching in disbelief the folly of men earning a living by betting on war and peace.

A wild and reckless scheme began to waken in my head. I wouldn't do it, of course. Wasn't I the timid and cautious accountant?

Me, Charles C. O'Malley, Scaramouche?

Me with the gift of laughter and the sense that the world was mad?

"Not trading?" John Kane asked me.

"Today's crazy," I responded.

"On days like this, fortunes can be made and lost."

I was not reassured.

As the closing bell approached, the price of October wheat soared back to its high of the previous day. That made no more sense than the fall earlier in the day. The war would end within the year, no matter who was nominated or elected. The market was far too high. It had been too high even at the day's low. Why couldn't everyone see that?

Probably because they were more concerned about the game than the real world outside the game, same as they imagined that world affected the game.

Jim Clancy was buying grain like it was about to disappear from the face of the earth. He was stupid after all, wasn't he?

In a few weeks everyone would know the grain market was too high. Why did I know it before the others?

I pondered that one. I wasn't smarter than they were, was I?

Yeah, maybe I was. Or perhaps only not as dumb as they were.

Enter Scaramouche, sword in hand. I sold every possible contract for October wheat that I could afford, given the potential capital I had calculated while on the El train. I was, after all, a natural "bear," was I not?

It was an angry, irrational, clownish decision.

I rode home on the train exhilarated. I had taken a long-term position. I would not have to range through that jungle every day. If my wife's wealth was wiped out, that was her fault for trusting me with it. We'd still have the house and money for college for the kids.

After my crazy adventure with the camera was ended, we could live normal lives like normal people.

Did I believe that?

Mostly, but not entirely.

I did return to the Chicago Board of Trade the next day.

With my camera.

"April." My wife moved our daughter from one breast to the other.

"Rosemarie," I insisted just as vigorously.

"See what a silly, stubborn man, Dadums is, honey? You and I will have to work real hard to keep him in line."

I winced as she poked playfully at our daughter's little belly. Already she treated the child like a live doll, part playmate and part plaything.

The little brat, content with her food, did not protest. Already I was outnumbered.

"You like the name April, don't you, Snookums?"

"Snookums doesn't get to vote. We'll name her Rosemarie, just because she's as beautiful as her mother."

"More so." She kissed the infant's head. "But flattery will not win the argument for you. April."

We were in Oak Park Hospital where, two days before, our first child had emerged happily and easily into the world. The doctor, ignoring the physiological impossibility, declared that she had appeared smiling. She certainly seemed to be a placid child. More like her father than her mother, right?

"Rosemarie. I insist."

"What you insist doesn't make a particle of difference. We had an agreement that I'd name the girls and you'd name the boys. You ought to keep your word."

That was such a bold lie that she didn't dare to look at me when she spoke it.

"Besides," she continued, talking to our offspring instead of to me, "Snookums loves her pretty grandmother and wants her pretty name, doesn't little April, Snookums."

Rosemarie's first pregnancy had been relatively easy. And free from drinking bouts.

Except the night she smashed the Buick into the tree in front of our house, the night that Vince had been reported missing in action. For a few terrible hours I thought I would lose all three of them.

"She shouldn't be drinking this way when she's pregnant"—the young resident in the emergency room at Oak Park Hospital shook his head in dismay—"and certainly should not drive when she's been drinking."

Rosemarie screamed obscenities at him. "I'm not pregnant, you god-damned fucking asshole. I'll never be pregnant again."

When I brought her home the next day, my wife had forgotten about her drunken screams and seemed more concerned about the damage to the "cute little tree."

I blew my top. For the first time in our marriage I raged at her. "You stupid little fool. If you want to kill yourself with your crazy drinking habits, that's up to you. But I will not have you risking the life of our child. This stupidity must stop. I will not permit you to drink ever again in my presence. Is that clear?"

Real swift, huh?

She ran off to her study, wailing hysterically.

It had been a bad week in late August. Our interlude at Long Beach was destroyed by persistent October weather come early. The first Chicago reviews of my book *The Conquered* had been patronizing and disdainful. I was making no progress with the prints for the option book *Trades*, unable now to make a satisfactory print to be seen by others as well as by myself.

All these were minor pains compared to the devastating wire from the Defense Department. Vince had been preparing to leave for R and R in Hong Kong. His letters said that the action was dying down in their sector. Then there had been a quick Chinese raid across the lines.

The chances that he was still alive seemed to me to be minute. However, from what we heard, it was better to be a prisoner of the Chinese than of the North Koreans.

Christopher, Leo, and now Vince.

To make matters worse, the following week, on the Labor Day weekend, Peg almost lost the baby. After a hurried rush to St. Anthony's Hospital in Michigan City, the pains stopped. Her doctor, who happened, thank God, to be at nearby Grand Beach, said that he didn't think there was any connection between her condition and the news from Korea.

"How does he know?" Mom asked with unaccustomed bitterness.

The prescription for Peg was to stay in bed for the rest of the pregnancy. "Don't even get out of bed to go to church in the morning," the doctor insisted.

"I have to pray for my husband."

"Pray for him, and your child, in bed."

It was a roller coaster of a summer for Mom and Dad. A second grand-son born (Theodore McCormack Jr.) two more grandchildren coming (one promised, with total faith, to be a granddaughter), a son-in-law missing in action, and a book of prints by their conventional son published to thun-derously bad local reviews.

"Dull and trite," said the *Trib*.

"Must be given credit for boldness to publish such amateurish efforts," argued the *News*.

"A sick exhibition of our corruption of defeated enemies," said the *Herald*.

"Anti-Semitic in its worship of German *volk*," opined the *Sun*.

We were all devastated. Rosemarie, just over her last spree and pathet-ically penitent in response to my fury, began yet another fling, but stopped it when I ripped a gin bottle from her hands and smashed it on her kitchen floor.

She ran away sobbing again, but this time to our bedroom.

"Don't hit me, please," she begged when I followed her. "It's all my fault."

"I'll never hit you, Rosemarie." I engulfed her in my arms.

Better, but still not very swift.

What astonished me about the reviews in the Chicago papers was their anger. Even if my photography was pretty bad, what was the point in their fury? I was hardly a threat to anyone, a twenty-three-year-old with a Leica and a Kodak and two years of service in Germany. Why use howitzers to slap me down?

I would later learn that the Chicago literati—the review editors of the papers and their friends who reviewed for them—were driven into parox-ysms of rage when someone in Chicago who was not one of their Lake Front group did anything that suggested talent or success. My talent might still be very much in question, but to have a book of prints published when many "much better" photographers (in their own social circles) were not published was an intolerable affront.

I am not kidding about the Lake Front either. A brilliant young intel-lectual, Isaac Rosenfeld, who died a few years later, wrote an extraordinary essay about Chicago in those days, contrasting the Lake Front culture with the barbarism of the rest of the city. It was a marvelously poetic exercise, thick with dazzling images and forceful metaphors. Even those who lived west of Halsted Street and read it were impressed, despite the fact that we were the targets.

For all its brilliance, the article was wrongheaded. There were a half dozen Frank Lloyd Wright homes within walking distance of our house on

Euclid Avenue, a fact that demolished Rosenfeld's argument all by itself—although it was the kind of poetic vision that cannot be demolished by mere facts.

A published photographer not quite twenty-four was bad enough, Irish and Catholic was worse, and from the West Side of Chicago settled the matter. How could I be any good?

I didn't much care, worried as I was about Vinny. What difference did reviews make when the photography was nothing more than a hobby anyway?

They troubled my wife and my family more than they bothered me. "Hell, Dad," I said, "I'm surprised they bothered."

I was locked into doing more books anyway. As the reader has doubtless noticed I am quite unskilled at extricating myself from messy situations into which I have stumbled, mostly through error and mistake.

More books would mean more bad reviews, tears from Mom and Rosemarie, and snide comments from some parishioners in back of church after Mass on Sunday.

As in, "I thought that was a pretty good review in the *Sun* last Sunday."

I'd smile and say thanks, though I would be tempted to reply that I doubted that the person ever opened the book review section of the paper except when he heard there was a review that suggested I was anti-Semitic.

To complicate the blend of light and shadows that summer, I was able to repay all her capital to Rosemarie before our daughter made her momentous appearance.

"A check for a hundred thousand dollars?" she gasped, for once surprised at something I'd done. "Rob a bank?"

"Made it on October and March wheat."

"But you never go to the Exchange anymore except to take those beautiful, terrible pictures."

I had, need I say, not taken any shots of her father. The temptation to do so, however, was gargantuan. I secretly prided myself on my great virtue in exercising such restraint.

"I took a short position and stuck with it. Every time I made a big gain, I simply put it back in more futures. It looks like the grain market will turn around with the shortfalls in winter-wheat goals, so I terminated the position."

"Oh, what does that mean?" She patted her large belly as if to assure the busy child within that Daddy was not necessarily a bank robber. "Do you have as much money as I do?"

"Nowhere near it, but enough for a while."

I had beaten the bastards and made more money from that one day's plunge than I would make in a decade with the two O's. I laughed in Jim

Clancy's ugly face when I terminated my position. I told myself that a lot of the money I had won was his.

I was the man who broke the bank at Monte Carlo.

"Wonderful," Rosemarie said. "Then you can concentrate on your photography for another year at least?"

And more if I wanted to. I didn't think I'd admit it to her. "Well, I won't have to live off of you for a while."

"Don't get on that subject again. It's crazy. Are you going to invest your profit again?"

"In blue-chip stocks—until I find a trader I can trust."

After he breaks the bank, the smart man quits, right?

"How marvelously brilliant of you, Chuck. I guess you showed Dad."

"Lucky."

Oh yes, very lucky indeed. The cautious, conservative, timid trader had plunged in where angels feared to tread and had made a killing in the process. Like the kid who won three dollars and fifty cents in the dime slot machine, I proposed to pick up my winnings and go home. Reckless bulls are commonplace in the exchanges, though most of them don't last long.

Reckless bears, however, are a rare breed. In fact, there are those that contend I exhausted the species. I wanted to get away from a battleground on which I did not want to belong. I wanted to terminate financial dependence on my wife. I was furious at those who thought of Heartbreak Ridge as an occasion to make money. So I made an appallingly bad investment decision in a moment of angry impulse.

And won.

What are you up to now, I asked the Deity that night.

John Kane said I was brilliant.

I insisted that I was lucky.

He disagreed.

So I did escape the Board of Trade and did end my dependence on Rosemarie's money by violating all my own rules of probity and caution. I wanted to be wiped out and I became modestly wealthy instead.

No, to tell the truth, I didn't want to be wiped out. I wanted to WIN! And I beat the hell out of Jim Clancy in the process, not knowingly, not deliberately, but nonetheless effectively.

John Kane, my red-faced Irish friend, told me that Clancy had taken a terrible beating in the falling grain markets.

"He hung on too long, a mistake the likes of himself never does. I think he was trying to catch you. Watch him, my lad, he's dangerous."

"You're handling my account from now on"—I patted his shoulder this time—"you watch out for him."

I had to keep a small account, mostly to justify my showing up at the Exchange a couple of days a week with my camera. Now that I was not screaming and waving in the pits and periodically losing my breakfast in the men's room, I found the Board of Trade a fascinating place. I thought that maybe I'd write a dissertation on it someday. Or an article.

Now I could spend more time on my doctorate. It was fun taking pictures at the Exchange. Despite my sobriety as a child, I always, as Mom pointed out happily, loved circuses.

They had clowns in them, you see.

And the Board of Trade was high comedy, filled with clowns, good and bad, happy and sad, greedy and generous.

That's what my pictures said.

None of the money I had "earned" by a combination of stupidity and good luck would bring Vince Antonelli back alive. What difference did my money make?

It made a lot of difference to Jim Clancy.

"Don't you aim that goddamn camera at me," he screeched at me one afternoon in the Trader's Inn, a bar across the street from the Exchange.

"I wasn't planning on it. I don't take pictures of drunks."

"Not taking any of that cheap little thing you're married to?"

"You're a fine one to talk," I fired back at him.

He elbowed his way through a throng of loud, gesticulating traders, who were still coming off the excitement of the session with their third drink in twenty minutes.

"You threatened me once," he snarled into my ear.

"The threat stands." I picked him up by his shoulders and shook him, like a cat would shake a mouse. "You leave her alone or I'll kill you."

"Big talk." He waved his drink at me, like it was a grenade with the pin pulled.

"You saw what I did to you in the pit, without even working up a sweat. Leave us alone or I'll wipe you out." Big talk. No substance. Dumb to say it with others listening. Very dumb.

"I'll get you before you get me, I promise you that. There's a lot you don't know."

"I'm quivering." I turned on my heel and walked away from him.

"And your pictures are trash, just like your father's paintings."

I had shot off my mouth once that afternoon. Leica in hand, I strode out of the tavern before I did it again.

The day after I had returned my initial capital to Rosemarie, I drifted into the house from a photo exploration of the Frank Lloyd Wright homes in the neighborhood to discover that Rosemarie was talking money on the phone.

"Absolutely not, we wouldn't think of it. I don't care if you are *Life* magazine. My husband will not agree to the use of his prints unless we're paid for them. What?" She grinned over the phone at me, and waved me to my assigned leather chair. "No, we won't charge for an interview. But you're going to have to pay five hundred dollars for each picture. You can afford it."

I closed my eyes and bowed my head. It was too late now.

Did I want to appear in *Life*?

Well . . .

What I wanted didn't matter anymore.

"Fine, you have a deal. 'Where is he now?' " She looked around the room. "Well, he's not here now. Maybe you can send your reporter around tomorrow morning about ten or so?"

I shrugged my shoulders, knowing, with my eyes still closed, that she was looking at me for agreement.

I might as well agree. Be a good boy, like you're supposed to, Charles Cronin O'Malley.

"Hooray!" she screamed. "They bought it!"

She thumped down on my lap, a heavier burden than she was eight months ago, but still a pleasant enough encumbrance. I put my arms around her and hoped that after the birth of our daughter (I knew enough not to dissent from that prediction) her once astonishing waist would recover its former slimness.

"We don't really need the money."

"Sure we do, if we want to establish that you're a great photographer."

"How did they find out about the book?"

"From the review in the *New York Times* next Sunday. Mr. Close called me while you were out to read it to me. It was great."

"What did they say?"

She waved her hand. "Oh, I didn't bother to write it down. You can read it Sunday."

"I guess I can wait."

"It'll be good for you. You'll have a bit of an idea of what I'm putting up with from this rambunctious daughter of yours."

Need I say that I still have that yellowed clipping that I picked up at Midway Airport first thing Sunday morning.

After one has explored at first quickly and then very
carefully this extraordinarily subtle and nuanced view of

Germans and Americans in Germany in the years after the end of the war, one wonders what sort of man the photographer might be. Quite senior, one assumes, a big, bearded man with broad shoulders and a bowed head and eyes agonized by the ambiguities of life. But the picture of Mr. O'Malley on the final page, taken by a certain Rosemarie Clancy O'Malley—one presumes his wife—reveals a slight, clear-eyed Irishman with freckles and, one wagers, red hair. His youthful good looks suggest laughter and charm.

One returns to the excellent book with heightened interest. If young Mr. O'Malley is so gifted today, what can we expect of him in the years to come?

The first printing promptly sold out. The book made a quiet appearance in the windows of a couple of Loop bookstores. A small ad, with the *Times* quote, materialized in the *Chicago Tribune*. It was more than either of us had expected.

"If only Vince is safe and Peg has her baby and the little brat here is all right when she gets tired of pounding on my stomach."

"A big order."

"God"—she tapped the breakfast table—"wants us to ask for big things."

Even God would have found it hard to mediate our argument the day after said brat had come into the world.

"It *is* April, isn't it, Snookums?" She tickled the little girlchild who, having exhausted the available nourishment, was now calmly sleeping. "We won't back off, will we?"

"The poor child is asleep."

"Nothing poor about my little April."

"Our little Rosemarie."

"No."

"Yes."

"Monsignor Mugsy likes me better than you."

"Compromise?"

"Well . . ."

"How about"—I thought for a moment—"April Rosemarie?"

"Doesn't scan."

"I gave you the first name."

"Don't like it. Here, you hold her for a minute. Don't be afraid, you're not going to drop her."

"She's so small."

"That's the way they come."

"I have to take her picture."

"Oh yes, that's right. You're the fresh-faced charming young Irish photographer, aren't you?"

"My agent spreads that stuff. . . . I've got it: April Rosemary!"

She arched her eyebrows thoughtfully. "Well . . ."

"It does scan."

"I *know* that."

"Well . . ."

"Give her back to me." She reached out her arms. "What do you think, Snookums?"

Snookums opened her eyes, thought better of it, and went back to sleep.

"See, she thinks it's beautiful too. We win, poor old Daddy, you lose."

Naturally.

"April Rosemary?" Monsignor Branigan peered over the top of his glasses ten days later.

"Mary the mother of Jesus," Peg, the godmother, was reciting her lines. "And two saints, Saint Rose of Lima and the baby's grandmother—"

"Who has to be a saint to put up with the lot of you galoots," the pastor chortled. "Okay, Rosemarie, you win, like you knew you would."

So, imperturbably asleep, our first child was introduced into Catholicism. I was taking pictures of her by then. Those would be some of the pictures that would change my life decisively and permanently.

Her maternal grandfather appeared at the baptism.

"What are you doing here?" I demanded.

"Your mother invited me. It's my granddaughter, isn't it?"

He ignored me and my family, fawned over Monsignor Mugsy—who was politely distant—and leered at April Rosemary.

"Prettier than you were at the same age, Rosie," he said. "A lot prettier. Looks like your grandmother."

Rosemarie's Grandmother Clancy, to judge by the painting that was preserved in our upstairs hallway, was the one from whom Jim Clancy inherited his ugliness.

"I'm glad you like her, Daddy. We're so proud of her."

"I hope we can all be friends now, huh, Chucky?"

He extended his slimy hand. Caught up in the spirit of the ceremony and feeling at peace with the world, I took it.

Later I found him pawing at Rosemarie in our kitchen as she was picking up a tray of dainty sandwiches to bring to the baptismal celebrants in the front room.

"Daddy"—she cowered, shamed and terrified—"*please.*"

I pulled him away and threw him against the fridge. "Leave her alone you sick little bastard."

He grabbed a knife from the sink and lunged at me. It was only a table knife that would barely have penetrated warm butter.

I twisted it out of his hand and threw him against the kitchen door. "Get out of here now and never come back or I'll kill you. This time I mean it."

"I can't go out in the rain without my coat." He was crying. "I just want to be friends."

"Rosemarie, get your father's coat."

She hurried out of the kitchen, too frightened to say a word.

"You sick, slimy little demon, what the hell do you think you're doing!"

"I'll get even," he sniveled. "Just you wait, I'll get even!"

A little boy who has lost his shooters in a marble contest. Yes, that was it, Jim Clancy was a spoiled child who never grew up.

"Here's the coat, Daddy." She turned and ran.

"Out"—I pushed him out the door, he skidded on the porch and slipped down the first couple of stairs—"and stay out."

He pulled on his tailor-made raincoat, hunched his bald head between his shoulders, and, bereft of all dignity, sloshed around the side of the house.

Evil, as we would all learn later when the Israelis tried Eichmann, and Hannah Arendt wrote her book about the trial, can be bland and pathetic. I remembered again his laughter when I started to vomit on the sailboat eleven years before.

His laughter and the chocolate ice-cream bar that made me sick again.

"Are you all right?" I whispered into Rosemarie's ear.

"Fine . . . I didn't tell anyone else. I said that Daddy didn't feel very well."

"I'm sure that's true."

"Poor sick man."

"I agree, Rosemarie. Poor sick man."

And as we would later find out to our dismay, dangerous too.

Rosemarie drank herself into oblivion that night.

I couldn't blame her.

1952—1961

I was in Korea when Kevin Patrick O'Malley was born eleven months and twenty days after his sister—a classic Irish twin.

I did arrive at St. Ursula's only five minutes late for the beginning of the baptismal rite. It was a baby boom baptistery, already occupied by Charley and Ted McCormack, Carlotta Antonelli, and a very dubious April Rosemary O'Malley, not at all sure that a little brother was a very good idea.

"Don't mind, Monsignor," his mother said, a touch of anger in her sweet voice, "it's only the child's father. He's always been a bit late."

"Galoot," Mugsy Branigan observed affably.

"He just wants to try for Irish triplets," the mother said. "Then he'll flit off somewhere else in the world. Serves me right for marrying a professional photographer."

After Kevin's baptism and just before Christmas my first exhibit was to open in a gallery on Michigan Avenue, more proof that I was a professional photographer.

Dwight Eisenhower had been elected (without my vote). Vince was on the prisoner-of-war list and his daughter, Carlotta, and our April Rosemary vied for attention at "poor little Kevin Patrick's" initiation into the Church. The "monster battalion," as his mother deliberately misunderstood my reference to the "monstrous regiment of women" ("and John Knox meant 'rule,' not a military unit"), had already begun to dominate his life.

It was the fault of President-elect Eisenhower that I was not present for Kevin's birth. The President-elect and Kevin himself, who arrived two weeks after he was scheduled to arrive.

"I see no problem with you going to Korea." Rosemarie was holding April Rosemary in her arms, fighting with the grinning girl-child about whether her index finger belonged in her own possession or in A. R.'s mouth. "This little demon came on time, I assume her brother will too."

Note that once again the question of the child's sex was not the subject to discussion. Poor little April was to have a brother "to take care of" and that settled that.

Dwight David Eisenhower was not my favorite president. On the other hand he was not certifiably mad, as were a couple of his successors. His treatment of Truman on inauguration day was bush league: he would not talk to the outgoing chief executive because the latter had arranged for Colonel John Eisenhower, the new president's son, to be assigned to duty at the inauguration. "Ike," incapable of being gracious himself, could not recognize graciousness in others and interpreted his son's presence at the inauguration as an attempt to embarrass him.

That should have been a tip-off of what was coming. Consider three important issues of his administration: McCarthy, integration, and Suez. "Ike" left it to Congress to deprive the drunken junior senator from Wisconsin of his powers to preside over anticommunist witch-hunts; he lent campaign support to Joe McCarthy and William Ezra Jenner even though both men had smeared his patron and mentor General George C. Marshall. He never spoke a word in support of the Supreme Court's school desegregation decision, other than to say that you couldn't change people's attitudes by law. Finally, he double-crossed our British, French, and Israeli allies when they invaded Egypt and, with barracks-room language, he pulled the rug out from under them, saving the hide of our implacable enemy Gamal Abdel Nasser, the scruffy Egyptian dictator.

He was also a drunk, as everyone in the Washington press knew and no one ever wrote. Mind you, he was not a compulsive womanizer like Jack Kennedy or a flaming nut like Johnson and Nixon. Dwight D. Eisenhower was a bourbon-swilling back-barracks gambler and a mean-spirited military bureaucrat who by accident had become a national hero. (The accident was that Roosevelt could not spare George Marshall from Washington to let him lead the invasion of Europe.) In his favor, it could be said that Eisenhower was not that other and even more dubious war hero, Douglas MacArthur, whom Truman had fired when he began publicly to disagree with his orders from Washington.

I often wondered during the hysteria of the welcome-home celebration for MacArthur whether the Republicans in Congress, the Luce magazines, and the people cheering in the street wanted to remove civilian control of the military—the issue at stake in the Truman-MacArthur fight.

Another good thing about Ike was that he probably will be the last war hero elected president. Televised politics has at least the merit of revealing the worst of the phonies and fakers.

All of this is by way of preliminary explanation of why I was not eager to accept *Look*'s assignment to accompany the President-elect on his promised trip to Korea.

The promise was a clever but petty public relations gesture—though more honest than Nixon's "secret plan" twenty years later to end the Vietnam War. Eisenhower would have buried poor, hapless Adlai Stevenson anyway, because the public was fed up with the war and the seeming corruption of the Truman administration. (The Communism-in-government issue, like the abortion debate years later, attracted much attention from the press but never much affected the way people voted.) Eisenhower could not, however, promise to end the war because peace requires two sides to agree and he had no control over the North Koreans or the Chinese. So instead he promised that if elected, "I shall go to Korea," a commitment devoid of meaning, but a wonderfully clever election campaign trick. (His secret warning to the Chinese that if they didn't end the war quick he'd drop atomic bombs on them was much more effective in bringing to an end the Panmunjom negotiations.)

Look wanted me to do a photo story, "Ike Goes to Korea."

"You're an artist, not really a photojournalist." Rosemarie considered the offer thoughtfully. "I suppose you have to do some of these things for the recognition. Your opening in December is more important."

"I'll be back in time for that." I wasn't sure that I wanted to go on a phony trip to Korea with a man I already considered a phony president. "I'm worried about being here when Kevin appears."

"I'm the one who gives birth." She frowned as though I had raised an unimportant question. "Who needs you?"

"If I'm in Korea, I'll never hear the end of it."

"Regardless." She waved her hand dismissively. About my career there was no room for jokes, not with Rosemarie anyway. "Well, I suppose you ought to do it. And"—she brightened—"maybe you'll be able to see Vince and tell him about his adorable daughter."

"I don't think they're going to be released that soon."

"Still . . . And, anyway, Kevin won't keep his poor Mommy waiting, will he, April dear?"

April, unaware of the possibilities of sibling rivalry, cooed soothingly.

The wire caught up with me in Pusan, Korea:

MY BROTHER KEVIN PATRICK BORN AT 3:20 A.M. I TOLD YOU SO. LOVE. APRIL ROSEMARY.

The year between the two births had been a frantically busy one for both of us, needlessly, I conclude with the sophistication of hindsight.

Rosemarie had help in the house. She need not have preoccupied herself so totally with her placid daughter, whose only goals in life were food, adoration, and sleep. Nor did Peg and Carlotta, still at home with Mom, need the constant concern from "Aunt Rosemarie" they were receiving. However, unlike Mom, who thought relaxed attention was the best you could give, my wife felt that you were somehow a failure unless your devotion to others was tinged by frantic anxiety. Mom and Peg (and Carlotta) didn't need the anxiety and our own brat ignored it. The last-named of the monstrous regiment was content when Mommy played with her, she chose to ignore all signs of maternal anxiety.

"Boring," the kids would say today.

For my part, I had decided that, now I was a photographer, I must pursue the career with the same compulsive intensity with which I once added columns of figures for the Double O's—and finish my course work at the University.

I was in the last, or perhaps the next-to-last, generation of photographers who did not "study" somewhere. I was also in the first generation who did not study under someone. The photographers before me learned by apprenticing themselves to someone (and often became unpaid slaves in the process). Those after me did what all the others in their generations do when they want to acquire a skill: they go to school—in the fifties and sixties for a bachelor's degree in fine arts, since then for a master's in fine arts. (I suspect that if I live a bit longer I will see the Ph.D. in fine arts as a requirement for earning your living with a camera.)

I had learned the craft and perhaps the art (I'm not sure even today whether I'm an artist) by the simple expedient of pointing a camera at people and places, releasing the shutter, and playing with the results in my darkroom. By the means of a little luck and a lot of my beautiful wife's charming persistence, I had, without any training or education, progressed sufficiently to publish one book, schedule a second for publication, and plan a one-man exhibition.

There were two possible reactions to this situation. I could have figured that I had earned my early success by sheer raw talent and that I ought to sit back and enjoy the rewards. Or I could have concluded that I had not deserved my initial good fortune and that I would therefore have to earn further triumphs by mastering all the arcane knowledge, vocabulary, and skills of my new profession.

I presume that I have been sufficiently candid about my personality that I hardly need tell the reader what was my choice. I bought and read all the books, did all the exercises, studied all the masters, touched all the bases, with the same compulsive faith with which natives of the South Sea Islands rub their amulets before they paddle canoes out of the calm waters of the lagoon and into the swell of the ocean.

"Why don't you do your own stuff instead of imitating others?" Rosemarie, visibly pregnant again, had complained as she mixed chemicals in my darkroom. "Did Mozart read books? Did Puccini? Did El Greco?"

"I like the comparisons." I kissed the back of her neck. "But I don't have that kind of talent."

"Kiss me again, please." She leaned her head forward to make her neck even more available. "I need reassurance . . . that's nice. Now what was I saying? Oh yes, I don't understand why you have to pay your dues by doing junk you don't enjoy or don't want to do."

"Everyone has to pay his dues," I insisted.

"Nonsense," she replied.

Her beautiful waist had reappeared as I'd hoped it would. It then disappeared again as Kevin grew inside her. She guaranteed its return. Having experienced her willpower I didn't doubt that for a moment.

There was only one problem that did not seem to respond to her good intentions and single-mindedness, and that had apparently disappeared, thank God.

Did I learn anything during that frantic year of self-education when I was trying to catch up with what I thought a successful young photographer had to know?

A little bit of history and some of the vocabulary, not much else.

At least I didn't try to imitate the masters. I didn't try to do a Matthew Brady with the Army in Korea. I didn't visit the national parks in the West like Ansel Adams. I didn't do classical nudes. (My "available model"—lovely even in pregnancy—didn't fit the classical paradigm either in shape or in personality). I didn't search the streets of the slums. I didn't experiment with various combinations of lines and hues. Yet I tried to imitate their work in my own context. If I didn't succeed in imitating the masters I studied, the reason is not that I felt I didn't have to. However, I failed in my efforts to discipline myself and become part of someone's "school."

I studied their work and tried to see through my lenses what they saw through theirs—but in my own environment. There was no El Capitan for me to photograph by moonlight, so in Oak Park, my Yosemite Park, I tried to capture the stark, liquid beauty of Adams's work by photographing Frank Lloyd Wright homes. It didn't work.

Then I turned to Minor White's more mystical documentation—with El stations as my targets.

The results were even worse.

Perhaps I thought I was really an impressionist at heart, like my father. Maybe I needed some of the misty atmosphere of the English in my shots. So I turned to D. O. Hill and Alvin Langton in the Thatcher Woods Forest Preserve on the banks of the Des Plaines River.

Disaster.

I tried to imitate Weston's shots of wrecked cars. A little better.

As Dad explained to me when I discussed the problem with him, "Chuck, you see what you see, not what Callahan or Stieglitz saw. And you see it pretty clearly. You can't blot out your own vision even when you try."

"Confusion, fear, hope," Mom interjected as she plucked something from Handel on her new harp.

"Pardon?"

"April," my wife, never silent for long, offered her exegesis, "means that is what your eye sees . . . and not a lot of silly calculation."

"In me?"

"No, silly, in the people. That poor little blonde in Germany; the young trader. They're both calculating all the time. And the thing is that they don't need to. Either God will take care of them or they'll destroy themselves. So they shouldn't calculate."

"I'm telling stories?"

"Don't all photographers tell stories?"

"Well"—I thought about it—"Ansel Adams says that something gets into his pictures beyond what he sees when he takes them. Some people think it's sex. But maybe it's only a story we have to read into every picture."

"What kind of story?" Rosemarie now considered me with interest—I was saying something philosophical for a change, no longer just the empirical shutter-snapper.

"Dad, do you know Fox Talbot's picture of his wife and kids, standing at a door that seems to be set in a tree?"

"I don't think so."

Now they were all listening to me, even, it seemed, a satiated Carlotta.

"Fox Talbot was one of the founders—along with Louis Daguerre—of photography. Indeed, his calotype or talbotype, unlike the daguerreotype which was a two-step process, really is a lot closer to what we do today. Well, anyway, he has this wonderful shot, one of his earliest, of the wife and three kids standing by what looks like a door in a garden. In fact, it is based on Richard Bentley's illustration of Gray's *Elegy*. Talbot conceals what Bentley reveals: the entrance is to the cemetery."

"Wow!" Rosemarie shivered.

"The passage in Gray goes something like this:

> *The boast of heraldry, the pomp of power,*
> *And all that beauty, all that wealth e'er gave,*
> *Awaits, alike the inevitable hour:*
> *The paths of glory lead but to the grave."*

They were silent, pondering that insight. I finally saw what I was driving at and continued. "So maybe every photographer tells a story of some sort, at least a story of trying to preserve something from the corruption of time and death."

"Precisely what I was saying," Dad agreed amiably.

"So maybe I see something of myself in those people who are so compulsive and I want to preserve them and me from our compulsions?"

Everyone laughed at that. Uneasily.

"The trouble with you, Chucky"—Peg was nursing Carlotta, as contentious and feisty a young woman as her cousin was genial and relaxed—"is that you do all the calculation and then disregard it by doing something outrageous."

"Like marrying me," Rosemarie put in.

"Or planning that wild show," Jane concluded.

"I think what they're saying"—Ted McCormack was now in his psychiatric residency and using baseball metaphors with his clients—"is that you carefully touch each base till you get to third; then you ignore the coach and race desperately for the plate."

"Sliding to make it just under the throw." Michael looked up from the French theology book he was reading. "Safe, so far."

"That part of it"—I thought they were all mad—"doesn't show in my work, does it?"

"Not yet." Dad filled my port glass; Rosemarie waved him away.

"Thank God."

"It will in the show," my wife added. " 'Rosemarie and April,' wow!"

"When do we get to see it?" Mom took her fingers off the strings.

"When it's ready."

"I hope Vinny is home for it," Peg said with a sigh.

We all promised her that he would be. Our guarantees, it would turn out, were not much good.

At least my year of academic self-training didn't hurt my work. I suspect Dad was right: I couldn't imitate anyone else. When I tried to the result was so bad that I threw the negatives away.

That night as we were undressing, Rosemarie returned to the subject of Fox Talbot.

"You were brilliant tonight, Chucky . . . unzip my dress, will you please . . . I mean about Talbot's picture."

"Didn't know I could be philosophical, did you?"

"I never doubted that. . . . Thank you." She shrugged out of her maternity dress. "I was surprised how deep . . . are you trying to preserve me from corruption?"

Tears stung my eyes. I kissed the back of her neck.

"Forever and ever, amen."

So I was busy learning how to do something I already knew and Rosemarie was busy being a mother, something that she did with natural and unselfconscious ease.

Her maternal preoccupations kept her out of the darkroom, where she had been learning how to develop and print with the same quick skill that she had acquired her competency in French cooking—now we had meat with Bernaise sauce in those weeks we didn't have pasta. Soon she would be better in the darkroom than I was.

"I can't do it," she complained tearfully one night in the darkroom after she had run upstairs to make sure that A. R. wasn't crying. "I can't raise kids and be your assistant at the same time."

"You can do anything, Rosemarie," I said cautiously, not having realized that she had signed on as my assistant.

"That's my line to you."

I bought more cameras, notably a new Hasselblad and an old Speed Graphic, experimented with color, and flew off to the Western Pacific with the President-elect and his massive entourage.

"Remember," Rosemarie told me as we fought our way through the crowds at Midway Airport (then the busiest in the world) this is *not* your career. You are not a journalist. You're an artist. You do studies and portraits, not candid pictures of presidents getting off airplanes for the cover of *Life.*"

"*Look.*"

"Whatever."

"Be careful."

"You too." She returned my fierce embrace.

Much later I would learn that she had been having twinges of pain that suggested that young Master Kevin might burst into the world early. Rosemarie was quite prepared to face childbirth without me if a trip halfway around the world was necessary for building my reputation.

As she said, the hospital was "right down the street."

"A mile and a half. How will you get there?"

"Drive, how else? Anyway, you'll be home in plenty of time."

When I noted the time of my son's birth in the cable I received in Pusan, I wondered if she did drive herself early in the morning to Oak Park Hospital.

Actually, Mom, who'd alternated with Peg in spending nights at our house on Euclid Avenue, did the driving.

"April almost had to deliver the baby herself," Rosemarie howled happily. "Wouldn't that have been fun, little Kevin?"

I suffered from time lag and motion sickness through much of the journey. Remember, we didn't have jet passenger aircraft yet, so the President-elect, his entourage, and the press suffered in DC-6s and DC-7s. I wore my battered old fatigues and my Legion of Merit ribbon.

"You should have flown in one of the C-47s during the war," a reporter from the *San Francisco Chronicle* told me. "That was real flying. I was evacuated out of Tulagi in one of them with a bullet in my ass. Lots of fun."

"No thanks." I reached for the vomit bag, but had nothing left to contribute.

"Were you in the service?"

"After the war. Germany. Constabulary."

"Pretty plush duty."

"Beats Heartbreak Ridge. Or Tulagi."

"What do you think of this guy?"

"Ike?"

"Yeah."

"Mean, unprincipled son of a bitch. Drinks too much."

"Typical peacetime military officer, huh?"

"Yeah."

"The people like him."

"The risk you take in democracy."

I didn't like him, and I'm afraid that I was not able to keep that feeling out of my photos.

He didn't like me either at first.

"Who's that stupid-looking redhead?" he asked one of his many yes-men on Iwo Jima. "What's he doing here?"

The man consulted his clipboard. "O'Malley, Mr. President, *Look*."

"Can we get rid of him?"

"He's an accredited journalist, sir. It would cause a lot of trouble."

"Well, keep him away from me."

"Yes, sir."

Despite my red hair, I am an inconspicuous photographer. Without even trying I disappear into the scenery. Probably a personality factor. Only the most insecure men and women notice me. The women I've been able to placate, even the nervous Hollywood actresses I would shoot later in the fifties. So President Ike was one of the few "models" who were always conscious of my presence; he would watch me irascibly out of the corner of his eye.

"Stay away from him," ordered his press liaison. "He doesn't like you."

"Yes, sir," I said, putting on my military face and manner.

I still got the picture of him driving up Mount Suribachi on Iwo Jima with Ed Power, a Secret Service man from Chicago at the wheel—Ed, as he would confess later to me, driving a jeep for the first time in his life.

The shot does not, to put it mildly, compare with the classic Iwo flag raising by the six marines. But it made the cover of *Look*. Ike was furious. He saw what the editors of the magazine and the American people did not see: an irritable old man who hated the discomfort and inconvenience of this ritual drive up a hill on which many brave young Americans had died.

Later historians and biographers, however, have seen that image for what it is. Some have excused it with the argument that Ike was not feeling well. One writer remarked, "Charley O'Malley, the famous photographer, was still in his young left-wing days when he took the picture."

Which led the Mayor (to my generation of Yellow Dog Democrats the only mayor Chicago ever had until young Rich was elected) to comment at an Irish Fellowship lunch, "Ha, Chuck, you are not even, ha-ha, as far left as I am."

"The truth," I once told an interviewer who kept pushing me about the shot, "was not that the President was sick on Iwo, but that I was."

"Did you dislike him?"

"Not as much as he disliked me."

"I'm glad I didn't vote for him," Rosemarie told me in bed that night after Kevin Paddy became a full-fledged Catholic (with rights to Holy Water, Collection Envelopes, and Christian Burial). "He is a nasty man."

"He will bring Vince home for us."

"So would that cute Mr. Stevenson."

"It would be a better country if he had won."

A position that I still hold.

To give President Ike his due, he tried later in the trip to be friendly with me. The man had a genial side too—authentic, not public relations. One minute he could be tough and mean and the next moment he was your friendly Kansas farmer. I don't think he could decide himself which was the real Ike. The second one, however, was the one people thought they were electing.

"Were you in the military, Irish?" he demanded at the airport in Seoul.

"O'Malley, Charles Cronin, sir." I saluted smartly. Well, as smartly as I ever did. "0972563. Master Sergeant, First Constabulary Regiment, Seventh Army, Bamberg."

"You know my friend General Radford Meade?"

"My C.O. for more than a year, sir. I worked directly for him. Liaison with C.I.D."

"Huh," he seemed to find it hard to believe. "Responsible work."

"Yes, sir. Fine man, General Meade."

The President's eyes narrowed. "You're the fellow who did that book."

"Yes, SIR."

"Good pictures, Sergeant." He returned the salute. "Carry on."

And walked away.

"Yes, SIR."

Then he turned around. "That the Legion of Merit you're wearing?"

"Yes, SIR." I saluted again.

"At ease, son," he said, with that famous and quite irresistible Ike grin. "What did you do to earn it?"

I told him in military terms what I had done, more than I told my wife and much less than Captain Polly had told her.

"Well done, son." He shook my hand.

The poor man even autographed one of my Suribachi prints. "Everyone else likes it," he said by way of explanation.

"Yes, SIR."

I sent him an autographed copy of *The Conquered*, but I never heard that he received it.

Anyway, I was not welcome at the White House for the next eight years and didn't mind that in the slightest. I was welcome, God knows, in the next presidency, but that gets ahead of the story.

So I took the pictures, collected my five thousand dollars, and rushed home to the baptism of my firstborn son, convinced for different reasons than my wife that I was not a photojournalist. She thought my eye was too strong to be wasted on journalism. I thought my body was too weak to be exposed to the strains of international travel.

I had barely recovered my ability to think reasonably when my new book, *Traders*, was published and my first exhibition, "Rosemarie and April," opened at a gallery in the shadow of the old Chicago Water Tower. A cover for *Look*, a book, and an exhibit, all in the space of a pre-Christmas week in 1952: not bad for a twenty-four-year-old, who, as I look back at him, knew almost nothing about life.

However innocent he might have been about life and about women, the young man was not the kind who would run for home plate without looking at the third-base coach for instructions. In this respect the family was completely mistaken. The third-base coach was my wife and the exhibit was her idea. Given the effect it had on her she should have regretted the sign she gave me as I came lumbering toward third base. Being my wild Irish Rosemarie, she never once expressed regret.

The gallery, much too prestigious for a young man, wanted to do its first exhibit of photos. Though cautious and conservative, the owner decided that if I was good enough for the *New York Times* I was good enough for him. He did not, however, want any prints that appeared in either of my first two books. Rosemarie, who had wangled power of attorney from me, signed the contract and then told me the details.

"I don't have any prints," I moaned.

"If you'd stop imitating other people and do your own work, you'd have prints."

"Ga, ga, ga," said my daughter, who was always present when Rosemarie sprang one of her surprises on me. "Ga, ga, GA!"

"Right. See, the kid agrees with me."

"Why don't you use some prints of her?"

"Baby pictures."

"Da, da, da, DA!" The little monster pointed at her mother, who was definitely not Da.

"Special pictures, magic pictures, bewitching pictures."

"Who's going to buy baby pictures, especially someone else's baby pictures, even if the baby"—I poked appreciatively at A. R.—"is the most beautiful in the world."

"Da-da," the kid announced, getting it right finally.

"We *do* have to sell pictures if we want the gallery to ask us back." Rosemarie paused thoughtfully. "I've got it! We'll do a show with the brat's pictures and me. Rosemarie and April, the progress from bride to nursing mother, a hymn to life and womankind! Isn't that wonderful!"

"Exploit my two women?" My stomach twisted into its usual dance of doom.

"Celebrate them!" She kissed me and April Rosemary and then kissed us both again. "I know just the shots. Leave it all to me. You have final approval, but—"

"You don't mind if people look at those shots of you?"

"Why should I? They're not obscene."

"They're you."

"So what? Anyway, they're me seen through the eyes of my loving husband. It will make your reputation, Chucky Ducky." She kissed me yet again. "It's your best work anyway, if we're doing an exhibit at all—"

"Which may be a bad idea."

"Regardless." She dismissed my wariness with her usual brisk wave. "We must use your best. Like I said, leave it to me and go back to imitating Stieglitz or whoever—"

"Ansel Adams."

"Regardless."

So I left it to her. In fact, I withdrew emotionally from the project and repressed all my curiosity about it. When she showed me the forty prints she had chosen, I merely nodded my approval. When she demanded new copies of them, I produced the copies with little attention to the content. It was her show, not mine.

It would make my reputation, all right, and it would also add a dimension of controversy to my reputation that I did not want. I suppose in the long run the controversy did more good than harm, though I didn't see it that way then. Rosemarie knew there would be controversy all right, she just underestimated how much. And I should have anticipated it.

Not that the pictures in that exhibition were poor. On the contrary, after all these years they are still hauntingly attractive. Some of the best work I've ever done. Immature perhaps, but then so was I. And they make up in vitality and love what they lack in maturity.

When our tired old DC-6 lumbered across the Pacific from Guam to Wake Island, from Wake to Midway, from Midway to Honolulu, and then, with a deep gasp for breath, from Honolulu to San Francisco, my priorities were, first, to inspect Kevin Patrick; second, to see my photo of Ike on the cover of *Look*; third, to examine my new book; and finally, last of all, to take an advance peek at the "Rosemarie and April" exhibit.

Kevin, I thought, looked like his uncle Michael; the *Look* cover did what I had wanted it to do, even if most of those who looked at it missed the point; *Traders* would stir up a hornet's nest at the Board of Trade; and the exhibit scared the hell out of me.

I was running for home plate, all right, and the throw from left field was coming right at my head.

Rosemarie's choice of prints was brilliant. The theme of celebration of beloved women as the source of life could not have been more powerfully traced. The gallery owners were so taken with her skill at arranging the exhibit—their prerogative, not hers, by the way—that they had actually offered her a job. But there was a lot of human flesh, wonderfully attractive woman flesh, in the display. In the swing of the pendulum today, few would object, but in that time, I knew there would be an outcry.

Even today, I suspect, some of the lobbies of Chicago bank buildings—willing galleries for art shows—would ban "Rosemarie and April."

The men in our family—Dad, Ted, Michael, and I—walked through our preview in embarrassed silence. None of us would have denied the power of the show. I think that for the first time I believed in the depth of my soul that Rosemarie was right: I did have some talent with a camera. But we all could hear the outrage of those who, to quote the novelist Bruce Marshall, think that God made an artistic mistake in ordering the mechanics of human procreation.

The womenfolk—Mom, Rosemarie, Peg, Jane—who ought to have been offended if anyone was, thought the exhibit was "wonderful."

Peg conceded, "You sure have guts, Rosie."

"Nonsense, darling." Mom examined very closely the cartwheel shot. "If you look like this, and you do, by the way, you don't have to be afraid of the camera."

"Guts is not what I noticed," I remarked in a stage whisper.

"Chucky!" The women screamed in chorus.

All except April Rosemary, who pointed at herself in every picture in which she appeared and uttered vowel sounds of uninhibited narcissistic enthusiasm.

Traders was reviewed with modest praise and it sold well for a book of prints. Many of my sometime colleagues at the Board of Trade would not speak to me for years after its publication. Others congratulated me on the "wonderful job you did, Chuck, great snaps."

Neither judgment was based on artistic considerations. Those who objected were convinced that anyone who photographed the pits was "against" commodities trading (like the Russian customs officials who banned G. K. Chesterton's book *Orthodoxy* in the conviction that it was about the state church and therefore almost necessarily against it). Those who approved were so convinced of the excellence of themselves and their work that they could not imagine any photo study being anything but favorable.

Both sides missed, I would like to think, the mixture of hope and terror I always felt in that place—in my own stomach and emanating from the bodies of the men around me.

I guess the pros won out over the cons. Three of my shots hang today in places of honor in the gallery overlooking the floor of the Board of Trade.

As my priest says, "Anyone can be a prophet in his own time, if he can arrange to live long enough. John Henry Newman lived to be ninety and was made a cardinal at eighty-nine when they figured he was too old to do any harm. But now he's always hailed as a cardinal. The secret of being hailed as a prophet is to outlive your contemporaries."

Similarly, the book that eventually came out of my first show is still in print and used as a text in many fine arts programs around the country. I suspect some kids are trying to imitate me the way I tried to imitate Ansel Adams's Yosemite in my Oak Park prints.

Give it up, kids, I say. Don't imitate anyone. Show us what you see. Not what someone else sees.

The cartwheel picture was on the cover of the catalog and also in the window of the gallery. It brought in viewers and clients literally by the thousands.

I don't know how many folk who stared at that shot—some in fascination, some in horror, some in admiration, some in outrage—realized that it was intended to be comic. It said, if it said anything at all, that my teenage wife was a funny, flaky, fun-loving creature. Mysterious, yes; possibly tragic, yes; radiantly lovely, yes indeed. But also, in her best moments, gloriously comic.

The Chicago critics were guardedly positive.

Tribune: "A hymn of adoration by the artist to the women he loves and to all womankind."

Daily News: "Young Charles C. O'Malley is a celebrant of life and the life-giving forces of the universe."

The art critics have always been a little less angry and precious than their colleagues in the book sections.

The good, gray *New York Times* sent its own august critic all the way to Chicago. He was dazzled:

> It would not be fair to this magical display of youthful talent to reduce Mr. O'Malley's work to a celebration of the stunning beauty of his wife and daughter. He praises their appeal and, through them, the appeal of the ingenious mechanisms by which our species attracts men to women. His work is a hymn to life, but it is a hymn that ends with a question mark. No one can deny the beauty of his Rosemarie or his April, but he knows, even more surely than we who walk hypnotized through the gallery, that such beauty is transient. It will not last forever.
>
> Will young Rosemarie and even younger April mature so that there is sufficient inner beauty to shine even more brilliantly as the years slip by? Is their loveliness a promise or a deception? At this most fundamental level, the art of Charles C. O'Malley is religious. Perhaps only a Catholic artist could see so much religious quest implicit in the bodies of two adored women. Mr. O'Malley is a photographer of sacraments.

Precisely, even if I could not have found those words to describe my intent in those days.

I suppose this whole story I'm trying to write is my way of answering, tentatively and ambiguously, the questions the *Times* man found posed in that first show.

I was sky-high after I read the review. Rosemarie wept for joy, not, I fear, because the writer posed a challenge to her even more than he had to me, but because he had understood my purpose.

"You did it, Chucky Ducky," she exulted. "You did it!"

"Right! I signed the contract, I picked the shots, I arranged the displays, I did it all!"

"What . . . ? You did not! Oh, you're kidding. I love you, I love you, I love you!"

We had much to celebrate that Christmas of 1952—two healthy children, success in my new career beyond any reasonable expectation, the promise that Vince would be home soon to meet his spunky daughter.

Leo Kelly had come home too, not dead after all. He had been brutally tortured by the North Koreans and had lost two fingers on his left hand. He was a physical and emotional wreck. Dad pulled some strings with someone at Fort Sheridan (he was *Colonel* O'Malley was he not?), who pulled some strings at Great Lakes Naval Hospital so that Rosemarie and I got in to visit Leo.

At first we did not recognize him. Then he opened his eyes, recognized us, and smiled.

"Hi . . . nice of you to come way up here. . . . You two married yet?"

"Two healthy children!"

"Wonderful." He closed his eyes. "Sorry I couldn't bring Christopher back for you, Chuck. He was the bravest marine of them all."

What should we say to him? We didn't dare mention Jane Devlin. Convinced that Leo was dead, she had married a real creep named Phil Clare. It was said that he cheated on her during their honeymoon.

"You're a photographer now, Chuck?" he opened his eyes again.

"Kind of."

"Would you send me your book up here? I've love to look at it. Not much good at reading yet."

He closed his eyes. He seemed to be asleep. Rosemarie and I looked at each other and turned to leave.

"I'm going to make it," he said. "I'll show them all. When I get out of here, I'm going to Harvard to get my doctorate in political science."

"We know you're going to get better," Rosemarie said fervently.

He smiled again.

"Stay in touch," I urged him.

He mumbled something that we didn't hear.

Then the nurse eased us out of the room.

I sent him copies of my two books. I don't know whether he ever received them. We didn't hear from Leo for many, many years.

The verdict wasn't in on my exhibition. The river wards had not yet voted. They weighed in with their verdict the day after Christmas.

Monsignor James Mitchell, the "spiritual adviser" (read "Boss") of the Archdiocesan Council of Catholic Action celebrated Saint Stephen's Day by branding the exhibit "an obscene insult to all virtuous Catholic women" in a statement carried in *The New World*, our Chicago Catholic newspaper (which, in an earlier and far more liberal manifestation, had supported the Loyalists in the Spanish Civil War).

The Monsignor was a specialist in dirty books and magazines. In fact, according to Father Raven, he was known in clerical circles as "Dirty Pictures Mitchell."

The Council of Catholic Action was a paper organization, a front for Monsignor Mitchell's crusade to keep drugstore magazine racks "pure enough for the Blessed Mother to look at them."

It seemed that art galleries were in the same category as drugstores.

"Don't pay any attention to him," Mugsy Branigan trumpeted. "He's a prude."

John Raven assured us that Mugsy, a master at ribbing, would hound Dirty Pictures for the rest of his life.

The Monsignor had not bothered to visit our gallery. "You don't have to look at filth," he told the secular press in a conference on Chicago Avenue across the street, "to know that it is filth."

Neither would the band of thirty or so Catholic women who picketed us come through the door. "It would be a mortal sin," one of them told the *American*, the Hearst afternoon paper that often appeared on pink newsprint.

CATHOLICS PICKET NUDE "ART" it announced in thick black headlines appropriate for the death of a pope or a president. Below the headline was a picture of the woman with a placard reading PUT SOME CLOTHES ON, ROSIE!

Next to that was a murky, dark, badly reproduced print of the cartwheel shot, copied through the window, which made it appear that instead of a two piece swimsuit, Rosemarie was wearing nothing at all.

The New World weighed in with an editorial damning the show on the grounds that children walking down Michigan Avenue during the Christmas season would be led into "grave sins of the flesh" by the lascivious picture in the gallery window.

In those days the avenue was not the Magnificent Mile it would later become; children did not amble down Michigan Avenue at Christmastime. Even if there were a few ambling kids, they probably would not have noticed the gallery if it had not been for the pickets; no one ever saw a young person peeking in the window, and, finally, the picture was utterly chaste.

But as I would learn in years to come, what matters often is not what reality is, but what the papers (and more recently TV) say that it is. The publicity was free and it brought us more patrons. All the prints in the collection were sold; we were assured that we would always be welcome at the gallery.

But none of us were quite prepared for the newspaper attention. We found it hard to believe that the press could so falsify the actuality of my prints and that our Church would engage in such irresponsible criticism.

Some things don't change. The great Godard film *Hail Mary* was picketed by Catholic women who refused to view it. They knew it was immoral and blasphemous because they had been told that it was. The opinion of Catholic reviewers, some of whom were priests, did not change their mind.

Rosemarie remained cooler than I did, indeed cooler than any of the rest of us. She simply walked in and out of the gallery as though the pickets were not there. None of them recognized her in her white mink coat. Mom and my sisters glared fiercely at the parading women but said nothing. Dad joined the line of marchers to sow discord.

I was the only one who took them on directly. I remember very clearly my words to them, but they were so childish and ill-tempered that I will not bother the reader with a verbatim transcript.

Well, I did say to one woman in her thirties, her eyes filled with hatred, "Don't you know the passage in the Gospel that says 'Judge not that you be not judged'?"

"Jesus was talking to the scribes and Pharisees, not to good Catholics like us."

I then said some very ungentlemanly things.

The next day I had a much better idea. I photographed the demonstrators.

Much later I would do a show called "Twenty-five Years of Protest," which portrayed marchers from 1952 to 1977. The striking aspect of the faces in such shots is that, whatever the cause, the hate is always the same.

I would see the same women many times in the next quarter century. I never did like them.

Then the *New York Herald Tribune* appeared. I suppose because the *Times* had liked the show, its rival, which had not deigned to send a critic originally, had to dislike it. He went out of his way to cast a different vote.

> One must admire the courage it takes for a man not quite twenty-five to display in a prominent Chicago gallery what are essentially family snapshots. Charles O'Malley has plenty of courage, no doubt. But like most men who achieve fame too young (in his case by working for *Life* and *Look*, journals that ought to stick with veteran photojournalists), he is devoid of sensibility and taste.

and-green trim, she was at the door defiantly welcoming both the serious patrons and the morbidly curious.

Virtually all the members of both groups liked the pictures. Scores of men and women told her that she was lovely, a truism that caused her to blush and smile happily.

Until her father, loaded to the gills as we Irish say, stalked in, an outraged little bull charging into a china shop with snow clinging to his black coat (with felt lapels) like oversized flakes of dandruff.

"You worthless little slut." He hopped up and down in front of her. "I'll never be able to show my face in a decent home in Chicago ever again. I'll be laughed off the Board of Trade. You've ruined my life."

He smelled like a cheap tavern on West Madison Street.

"Please, Daddy, don't—"

He slugged her in the chest and sent her reeling against the wall.

"Cunt!" he shouted, and whirled around to leave.

"No impulse control," Ted would explain later. "Indulged totally as a child. Never learned to delay satisfaction of instant urges. He has the money to gratify himself, but is hampered by his physical appearance. That increases his rage impulse."

I had my own rage impulse. I grabbed his coat on the way out. "I'll kill you!" I shouted, intending only to throw him bodily out of the gallery.

Michael and Ted pulled me off him.

The American's headline said:

DAD DENOUNCES
DAUGHTER'S
NUDE "ART"

Rosemarie's binge lasted six days.

21

"I don't know what to say." Ted McCormack tapped his pen on the desk in his office. "She's not a classic alcoholic, that's certain."

"A.A.?"

"I'm sure that it won't hurt. I'm glad she's decided to try it. But her problem is more complicated than most. A.A. works by changing behavior. It doesn't deal with underlying problems. In many cases that works. For Rose"—he shrugged—"God, Chuck, I'm not sure."

It had been the scariest of Rosemarie's explosions. It had lasted for almost a week, during which no one was able to talk to her, not even the good April.

She was not abusive or obscene as she had been after the oak tree collision. Rather she wept, continuously it seemed.

Mom and Peg took turns holding her in their arms and telling her how wonderful she was and how everyone loved her.

I searched the house for the bottles of gin and bourbon she had hidden before the binge began. She had carefully prepared the logistics of her drunk.

I found half a dozen bottles, but I must have missed at least that many more. She consumed a bottle a day for the six days and then stopped drinking and locked herself in her study for another day.

When she finally emerged, wasted and looking at that moment like she had aged ten years, she apologized to all of us, hugged her children, swore she would never drink again, and promised that she would attend A.A. meetings.

We all rejoiced, I with somewhat less conviction than the others.

"She doesn't like booze, Ted," I said to my uneasy brother-in-law. "When she's ... well, when she's stable, she doesn't touch it and doesn't seem to miss it. I don't think that it's hard for her not to drink most of the time."

"Then something snaps, and like it or not she tries to destroy herself with it."

"Exactly. Probably it's the result of her early family life."

I was not ready to tell him about her father's raping her.

"Everything is the result of early family life." Ted smiled ruefully. "I don't know what to say, Chuck. She may need long-term psychotherapy. Analysis even. And there's no guarantee that would work."

"I don't think she's ready for that now."

"It's a solution you should keep in the back of your head for the future. In the meantime maybe A.A. will do the trick. It often does."

I thought of the untidy, slobbering, red-eyed, manic woman that my wife had become during that terrible week. She had degraded herself more than her mother had, poor woman. Would Rosemarie fall down the steps someday?

I shivered.

"What can I do, Ted?"

"Stand for reality, Chuck. Love her, but don't tolerate another binge. Make it clear that you will think of ending the marriage if she does it again."

"Ending the marriage?"

"You may have to threaten it. But don't threaten unless you mean it."

I left his office frightened. I could not lose her, could I? Wasn't that unthinkable?

A.A. had to work.

It did for a couple of years. Rosemarie went to her meetings faithfully, though she never discussed them with me. And she did not drink.

What would happen when another incident triggered her terrible self-destructiveness?

As the months went on, I persuaded myself that the problem was behind us.

I hardly noticed when she cut down on her A.A. meetings and then stopped going to them.

22

"You won't believe this, Cordelia"—Ed Murray beamed over his glass of burgundy—"Chucky knocked me out in a high school football game."

My big blond nemesis from high school and my little blond friend from Notre Dame were enchanted with each other.

Cordelia Lennon smiled back. "Almost nothing about Charles would surprise me." She was thinner than in the days when I'd first kissed her in the office of her magazine at Notre Dame. So she seemed little, almost tiny—a blond girl-child with haunted eyes.

Since the very first moment Cordelia had come through the door of our house, Ed had bathed her in a warm and gentle smile, admiring, protective, and hungry. Cordelia, still hurt and discouraged from her professional failure and the death of both her parents, resisted his tall, strong, South Side Irish charm for about a minute and a half. Then she gave herself over to his caressing expressions and began to reply in kind. They melted in each other's warmth like butter in warm maple syrup.

Not instant love, surely; but instant chemistry between two hurt and lonely people.

Rosemarie had won again.

"I talked to Cordelia Lennon this morning," she had informed me on an autumn day in 1953.

The war was over. Vince had come home—haggard and haunted but apparently happy. Carlotta was unsure of him at first, but now adored him. And another child was on the way. We were settling down to what some historians today, without much data, think of as the quiet Eisenhower years.

"From New York?" I kissed her and sank into my audience chair in her study.

"No, she's come home. Someone finally told her the truth. Finally. She will never be a successful concert pianist."

"Poor kid."

"And she's had some kind of unhappy love affair too."

"She never had much taste in men."

"Chucky, I'm being serious."

"Yes, ma'am. Well, I'll try to be serious too. Cordelia doesn't make it quite into the top one percent of American pianists, but that doesn't mean her talent and work are worthless. She can teach, she can direct parish musicals, she can bring joy to her family and her friends, just like Mom does with the harp without ever being a concert harpist."

"That's a good way of looking at it." Rosemarie was working on some sort of schedule on the desk as we talked. What was she planning for me now? "Anyway, I hope you don't mind, I invited her for dinner tomorrow night. Poor kid needs some friends."

"Fine with me."

"I *always* liked her, even when she was sort of chasing you."

"I thought it was the other way, but I won't argue."

"And I asked Ed Murray too."

"Rosemarie! They're oil and water. He's a big lug and a political lawyer and he's from Little Flower"—the most South Side of South Side Irish parishes. "She's an aristocratic doll, an artist, a rich kid from the North Shore. That's crazy."

"Poor Ed. I can't believe that dumb girl jilted him the night before her wedding."

"Ran off with another guy. He was lucky to be rid of her."

"But all those months in Korea dreaming about her . . ."

"Regardless, as you would say, he's well rid of her."

"They're both lonely. I'm sure they'd always be good to one another."

"They're both good people, Rosemarie, but they just don't match."

So it turned out that they matched perfectly. Rosemarie's aloof smile at me was a happy I-told-you-so.

"That's a bit of an exaggeration, Cordelia," I pleaded. "First of all, he hit me first. Secondly, he hit me so hard that I lost all consciousness of what I was doing. Thirdly, the reports of my hitting him back were made up by those who knew I couldn't remember the last few seconds of the game. I don't really credit them."

"The story was in the paper, Delia. And the clipping is downstairs with all the papers Chucky saves, including his idea notebooks."

"I'm fascinated," Cordelia said, drinking Ed in with her eyes like he was a mug of hot chocolate on this winter night. "Tell me more."

"Well," I rushed in to give my version, "the first three string quarterbacks were out because of sickness or injuries, so the coach sent me in to call the plays. He told me to call anything but my own number. There was no danger of that because I didn't want to get hurt by the big lugs in the Carmel line, like him!"

"And he marched them straight down the field," Ed took up the story, "on fourth down at the twelve-yard line. His current brother-in-law threw a pass. I blocked it and somehow it fell into his hands."

"Need I say I was terrified? My only thought was to run as fast as I could to escape the ten-foot-tall Carmel giants who were chasing me."

"He escaped toward the coffin corner—"

"Where I would have run out of bounds, if this ape had not tried to tackle me. Alas for the Caravan, his impact not only knocked me out and the ball out of my hands, it also propelled me across the goal line. After that I remember nothing."

"Then, Delia"—Rosemarie had been waiting for her chance—"Chucky held the ball for the point after, something he'd been afraid to do all season. But they didn't have anyone else because all the other quarterbacks were out. Anyway, Chucky held the ball perfectly and we were ahead by one point. There was twenty seconds left, so Fenwick had to kick off with Chuck holding again. We were all cheering like crazy."

"Chucky! Chucky!" I imitated the shrieking voices of teenage girls.

"And he blocked me so hard"—Ed was laughing as though it were the greatest joke in the world—"on the run-back that I was knocked out."

"Unnecessary roughness," I murmured. "Could have cost us the game."

"That's Charles Cronin O'Malley the street fighter," Rosemarie crowed.

All three of them were laughing.

"It wasn't that funny."

"That's how friendships are born among men," Rosemarie sniffed.

"I'm sorry we never met at Notre Dame," Ed said gently to Cordelia. "I guess I didn't read much then. I'm trying to make up for it now. . . . You were studying piano in New York?"

"Yes, I was, Ed." She winced. "I thought I was good enough to be a concert pianist. I guess I'm not."

Ed's wide face melted with compassion.

"Still, Delia"—Rosemarie took over the conversation—"you're probably better than ninety-nine percent of the pianists in the country. You can enjoy your music and make others happy with it for the rest of your life. Like Chucky's mother does with her harp. Think of your parish and your school and the family you'll have. It might even be a blessing in disguise for you."

My lines, the bitch had stolen my lines.

"My head tells me that, Rosemarie. And it's good to hear someone else say it. Thank you. I'll be all right, I'm sure. It will just take time."

"Would you play for us tonight?" Ed asked impulsively.

In nine hundred and ninety-nine cases out of a thousand, that would have been a dumb question. In the chemistry of our dining room it was the perfect question.

She did play that night—Chopin, and with more feeling than I thought she had. She must have missed the concert trail by a hair's breath.

Or maybe she was playing for Ed.

"I could listen to music like that all day," the big lug sighed.

Rosemarie and I peeked through the drapes as they left our house. Halfway down the walk, Ed put his arm around her shoulders. She leaned against him.

"Done." Rosemary clapped her hands.

"If it doesn't work, you'll be responsible."

"Oh, it will work all right."

Later as she was combing her hair, she said casually, "Would you like to spend a few days in Connemara?"

"Connemara? Where's that? In Africa?"

"The West of Ireland, silly."

"You think it's time to drag Timmy back?"

"To give it a try. . . . Jenny Collins doesn't date anyone any more."

"How old is she?"

"Twenty-four. A year older than me."

"You've bought the tickets?"

"Naturally . . . but I can take them back."

"Don't do that!" I sat up in bed. "I'll never refuse a few days alone with my wife."

"We won't be alone."

"The kids?"

"Peg and our nanny will watch them."

"Who's coming with us?"

"Your parents."

"Mom and Dad?" I could hardly believe my ears.

She was brushing her hair now in rapid motions, and talking with equally rapid speed. I was distracted from her words by how lovely she looked in bra and panty—always a new and wonderful sight for me no matter how often I'd seen it.

"The war has been over for ten years and they've never gone abroad together. Your dad travels on business. The good April watches the office. I think they're a little afraid of a vacation just with each other. They're still young, Chuck. They still love each other like two crazy kids—"

"Two crazy O'Malleys."

"Regardless." She waved off my interruption. "They wouldn't think of flying off to Ireland unless we push them into it. Then when we get them there, we'll sort of drift off and let them get to know one another again."

"You astonish me, woman."

"I don't think it's astonishing." She jabbed at an uncooperative strand of hair. "I think it's common sense. Will you do it?"

"Sure. Why not?"

Nonetheless, I was uneasy when we finally settled into the Royal Hibernian, Mom and Dad on one floor and Rosemarie and I on another. They were awkward and uneasy for the first day, and then they drifted away from us on the second day before we had a chance to drift away from them.

At breakfast the third day, Mom, glowing complacently, remarked, "You know, dear, I think we ought to do this every winter."

"I couldn't agree more."

Rosemarie winked at me.

Right, you go to Ireland in the winter, to a poor, desperate, rain-soaked country. Ireland should not have been poor; before the Easter Rising in 1916 its standard of living was high, almost as high as that of England. The ravages of the next seven years of war and then the reactionary government of Eamon De Valera curtailed economic growth. Ireland had become a backward peasant country again, which is what Dev wanted.

We told Mom and Dad that we wanted to go out to the West of Ireland to see if we could find Tim Boylan. They thought that was a wonderful idea.

We came across on an Aer Lingus 707. I was sleepy from the Marezine I had gobbled down. However, there was no turbulence. I was still groggy when we left for Galway in a run-down and bumpy train.

"This country," I told my bride, "is awful. It's down-at-the-heels. Everything and everybody is worn out."

"The people are wonderful and the pub conversation is sensational."

"You say that because they like your singing."

"Our singing."

Our reservations were at the Railroad Hotel, above the dank, smelly station in the center of the town. The hotel had been elegant once. Now it was damp and threadbare. The chairs in our room creaked and groaned when we tried to sit on them. The bed was lumpy and it sloped to one side. The mist outside obscured Eyre Square.

I must add that everything about Ireland and Galway has changed completely in the last forty years.

"Are you going to sleep right way, Chucky Ducky?" Rosemarie asked as we huddled under the covers.

"Not if there is something better to do."

"I need someone to keep me warm."

I obliged, assuming that it was one of the carefully calculated times that it was safe to do so.

That evening we wandered around the Eyre Square and its fringes looking for Brandon's Pub. We learned that it had closed six months earlier.

"Times are hard," we were told repeatedly.

Rosemarie, using all her charm, asked in each of the other pubs if they knew a Tim Boylan. Lots of publicans and their patrons knew a Jim Boylan, a Joe Boylan, a Mick Boylan, and even a Tommy Boylan. None of them remembered Tim Boylan.

"He worked at Brandon's before it closed," Rosemarie would say patiently. "A big, dark American with scars on his arms. He was learning to speak Irish."

They also knew many big, dark Americans, but they weren't sure about the scars on his arms. And why would a Yank want to learn to speak Irish?

Fair question.

We learned nothing.

"Did you have the impression they were covering up?" I asked.

"No, they were just being Irish—offering help when they didn't have any."

The next morning after breakfast—which was astonishingly good—we walked out the door of the hotel into bright sunlight.

"Lovely day," the doorman said.

"It won't last," I replied.

"Sure, shouldn't we thank the good Lord for what little of a lovely day we have?"

Rosemarie agreed with a charming smile. The man agreed to let me take his picture.

Then my wife bounded back into the hotel and struck up a conversation with the blond young woman at Reception.

"I don't suppose there's many Americans living here, are there now?"

"Why would a Yank want to live in this gloomy place, and there not being enough jobs for those who were born here?"

She sighed, and Rosemarie sighed in sympathy.

"I suppose you wouldn't remember a big Yank who worked at Brandon's Pub across the square before it closed?"

"Timmy, is it?"

"The very same."

"A grand man. Scars on his arms. Sang a lot, like he was trying to be happy but couldn't quite make it. But always very nice and respectful. Never touched the creature either."

"Isn't that the man we're looking for, Charles?"

"Isn't it just?"

I could imitate the local style of speech as well as she could.

"And why would you be looking for him?"

"Isn't there a young woman back home in America who gave us a message for him?"

"Does she love him, now?"

"Ah, that would be telling, wouldn't it?"

They both sighed again.

"Is it a message he'd like to hear?"

"Won't he be delighted?" I chimed in.

The young woman sighed again. "Well, he's a real gentleman and himself so sad and doesn't he deserve good news?"

"He does," my wife and I said in unison.

"Well"—she looked both ways to see if anyone was listening—"if you take the coast road beyond Salt Hill and on to Clifden and look for a small hotel called the Clifden, you wouldn't be far from wrong, would you?"

"We wouldn't, would we?"

"Isn't it Gaeltacht, Irish-speaking, if you take me meaning . . . course, don't they speak English too?"

"American," I said.

For the first time the young woman smiled.

"I don't suppose you would be able to find us a car?" Rosemarie asked.

Certainly she could.

"God go with you," the young woman blessed us as entered our very old Morris.

"And may Mary remain with you all this day," Rosemarie blessed her in return.

We sang "Galway Bay" all the way out to Clifden. Rosemarie naturally did the driving. I was told that I was bad enough when I drove on the right side of the road. We'd be taking no chances on the left side.

The sky and the bay were breathtaking. The poverty on either side of the road was depressing. Misery under glory. We had no trouble finding the Clifden Hotel. It was a neat, freshly whitewashed little place with a brightly painted sign.

"Lets go in singing," Rosemarie urged.

So we charged in, still singing "Galway Bay."

Behind the Reception, Tim, who had been working over some papers, froze.

"May God and Mary be with this house," Rosemarie announced brightly, and then added, *"Dia's Muire dhuit."*

Tim said something in Irish. Rosemarie would later tell me that it was *"Dia's Muire dhuit's Padraig."* Then, with big grin, he translated for us: "May Jesus and Mary and Patrick be with those who come into this house."

He swept Rosemarie up in his arms and then shook my hand vigorously.

" 'Tis yourselves!"

" 'Tis!"

"Would youse ever like a pot of tea and some scones?"

"We would."

We were ushered into the tiny dining room, clean, neat, and smelling of fresh bread.

"Granne, me girl, these are friends of mine from across the sea, would you ever be able to find them a pot of tea and a plate of fresh scones?"

The child—thirteen at the most and scared of her shadow—admitted she could and dashed off.

"You didn't bring Jenny, did you?"

"We did not."

Timmy sighed.

"Sad or glad?" I asked.

"Both, I guess." He shrugged. "She should forget about me."

"She never will," Rosemarie insisted.

"That's not my fault, Rosemarie H."

"It is too."

"Maybe it is. . . . Does she know where I am?"

"No."

"You didn't tell my family?"

"No."

He sighed again.

"I can't go back home. I can't. Out here the horrors kind of fade away most of the time."

"You should go home to Jenny and Dr. Berman," Rosemarie said flatly.

"Maybe someday," he said sadly. "Not yet and probably never."

"You'll come back someday," Rosemarie said confidently. "I know that."

He laughed genially, a much warmer laugh than what I used to hear in the Magic Tap on Division Street.

"So what's going on in the neighborhood? How many kids you guys have?

Rosemarie showed him the pictures of April Rosemary and Kevin Paddy.

"I see gossons and colleens like them out there every day . . . not quite so healthy-looking or as well dressed, sad to say."

We filled him in on the events of the neighborhood. Granne brought us another pot of tea and a second plate of scones. With a saucy tilt of her head in my direction, she said something in Irish.

"She was making fun of me."

"Ah now. All she said was that the cute little redhead could eat all the scones in Connemara.

"Try me!" I shouted after her.

We continued our conversation.

"We should be going now, Timmy," my wife said, "not to overstay our time, if you take me meaning? But we won't forget about you and we won't let you get away."

"I won't even ask if that's a promise. . . . Hey, Charles C., put away your wallet. It's on the house!"

" 'Tis for herself, even if she is fresh."

I put a five-pound note on the table.

"Would you want to be taking her picture?"

"I would!"

"We'll take it first and then I'll give her this after you leave, so we won't embarrass her altogether."

I got a marvelous roll of her, including a shot that I flatter myself is a bit of a masterpiece. Despite my wife, I entitled it "West of Ireland Matriarch in Training."

"*Go dte tu slan,*" Tim said as he helped Rosemarie into the car.

"*Beir dua's beannacht!*" she replied.

Where did she learn Irish greetings? I had given up asking those questions of my wild Irish Rosemarie.

"He'll never come," I predicted as we bumped back to Galway Town.

"Oh yes he will, Chucky. He still loves Jenny. He's just afraid of what he'll have to work out with Dr. Berman."

While we were in Ireland, probably when we were in Galway, Rosemarie conceived our third child and second son, James Michael (Jimmy Mike) O'Malley.

The rhythm method of birth control is not suitable when you are feeling chilled in a damp and threadbare hotel.

23

"As a card-carrying member of the Pepsi Generation"—my wife sipped her Pepsi blissfully—"husband mine, I could get used to this life."

The P.A. finished the soothing and suggestive sounds of "Hernando's Hideaway." The next song was the appropriately romantic "Three Coins in a Fountain."

"Hmmm . . ." The Southern California sun, compassionate and gentle, penetrated my muscles and bones, caressing and renewing my soul. "You think you could live in the Beverly Hills Hotel for the rest of your life?"

"And eat in the Polo Lounge Bar every day. Order me another Pepsi, please."

"Yes, ma'am." I waved my hand like I was perhaps a Turkish sultan or a degenerate Roman emperor. "And people would stare at you during the lunch hour every day because they would be sure you were some famous actress only they didn't quite know which one."

"Any mother of three children"—she shifted on her lounge—"would be flattered to be confused with a star, even more so with a starlet. . . . How old do you have to be before you are no longer a starlet?"

"Twenty-five," I made up the answer. "It is written in the ordinances of Beverly Hills. You have another year."

"I did say three children, didn't I? Do I really have three children?"

"You do. In fact, we do." I ticked them off on my fingers: "April Rosemary, Kevin Patrick, and James Michael, aged three, two, and six months. Not quite Irish triplets."

"How did that happen?"

"Beats me."

We both laughed. Our February 1955 trip to Southern California, in later days known appropriately as LaLa Land, had begun as business and was now ending on a note of intensely renewed sexual pleasure. Rosemarie and I had fallen in love again. We were experiencing the natural rhythms of married love without yet realizing that there are such rhythms and that the secret of happiness in marriage is to be sensitive and responsive to their ebb and flow.

She opened one eye. "You ought to rub on more suntan cream. You know what sun does to your skin." She removed *Vogue* from its fortunate place on her belly, sat up, and reached for the tube. "I know, you're waiting for me to do it."

The subtle shifts in her body as she moved recalled the powerful emotions of the previous night. Rosemarie was a woman of infinite willpower. She had determined that three pregnancies would not noticeably affect her figure and that was that.

Only one human frailty seemed immune to the strength of her will—her occasional disastrous drinking bouts. And that had not been a major problem since the terrible week after the scene with her father at my first exhibition.

"I'm not an alcoholic," Rosemarie had insisted without rancor when I finally asked why she had stopped going to A.A. meetings. "It might be easier if I were."

I let the matter drop.

We pretended by mutual and implicit agreement that her father did not exist. He was excluded from family rituals and celebrations, stricken from the Christmas card list, banned from conversation. We dealt with him through lawyers and heard on the grapevine that he was spending more time in Las Vegas.

Vince Antonelli, who now held my seat on the Board of Trade, reported to me that Jim Clancy rarely appeared on the floor. His old ring of cronies had broken up; Jim was now more than ever a lone wolf trader, a fat, angry, reckless little man who, for all of his lack of "impulse control," still possessed the instincts of a successful bandit and continued to pile up profits.

Vince, worn and haunted, had come back from Korea with a hero's medals and a determination, more furious than mine, to make up for lost time. He'd abandoned his plans for law school and plunged into the commodities game with passionate enthusiasm. The redolute tenacity that kept him alive in the P.O.W camp served him well on the Exchange. He learned quickly and soon was making as much money in a month as his father, a shoemaker on Division Street, would make in a year. I turned over my account to him with instructions that I didn't want to worry about it anymore.

"Unless I see Ed Murray charging after you."

"If you can't beat 'em, hire 'em. Ed and his father are my lawyers. Now that Ed's married to Cordelia, he's settling down to become one of the best lawyers in town."

"Still the clever one," Vince said with a grin. "Always thinking and planning?"

"Just a simple snapshot taker, trying to earn an easy buck."

Despite the torments of the Korean camp, Vince seemed to adjust easily to civilian freedom. Peg and Carlotta were clearly happy, and now the latter had a little brother, Vincent, to complain about to her cousin April Rosemary, who knew all about the problems of little brothers.

There were times, however, when the distant, haunted look in Vince's eyes worried me, as did the strained silences between him and Peg. I kept my worries to myself.

My parents were showing their years at last. Dad was fifty-five, Mom fifty-one, young by my standards today, but terribly old when you're twenty-seven and basking under the sun of Southern California in February. They were aging elegantly, however, Dad with a white beard and Mom with carefully groomed silver hair that made her look even more like an exiled duchess. With their whole generation, they were still making up for the lost time of the Great Depression, never quite forgotten; but their vacations and cars and fur coats and new furniture were never vulgar. The two of them were, I thought, entitled to it.

Try as I might, I could not exclude the fear that my growing old would not have such grace.

At the side of the Beverly Hills pool, my wife rubbed the suntan cream into my skin as tenderly as she would rub baby oil into the skin of James Michael, a premature baby who seemed mortally terrified of the world. Her fingers gradually became demanding.

"I think you're more interested in seducing me than protecting me from the sun." I pretended to twist away.

She leaned toward me. "Southern California sun is dangerous. We have to do a good job of protecting the poor little redhead's sensitive skin, don't we?"

"You know what's going to happen to you if you keep protecting me that way?"

"No, what?"

"You'll be ravished."

"Can I count on it?" Her caresses assumed a lascivious rhythm, her eyes grew soft and round, her lips parted, her body tensed. I imagined her loins moistening in preparation for me.

"Keep on, woman, and we won't make it back to our cottage."

"*Really?*" Her hand darted underneath my trunks. "I thought you were a rational man who wrote down all his bright ideas in a notebook."

In the two years since Kevin's birth, Rosemarie and I had begun to experience the same problems that affected most couples in our generation. On the one hand, we had invested our emotions heavily in the vision of domestic happiness—family, home, suburban affluence. On the other hand, the demands that we imposed on ourselves made sexual bliss at the family hearth almost impossible.

For us there was less excuse than for most.

Rosemarie had help with the children. We had more money than we needed. We were good at our sexual *commedia* when we bothered to play it out.

Nevertheless, I worked long and hard at my new profession. I did portraits for affluent Chicagoans who did not understand my vision but liked the results. I flew around the country on assignment for magazines. Occasionally I found time for my own "studies"—meditations and reflections like "The Conquered" and "Traders" and "Under the Golden Dome." I stayed up often till after midnight working on prints for my books and exhibits. I had finished my course work at the University and was grinding away at a dissertation on the Marshall Plan. I would try to explain why the relatively small contribution from the United States had jump-started (as we would say now) the German economy.

Why did a professional photographer need a Ph.D. in economics? There was no good answer except that I had started it and I would finish it.

I realized even then that Rosemarie was right, as by her own admission she always was: the studies and the portraits were my strongest skills. Still I felt that I was not proving myself as a photographer unless I could earn a decent living for myself and my family with my camera, a monumentally difficult task as any photographer will tell you even today. (Unless you are among the few who can charge in five figures for two hours of work!)

For all my frenzied work, I still fell short of that goal. I would not listen to Rosemarie when she pointed out, not without acerbity, that I didn't have to work that hard. The money from my investments, not to mention hers, was more than enough to supplement my earnings.

"The photographer is, or at least ought to be, a member of Plato's leisure class, a man who does what he wants to do because he doesn't have to do anything." She then developed a long argument from Plato's *Republic* about leisure as the basis for society and culture.

It was a powerful argument, like all her arguments, although I cannot, to tell the truth, remember its details.

"They had slaves."

"We don't need them because we have a much broader base of capital. You're the economist. You should know that."

She was right, naturally. I was exhausting myself to honor standards that I had made up, probably because I did not know any other way to live. In the process of chasing this new will-o'-the-wisp, however, I did learn some things about the eye of the photographer that would serve me well later on.

"Well," I took the offensive, "you don't have to work as hard with the kids as you do. You have help and you have Grandma."

"I don't want to ruin it for April." Her lower lip turned down stubbornly. "And the help are not the kids' mother."

Rosemarie was a superb mother until she became compulsive about the role. She led the kids as the first among equals rather than trying to rule them like the empress she was with me. She presided over the revels, organized the gang, laid down the rules for the game, and rallied the population against "him."

Meaning Daddy, who had to be treated very gently lest he break.

Then her conscience would catch up with her and she would become "responsible," compulsively watching, supervising, worrying.

"Mommy, go take a nap with Daddy and leave us alone," April Rosemary told her, maybe a little after 1955.

Paralyzed with laughter, Mommy did what she was told. Delighted with her success, the little monster often used the same line on her mother in later years.

The two older children treated me like I was a sibling too, a younger brother who was funny and entertaining, but hardly to be taken seriously.

When I tried to be angry with them, they laughed at me.

As the man says, you get no respect.

We would both have done better in our self-assigned roles if we had been able to approach them with greater relaxation and self-confidence. I should have given myself time to think and wander and reflect and observe. Rosemarie should have pursued her singing and her reading and her sometime role as my assistant. The culture of the 1950s and our own personalities did not permit such relaxation.

It is fashionable now to ridicule and blame the fifties for their emphasis on suburban domesticity and material affluence.

To which I reply, often infuriating April Rosemary and Kevin and their siblings, that suburban domesticity is preferable on both aesthetic and ethical grounds to the relentless narcissism of Halsted Street yuppiedom.

And I add, above the uproar, that the decision made by our society in the postwar years to provide higher education for everyone, including women and blacks, was the most important social choice of the century and is responsible for the shape of American society today more than anything done during the *Big Chill* years.

Except possibly, I sometimes add, the interstate highway program.

I defend the right of women to have options. I'm glad my daughters have other models available as alternatives to the suburban domesticity of our time—a domesticity in which, as someone said, women agreed to have more children in less space and with less help than their mothers, in return for the promise that men would provide for them with greater affluence.

Yet I am not sure that the availability of options has made women any happier, on the average. Those who are capable of making choices are surely happier, but those who are not are much less happy, drifting as they do through life with neither career (in any meaningful sense) nor family. The one option offered for women in our time at least protected some of the weaker from having to make their own decisions.

There are costs to freedom. And casualties in a revolution that offers more freedom.

Nonetheless, while I will defend the fifties from the criticisms directed at the lonely crowd (a reality only long years after David Riesman wrote about) produced during the "me" decade and from the slander of shallow reporters like David Halberstam, I still have to admit that Rosemarie and I messed up badly during the fifties—that era of bobby sox and hula hoops, of *Ozzie and Harriet* and *The Honeymooners,* of Billy Graham and Elvis Presley, of tail fins and conical bras, of Estes Kefauver and the Davy Crockett craze, of the Bunny Hop and *Sputnik.*

We messed up because we compulsively assumed unnecessary responsibilities, as did most of our generation (better behavior, I would still argue, than the compulsive rejection of necessary responsibilities that marked our successors). There was nothing wrong with the vision of suburban domesticity. The mistake was in blighting the vision with our own hang-ups.

"I made a mistake," she said in bed once. "I was completely wrong, that's all."

"Call the press, sound the trumpets!"

"Silly." She slapped my arm and closed *The Blackboard Jungle,* which she had been reading. "The mistake was about you and it was really dumb."

"About me?"

"About you." She sighed and took off her reading glasses. "I assumed that because you are an artistic genius, the accountant part of you was just an act. It took me all these years to figure out that it isn't an act and that the picture taker needs the accountant too."

"Uh-huh." The idea had never occurred to me.

"So you probably ought to do what you want to do."

"And, other than disrobing you and ravishing you, what is that?"

"Finish your dissertation. It will make your pictures even better. I'm not sure why, because I haven't figured you out completely yet. But I know it will."

"You read minds too?"

"Only about sexual desires in men, and that's pretty easy. Don't tear my gown, please."

Thus it was decided—even if it took me several months more to wrap up the first draft.

So Rosemarie and I were close and loving partners, but in marriage that's not quite enough, not when there are serious problems that are never discussed.

We joined the Christian Family Movement, as did many Catholic couples in that era. We were the "babies" of the group, assured by the other couples that we had no idea yet what "life is really like."

Given Rosemarie's experiences with her father, I found that argument ridiculous if not offensive.

The religious ideals we discussed in our analysis of the Bible and the liturgy and the world around us (in the paradigm of See, Judge, and Act) were a direct challenge to the compulsive suburban life. If we really trusted a good and loving God, if we really believed in the worldview of Jesus, if we really thought that we lived in the palm of God's loving hand (as the old Irish blessing puts it), then we would have been less compulsive, less preoccupied, less hassled, less impatient with one another and our kids, less irritable when the perfection of our vision was marred by the imperfection of the human condition.

Ted McCormack—also a C.F.M. veteran—would contend later that the movement came apart because of the demands of intimacy. The groups became surrogate families in which all the unresolved childhood conflicts with siblings and parents reemerged to bedevil the community. The vast area of relational problems that husband and wife had ruled off their personal agenda surfaced, if indirectly, at our meetings and scared the hell out of everyone.

"If you really loved one another that way," Jane said with a shiver, "you could get yourself fucked to death."

It was a colorful way of describing the risks of intense intimacy, really intense intimacy, that seem to lurk at the core of the Christian message. (Small wonder that priests, even men like John Raven, didn't dare preach it.)

"And that's the real problem, Ted," I would add to his analysis. "The unresolved family conflicts are bad enough. Once you understand what Jesus really meant, you run for your life. It would be too scary to live that way."

Anyway, at twenty-four and twenty-seven, with three kids and my seemingly dubious career as a camera artist (Rosemarie's description), neither my wife nor I was capable of taking Jesus seriously. We had, we thought, lots of excuses and plenty of time.

A dangerous argument whenever you use it.

Our trip to California was courtesy of *Vogue*, which had been making up its mind for some two years whether I was a fashion photographer or not.

Curiously, it was an assignment that my wife, who disapproved strongly of my ventures into photo journalism, strongly advocated, and one that I resisted.

I came up from the darkroom to find her nursing Jimmy Mike and talking on the phone.

"My husband might not be worth fifteen hundred dollars a day"—she shifted her son—"but that's what he gets. If you want him to shoot all those beautiful women, you simply will have to pay his rates."

She was lying through her teeth about my rates.

"What? No, that doesn't include expenses. Seventy-five hundred for five days, *plus* expenses. That includes me. I'm his assistant and I'm *very* expensive. Huh? My dear young woman"—she winked at me—"I assure you that I am not about to permit my husband to associate with those gorgeous models without my being there to protect him. Ten thousand? Well, that's more like it."

"*Vogue?*"

She nodded cheerfully. "Lingerie shots with ten of the most beautiful women in Hollywood. Sounds like fun."

"Cheesecake."

"Dear God, Jimmy Mike"—she disengaged the frail little punk from his source of nourishment—"will you listen to your daddy, the prude? So what's wrong with a little cheesecake?" she said, giving me a look. "You like it well enough. Anyway, it will be interesting to see how you do. Maybe you should devote your life to studying beautiful women."

"I've already done that." I kissed her.

"Hmm. . . . Isn't Daddy a nice man, Jimmy, even if he spends all his time with those terrible chemicals? You won't mind if three months from now I go away with nice Daddy for a tiny little week to protect him from all those predatory women, will you?"

He didn't protest, God knows.

His mother changed her mind several times before we caught the noontime DC-7 from Midway to Los Angeles.

I had to practically drag her out of the house. She sulked for the whole flight.

She wasn't sulking a week later when she led me from the pool back to our pink-and-green cottage.

I grabbed her arm in front of the steps, whirled her around, and, surrounded by azaleas and palm trees, ravished her with a savage kiss. "That's what happens to women who tease their husbands at the side of a swimming pool."

"Oh . . ."

I recaptured her lips, grasped her bottom with my hands, and overwhelmed her. Somehow the straps came off her suit in our fierce tussle.

"Are you going to make love to me here outside?" She inhaled frantically. "Not that I mind, but I think they have laws out here—"

"Inside, woman." I boosted her up the stairs.

She had not accompanied me to Washington for my shoot of the Army-McCarthy hearings.

"Why should I leave three children home alone, just so I can go to a dumb city while you take dumb pictures of a dumb senator?"

"You won't leave them home alone," I had shouted at her. "And this is not just a dumb senator. This is a historical episode of major importance. And only we photojournalists can reveal what kind of a man he is. The newspapers are paralyzed because they have to play the news stories straight."

"Fine. Maybe. Only you're not a photojournalist. How many times do I have to tell you that?" she shouted back, confident that she would win any shouting match. "You're a camera artist. That's spelled—"

"I know how it's spelled, goddamn it. I have to do this anyway."

"Well, you can do it without me. In case you haven't noticed, I have an infant son to protect. He's lucky, poor little thing, to be alive."

She stretched the truth a bit there. Jimmy Mike was a frail preemie, but he was healthy enough. There never had been any real danger that he might die.

Exactly how healthy, he would prove in his tight-end days as an Arizona Wildcat, but that comes later.

So I went off to D.C., into the maelstrom of National Airport, over to the gracious old Hay-Adams (selected by my wife, who was also my travel agent, even when she disapproved of my reasons for travel), and finally up to the Hill.

I will not trouble you with the technicalities of the fight between the junior senator from Wisconsin and the United States Army over his two staff members who, it appeared to some, were homosexually involved with one another. The press couldn't say that. It couldn't say that the Senator was a blowzy drunk. It couldn't say that he was a contemptible bully, a cheap ward heeler, and a total fraud.

It couldn't say that for all the lists of known Communists in the State

Department (varying in number from 57 to 81 to 205), he had never uncovered a single real Communist.

He was not, however, wrong: there had been notable Communist in-
filtration of the American government during the 1930s. "Tail Gunner Joe,"
however, did not know the name of a single Communist infiltrator.

So he had become the principal hunter in our national hunt for "red"
witches. The search for "pinkos" hurt a lot of innocent or mostly harmless
bureaucrats and film writers and other such folk who were only exercising
their freedom of political thought.

And General George C. Marshall, Eisenhower's mentor.

I had no sympathy then and I have none now for Communists or fellow
travelers who were Russian dupes (even when they wore Roman collars).
Yet I could tell after the first five minutes that Joseph R. McCarthy was an
incompetent fake. Nonetheless, such was the temper of the time and the
need to find scapegoats for the "loss of the peace" and the "loss of China"
and the "Korean mess" that the former tail gunner, who apparently never
fired his weapon once in combat, had terrified the rest of the United States
Senate, paralyzed the federal bureaucracy, threatened the rest of the country, kept our war-hero president at bay, and was spoken of as a possible
presidential candidate in 1956 or 1960.

And, despite his rating in a press poll as the worst senator in Washington, he became the hero of every nun and anti-Communist cleric in the
land, much as the Berrigan brothers would later become heroes of the Catholic left (made up in part of the same people who had worshiped Tail Gunner Joe).

McCarthy, mostly by luck, had learned how to manipulate the mass
media, which in those days included the newspapers, the newsmagazines,
radio—and television.

I have thought often, in the years since, that the eagerness of Democratic liberals to prove that they were as "tough" on Communism as men
like McCarthy and William Jenner and Kenneth Wherry (a senator who
had made his money in the undertaking business) was one of the principal
reasons they involved themselves in the Vietnam quagmire.

The Luce empire was uncertain. Its working journalists knew what Mc-
Carthy was. Its boss, still smarting over the "loss of China" (where he was
born, the son of Protestant missionaries) and quite ready to consider the
possibility that total war with China and Russia might be a good idea, was
inclined to be more sympathetic.

I was hired as a compromise. Irish Catholic like the Senator, I was
assumed to be anti-Communist. Known as a liberal Democrat (unfairly, I
was merely a Democrat, the kind that would later be called a Yellow Dog

Democrat—someone who would vote for a yellow dog if it ran on the Democratic ticket), I could be assumed to have reservations. Why not have that little O'Malley kid get some shots? He's good, whatever they say about him. Gorgeous wife too, can't figure what she sees in the little punk. Anyway, everyone liked that cover he did for the other guys, with Ike riding up the mountain.

So off I went to Washington, Nikon in one hand, Hasselblad in the other.

"You want to meet the Senator personally?" Roy Cohn, sleaze already carved deeply into his young face, challenged me during the first recess.

"Maybe after I'm finished." I retreated a step or two. "I don't like to meet subjects till my shoot is finished."

"We could take a look at your father-in-law's operations in Vegas, you know."

Phony ruthlessness. Any reporter from Chicago could have told him about Jim Clancy.

"Go right ahead. It wouldn't bother me in the least."

Later Bob Kennedy ambled over. He was the minority counsel for the committee—of which his brother was a member—and hence no friend of the Tail Gunner.

"Hiyah, Mista O'Malley."

We shook hands gingerly. I thought that he very possibly was a dangerous reptile, but a reptile with a charming smile. About my age, he had the reputation among the reporters of being a more ruthless politician than his brother. "Bobby," they said, "is a real hater."

"You talk funny," I told him.

"Nah," he smiled again. "Yah talk funna."

"I'll send you some prints. Free."

"Wanna meet mah bratha?"

"Will I need a translator?"

I agreed that, yes, I did want to meet the Senator, who I assumed along with a lot of others in those days would be the first Catholic president. After the pictures.

"Wadya think of this affah?" He nodded at McCarthy and Cohn, who were walking by us.

"Crooks."

"Yah." He smiled for the third time. "Nice to meetcha, Mistah O'Malley."

"Chuck."

"Bobby." He shook hands, favored me with his stunning smile again, and wandered away. It was a long, long time before I learned to like and even admire the man. I prayed for his nomination in 1968 and stood help-lessly sobbing over his body that terrible morning in Los Angeles.

At the Army-McCarthy hearings, I had taken enough shots the first day for *Life*'s purposes, but I could hardly collect a week's wages for a day's work, so I lingered in Washington. That evening, feeling as though I had been isolated from the rest of creation, I called home. Rosemarie, always one to take advantage after her point was made, reported cheerfully on the day's events and put each of the kids on. They all missed Daddy. Which may or may not have been rehearsed. Even Jimmy's babble was interpreted with that message.

"He's a terrible man," Rosemarie observed when she had reclaimed the phone. "I can see why you don't like him."

"How do you know he's terrible?"

"I've been watching it on television." She sighed. "A woman has to do something when her husband isn't around. He's a real slime, isn't he?"

"Yeah, he really is."

I hung up thoughtfully. Television. We had one—relatively small, maybe a little bigger than the kind kids today bring to the Bears games at Soldier Field. We watched Milton Berle, Sid Caesar, *The Ed Sullivan Show*. You couldn't see the Bears during the season, since home games were not telecast in those days and away games were banned because the Cardinals (still my team) were playing at home. One could go to taverns and watch the game on sets with antennae high enough to pick up Rockford or South Bend.

I had no time for that. And neither Rosemarie nor I thought we had time to watch the newscasts. We could read the news in the papers and in more detail too. Most of the rest of the stuff, except for an occasional fine drama on *Playhouse 90* or *The Hallmark Hall of Fame*, was junk anyhow.

As I pondered her words, I turned on the small set (black-and-white, as they all were in those days, as hard as it is for kids to believe now) in my room in the Hay-Adams. There was Tail Gunner Joe ponderously de-manding a "point of order." Perfect title for the shot (developed in *Life*'s Washington lab) that I was sure would be their cover picture. I watched the replay on the news program with fascination. So that's the way things were going.

I stayed the rest of the week, shook hands with Jack Kennedy, who was even more difficult to understand than his brother, wandered around the Senate taking shots that might make a study someday, and developed my prints late in the evening. It was all over, however, a waste of time.

I later won a Pulitzer Prize for "Point of Order." My wife admitted that she had been wrong—a rare admission, one to be treasured.

"But only accidentally," she added.

She was right fundamentally—a concession I did not need to make when I won the prize. For I had acknowledged her superior wisdom when I returned home that Friday afternoon, having crept away from the Capitol after a token appearance in the morning.

"Home early?" she called, when I stumbled into the house, deathly ill from motion sickness.

"To catch my wife with her lover."

"A lot of opportunity with three kids around."

"You were right." I slumped into my leather chair. The three offspring had turned Mommy's study into a playpen.

"Naturally. But how so?"

"TV will do in the Tail Gunner, regardless of *Life*'s cover. Indeed, eventually it will do in *Life* and photojournalists too. Oh, we'll take pictures, but TV will shape life in the sixties and far more effectively than the picture mags do now."

She pondered. "Sure. I only realized that you were right about McCarthy when I saw him on television. It will sort out the phonies."

One kind of phony would be finished. Another kind, the fakers who knew how to appear sincere on TV, would replace the Tail Gunner Joes of the fifties.

I'm not sure that American life and politics are any better because Ronald Reagans can replace Joseph R. McCarthys. There's been change, if not progress. The demagogues have to be smoother.

A man with a camera, whether photojournalist or camera artist, would not be the man of influence he had been in the thirties and the forties and the fifties.

Photographers would never be able to set up a scene like the one in the Bohemian Alps where we hunted Nazi werewolves for *Life*. By the late 1960s, however, different setups would be possible, as the camera crews at the Democratic convention in Chicago proved. And the emergence of such national "personalities," whose sole claim to influence is their ability to manipulate TV, proves that the phonies are still around and maybe as powerful as ever. Different phonies. I would not, in the ordinary course of events, be taking their pictures.

Which did not make me any more eager to photograph Hollywood women in high-fashion underwear.

When we set up camp in the lush California ambience of the Beverly Hills Hotel, I decided that it was not such a bad idea after all.

Rosemarie agreed completely. "I think I could grow to like this vulgarity," she said as we were ushered through the lobby and out into the garden toward our cottage. "Particularly in the winter."

"Without the kids?"

"April is entitled to her time with them."

Once she was away from them, Rosemarie's compulsions faded rapidly.

We had accidentally stumbled into a romantic renewal interlude, of the sort that is essential to keep a marriage from deteriorating. More accidentally for me, perhaps, than it was for Rosemarie.

We were practicing rhythm, Catholic birth control, without too much difficulty given our preoccupations with career and family. Rosemarie had scheduled the California shoot so that it would occur during the "safe period"—the right half of the month, as she called it.

To regulate human love by the calendar, especially when you excluded anywhere from a third to a half of the month, seemed like "natural law" to the old men in the Vatican. It didn't seem natural at all to married people or the priests who heard their confessions. Which is why eventually they turned their backs on the Vatican on this issue—and later on almost all issues of sexual morality.

Our first night together in the decadent luxury of LaLa Land (a perfect name even if I use it anachronistically) was warm and pleasant—two long-separated lovers becoming acquainted again.

The second night was another matter.

"How did you feel during the shoot today?" Rosemarie, striking in a white linen suit, asked me at supper that night.

"What do you mean?" I was gobbling a steak, enjoying more of an appetite than I had experienced for months.

"With those women."

"They were both very lovely, a little old for me, but quite striking. A lot of tastefully applied makeup. Probably requires a lot of time."

"Bodies?"

"Wonderful. Not in a class with yours." I tentatively reached for her thigh. I was not rebuffed.

"Not my question . . ."

"What is your question?"

"Would you like to sleep with them?"

"Well, in principle, sure. I'm a male member of the human race. I know from the philosophical tone of your voice"—my hand crept up and down on her thigh—"that you have thought something out. What is the insight this time?"

"Don't stop what you're doing or I won't talk. Okay? My insight is that the relationship between an artist and a model, woman model anyway, is affective. It's a love relationship. She must give herself to you, if only to your camera. You must win her over to yourself, if only to your camera. Those two women came into the studio uneasy and defensive. They live by their beauty and they're scared to share it with a camera they can't control. Morever, although the lingerie is absurdly chaste, they still are undressing for you. So you have to be warm and tender and gentle with them, so affectionate that after a while they want to share themselves with you."

"Ah."

"You're *very good* at it.—Yes, chocolate ice cream and coffee, please.—*Very* good."

"Really?"

"Really. I think they both would have liked to go to bed with you. I don't mean they would have. They have the look of happily married women. And the demure, self-effacing wife was there with her lights and film. But they found you very attractive."

"Little red-haired runt?" My fingers had found an appropriate place to rest—between her legs.

"Sensitive, considerate, *cute* redhead."

"So it's a good thing you came?"

"What troubles me is that your best talent might be for photographing women." She sighed. "I will have to travel a lot in that case."

"Do you really want that ice cream?"

"Have them send it over to the cottage. I have the impression I may need nourishment before the night is over."

As I look at the pictures of those glamorous women many years later, I am more convinced than ever of the correctness of Rosemarie's insight. There was indeed an affective relationship between me and them. There still is, lingering in the memory traces of my brain. And with every woman I have successfully shot. (It doesn't work with everyone.) The subdirectory on the hard disk inside my head where those experiences are stored is a pleasant one indeed.

It was also wise for Rosemarie to accompany me.

I would not have been unfaithful, but it would have been much more difficult to do the shoot well.

By happy chance our romance was renewed, imaginatively and powerfully, during the spectacular nights of that week.

During which I did indeed call my adviser at the University to tell him I would have the second draft ready in two weeks. For some odd reason he seemed delighted.

On our last day of shooting, before Rosemarie seduced me with the suntan cream at poolside, the starlet (the only one of the two models allegedly younger than we) canceled at the last minute. The editor from *Vogue* was dismayed. The set had been arranged, the lights were ready. No model.

"This is terrible," she said. "We'll never ask her again. I'm afraid we'll have to end the shoot."

"Can I make an alternative suggestion?"

"Certainly." I nodded toward Rosemarie, who was bustling around with the lights, alternately fighting and flirting with the technicians. "Wonderful! Her rates?"

"Same as the girl who canceled."

"All right."

"Rosemarie . . . come here, darling . . . see that blue corset, the strapless one?"

"Foundation garment, dear, let me see." She consulted her clipboard. "Sapphire blue foundation, panel in nylon lace, satin, net, with a latex back section—makes the skin look like alabaster."

"Right. Put it on. We need a model."

"No! I never wear *that* kind of thing. Ugh. It makes me feel all cramped-up just to look at it."

"Hurry up, we don't have all afternoon."

"No." She did not speak with too much conviction, however. Her refusal was merely for the record. As I knew it would be.

"The actress's rates, dear," the editor from *Vogue* chimed in.

"Do it, Rosie!" a technician yelled.

"All RIGHT."

Rosemarie played it for laughs, overcoming whatever shyness she might have had. It was the best shot of the series, not a comic figure, but a mysterious, dark-haired, alabaster woman of the world. Afterwards she received several modeling offers, which she promptly and firmly turned down.

"I only work with my husband," she assured them primly.

Her suggestion that I do the shoot was wise, quite apart from the renewal of our married romance it occasioned. I was very good indeed at capturing women in the eye of the camera. What might have been cheesecake, though in *Vogue* high-class cheesecake, became art. If I do say so myself.

So there was a lot on our agenda at poolside as the sun began to fall behind the trees. She managed to drag me into our cottage as I frantically kissed her neck and shoulders, but we didn't make it as far as the bedroom. Not the first time.

We had supper sent to the room. Rosemarie phoned my mother, who was delighted to preside over the playroom till Monday evening.

I was a genuinely happy young man. Despite our compulsions we were still very much in love. I was improving in my career. Rosemarie was a wonderful mother and an ingenious lover. All was right with the world.

I often wonder how our life would have been different if we had been able to stay that weekend.

At eight o'clock the next morning I was shaken out of my well-deserved sleep by a phone call. Where the hell was Rosemarie? She was the early riser.

The shower was running.

Damn the self-indulgent woman.

I picked up the phone. "Yeah?"

"Ed Murray, Chuck. Sorry to bother you. I'm afraid I have some bad news. . . ."

The kids? My parents? Peg and Vince?

"Jim Clancy got himself blown to kingdom come this morning."

— ⁓ 24 ⁓ —

"As I understand it, Mrs. O'Malley"—Lieutenant Arthur H. Rearden was three-quarters of a foot taller than me, lean as a street lamp, and had long unruly silver hair, excessive dandruff, and bad breath—"you inherit all your father's money. Mr. Joseph O'Laughlin, who I believe is your father's attorney, confirmed that to me."

"You understand more than I do." Rosemarie, demure and pale in a black suit, but dry-eyed, spoke calmly enough. She was dangerously close to an explosion.

So was I. Closer perhaps.

"You are not familiar with the provisions of his will?"

"My father and I have not been very close for the past several years."

"Since"—he flipped his notebook with the hand not holding the cigarette—"since the public, uh, altercation at one of your husband's exhibits."

"Since my mother's death, really."

"I see." He finished his cigarette and lighted another.

We were sitting in the office of Conroy's Funeral Home at Lake and Austin. If you were not buried from those precincts, steeped in the smell of mums, you were not buried properly as a West Side Irishman.

"Is it not true"—he was standing at the door of the undertaker's office—"that in that exhibition you were depicted in the nude?"

"No, it is not—"

"What's the point of this, Detective Rearden? You sound more like a state's attorney than a homicide detective."

"I'm trying to establish motives for the crime," he sneered, "MISTER O'Malley. Your wife has powerful motives. She inherits an enormous amount of money. She hated her father. You threatened him repeatedly, three times at least." He flipped the pages of his notebook. "She also inherited money from her mother when her mother died. She claims not to have been in the house when her mother fell—or was pushed—down the stairs. The only witness who can establish her presence elsewhere is, marvelous to relate, your sister, Margaret O'Malley. Now Mrs. Vincent Antonelli. Married a wop, huh?"

"So?" I half-rose from my chair.

"Charles!" her voice cracked like a rifle shot. My temper simmered down. I sat back in the chair, my fists still clenched.

"So all you have to do is to prove that while we were in Los Angeles we wired my father-in-law's Cadillac with TNT."

"You could hire people to do that"—he shrugged—"and then go away because you thought it was an alibi."

"So you need to find out whom we hired."

"Which I intend to do." As Art Rearden leaned forward, his bad breath almost choking me, Ed Murray and his father, Dan Murray, and his wife Cordelia appeared silently behind him. "All I know is that your wife's parents are both dead and the two of you have inherited a lot of money. I intend to send you both to the electric chair. Your wife won't look nearly so good after they've fried her."

Rosemarie screamed, a little, plaintive cry of terror. I went after him. Ed stepped in between us. He was still substantially bigger than I was.

Cordelia embraced Rosemarie.

"We heard that," said Dan Murray quietly. "And we aren't about to forget it, Art. The Commissioner and the State's Attorney won't be at all pleased."

Art Rearden turned on his heel and departed, trailing his various smells behind him.

"What was that all about?"

"A burglar killed his wife while he was on duty." Dan Murray—a robust older version of his son—was frowning thoughtfully. "Accidental murder, she surprised the guy. Rearden has been a little nuts ever since. This time he's gone too far. That was unprofessional and ugly. I think I will have a word with a few people. He should be regulating traffic over at Midway. Something like that."

"Everyone in town knows," Ed added, "that Jim Clancy was in bed with the mob the last few years. You hear on the street that some of our friends over on the West Side were upset with him because he was trying to pull something slick on them. Our friends don't like that. Sorry, Rosie."

"Ed, there was so much hate in that man's eyes. He really does want to see me die."

"Don't worry, kid, they don't have even the beginning of a case. The State's Attorney's office knows that. Art is acting on his own."

We had flown home from L.A. on the first flight we could get, but it was still ten o'clock at night when we arrived at Midway. Vince and Peg met us, radiating the tenseness that so often seemed to accompany them.

Ed and Cordelia hovered behind them, their eyes on Rosemarie, horrified, I was sure, by her obvious pain.

Jim Clancy, they told us, had bounded out of his house, on the run, according to the woman who lived on the opposite corner of Menard and Thomas and who watched everything that happened in that street from sunup to sundown. He jumped into his brand-new car, parked in the driveway and not in the garage despite the bad weather, turned on the ignition, and disappeared in a burst of fire and smoke. The watching neighbor was taken to St. Anne's Hospital for treatment of wounds to her face from the breaking glass of her windows.

There was enough of him left for an autopsy. The body would be released to Conroy's the next day, after the autopsy. The papers had reported on Clancy's recent relations with the mob. There was no mention of the art exhibit. The obituary referred to his long association with the Board of Trade.

"Will there be a big wake?" I asked Vince.

"Lots of people from the Board will come because of you and Rosemarie and there will be some curiosity seekers too. There'll be cops hanging around to see about the Outfit, but the word is they won't show. Don't want anyone to infer a connection."

"So I'll have to stand there for two nights," Rosemarie began.

"One night. April decided that promptly," Peg cut her off. "She makes decisions for all of us that we don't want to make ourselves. . . . How do you feel, Rose?"

"Numb. No feeling. You can't miss what you've lost already. I felt sorry for him when he was alive. I gave up on trying to save him long ago. Still, he was my father."

The numbness continued the next day, until the scene with Art Rearden. I couldn't reach her. I could never reach that distant, frigid part of her soul where Rosemarie dwelt with the memories of her mother and father. Each time I thought about those memories—which wasn't very often—I marveled that she could have matured into the usually self-possessed woman that she was. The astonishing thing was not that she drank too much occasionally, but that she didn't drink all the time.

The wake was a strange one even for an Irish wake. The usual people showed up—politicians, distant women relatives who had not missed a wake in forty years, officers of parish societies, older priests who had once served at St. Ursula's for whom wake attendance had become their only remaining priestly function, married couples who had known Jim and Clarice Clancy in their younger days at Twin Lakes, old-timers from the Board of Trade, nuns from the grammar school, our own friends and neighbors, including our C.F.M. group, and unidentified characters who may have wandered into the wrong wake.

The greeting was the same as at "ordinary" wakes: "Sorry for your trouble." Monsignor Branigan's bluff good cheer, as always, exorcised the specter of death for a few moments. "Those galoots of yours playing football yet, Rosie? We'll be needing them at Notre Dame soon."

It was all off-key. No one could observe, "My, doesn't he look natural?" or "Didn't Joe Conroy do a wonderful job?" because even the magic of the ancient funeral director could not assemble the scattered fragments of Jim Clancy's body. The casket was closed, a phenomenon that didn't seem right at an Irish wake, as fashionable as it had become for other groups.

Moreover, just as there was less sorrow at this wake for a man who had earned little in the way of mourning, there was also less of the crazy, archaic, cheerful hope that the Irish demand at their wakes. It was a quiet, gray-tinged ritual, a hesitant tribute and a very hesitant hope, at which my wife presided with a pale, tense graciousness.

Jim Clancy's lawyer Joe O'Laughlin tottered in—a little old man with dirty white hair. "Sorry for your trouble, Rosemarie," he said, sighing. "Sorry for your trouble."

He was the only one with tears in his eyes.

He himself would be dead two months later, leaving Jim Clancy's estate in a mess that took Ed Murray years to straighten out.

Only Father Raven, now transferred from St. Ursula's, broke through the gloom.

"God loved him, Rose; no matter what happened God never stopped loving him."

A tiny tear appeared at the corner of each of those marvelous dark eyes and slipped down her cheeks.

"Thank you, Father."

The last visitor departed at nine-thirty, half an hour before wakes were supposed to end. Only Ed and Cordelia (she pregnant, and back looking very happy) and my family remained.

"It wasn't much of a wake at all," the old-timers would say. "But, ah, herself is a fine woman, now isn't she?"

They might then add words of astonishment that Jim had fathered such an elegant daughter.

Ed Murray took Rosemarie and me aside as we were preparing to leave. "Did you know your father had terminal cancer, Rosemarie?"

Her eyes widened. "No, I had no idea . . ."

"They found it all over the organs on which they were able to perform an autopsy. His doctor told the coroner that he had diagnosed liver cancer three weeks ago. It had already metastasized. Your father would not have lasted more than a couple of months."

"But why then would they kill him?"

"Those folks have their own code—if they knew, which maybe they didn't."

"I suppose," she frowned, "they did him a favor."

Later, when we were driving home from Conroy's in Rosemarie's gull-wing Mercedes 300 SL, with me at the wheel, she began to talk about her father.

"Losing his hair was the worst event in his life," she said thoughtfully. "Mom always said that was the turning point. He had a big mop of curly black hair—a cute little boy with long eyelashes and pretty hair. Being short wasn't bad as long as you were cute enough to be spoiled by everyone. When he lost his hair he stopped being cute."

"Poor man." We parked in the driveway. I'd let Rosemarie talk as long as she wanted. A February thaw was melting the snow piles and had turned the drive into a small lake.

"It was a bitter pill to swallow; one year he was a cute little trickster, the next year he was an ugly little practical joker. Somehow his greed for money, which didn't offend anyone when he was cute, became terrible when he was ugly. He sensed that those who once admired him, or at least tolerated him, now despised him. So he began to overeat and became obese."

"From an indulged, pretty child to a fat, ugly child?"

"That about says it, doesn't it, Chuck? Losing his hair didn't bother your father."

"He wasn't short and he sure wasn't indulged. Anyway, people are different."

"They sure are." She sighed.

"I didn't know about the practical jokes."

"Mom told me that he had always been prankster; his mother thought it quite amusing when they were courting. I have a picture somewhere—he was really an adorable little man with laughing eyes. He was always playing harmless little jokes on her. He gave her a dime-store ring before he gave her a real diamond—"

"Doesn't sound very funny to me. Did he play tricks on you?"

"Oh sure, my dolls would disappear and then turn up in the attic or the coal bin. I'd laugh because he wanted me to laugh. If you didn't laugh, he'd put you on his enemies list and not talk to you for days."

"Enemies list?"

"He had a list of all the people who had ever offended him and his plans to get even. The last time I saw it was up at Lake Geneva. He kept it in an open safe on the wall behind the big painting of Mom, you remember, in the room—"

"Where you tried to seduce me for the first time."

We both laughed.

"I remember"—the smile vanished quickly from her weary face—"one Christmas I pleaded with him for a horse. I was about ten or eleven, the age when little girls want horses—substitute for a man under you, I suppose. I did a lot of riding that spring out in the Forest Preserve and then later on at the lake. Do you remember? Peg came sometimes."

I nodded, though I did not remember.

"He promised that he would bring me one on Christmas day. So he gave me a little box, fancy one, with a toy horse wrapped up in red tissue paper. He thought it was a wonderful joke and became very angry when I cried instead of laughed. . . . I lost interest in riding after that."

"How did you survive, Rosemarie? And survive to become the wonderful woman you are?"

"You're sweet, Chuck." She touched my hand, still on the steering wheel, affectionately. "Sometimes I don't think I survived at all."

"But you did." I captured her hand and held it tightly.

"Well, *if* I did, the reason was your family, mostly. I don't suppose that as a little girl I thought about it that way, but I knew I *had* to be with the O'Malleys. That's why I was such a nuisance."

I put my arms around her and kissed her as passionately as I could while still being very gentle. "Pesky little brat that I wanted to strangle. Or kiss till the end of time."

"I think I wanted to kiss you the second time I saw you. Even though I hated you because you were a crude, ill-tempered BOY!"

"And I wanted to take your clothes off ever since I was twelve."

"Dirty-minded little boy." She kissed me. "I think I would have let you do anything you wanted—anything you could work up enough nerve to want."

We laughed again.

"You go in the house, I'll put the car away."

"Thanks for listening. Sorry I ruined the weekend."

"Don't be silly."

I parked the car and went up to our bedroom. Rosemarie, in a black slip (tolerated only at times of mourning), was listlessly combing her long hair.

Knowing that she wanted to talk more, I sat on the edge of the bed and waited.

"I've never lied to you, husband mine, have I?"

"Lord, no, Rosemarie. If anything, I've thought, you may be too honest." (Although sometimes, when you have that far away look in your eye or when you wake up at night crying as you did on our honeymoon, I wonder if there is yet another secret.)

"Then believe"—she placed the brush on her vanity table—"please believe that what I will now tell you is the truth."

A sharp knife of fear jabbed into my gut. What now?

"Of course."

"That terrible policeman knows something. Or thinks he knows something. Or has a hint of something. You see"—her breasts rose and fell in a quick spasm of breath—"Peg and I were in the house the day mother died . . . I mean before she died . . . and"—her voice caught—"when she died."

"What?"

"You were in Germany and there was never any reason to tell you when you came home. We were two frightened, silly little girls." She played lifelessly with her brush. "We hadn't done anything wrong, but we were terrified, especially by the police."

"Tell me what happened." My heart thumped irregularly. I too was terrified.

"Mom and I had been fighting, we usually did when she was drunk, which was almost all the time when I was in high school. She would hit me and I'd run away screaming."

"Hit you with what?"

"Oh, a hairbrush"—she lifted her own and began to brush her hair again—"or a broom or something like that. She was such a quiet, sweet, sad lady when she was sober. She'd hug me and cry and laugh. And I'd hug her back. I loved her when she was that way, I really did. And when she wasn't drunk she didn't remember what she did to me. And I didn't have the heart to tell her."

"Peg knew?"

"Sure Peg knew. What doesn't she know? She's as bad as April for knowing everything. Anyway, she saw the black-and-blue marks."

"Black-and-blue marks?"

"When Mom would beat me. Sometimes I'd let her do it. I thought maybe I was wicked and deserved to be punished and . . . and I didn't want to hurt her. You know what kind of a temper I had in those days."

"Poor kid."

"I don't know. I survived, I guess. Anyway, that day she threw a mirror at me. It hit me, not very hard. I didn't feel like taking the punishment this time. I picked it up and threw it back. I missed like I intended to do. One of the maids saw us. I'm sure she told Dad and maybe he told the police.

Anyway, I ran out of the house screaming and down to your house. I didn't mean to tell Peg, but she guessed."

"I'm sure she would—"

"So later she walked back with me. I begged her to come in. Mom would never do anything when there were neighbor kids in the house. So we went in the door. Mom was at the head of the basement stairs and saw me, she began to shout and kind of staggered toward me. I huddled against the door. She hit me with a hairbrush she had been carrying. Peg pulled it out of her hand. Mom ran back to the coat stand and grabbed an umbrella. She rushed toward the two of us—we were both too scared to move—and tripped on her robe just as she passed the door leading to the basement. She fell down the stairs. Peg and I screamed. We ran out of the house and back down Menard to your apartment. Your mom was playing the harp, so she never noticed that we'd left. We crept back to the house later and down the basement stairs. Peg picked up the umbrella and put it back on the coat stand. Then we called Doctor Vaughan. We were pretty clever little plotters, but you of all people know that, don't you?"

"Contented victim . . . Did you know your mother was dead when you ran away the second time?"

"I think I did." She put down the brush again. "We looked down the stairs and saw that she was awfully still. I was afraid she was dead. I dream at nights sometimes that if we had called the doctor right away she would have lived. I know that's probably not true. Still, I feel guilty, sometimes terribly guilty."

"You shouldn't feel that way."

She seemed not to hear me. "Peg and I promised each other we'd never tell anyone what had happened. The police were a little suspicious, but all the neighbors knew that Mom was drunk most of the time, and there was no sign of violence. I think they talked to your mother on the phone to make sure. We were terribly scared for a few days, you know how kids that age are—quick and shallow terrors, and then we forgot about it. I was sorry about Mom, she was a sweet and pretty lady, but so unhappy. We were never very good friends. She knew what Dad was doing to me, but she pretended she didn't. So I guess I hated her. . . . Sometimes."

I pondered with as much dispassion as my pounding heart and churning stomach would permit. Was this the whole truth?

"The reason you didn't tell me this before?" I asked as gently as I could.

Rosemarie was not offended. "I didn't even think of it, Chuck. The . . . the other was so much worse. And in my head I knew that I hadn't done anything wrong. I mean, I often wished poor Mom was dead, and I still feel guilty, sometimes I even think I actually pushed her. But Peg insists that I never touched her. I was hysterical, so it's hard for me to remember. I know, when I'm being sensible, that it was just a terrible accident and that I didn't cause it."

It seemed a reasonable explanation, but part of me resisted it. However, Art Rearden was the immediate problem.

"So Rearden read the records of the cops who investigated your mother's death, and he bluffed. He doesn't know anything more and you didn't confirm any of his hunches. I don't think it's anything to worry about."

"You do believe me?"

"Certainly I believe you."

I did, about ninety-five percent. And in the other five percent I said to myself that if she had shoved back, she was acting in self-defense.

"Sometimes I dream that I pushed her down the stairs." She repeated her plea: "But I didn't. I know I didn't. Peg was there."

Good old solid, tough-minded Peg, the one member of the family who had what I wanted and lacked—stability of character.

"It's all over, Rosemarie. Don't worry about it."

There was, however, a tiny doubt in the back of my head, despite my best efforts to banish it.

"Thank you for believing me." She stood up and pulled the slip over her head. "Would you please make love to me, Chuck, slowly and gently, so I can forget it all for a while?"

"I was hoping you would ask."

Later, when Rosemarie, cuddled in my arms, was sleeping peacefully, I lay wide awake pondering what I was beginning to see—and not liking it at all.

I had begun to realize that the reason I could earn money and please patrons and critics with my photographs was that I saw things the way other people don't see them—the essence of the artistic gift, I suppose. When I recorded the instant of glee on a trader's face when he has made a sale, I did so because I saw the transient gleam in his eyes and the triumphant curve of his lips not as part of a continuous passing parade of emotions but as a moment of exploding illumination—a skyrocket on the Fourth of July. Or when I captured Rosemarie standing on her head, with a crazy smile on her face and her delectable body offered as an overwhelming gift, I saw not a brief segment of a nutty cartwheel, I saw in a dazzling burst of light a woman's soul transparent in her body.

At first I thought that everyone experienced these brief instants of— what should I call it?—physical luminescence. Then I realized that not everyone did, not even every artist or photographer. It didn't seem fair that such insight, which was a given for me, should be a will-o'-the-wisp for others. Fair or not, I had it.

Then I understood why I was able to plan the Wulfe's escape, make love properly to Rosemarie on the day after the wedding by the ice dunes, and say the magic words to her at the end of our honeymoon, words that I had not even heard in my own brain till I spoke them. I SAW the world occasionally in bites of illumination—I can think of no other words to describe the experience—not unlike I saw my subject through the lens. No, the luminescence of the lens was merely one form of the gift, frequently unwanted, of sight.

The lights would suddenly turn up and I would see everything on the stage, not only the present act, but those before it and those yet to come.

In bed that night I SAW on the brightly lighted stage something I very much did not want to see. I also saw, in vague outline, what I must do about it.

John Raven's sermon at the funeral mass the next morning was brilliant, a message of hope in the middle of the night, of God's implacable love surviving even on the edge of the swamp of despair.

There were only a handful of mourners in the church to appreciate the sermon. Most of our friends felt that they had discharged their obligations to ambiguous sympathy by coming to the wake.

I listened to John out of one ear, as my mother would have said, and with the other ear listened to the rushing voices inside my head. It was one of the wildest ideas I had ever considered. Unfortunately the pieces all fit too neatly into place, pieces of an elaborate and cruel practical joke. The memory of my sickness on his sailboat was as vivid in my mind as the day it happened.

I was one step ahead of Art Rearden because I was an artist and I saw the joke in its entirety. He saw only some of the parts.

Rearden was at the graveside in Mount Carmel Cemetery, hatless and huddled against the strong winter winds sweeping down from the northwest and turning the melted snow back into ice.

"Has he searched the house at Menard and Thomas?" I asked Ed Murray as we carried the casket toward the grave site.

"Sure. The morning of the explosion."

"Find anything?"

"We would have heard about it if he did."

"The house at Geneva?"

Ed looked at me and scowled. "That's not in his jurisdiction. He'd have to persuade the FBI to get a federal warrant or ask the Wisconsin State Police, I suppose, to cooperate. Why?"

"He scares me, that's all."

Would a man like Art Rearden hesitate to break a law himself to find evidence? Especially if he knew where to look for it?

I doubted it. The courts might be hesitant to accept illegally obtained evidence (they were less hesitant in those days than they are now), but I didn't want it to go that far.

It was becoming quite clear what I had to do. The logistics of my effort were still obscure.

I was, mind you, still a very young man. When my sons were twenty-seven, I thought, not without some reason, that they were mere children. Yet, to be more honest than I ever was with them on the subject, they were a good deal more mature than I was at that age. My actions in the next few hours were wildly impulsive. There were, there must have been, better ways to do what I saw had to be done. But, as with the escape to Stuttgart, I could see only one way.

If it didn't snow, I calculated, I would need six or seven hours to carry out my plan. It could be done, if I could figure out a way to keep my emotionally paralyzed wife asleep till eight or nine o'clock the next morning.

And to get out of the house without being observed by anyone watching from the outside.

I needed co-conspirators.

As we left the graveside after Father Raven's final prayers, Art Rearden sidled up to us.

"You folks are really rich now, aren't you?"

"Please go away, Mr. Rearden," Rosemarie begged. "We don't need the money."

"Some people never have enough."

"Get out of here." I stepped forward to push him away.

"Don't hit a police officer, Mr. O'Malley; it's disorderly conduct."

"You want to get busted, Art?" Ed Murray stepped between us again. "You're in hot water already."

"Not as hot as your clients." The cop slipped away, having delivered the message he came to leave.

Dan Murray joined us. "He was hoping the press would be here."

"Why aren't they?" I looked around for the first time. Like the funeral mass, the burial was private. The papers had left us alone, except for one photographer.

"Jim Clancy is not a very interesting subject anymore. A headline in the evening papers, some speculation in the early editions of the morning papers, a clip of a blown-up car on the evening news—that's about all his death merits, maybe one more picture in the back pages of the late editions tonight. Rearden has forgotten how the game is played. The guy is really slipping."

Probably counting on a big recovery, I thought.

I cornered Ted McCormack and asked for a prescription that would help Rosemarie get a good night's sleep.

"Pretty strong stuff?" he asked.

"Yeah."

"Don't leave it lying around the house." He wrote out some illegible words on his prescription pad. "This medication can be kind of dangerous."

"I'll throw it out by the end of the week." I took the piece of paper, shivering. "Getting cold again, huh?"

Ted looked up at the sky. "We're supposed to have snow before tomorrow morning."

Just what I needed.

We ate the obligatory lunch at Butterfield. I asked Vince for the loan of his Fairlane that night. "I'll explain someday what's up. Just trust me."

"Sure," he said.

"I'll call you tomorrow morning when it's all right to pick it up."

Back home, I went to the darkroom.

Rosemarie went to the kids. "I'll have to explain to them why they're not going to see anymore a grandfather that they haven't seen anyway. I'll join you later in the darkroom."

"Not necessary."

"I don't want you drooling over those Hollywood broads."

She did work with me for a while, establishing once again that with chemicals, as with almost everything else, she was more skillful than I was.

Mrs. Anderson, our efficient housekeeper, put the kids to bed. We ate a cold supper, mostly in silence, went up to the bedrooms to kiss the kids good night, and returned to the chemicals.

"I want to work till I'm exhausted, so I'll fall right to sleep," Rosemarie said as I closed the darkroom door. "With dreams of the pretty broads filling my head."

"You know as well as I do"—I pointed at the Rolleiflex transparencies of her—"who was the prettiest broad in the shoot."

She picked up the magnifying glass. "I always have a hard time linking her"—she gestured with a touch of contempt at the transparencies—"with me." She pointed the glass at herself. "Two different women."

"One broad." I patted her backside affectionately.

"I know that." She giggled. "It's just hard to comprehend it. Know what I mean?"

"Sure. It's the other way with most people. They don't like their portraits because they think they are better looking than the picture."

"I'm a confused young woman." She giggled again, but picked up one of the transparencies.

"Note the long black hair on the alabaster shoulders," I recited as from a text, "which contrasts with the sapphire blue garment—"

"Ugh. Tight little thing."

"Does the job. Not that, in the case of this model, a job is needed. She is a widely traveled, experienced woman of enchantment and mystery. A woman seeing the picture in *Vogue* would wonder whether, in the same garment, she too might look mysterious."

"She'd wonder," Rosemarie tilted it again, "until she found that it was only the photographer's wife, a dull suburban housewife with three children."

"And a gull-wing Mercedes."

"A point . . . actually, no matter how I look at the transparency, she is a knockout."

"She?"

Rosemarie put the slide back on its viewing stand. "I'm not *that* gorgeous," she said slowly. "My husband took the picture and he's prejudiced. But"—she paused, took a deep breath, causing her breasts to rise attractively under her gray darkroom smock—"I'm really not bad-looking."

"Progress of a sort," I sighed. "You'll agree, I take it, that we don't have to retouch this one?"

"Don't you dare even think of it."

We kissed quickly and went to work.

Hours later, about eleven o'clock and right on my schedule, Rosemarie yawned. "Please, Mister Overseer, sir, can this slave go to bed now?"

"I suppose so. You can't get the quality of slaves you used to be able to get in the darkroom. I'll come upstairs with you."

"Not necessary."

"Ted gave me some medication to help you sleep."

"Don't need it." She hung up her smock on the peg outside the darkroom. "Dead tired."

"Ted said you should take it so you won't wake up in the middle of the night."

"Don't want it."

I had to insist when she was under the covers, almost forcing the pill and the water tumbler into her hands.

"Don't leave these lying around."

"I won't."

"Promise me you won't stay down there with those smelly chemicals too long. You ought to get some sleep too."

"I'll be up in a half hour."

I did not, however, return to the darkroom. Instead I phoned the weather service. The recording assured me that there would be snow by morning, an accumulation of two to four inches. Great.

Why did my comic adventures have to involve cars? I was as rotten a driver as I was at everything else requiring physical skills. No matter how hard I tried to concentrate on driving I would never be as good as Rosemarie—and she always drove with relaxed ease.

Had I made a mistake in excluding her from the operation—if one could use that word for a venture so mad?

No, she had enough trouble as it was.

I never doubted, by the way, the accuracy of my reading of Jim Clancy's practical joke.

I looked out the front window of the house. As I had anticipated, there was an unmarked car a quarter block down the street, lights out. Either Chicago cops or Oak Park cops watching us at Chicago's request. Probably Chicago. Rearden was not the kind of man who would want to cooperate with others, nor, unless I misread them, were these the kind of Chicago cops with whom our fiercely independent Oak Parkers would like to work.

I put on dark trousers and a black turtleneck, dug out some old, soft-sole boots and a black jacket Rosemarie had given me at Christmas. If I had worn a beret, I would have looked like a Corsican knife in the *le milieu*. Instead I found a thick fur cap that would obscure my red hair and keep me warm.

Vince's keys were on the back porch where I'd suggested he leave them. Now all I needed was the other set of keys. They would be in Rosemarie's jewel box.

Only they weren't there.

Rosemarie was sleeping quietly, but I did not turn on the lights. There was no point in taking a chance that she would wake up before the pill took effect. Thus I walked carefully and worked by the illumination of the night-light. I felt around in the box again. Not many jewels—my wife believed in expensive jewelry but not much of it. I felt the chain of pearls for the third time: no, there was no key tangled in it.

I closed the box thoughtfully. What the hell?

I sat on her vanity chair. Where had she put the keys? I was quite sure that, like the house on Menard, the Lake Geneva place would quickly be put on the market and replaced, even before it was sold, by a house in Long Beach or Grand Beach, close to Mom and Dad.

Might she not have put the keys with the papers that were pertinent to Jim Clancy's estate so that all of them could be turned over to the Murrays tomorrow or the next day?

I left the bedroom, thought of another angle, and returned to the bedside. I brushed my lips lightly against hers. Only a hint of response. Sound, sound asleep. I mussed my side of the bed to make it appear that I might have slept there for a while and then—last brilliant thought—turned on the light in the bathroom.

A sleepy woman, waking and wondering where her husband was, would see the light and slip quickly back into her drug-induced nothingness.

Brilliant, O'Malley, brilliant. You have improved at this comedy through the years. Your improvisations are not as stupid as they used to be.

I had opened the back door and shivered in the cold when I remembered that I'd forgotten to look for the key to the summer house in Rosemarie's key box in her study.

Idiot!

I stole quietly back into the house, crept into the parlor and then into the study, and turned on her desk light. I fished the key box out of the drawer in her desk, and opened it. No key for the summer house.

Then it dawned on me that she might just possibly have left it on the key hanger that I had placed at the front door with the curt observation, "If we get into the habit of leaving all important keys here, we won't have to search for them when we need them. Isn't that true Rosemarie?"

She had sighed patiently. "Yes, dearest husband mine."

Well, there's nothing wrong with a little neatness, is there? Since we never used the house, we had little need of the key. Perhaps now Rosemarie would sell it and we would buy a house in the dunes.

Sure enough, the key to the summer house, with my tag on which SUMMER HOUSE had been neatly inked, was just where it ought to be.

I slipped out the back door, crept in the shadows alongside our garage into the alley. Yes, we have alleys in Oak Park.

Then I remembered that I had forgotten to take a flashlight. There would be one in Vince's car, would there not?

Don't bet on it.

I returned to the house, found a light after considerable searching, on a shelf outside my darkroom, decided I had to make sure I had reserve batteries, found them in the tool cabinet (totally unused by both my wife and me) in another corner of the basement, and crept out again into the winter night.

Once I was back in the alley I walked the full length of the block to Berkshire, turned west, crossed Oak Park Avenue, and, shivering with the cold, walked three more blocks to the Horace Mann School on Berkshire and Kenilworth.

There was the dark blue Fairlane, waiting for me as promised. It needed a wash, as did most cars in the Chicago area after a winter thaw. Neither my sister nor her husband was as compulsive as I was about keeping cars clean.

Or changing the oil.

I looked in either direction. No sign of activity. The Oak Park police would be around in another hour to ticket cars illegally parked on the streets after dark. Residents would know that, so any car on the street would say "cop" very loudly.

I switched on the ignition, waited for the motor to warm up, turned on the lights and the heater. It would take two hours or so to drive to Lake Geneva, maybe a little longer depending on how bad the roads were. I figured I would go as fast as I could on the way up in case I had to take it slow coming home.

There were many different routes to Lake Geneva in those pre-expressway days, the most favored being Illinois 41 (Cicero) or Illinois 42-A (Harlem) north to Wisconsin 50 and then left to Geneva City and along either side of the lake to the home you were seeking.

Those who lived, as did the Clancys and, once long ago, my father's family, at the west or Fontana end of the lake sometimes argued for either U.S. 14 (Northwest Highway) or U.S. 12 (Rand Road). The latter wended its way through Fox Lake and Wonder Lake before it crossed into Wisconsin. The former took the long way around through Harvard and Woodstock and Walworth and came in to Fontana from the west; the distance was longer in miles but, according to its advocates, not in time because one missed the concentration of resort towns on the other routes.

I chose this route because I figured that the fewer people who had a chance to see me in the middle of the night the better off I would be. I drove up Harlem Avenue, turned left on Northwest Highway, and settled in for the long ride, WIND blaring popular music on the car radio to keep me awake. I winced when they played "Three Coins in the Fountain." That interlude at the Beverly Hills Hotel must have happened in another incarnation.

The suburbs on the road, Des Plaines, Mount Prospect, Arlington Heights, Barrington, even Crystal Lake, had expanded enormously since the last time I had been on those roads before the war (and have grown even more incredibly since then). Small towns on the Northwestern, they had become part of the metropolis now. An idea for a study tickled the back of my head. I dismissed it for the present. I had other fish to fry.

Only in the Woodstock area and beyond did I find the familiar farmlands of yesteryear, now barren and blanketed with snow as they sped rapidly by on either side of me as I cut through the night.

I still had not dismissed the tiny scruple in the back of my head. Certainly I believed Rosemarie. Still . . .

If she had killed either or both, she had ample reason. Didn't she?

So far it was all going easily. No flat tires. No red-haired French border guards. No black Zouaves.

I thought of Trudi again, for the first time in years. Eight years this coming summer I had driven them to Stuttgart.

I would never know what had happened to her, but it was, somehow, a comfortable mystery to eat up the time during my race through the February night.

North of Woodstock I opened up the car to seventy, but slowed down carefully to observe the speed limits in Harvard and Walworth, though it was most unlikely that the local police would be anywhere but in their beds.

As I told you, however, I am a careful man—given the mad assumptions of the context in which I found myself.

I had left Oak Park at 11:30. At 1:35, I turned the corner of the Walworth road, climbed over the hill, and entered Fontana, nothing more than a beach and a street or two of houses behind it in those days before the construction of the big hotels and marinas. The lake, in summertime a turquoise mirror nestled in the hills, was now a smooth dark patch surrounded by snow and an occasional streetlight.

Though I wanted to rush down, do my work, and return to the comforts of my bed, I forced myself to stop the car at the beach and think.

The only possible problem would be that Rearden might be lurking in woods, waiting for me. That was not very likely, but neither was it impossible.

I drove away from the beach, parked in the public lot near the town hall (jammed on summer weekends and, I was told, a marvelous place for necking at night), locked the car, and began to trudge the half mile along North Shore Drive to the Clancy house.

How many lifetimes ago since the prom?

Only nine years since I had fished her out of the lake and kissed and caressed her, with savage delight, to tell the truth, in the two-story "den" of this house?

It must have been longer than that, must it not?

My initial impression then had been correct in one respect: she was indeed a very satisfactory partner in the kissing and caressing business.

I wished I was home in bed with her, not making love, because she would be sleeping so deeply, but perhaps holding her hand.

It was bitter cold; the temperature must have fallen more than the Weather Bureau had anticipated. And the snow, off North Shore Drive, was higher than my boots. So a wet, insidious chill slipped into my stockings and then into my feet. If I was not careful, I would give myself a fearsome cold.

(I am aware intellectually that colds are caused by a virus, but I was raised in such profound faith that colds were caused by wet feet and un-wrapped mufflers that I cannot shake those convictions.)

I had decided that if I was to continue to avoid even the unanticipated risks, I would not enter from the driveway into the Clancy house, but rather from the front door on the lake side. This would mean I would creep in over the property of the next-door neighbor and cross his front lawn. I assumed that the neighbor would not be on the premises during midweek in February.

Resorts in the dead of winter are ugly, naked places, bereft of their charm and glitter. A great idea for a study, wasn't it? Well, even if this was a wild-goose chase, at least it wasn't a completely wasted night.

I paused in front of the Clancy house. The lake was frozen, the pier removed so that it would not be damaged by the ice.

The scene was totally different, but, yes, I did fish her out of the water right there. It had turned out, on balance, not to have been such a bad error, even if it had brought me back here tonight under such preposterous conditions.

I put the key in the door, tried to open the lock, and discovered that it wouldn't move.

Frozen?

One was supposed to heat the key with a match, then try again. Alas, O'Malley, who doesn't smoke, virtuous and wholesome lad, doesn't carry matches.

Well, the next step was to rub the key in your hands so that it would absorb some body warmth. Right?

I pulled off a glove and I began to massage the key, but it was cold and elusive. After a few brisk rubs, it slipped out of my hand. I reached for the flashlight, fumbled with the switch, and turned it on.

Beneath me was nothing but trampled snow.

I searched frantically with my bare fingers, ignoring the sharp pain from the cold snow and ice. I thought I had found it in a clump of snow, but it slipped out of my fingers. I dug deeper, but uncovered only a twig.

Had I not done the same thing in the forest between Bamberg and Nuremberg? Still clumsy.

Now nearly frantic, I flashed the light in all directions and, my knees digging into the wet snow, searched desperately in the mess I myself had created.

Finally I found it, wedged up against the screen door.

This time it turned the lock easily and the door swung slowly open. I was still thinking clearly, despite my clumsiness. The daimon, I suppose, was at work. Don't leave any clues (other than your footsteps on the lawn and the trampled snow at the doorway!). Take off your boots and leave them inside the door.

So with wet stocking feet I padded down the corridor and into the big den. I paused in the dark to orient myself. On my left, where there was a massive patch of gray, would be the big window overlooking the lake. Dead ahead would be the fireplace with the moose's head on the wall. Beneath it the rug on which I had romanced the young Rosemarie. On the right would be the massive desk and the library shelves with leather-bound books that Jim Clancy probably never opened.

Lord have mercy on him, as Mom would have said.

So, immediately on my right, hard right, would be the wall with the painting of Clarice and a safe behind it, usually left open because, according to Rosemarie, it contained nothing of value except Jim Clancy's enemies list.

I flicked on the light quickly, flashed it on the wall, found the picture, and turned the light off.

Presumably there would be no one on the lake with field glasses focused on the Clancy windows, but why take chances, right?

Pull the shade?

And leave fingerprints?

I groped around in the dark, found a big, plush chair against the wall, climbed up on it, fished for the picture, discovered it, and, ever so gently, lifted it off its hanger.

Then I flashed the light on and off again to locate the safe.

Everything was going according to plan, I told myself. I touched the combination lock of the safe and eased it toward me. It swung open easily.

I probed around inside with my hand—several stacks of paper. I reached for them with such vigor that I fell off the chair.

And hit the floor with a noisy clatter and several appropriate obscene and scatological expressions.

Several parts of my anatomy, most notably my posterior, felt like they had been damaged for life. Moreover, I was dazed and confused. Where was I? What was I trying to do? Might I not need a little nap?

I struggled to my feet, limped around in the darkness to find the overturned chair, and tried again.

Dummy.

Steadying myself, I made sure that I had all the papers and then, much more carefully this time, eased my tense and aching body back off the chair.

I flicked the light on. A few bills, some prospectuses from Las Vegas hotels, and an unsealed envelope.

It was labeled, "For the police, in the event of my death."

Nicely put, huh?

I opened it and glanced at the contents. Sure enough, a long letter claiming that Rosemarie had killed her mother and expressing fear that she and I would kill him. A list of servants who could testify to the strange events of the day of Clarice's death and of witnesses who would testify to my many threats to kill him.

Nice practical joke, huh?

Still running on my daimon's automatic pilot, I put the irrelevant papers back in the safe, closed it, and hung the picture. I flicked the light over the floor to make sure that I had not left any papers on the floor after my fall.

One of my shins began to hurt. A skinned knee probably, of the kind I thought I had left behind on my fourteenth birthday.

I had banged up my knee in Bamberg too. For a moment I thought I was back in the woods. I shook my head to clear the fog. Had I hit my head when I fell?

Mrs. Clancy—Clarice—I reflected, was a lovely woman, not as striking as her daughter but still lovely. Dear God, why did she have to suffer so much?

No answer.

I turned off the light to reflect. Would the practical joke have worked? Maybe. Maybe not? The Murrays would have found many witnesses to testify to Jim Clancy's emotional aberrations. There could be no proof that Rosemary had killed her mother; his charges would not be enough to establish that. Who were the witnesses? Might he have paid them off to commit perjury? Would they be ready to take that chance after he was dead?

That did not seem likely.

And, as to his own death, the mere fact that he expected his daughter and son-in-law to kill him would not prove that we actually hired the hit man who planted the bomb in his car.

No, neither he nor Rearden had enough to fry us. Still, there was enough to drag us through the courts for months, maybe years, and to destroy our reputations and make our lives miserable. And the lives of our children.

Great little joker, Jim Clancy. Quite amusing, as his mother had said. *Requiescat in pace.*

Who were the witnesses?

I flicked on my flashlight and watched the light die. Ah, but O'Malley is provident. I pulled the fresh batteries out of my pocket and, bumbling and fumbling in the dark, tried to install them.

Finally I got all the parts of the light more or less properly screwed back together. Proud of my skills, I flicked the switch again. It didn't work.

Provident O'Malley didn't bring a fresh bulb.

Then I made a terrible mistake.

The most callow of readers will say that, having found what he expected to find, O'Malley should now redeploy. Instantly. Get the hell out. Who needs a flashlight? You can read the stuff in your car. Go home. To your warm bed. And your warmer wife. Right?

So O'Malley spends fifteen precious minutes groping and fumbling for a flashlight.

Fifteen stupid minutes.

Finally, I found a light in one of the drawers of Jim Clancy's desk. I was about to turn it on when a searchlight swept across the room, nailed me behind the desk, and then passed on.

Now what?

Whose searchlight? And from where?

A car door slammed. Voices crackled in the cold night air. The searchlight had been auto headlights. Had they seen me? Where should I hide? They were coming in the back door. So if I . . .

I rushed madly, banging my shins a couple of times, across the jet black room, and out the door into the corridor leading to the front entrance.

Should I try to make my escape, hoping that I hadn't been seen? Or should I wait to see who they were and what they wanted?

With Clancy's letter crammed into my trousers pocket, the better choice—and I admit it was a close judgment call—would have been to run.

So I stayed to listen.

The visitors had a hard time with the driveway door. One of them was, with considerable obscenity, trying to pick the lock.

Cops?

Or robbers raiding the house of a dead man?

Which did I want?

Professional thieves would not be so blatant or so clumsy.

Cops. Five will get you ten that it's Rearden and a buddy. I would recognize him shortly, perhaps, by his smell.

Instead I recognized the voice. I omit the obscene language from the conversation because it would be tedious to record it all.

"I hope you know what you're doing, Artie; this is breaking and entering. And in another jurisdiction."

"You read the letter, didn't you?" The light went on in the den. "The evidence we want is here. We'll take it and get out. Who's to know where we found it? We'll tell them it was in the old guy's home in Chicago."

"Geez, look at the layout, the guy must have been loaded, know what I mean?"

"And it's all going to that little cunt and her faggot husband. I'll laugh when they both fry."

"You think you can fry them, Artie, really?"

"Him for sure. Her . . . well, it might be better than being raped by butches for the rest of her life. I'd enjoy thinking about that more. Serve the rich bitch right."

"That's for sure—hey, is that the picture the letter talks about?"

I'll admit that I'd been pretty clumsy. But I was an amateur, not a pro. These two were as bad as Special Agent Clarke, the FBI man who wanted to turn Trudi and her mother and sister over to the Ruskies. Suppose some local police come by and see the car in the driveway and lights on in the house. Suppose they are a little trigger-happy. Suppose they come in with guns drawn, without warning. Suppose that Artie and his rasping buddy try to reach for their guns.

Then what happens to your genial red-haired eavesdropper, poor innocent Chucky, you ask?

Better that you don't ask.

There was a rattle and then a bang as the picture was pulled off the wall and dropped on the floor.

"Yeah, there's the safe. Hey, we're home free!"

Then a string of very tedious and unimaginative obscenities.

"I don't get it, Artie. The letter said all the proof would be here. How come there's nothing but bills and ads for expensive hotels, know what I mean?"

"Because someone got here before us, that's why."

"Who? Not that O'Malley squirt. He's still in his house."

"Yeah?"

"Look, Artie, you know what they're saying on the streets, that the old guy put out a contract on himself because he knew he had cancer and he wanted to go out with a ha, bang. Maybe this is some nut letter, know what I mean?"

More obscenities, again showing no creative imagination.

"Let's search this place, tear it apart, the stuff must be here."

Movement in my direction. I rush, as quietly as possible, for a closet that I remember is at the other end of the corridor.

I remember wrong.

"Hey, wait a minute, Artie. We got no warrant. This is out of our jurisdiction. What if the local cops show up? What if we don't find anything? We've left our prints all over the place. What if the squirt goes after us? We could be in a whole lot of trouble."

"I know they did it. I want to see him fry. I want to see that cunt turned over to the butches."

"Yeah, sure, Artie, but cops don't turn out so hot in stir either. Come on, let's get out of here."

"You losing your nerve?"

"You said right in, right out. You didn't say search. Besides we'd need ten guys to go through this place. It'd be like looking for a needle in a haystack, know what I mean?"

"You *are* losing your nerve."

"Come on, Artie, use your head. This isn't working out, let's get out of here before we're both in real trouble. Know what I mean?"

Cursing and protesting, Artie apparently did know what his friend meant. They turned off the light, stumbled down the corridor, slammed the door shut, and started their car.

It was stuck in the snow.

The friend had to get out and push while Artie rocked it back and forth from second to reverse and finally got it moving.

Add multitudinous monotonous obscenities.

Finally they left, their headlights once more cutting a path across the den.

This time I was safely hidden in the corridor.

Three-thirty according to my watch's luminous dial.

Give them a half hour and hike back to Fontana.

What if they recognize Vince's car?

How many blue Fairlanes are there in America?

The license numbers?

Those two remember a license and then see it in the dark up here?

You've been reading too many mysteries.

I hiked back through the snowdrifts. Lazy flakes began to swirl around casually, white fireflies in the cold air. I huddled under my jacket and shivered desperately. What, I wondered, if the two bent cops were lying in wait for me.

I encountered not a single living being as I pushed my way through the snow and the cold. I imagined that I was Robert Scott struggling toward the South Pole. Where were the sled dogs? Oh, yes, we'd eaten them.

Finally I stumbled into the parking lot. Where was the Fairlane? What happened to it? Oh, there it was, covered with snow. Would the car door open? Or would the lock be frozen?

It opened just fine. Unfortunately the car wouldn't start. The ignition turned over dubiously a couple of times and then gave up. When was the last time Vince had a tune-up? I pushed the gas pedal desperately. It still wouldn't start. I smelled gasoline. I had flooded the engine.

Shivering uncontrollably now, I climbed out of the car and tried to clean off the windows. Even if I got it started, would it be able to plow through the snow out of the parking lot?

I returned to the car, depressed the gas pedal to the floor, and turned the key. There was a promising sound. I tried it again. A more promising sound of an ignition almost catching. You got me into this, I informed the Deity. It's your job to get me out.

Apparently he heard me. The engine started briskly, as though asking why I had messed it up the first time around. Just to show me that it was alive and well, the car lurched out of the parking lot, skidded across the highway, and paused at the edge of a snowbank.

Gently now I eased us back on the snow-covered highway and began the slippery ride to Oak Park.

I waited till I was on the outskirts of Woodstock to read the papers Jim Clancy had left as part of his practical joke. I memorized the names of the witnesses, in case we ever needed them, and then tore the pages into small pieces and trailed them out of the window of the car over the next thirty miles.

All except the brief description of how his wife died. Driven by a demon—and not my woman-loving daimon, who would be disgusted about such behavior—I folded those sheets and put them in my pocket.

Everything but the ice-cream bar. Did he have one more practical joke to spring?

I shifted uneasily. It would be like him to have one final trick in reserve.

The snow was falling hard now, just as predicted. I drove very carefully. I wanted very much to arrive home safely and fall into bed next to my wife.

I beat you, Jim Clancy. I beat you. She's mine now.

In retrospect, my pride was hardly justified. I had simply made less mistakes than the two cops, just as I had made less mistakes than Agent Clarke.

Arthur Rearden was killed in a shootout in a bar on Seventy-ninth and Racine the next year. He was off-duty and drinking in the bar when two young black kids tried to rob it. He killed both of them. I hope somewhere he has found peace.

It never made the papers, but the police generally accepted the explanation they received from their stool pigeons: Jim Clancy had put out a contract on himself because he knew he was going to die.

He did indeed go out with a bang.

No one ever made the suggestion again that Rosemarie and I might have tried to kill him—until a rather recent article in a Chicago underground paper called *The Feeder*. A young woman photographer, convinced that my continued success was depriving younger photographers, "especially women with a feminist's vision," their justly merited success, assembled every nasty word ever printed about me in my whole career.

A labor of love, you might say.

> Many Chicagoans have not forgotten that most of O'Malley's wealth was inherited from his father-in-law and mother-in-law, both of whom died under mysterious circumstances. His mother-in-law, Clarice Clancy, was pushed down a flight of stairs. His father-in-law, James Clancy, was blown up by a car bomb. While police were never able to find evidence conclusively linking O'Malley to these killings, neither were they able to completely exonerate him. Given the paucity of his talent and the ambition that has driven him to the heights of success, one could expect almost anything from Charles Cronin O'Malley.

Not libelous, not quite. And the operative word, gentle reader, is not "exonerate"; it is "success."

In *The Feeder*, hatred, so long as it is ideologically correct, covers a multitude of sins.

Back in 1955, that episode of my life was not quite finished. One small, suspicious, Othello-like part of me still did not quite believe Rosemarie's account of her mother's death. Was not the fall down the stairs too fortuitous, too much of a coincidence?

It was then, however, that I began to gather my little secret dossier about the deaths of her parents—against what event I was not sure, but so that I might have the data at hand if I ever needed it.

It was an almost harmless obsession, a tiny infection, a small wound that, I told myself, could not ever become serious enough to cause gangrene.

I had seen a look of fury occasionally in her eyes, almost always when she was drunk, and momentarily feared for my life and for the lives of our children. Sober, Rosemarie would not hurt even a bug—she chased flies out of the house rather than swat them.

Drunk . . . might she be a killer?

It was only a tiny fear, one to which I paid little attention. But it was there, as small as a virus that carries a deadly disease.

I drove slowly up to Greenwood and Euclid at seven-thirty, parked the car a block away, slogged through the falling snow down the alley and into our back porch. I returned the key to key ring, threw the sedatives down the toilet, and collapsed into bed.

Hours later, freshly showered and morning bright, she brought me my breakfast.

"Did you take one of those nice little pills too?"

"No." I had learned that you should not roll over in dismay when your wife brings you breakfast in bed.

"You were out like a light all night long."

"Was I really?"

Rosemary did not get drunk the week her father died.

But she did the following week, when she discovered that she was pregnant again.

And I continued to worry about the ice-cream bar.

~⚬ 25 ⚬~

I will now tell you the story of my wife's death. The true story.

He had typed the document himself. It was sloppy, marred by erasures and misspellings—and thus seemingly more authentic.

I have attached the names and addresses of my servants at the time, who will testify to the truth of my story.

My daughter Rosemarie was a difficult, spoiled child. My poor wife indulged her and then, when our child became a hot-tempered little monster, feared her. With good reason.

In her rages she frequently assaulted my wife physically. I felt that the child needed psychiatric attention, but Clarice objected that such attention would suggest to others that we had 'bad blood.'

I lived in terror for many years that in one of these assaults she would do serious harm to my wife. I never suspected how much harm she might do.

On the day of her death my wife had been ill with a serious headache. She forbade Rosemarie to go out with Margaret O'Malley, whom we both felt was a bad influence on our daughter. Her parents tended to be lax with children and we were convinced that Margaret encouraged my daughter to resist her mother's wishes.

Rosemarie disobeyed my wife's orders, in the hearing of our housekeeper. Later, she returned to the house, with the O'Malley girl. My wife reproached Rosemarie for her disobedience. Rosemarie attacked her and in the ensuing struggle pushed her mother down the steps to the basement. Then she and the O'Malley child fled back to the O'Malley residence. They either persuaded or deceived

Mrs. O'Malley to tell the police that neither of them had left.

I was aware of what happened, but instructed my servants not to speak to the police about the actual events of that day. I had lost my wife. I did not want to lose my daughter. Moreover, I believed that the tragedy was an unfortunate accident and that no useful purpose would be served by inflicting punishment on my daughter.

Since I made that decision, however, I have often wondered whether I misinterpreted the facts. Was my wife's death—with so many years of life still hers by right—a tragic accident or the result of a deliberate and cold-blooded murder?

I am now prepared to say that the latter is the truth. And that I am the next target.

Thanks,

James Patrick Clancy.

26

The volcano smoldering under Vince and Peg finally blew up.

At our house at supper.

They probably should have called and canceled the evening. But it was only two weeks since the death of Jim Clancy and they doubtless felt that they owed it to Rosemarie to come to the Syrian meal she had promised them.

The strain between them was so strong when they came into the house that even I noticed it.

We chatted about the *Vogue* shoot. They both admired my proofs and were properly impressed with my wife in the blue "foundation garment."

"I always said you should be a model, Rose." Peg beamed approvingly.

"If I ever have a career, which I doubt"—Rosemarie began to distribute the spicy meat dish that, at the risk of my life, I had earlier called Irish stew—"it would be doing something, not just posing for a camera."

"Gourmet cook," I suggested, shoveling the tasty meat into my mouth.

"Human garbage scow"—Peg smiled indulgently—"you don't count."

"As long as it isn't moving," Rosemarie agreed, "Chuck will eat it."

Vinny was tense and silent, his eyes dark, his lips thin.

"Do you like it, Vince?" I asked tentatively.

"Great." He smiled like the Vince of old. "Rosie's a wonderful cook."

"Thank you." She bowed in gratitude.

"Peg's a wonderful cook too." Vince relaxed and smiled. "Not a gourmet chef like you, Rosie. Not everyone has time for that."

Peg turned white. Somehow her anger jumped across the table. Vince, who had meant a sincere compliment—well, eighty-five percent sincere anyway—turned dark again. "I mean"—he tried to recapture his composure—"you're not busy with a musical career like Peg, are you?"

"She's my agent," I said, ineptly trying to smooth things over.

"That doesn't take her out of the house all the time, does it?"

"She's home more than a lot of women." Rosemarie was about to join the brawl. I wished I could find that plane which was leaving for Katmandu.

"Women that have to work for a living"—his voice rose—"women whose husbands are not able to support them."

Oh boy.

"There is nothing wrong with a woman having a career," Rosemarie fought back. "Just because I stay home, it doesn't mean—"

"Why don't YOU become a professional singer?" Vince yelled. "Then you can leave your kids alone as Peg does."

"I'm with them more than you are." Peg's fingers gripped her Waterford claret glass.

"It's my job to earn the money, yours to raise the kids." He pushed away from the table. "A woman belongs at home."

"Bullshit," said my wife, pouring oil on the flames.

"Your children are never neglected, Vinny," Peg said wearily. "You know that."

"They need a full-time mother."

"And a father," she fired back, "who keeps his agreements."

"What do you mean by that?" He leaped out of the chair.

"I mean"—her voice was icy—"that you agreed before we were married that it was all right if I continued with the violin. You urged me not to give it up when I was willing to do so. Now you've changed the rules."

"All those months in hell in Korea"—he was sobbing now—"I dreamed of peace and happiness at home. I should have let myself die that night they soaked me and left me out in the cold. If I thought I'd return to a wife who loved her fiddle more than she loves me and our children, I would have died."

"Always Korea, Vinny," she stared at him coldly. "Always Korea, when you want to intimidate me."

"You weren't there. You don't know what it was like."

"If I'd thought it would be held over my head throughout my marriage, I would have volunteered as a Red Cross worker."

"Bitch!" he screamed.

"Not in my house!" Rosemarie screamed too. "You don't call your wife that in my house."

"Calm down, Rosie." Peg did not take her eyes off her husband, who was rampaging back and forth on the other side of the table from her. "It's been coming a long time. I'm only sorry that it had to happen in front of you."

"You've all looked down on me because I'm Italian." Vince pounded the wall. "Not good enough for a shanty Irish wife."

"Venetian-blind Irish," I murmured.

"That's the last cliché, Chucky. First it's neglecting the kids; second it's Korea; third it's the despised Italian people."

"Bitch!" Vince screamed again.

"You can think of better words than that, Vince." She glared at him. "All right, it's been building up. I might as well say it in front of witnesses: This has to stop. Either we find help to put our marriage back together or you get out. I will not have my children subjected to these foolish rages of yours. I love you and I always will love you. I'll fight with you as often as I need to, I'll ask for forgiveness whenever I'm wrong, which is often, but I will not, Vinny, not, tolerate this rage of yours anymore."

"You'll have to tolerate it," he sneered. "I bring home the money. I'm the breadwinner."

"Go home, Vinny," she replied composedly, "and calm down. Or don't go home. Spend the night at your mother's. She won't put up with it for long either. And don't come back until you agree that we both need help."

"Fuck you!" he roared and bolted from the house.

"Sorry, Chuck." She glanced at me. "I know how much you respect him."

"I could tell there were some troubles," I said lamely.

"It's Korea, as I'm sure you've guessed. He's never quite recovered his confidence since they tried to break him. Law school was supposed to help and it made things worse."

"He's always this way?"

"Dear God, no, Chuck. Most of the time, he's the sweet wonderful man who took me to his senior prom. But it's getting worse. I had to lay down the law. I'm not sure it will work."

"I'll drive you home, Peg." Rosemarie laid aside her napkin and stood up. "You don't mind, Chuck?"

"Huh? Oh, no."

The two of them needed to cry together.

I finished the rest of the "Irish stew."

That night, Rosemarie and I lay silently next to each other in bed, the lights still on.

"Has it been going on long?" I asked, sure that Peg had told her everything through the years.

"Up and down. Never this bad. I didn't tell you because you'd feel you had to do something, like you always do, and there's nothing that can be done until poor Vinny is ready."

"Do you think they'll separate?"

"I hope not. Peg has to mean it, though, or it won't work. If she bluffs and he calls her bluff it's curtains."

More silence.

"Am I ever that way?"

"You! Oh, Chucky, how funny!"

"Well . . ."

"No, no, no." She punched my arm. "You're the one who puts up with the nut in the family."

I didn't know what to say, so I said nothing at all again.

"Thanks," she continued "for taking care of the dishes."

"I figured I should, since I ate all the food. . . . What can I do to help them?"

"Nothing!" she gripped my arm fiercely. "And please, please, don't even try. You'll only make matters worse."

"You're going to intervene?"

"Certainly."

"With Vince?"

"Naturally."

"Poor man."

"He has it coming."

"All right." I felt rebuked. "Will they make it?"

"I'm not sure."

"Bet?"

Her outrageous leprechaun grin cracked her solemn face. "Never, husband mine, bet against Clancy when she's about to lower the boom."

27

"You don't really want to return to your motel"—Millie tilted her brandy glass in my direction—"do you? Why don't you spend the night here with me?"

Her invitation made explicit what the situation already conveyed—a fire crackling against the early spring chill, two people alone in a suburban parlor outside of New York, a sumptuous woman clad in a shimmering black robe under which there was almost certainly nothing but her, a man who had been wined and dined into insensitivity, four days of close cooperation that had eased into intimacy, an absent husband, an atmosphere of recklessness and adventure.

Why not? It was, after all, June of 1958 and I was a sophisticated man of the world, was I not? Especially with two-thirds of a bottle of wine in me. All right, I don't drink, but this was a special situation, wasn't it?

"That's an interesting invitation." I looked at my empty glass.

"You're temporizing, Charles."

You bet I am.

Holiday had asked me to do a "portfolio" on "life in the suburbs." "We've heard too much that is critical of the suburbs," Millie Edwards said to me over the phone. "We want this piece to be a celebration of the freedom and the culture and the togetherness that suburban life has made possible. We know you are a suburbanite yourself and that you reject much of the criticism. We thought some quality shots from you would make the piece a really major contribution to the discussion."

"What suburb?"

"The one I live in. That way we will have no trouble finding the people and the places."

"I have approval on what you use." Rosemarie was no longer acting as my agent, but I knew what she would say.

"Surely. We don't want to violate your integrity."

"Integrity" probably didn't mean the same thing to both of us. My "portfolio" would probably be four pictures at the most. I liked the idea. And I could use the shots in the suburb project that was in my idea notebook.

So, I agreed. Rosemarie thought it sounded good. No, she couldn't come. Not at the end of the school year when she had to get the family ready for Grand Beach.

How much of a West Side Irish Chicago local I was became obvious almost on arrival. The chosen "suburb" was much like John Cheever's Shady Hill, utterly unlike Oak Park and River Forest and not at all the "ticky-tacky boxes" of the social criticism and the songs. It was supposed to be a slick piece defending the people who read the magazine.

They, in their turn, were not like my friends and neighbors. They were from all over the country, rootless, driven, bright, sophisticated, and—to my quickly jaundiced view—both supercilious and amoral.

Millie Edwards ("my professional name, Wright is my husband's name") was also unlike any woman I had ever met, the WASP beauty after whom Woody Allen chased and about whom I was ignorant. She was perhaps ten years older than me, tall, both svelte and voluptuous (I mean really voluptuous), and iridescent sexually.

I tumbled quickly and, I fear, completely. She knew that she had awed the red-haired runt from Chicago and was frankly amused by her conquest.

Acutely conscious of her presence behind me, I clicked away with my Rolleiflex and Hasselblad. Westchester County or Cook County, Dutch Colonial or ticky-tacky, my kind of people or other kinds of people, the themes were the same: domesticity, "togetherness" in family life, gadgets (electric carving knives, washers and dryers, tail fins on cars, hi-fidelity stereo systems, ever larger TV sets), child-centered living, religious devotion, commuting fathers, Bermuda shorts, chauffeuring mothers, conformity, etc., etc.

So I took pictures of PTA meetings, barbecues (around swimming pools, which at that time you couldn't find in most suburbs, even modestly affluent ones like Oak Park), wives greeting husbands at the seven-thirty train, martini-drenched cocktail parties, pastors in turtleneck sweaters leading bible discussion groups in luxurious homes, tail fins in front of churches, T-birds in high school parking lots, mothers delivering children to their respective post-school activities, waiting rooms in maternity wards, new homes on the fringe of the expanding suburb—read about all of it in the popular histories of that era.

Change the hairdos and the clothes, the car styles and the slogans and you could take most of the same pictures today. Suburbs, then and now, are a nice symbol by which one group in the upper middle class (professors and journalists) can scapegoat another segment (businessmen and professionals). Moreover, they also were an excellent inkblot in which those who fancied themselves a cultural elite could see—and protest against—the weakening of their monopoly on the good, the true, and the beautiful.

The more affluent members of the middle class have always wanted the "good life" that the postwar suburbs made possible. The difference between the pre-1950s suburbs and the myth I was trying to capture was size: prosperity gave many more people a share in affluence. And the difference between then and now is that far more people (too many, probably) take affluence for granted today.

My generation, born or raised in the Depression, was catching up; because of the flourishing economy a lot more of us caught up than were ever expected to do so.

Suburban "lifestyle" a dramatic social change in the fifties? Not in quality, only in quantity.

I grew angry at the stereotyping as I wandered through Westchester County, watching Millie Edwards out of the corner of my eye, especially because scapegoating was the work of those who were enjoying the affluence as much as anyone else.

The *Holiday* project was ambivalent in its essence: it was supposed to celebrate suburbia as well as critique it. I did my best to celebrate Prosperity, which is much better than Depression.

I know, I've lived through both.

I think I did a pretty good job despite my distractions.

I saw some of my shots cited in a "social history" book the other day as evidence of how "complacent and conformist" Americans were in those days.

Only in those days?

Millie is in one of the shots in the book. My memories were accurate enough: she was a devastating woman.

Her allure was not merely physical, though there was plenty of that, God knows. She was bright, sophisticated, accomplished. Wasn't my wife worthy of all of those adjectives too?

Yeah, except Rosemarie, like all the other women in my life, was anything but cosmopolitan. West Side Chicago Irish to her painted fingernails. Aware of the outside world, but not deeply involved in it and not even eager to be.

Millie was part of the Big World—whatever the hell that was. She'd graduated from Radcliffe, she'd done graduate work in Paris, and she skied in the Alps every year after Christmas, vacationed in Corfu, bought her clothes in Paris, knew Frank Sinatra, spent weekends on Martha's Vineyard.

Cortina, Corfu, the Vineyard—and we had Grand Beach!

"Chicago sounds like such an interesting city, I really want to visit it sometime. Tell me about your Major Daley. He is an interesting primitive type, isn't he?"

See what I mean?

All of which is to say that she was different. That may have been the strongest part of the temptation.

Would my Rosemarie have been attractive to a visiting artist from Westchester?

He probably would have thought her the Irish serving girl type. Poor man.

"Your wife sounds like a fascinating woman, Charles. Looks like one too. Oh, yes, I saw the picture in *Vogue*. Simply adorable. You're a very lucky man."

In a tone of voice that made me wonder whether I was in a rut.

Clever.

If I hadn't been tempted, I would not have been human.

I would enjoy the flame of her company, I told myself, without flying into the fire of infidelity.

Right?

Rosemarie and I had drifted apart again by the late 1950s. We would have denied it then. We both would have asserted pugnaciously that we were very much in love. But the truth is that love that is not tended grows cold and perhaps dies. Can it be reborn?

Perhaps. If the opportunities are seized.

We had stumbled into an opportunity in Beverly Hills. If there were any other opportunities we missed them. We slept in the same bed—when I was home. We were not unfaithful to each other, heaven knows. We made love—nice, safe, unexciting married love—when we were not too tired at the end of the day, which we were most of the time.

We lived the kind of life in which you begin every day rushing and at the end, even though you have never once slowed down, you are even farther behind than when you started.

Rosemarie had not reached her twenty-fifth birthday when Sean Seamus O'Malley, our third son and fourth child, was born. She was sick through most of the pregnancy, the delivery was more difficult than the first three combined, and she was depressed for several weeks after Seano's birth, so depressed that the task of restoring her body to its previous perfection was delayed for several months.

"I could have fifteen more before menopause," she said. "Do you want a family that size?"

"I think not."

"I love every one of them," she said as she soothed "poor little Seano," who as far as I could see was neither poor, nor, even then, particularly little. "I wish there was a bit more time to breathe."

Jane and Peg and our whole generation were having children at about the same rate—gamely, enthusiastically, even joyously. At first.

When they found that perennial pregnancy was ruining their bodies, their nervous systems, their marriages, their lives, many of them became angry—at the Church, at their husbands (first available target), and at themselves. I read somewhere that until the early part of the last century in Western Europe (and much more recently elsewhere) 6.38 pregnancies were required on the average to produce two adults, in other words, for the married couple to reproduce themselves. When we were having children, 6.38 pregnancies would produced seven children (since one must round to the nearest whole child).

I've never been able to figure out how much the Church's birth control teaching contributed to the breakdown and collapse of many marriages of our generation. Some marriages would have fallen apart anyway. Other marriages survived and flourished. But in between were a lot of marriages that might have continued to be love affairs, but became conflict and hate affairs because of exhausted women and little or no healing renewal from sex.

The Church, ignoring the experience of married people, didn't think that healing and renewal of love were what married sex was about. Sex was for having children. If you didn't have children it was dirty.

I must be candid about the deterioration of our love during those years. If the puritanism and insensitivity of the Church leadership at the time aggravated our problems, they did not cause the problems. I could hardly plead, as did many of my male contemporaries, that I was working day and night, not for myself but for my family. I could not claim that I was doing it all for my wife and kids.

For they didn't need any more money than we already had.

Nor could I complain that my wife was a nag. Save on the subject of photojournalism, she almost never harassed me. Her "ought tos," as I knew well by now, were suggestions and not conditions for continued love. She was still beautiful, still witty, still mysterious. I had little time to appreciate any of these characteristics.

She did drink too much on occasion, but her binges had settled into a pattern that did not seem especially dangerous: once every six or eight months she would drink herself to sleep in the quiet of her study, sometimes spending the night there, sometimes staggering up to bed later on. The next day she would be quiet and wan, perhaps apologetic. The day after, she was herself again, mistress of the revels with which she and the foursome kept themselves busy.

I consoled myself with the piety that the problem had lessened and that soon it would disappear completely.

The children tired her, but she did have two helpers and was never physically prostrated like other woman of her generation. She could always sneak out for a movie (like *The Seventh Seal* or *The Man with the Golden Arm*) or a concert or a recital with Mom and Peg—much more freedom and self-realization (or whatever you want to call it) than other women could enjoy.

She was compulsively responsible about the kids, but, the children, led by the indomitable April Rosemary, knew how to deal with her. They were developing distinctive personalities of their own. April Rosemary was a serious, all-wise little mother; Kevin a clown; Jimmy a dreamer; Seano a resourceful, self-possessed foil for everyone else.

My Rosemarie governed them all like she was their big sister. I was terribly proud of her skills at motherhood. I told her so. Right? Wrong. I was not too busy to notice. I was too busy to comment. Though the children continued to treat me like a very funny baby brother, they worried that I was not like other daddies: I didn't go to work in the morning.

"Taking pictures is *not* work," A. R. insisted, hands stubbornly on her hips.

"I agree, honey, but I get paid for it."

"Really?"

"Really."

They were fully prepared to offer me their best thoughts on what to shoot and how. April Rosemary even began to say, "Daddy, you ought to . . ."

I took them to a circus once. They agreed on the way home that I was funnier than any of the clowns. Their mother did not dissent.

Nonetheless their mother and father drifted apart, not because the deck was stacked against us but despite the fact that the deck was mostly stacked in our favor. We did not talk about our dwindling sexual activity because we accepted the folk wisdom that such diminution was natural and inevitable. To discuss that most poignant aspect of marital intimacy requires a willingness to be vulnerable and to put the whole relationship in the balance. Husbands and wives are mostly unready, I have learned from experience and observation, to take such a chance.

The Church's teaching, bad enough as it was, also became an excuse not to face what I call the romantic imperative of marriage: To wit, you take periods of romantic renewal out of marriage and it isn't marriage anymore.

The realist argues that marriage and romance are two different phenomena. Marriage is too serious a union to confuse it with romantic love. I respond that it is so serious a union that you must have romantic love to sustain it.

My book *The Romantic Imperative* has sold more than any of my other works, more than most of them put together. More about that later, however.

So Rosemarie and I were doing what most people our age were doing: we were using career and family as an excuse to avoid the challenge of maturing intimacy.

The Church sure did help us in this evasion.

In my more reflective moments, I envied Peg and Vince their bitter fight. They could not continue to drift. They had to face the issues and talk about them.

A few weeks after the night I demolished the Syrian meal, in the early evening, I was walking by their house and, disobeying my wife's strict orders, I impulsively walked up the steps to ring their doorbell. On the porch, I hesitated. There was no noise inside. The house, with a single light in the living room, hinted that no one was home. I glanced in the window to see if anyone was home.

My sister and her husband were huddled on the couch, her arms protectively around him, his head resting on her chest. From a distance and through the thin drapes, it was obvious that he was weeping.

I tiptoed away.

What a wonderful picture of forgiving love it was. Too bad I could not take a picture of it, especially of Peg's tender affection, big enough in the scene briefly observed to embrace the whole world and all of a lifetime.

Some woman, my sister.

A day or two later the phone rang. No one was around, so, against strict orders that artists don't answer phones, I picked it up. "O'Malley residence."

"You're not supposed to answer the phone." Peg, the purest sort of joy in her voice.

"Only when I know it's good news."

"That obvious, huh?" She sounded ecstatic.

"So obvious that even dumb Chucky notices."

"Dear God, brother, it's wonderful to fall in love again."

"I'm glad it worked out," I said with more than my usual flair for an original phrase.

"The guy is so ashamed of the other night. Be nice to him when he calls."

"Unlike the other times when I was not nice to him."

"What? Oh, don't be silly! Tell Rosie I called."

"Surely."

"Don't forget."

"I won't."

A half hour later my bride entered the house with the same stillness that would have marked the arrival of the First Cavalry Division.

"Call Peg."

"You're not supposed to answer the phone."

"Only for good news," I repeated my prepared defense.

"Good news?" she bellowed.

"Oh, yes."

The armored division thundered across the house toward her study and the phone.

When a sheepish Vince called me the next day, he sang the praises of reconciliation. "You can't beat falling in love with your wife again, Chuck. Greatest pleasure in the world."

"I can believe it."

"And that's some woman you're married to."

"Especially when she lowers the boom?"

"Wow!"

"Indeed."

Both Rosemarie and I missed the lesson in the Antonelli reconciliation.

And there was another lesson I missed, and would for years to come, until disaster forced me to see it.

So Rosemarie and I drifted through the late fifties and there I was, hardly Burt Lancaster, but still a housebreaker in Shady Hill.

Rosemarie never came into the darkroom anymore, and she withdrew after the arrival of Seano from her role as my agent, thus cutting two of the links that held us in common beyond ordinary ones of bed and board.

I did not have the nerve either to ask her formally to continue to be my agent, or to hire another. I was afraid, I think not unreasonably, that if I hired another she would take such action as grounds for divorce.

I had learned her style well enough: ask for more than you think you can possibly get and more than you can possibly believe you're worth and then refuse to negotiate.

It worked quite well.

If she had been playing the agent role, however, the two big fights we had in the late fifties would have never occurred.

She would not have accepted my assignment to cover racial integration in Little Rock in the fall of 1957 for *Look*.

She was furious at me when I left.

"Why do you waste your talent on something that you know is not nearly as important as it used to be? How many times do I have to tell you that you are not a goddamn photojournalist?"

"This is a historic event, Rosemarie, I have to be there."

"Who says?"

"My conscience."

"Does your goddamn conscience have anything to say about walking out on your wife and kids in September when two of the kids are going to school?"

"It won't happen again."

"Bullshit."

I have said that she was not a nag. I realize she sounds like one in this exchange. I must insist that both her fury and her language were unusual. And note that the anger was not about my trip to Arkansas at the beginning of the school year. That was flimflam. The real reason for her anger was that I was, as she saw it, wasting my talent.

I would win another Pulitzer for my shot of the black and white tots looking up with awe, but not fear, at a rifle-carrying national guardsman. Need I say that my prize did not change Rosemarie's judgment about wasting my talent?

The shot has been criticized in years since for being "sentimental"; some of those who don't like it even suggest that I staged it.

I didn't stage it, as those who were with me when I shot it will testify. Was it sentimental? I would like to think rather that it was a statement of hope, one of the few more or less explicitly ideological photographs I've ever made. I don't think that was a false hope. Black and white children go to school in relative peace now. Most Americans accept school integration as a matter of course. Our racial problems are far from solved, but we are in some respects in better shape than we were thirty years ago. That is a modest achievement. It was all I expected in Little Rock that day. Not to mention the next day, when I was in the hospital.

It's hard when one looks back on that era to understand whether the Southern white leaders expected to get away with their policy of "massive resistance" to the Supreme Court's 1954 school desegregation decision. Did Governor Orval Faubus really think that the federal government would back down in 1957 when he tried to "interpose" the Arkansas National Guard between the courts and the Little Rock school system? Or was he merely running for reelection?

I think the wiser and more cautious southern leaders knew that they could only postpone implementation of the decision, not block it permanently. Eisenhower was, after all, a conservative president who had never expressed support for the 1954 decision; if he would send in paratroopers and federalize the Arkansas National Guard, then a Democratic president would act even more strongly. In the long run, Jim Crow's days were numbered.

But you still had to run for reelection in the short run, didn't you?

(While I'm talking about school desegregation, let me note what I think of that greatest faker of them all, Chief Justice Earl Warren, who went around the country taking credit for the decision and lecturing the rest of us on the need to grant complete racial justice. I suppose he did deserve credit for the unanimous decision in *Brown v. Board of Education*, but I never heard him apologize for his activities during the Second World War when, as attorney general of California, he was one of the leaders of the campaign to ship Japanese Americans to concentration camps. Everyone makes mistakes, but Warren would never admit that mistake. I know, I asked him at a conference and he walked off the platform.

I sent off the picture to *Look* knowing that it was a sure cover and maybe a prizewinner. If I'd had any sense, I would have flown back to the new O'Hare Airport, which had just opened in Chicago. I had seen Little Rock. I knew that the good guys would win. I had made my contribution. There was no reason to hang around looking for "one more shot."

I knew my wild Irish Rosemarie was right. I was not designed to be a photojournalist.

So the next morning, I showed up early at the high school. Too early. The police and the troops were not in place. I was loading film when I saw four lean, hard men bearing down on me, classic rednecks if I had ever seen one.

The Little Rock folk did not like either school integration or national publicity. They blamed the press for both. I was the press, a Yankee with a camera.

I was too dumb to be frightened.

"Let's kill the fucking peckerwood!" one of them shouted.

It dawned on me that I was the peckerwood. I was too scared to run.

One of them hit me in the groin, another pounded my jaw. Then, as I fell to the ground, they stamped on my Hasselblad and started to kick me.

I think they really would have killed me if a Little Rock squad car had not turned the corner.

The rednecks took flight. The cops did not chase them. Indeed they were none too gentle with me as they drove me off to the hospital.

"You should have stayed up north where you belonged, fella," the sergeant next to the driver told me. "You only got what you deserved."

"Yes, sir," I said politely, hoping I lived long enough to get to the hospital. I remembered the man's name and gave him full credit for his quote in the article in *Look*.

The loyalty of the press to its own being what it is, an assault on a Pulitzer Prize–winning photographer was national news that night.

I was described on TV that night as suffering from a brain concussion, two broken ribs, a dislocated jaw, broken teeth, and possible internal injuries.

Attention on the national news that night was quickly shifted from me to my wife. She was asked, when her plane landed at the Little Rock airport, whether she blamed the people of that city for the attack on her husband.

She drew herself up to her full five feet five-and-a-half inches of Irish pirate queen dignity and snapped, "Certainly not."

"Who do you blame, Mrs. O'Malley?"

"Well"—she glared handsomely at the red eye of the camera—"let's start at the top. I blame President Dwight David Eisenhower, who has never once expressed solid support for the school desegregation decision."

"You were great on the tube," I told her when she came into my room. "Upstaged me completely."

I was favored with the same disapproving stare she had directed at the TV camera.

"Go on, say it," I muttered through my wired jaw, " 'I told you so.' "

She burst into tears and threw herself on her knees next to my bed.

"Is there anyplace I can kiss you," she sobbed, "without hurting you more?"

"All kinds of places," I acknowledged.

She never said "I told you so" when I finally came home, mostly in one piece again.

What she did say was, "Don't ever try anything like that again, not unless I'm along to take care of you."

My response was a docile "Yes, ma'am."

I suppose that was one of our moments of possible renewal lost. I told myself I ached too much to make love.

Finally, on September 23, after I had returned to Chicago, still aching, the President spoke out: what was happening in Little Rock was a "disgraceful occurrence." The orders of a federal court were not to be "flouted with impunity" by any individual or mob of extremists. He issued a proclamation ordering that the opposition "cease and desist therefrom and disperse forthwith." To back up the proclamation he sent in a thousand paratroopers, whom Senator Richard B. Russell of Georgia likened to "Hitler's storm troopers."

I will always argue that if the sainted Ike had acted that vigorously earlier, much of the racial conflict of the next decade might have been avoided. I suppose he had enjoyed a bit too much the privileges of a racist military life.

My photography did improve. I was now famous enough at a very young age to merit serious criticism, that is to say the kind of criticism that you should think about. So I thought about it and decided that for the most part it was either wrong or irrelevant. I continued to do what I had been doing.

As my Rosemarie put it, "You're the one who sees the form shining in the proportioned parts of the matter."

"Huh?"

"Aristotle."

"Oh."

"Again, you're the one who sees the sacraments more clearly, God lurking in the world."

"Who's that?"

"Rosemarie."

"I like her better than Aristotle."

Neither Rosemarie nor Aristotle was present in Millie Edwards's parlor, however.

Millie crossed the room and sat next to me, her eyes glowing expectantly. Her face, underneath skillful makeup, showed lines that hinted at sadness. Her two children were still away at boarding school. Life had not been good to this bright, brittle woman.

She leaned toward me and revealed two magnificent breasts—and myself with a breast fetish, in common with most Irishmen.

"I want you, Charles," she whispered. "I intend to have you."

I ought to find out what her powerfully erotic perfume is, buy some for Rosemarie.

She began to kiss me, at first gently and then with savage persistence. Her fingers began to work on my shirt.

Why not? Who would know? What harm would be done?

I was saved not by my virtue, but the sudden collapse of my ardor. I realized that I could not make love even if I wanted to.

When I'm being kind to myself, I add that maybe the memories of Rosemarie's fingers on my shirt at Long Beach on our wedding night forced all other images out of my brain.

"I'm sorry, Millie." I slipped out of her grasp with as much grace as I could muster. "I'm a Catholic."

Can you imagine a dumber excuse than that? In Westchester County?

Millie was hurt and sad, but a good sport. She went to her bedroom, dressed, drove me back to my motel, and kissed me good night with a quick brush of her lips.

How often had she been rejected?

I felt sorry for her.

And did not sleep for a single minute that night. I tried to pray but, for the first time in my life, God was not interested in me.

I didn't blame him.

I was pretty much of a bum.

I was exhausted and guilty when I arrived late that Friday afternoon at our house in Long Beach.

It was one of those glorious June days when summer exists in gentle promise and not yet in its mature heat.

"Charles Cronin O'Malley!" Rosemarie shouted from the front porch. It was her Clancy-is-about-to-lower-the-boom voice.

"I have to leave for Miami tomorrow morning."

"No, you don't."

"I do."

"I canceled the shoot."

I stuck my head out on the porch. She and Seano were watching the lake roll in on our beach in big, self-satisfied rollers.

"I'm going to put this little ape to bed—right, little ape? Then we talk. This is Daddy, Seano, remember him? Yes, that's right, kiss him. It may be the last time because I propose to push him off this porch shortly and into the lake."

I sat down on the swing, knowing that I was in trouble.

Rosemarie reappeared, a thin blue robe over her bikini. So there wasn't going to be any sex. Well, that figured. I was too tired for it anyway.

"Wanna drink?"

"Not now."

"Good." She sat down on the porch swing across from me and pointed an accusing finger at me. "Charles Cronin, this has to stop."

Did she know about Millie? Even if she didn't, I was still in deep trouble indeed.

How deep would be clear before that summer was over.

28

"To begin with"—she crossed her legs and drew the robe tightly around them—"I love you and I don't propose to lose you."

The stereo system inside was providing waltz music, soft and quiet waltz music. "Rosemarie," I said tentatively, "there is no one else."

Not my fault, maybe, especially after last night.

"There goddamn well better not be." She smiled ruefully. "I know there's not, Chucky, no thanks to me."

We'd been married seven years and she was still a fascinating and un-predictable puzzle.

"Then you're not going to lose me."

"We are going to establish some new rules." She waved away my comment as utterly beside the point—and probably dumb too. "First of all, I'm your agent again, check?"

"I didn't know you weren't."

"When was the last time I arranged a shoot or signed a contract?"

"I didn't fire you." The cool breeze off the lake was not helping my body temperature. I felt sweat begin to ooze into my brown poplin suit. Wash-and-wear for traveling.

"I know *that*." She dismissed my point as irrelevant with a brisk wave of her hand. "I fired myself. I'm rehiring myself? Okay?"

"Sure." I took off my coat, folded it neatly, and placed it on the deck beside my chair.

"Secondly"—she ticked the number off on her finger—"in my capacity as your rehired agent, I arrange *our* schedule so that I accompany you on half your trips and work at least two days in the darkroom, okay?"

"Do I have a choice?"

I knew I had no more a choice than I did when it was decided that I should marry her. The difference this time was that I no longer pretended to myself that I wanted a choice.

"Sure you have a choice." The wind went out of her sails. "I mean these are just strongly worded suggestions. You can say no."

"I haven't yet. Thirdly?"

"Huh? Oh, thirdly"—the sails filled with wind again—"lemme see . . .

well, thirdly you stay here for the next month, enjoy the scenery"—she waved at the lake and the beach and the sky—"and get to know your wife and children again. The Michigan dunes are one of the most beautiful places in the world and you've never really bothered to appreciate them."

"There was a winter night years ago—"

"That does not count." She actually blushed. "Besides we still do provide those entertainments if you want."

"I see."

"Well?"

"There's the problem of the study I've promised for our autumn exhibition."

"Oh, *that*." She waved her hand airily. "Do something up here."

"Like what?" I would be inside her very soon, no doubt about that. She knows too, I can tell the way her eyes are darting.

"Like"—she paused and then leaned forward eagerly—"I've GOT it. Do another one of those foggy things with the kids. Up here. Call it . . . "Angels in Summertime"!

"You know"—I reached for my jacket and removed from the inner pocket my ever present notebook for recording ideas—"that's actually an excellent idea."

She smiled tolerantly at my compulsive note taking. "Am I not worth the cost as an agent?"

"Among other things." I carefully replaced my notebook in its proper place.

"The kids are over at Mom's." Her voice lowered to a whisper. "Sean is asleep."

"Fourthly?"

"Fourthly . . ." I had distracted her. She counted on her fingers again. "Oh . . . well, I think five kids are enough, don't you?"

"Five!" it was my turn to count on my fingers. "We have four, don't we? April Rosemary, Kevin, Jimmy Mike, and the little punk? You're not—"

"Certainly not." She dismissed this possibility as so absurd as not to be discussed. "I'm speaking of an upper limit. I mean I can do five like we agreed at our pre-Cana, I think, and keep my sanity. But at the present rate, it could be fifteen."

"Easily."

"So I'll have another one sometime, but that's enough. I love them all. I wish there had been a little more time, but that's neither here nor there, right?"

"Right."

"So five is enough?"

"If you say so."

"I want more agreement than that."

"I agree. I mean four would be enough too."

"Five."

"Okay."

"So that means birth control."

I knew we'd come to that.

"But we're Catholics!"

"What does the Pope know about marriage?" She began to move the swing back and forth, fixing for an attack on the Pope.

"Not much."

"You know what happens when we try rhythm?" She was adopting her Maxwell Street merchant persona, making me want her all the more powerfully.

"We either don't make love or you get pregnant."

"Right. And what about times like this when we both know that the best thing possible for our marriage would be for you to ravish me from now till supper?"

"Or you ravish me."

"Regardless." She waved my cavil away.

"We'd either look at the calender or give up the idea because we'd be afraid to ask."

"Can we live that way?"

"Dear God, Rosemarie." I shut my eyes and saw through my camera eye the failures of the past five years. "I don't think so."

"So?"

"We stop receiving the sacraments, I suppose."

"I won't do that!" Her lips tightened. "I won't let a pope or a priest tell me that saving my marriage is a sin."

I had never quite thought of it in those terms before.

"I'll take care of it," she went on. "You don't have to worry your conscience about it."

"That wouldn't be fair," I protested.

"Well then talk to some priest who will tell you that saving the marriage is more important. That's what John Raven is saying."

"You talked to John?"

"*No*, I made up my own conscience, like an adult should. But I know John is telling people that too. Michael says the same thing."

"My brother?"

The robe had fallen away from her knees. I found myself slipping deeper into a luxurious swamp of desire. My manliness had recovered from its disgrace last night.

"It's probably not fair to cite him because I told him to say that."

"You told him?" I loosened my tie. Yes, she would have to ravish my body this time, having done in my mind and my conscience as foreplay.

Michael had been ordained in early May, a proud day for my parents: nine grandchildren and now a priest in the family, a serious, devout, and dedicated young priest. Mom and Dad were, need I say it, late for the ordination ceremony. Some things never change.

"Sure, they put the poor kid in a parish after locking him away for seven years and expect him to work intelligently with men and women who are older than he is and more experienced and better educated. So"—she shrugged, the Maxwell Street merchant—"he needs someone to ask about women and marriage and stuff like that."

Rosemarie as confidante to the clergy. Wow!

"Do you object?"

"Me? Hardly. I was merely admiring his good taste."

She blushed again and stayed crimson. "You'll talk to John. He says, I'm told, that if the Pope doesn't change the rule, the priests and people will change it for him. Married people can't and shouldn't live the way they told us we had to live. God understands that, even if the Church doesn't."

I thought about it. "I'll ask John what he thinks the next time I see him. But it's obvious that you're right, as always. The trouble with our marriage, like most, I suppose, is not that we have too much sex, but that we don't have nearly enough."

She sighed, her robe now open from top to bottom. "I couldn't agree more."

Thus did we change our attitude on family limitation, a few years before most Catholics and most priests. As I write these words, the Pope and some of the bishops, more than forty years later, are still kidding themselves into thinking that if they are clear enough about the Church's teachings, we lay folk will put our marriages in jeopardy at their say-so.

You don't have to be married very long to know that the frictions and the tensions of the common life in which a man and a woman occupy the same house and the same bed are only tolerable when the pain can be healed and the love renewed in physical pleasure. From inside a marriage that fact is so evident, so "natural," so undeniable, that you wonder how anyone can doubt it.

Even if your wife is a splendid woman such as my Rosemarie, maybe especially if she is a Rosemarie, you simply have to love her physically or you go out of your mind with tension, conflict, avoidance, and frustration.

If the Pope doesn't like that, he should take it up with the God who made us that way.

"Fifthly?"

"Fifthly, I love you, Charles C."

"Then take off your robe, it's too hot out here anyway."

"You're the one who is too hot." But she obeyed my command.

Bikinis in those days, as I have said, were considerably more substantial than they are now. But there was still a lot of Rosemarie, nicely emphasized by white fabric and long black hair. It was such a comfortable swamp. Why not stay here all summer?

"Thank you, Rosemarie." I would wait a little while longer before joining her on the swing; a little more anticipation seemed appropriate.

"For taking off my robe?"

"That too. But mostly for lowering the boom. I would never have had the nerve, not in a million years. I'm glad my wife did."

"I was scared"—her voice caught—"you'd be mad."

It was a perfect time and occasion, was it not, for talking about the remaining problems on our marriage-problem agenda: her drinking habits and the mystery (in my head anyway) of her mother's death?

I thought about it, wondered how to raise the issue, and then, not nearly as brave as my wife, I postponed talk about her occasional drinking bouts to another occasion. It was a loss of nerve that would cost us both dearly.

"Are you really going to stay with us all summer?" she asked.

"Looking at you this moment, young woman"—I rose, walked to the swing, and sat beside her—"I think I'll find it very hard even to drive into New Buffalo to buy the paper."

"It's delivered during the summer." Her voice was soft now with desire. "Let me take off your shirt."

The screens around our deck provided sufficient privacy to protect us from any voyeurs who might be offshore in cruisers watching us with binoculars.

"I knew, deep down, you wouldn't be angry." Her lips roamed lightly over my body, rewarding me for my cooperation.

"I'll never be angry when you say truths I need to hear." I unhooked the back of her bikini top. "I can't promise that you won't have to do it again."

"It'll be easier next time. . . . The little slob left some nourishment in there if you want it."

I turned her head and looked deep into her eyes. It was a fantasy that, I would learn later, many, if not most, husbands and wives have, but which few are able to discuss: nursing your own husband/son and being nursed by your own wife/mother.

"You're sure?"

"Please," she begged me, her back arching in anticipation. "I really want you to."

My lips circled her salty nipple and gently drew on them, sweet warm fluid slipped into my mouth. Rosemarie moaned softly. I felt like I was floating on a sweet-smelling, snow white cloud. I could stay here forever.

She held my head against her breasts. There was no milk left but I did not want to leave. Not ever. Our renewed love was sealed. We would always be together.

Rosemarie's fingers began to fumble with my belt buckle.

The renewal of married love that glorious summer was profound and powerful. Unfortunately, it was not strong enough to resist the storms that would assault it later on in the year.

In our bedroom—to which we had eventually repaired—lying peacefully and happily in my arms, Rosemarie continued her litany.

"Sixthly—"

"I thought we were finished."

"No, but you seemed too preoccupied with other matters to listen."

"All right." With my fingertips I skimmed her lips, back and forth, several times.

"I can't talk if you keep doing that."

"Sixthly . . . ?"

"Sixthly"—she drew a deep breath—"we're flying to Germany at the end of August. You have a contract to do an update of *The Conquered*. A big, big advance. They'll print your old pictures with the new ones and you can write a long text too. It'll be a major work, right? You can put in all that stuff from your dissertation about the Marshall Plan—which by the way we're going to finish real soon, are we not?"

"Yes, ma'am. Before Christmas."

"Labor Day. And then they've planned an important exhibition of all your work. So we *have* to go, don't we? I mean we've never traveled on the continent together . . ."

"Where"—my heart was sinking toward the bottom of Lake Michigan because I already knew the answer—"is the show?"

"In that cute little city where they make the Benzes, you know, Stuttgart."

━━୫ 29 ୫━━

Our trip to Europe was great fun, so much better than I would have dared to expect, that when it finally exploded I was caught completely unprepared.

Rosemarie was pure delight, protecting me from reporters and groupies (as we could call them now), nursing me in my travel ills, amusing me with comic commentary in dialects appropriate to the country we were in, encouraging me when I was discouraged, and loving me body and soul. She was the perfect agent/assistant/wife/mistress.

I told myself that my fears about returning to Germany were quite irrational.

I looked for Trudi in the faces on the railroad platforms and at the same time I was sure I would never find her.

Our German hosts were pleasant and obsequious. Even today, but more so then, they were not quite sure how to relate to their conquerors turned allies and protectors. They seemed to want to say, See how we have recovered from the war, see the spirit and the energy of the German people, see how good we are, see how efficiently we have thrown off the yoke of our Nazi past.

And you wanted to say to them something like, Yeah, but . . .

They were delighted that I had returned to "record the progress in the Federal Republic since your last visit." Progress there had surely been. There were few traces left of the war, an occasional ruined house or legless vet of the Wehrmacht. The country was bursting with progress and prosperity, the German economic miracle was in high gear. So successful was the recovery that already the German literary left (Böll and Fassbinder, for example) were complaining about it, without, as befits the literary left, proposing any particular alternative.

We were presented to Herr Reichkanzler Adenauer in Bonn. He remembered me.

"*Ya, ya, Herr Roter!*" He exclaimed, embracing me, much to the astonishment of his attendants.

"Frau Roter," he said, kissing my wife's hand, much to that young woman's blushing delight.

"You will see our Kurt and Brigitta?"

"Ja, ja!"

"Ja, gut!"

As an American artist, one who had studied Germany after the war with his camera (not knowing at the time that this was what I was doing), I was offensive to both the left and the right. The former saw me as a representative of American capitalism (which, God knows, I was) who had come to celebrate the "materialistic" economic miracle. The latter (much more quietly) saw me as someone who had come to probe beneath the surface of prosperity to remind the world of the Nazis and the Holocaust.

Hence, my exhibition in the gallery in Stuttgart, which looked like a concrete Zepplin hanger, was a retrospective on all my work, putting *The Conquered* into its proper context, as it was explained to me.

Thus the right could say that I was as critical of America as I was of Germany, and the left could rage more furiously than ever about American capitalism (which had provided the money that had in turn produced the resources that supported the university system off which the left lived).

I found these attacks more amusing than offensive. I suppose that both the left and the right were correct about me. I was indeed a celebrant of American capitalism, but a celebrant who saw the flaws. A quiet reference to what happened to me in Little Rock usually put down a reporter who suggested that I was nothing more than an agent of American imperialism.

Rosemarie, who was my interpreter, among her other roles (somehow she had managed to pick up enough German so that she became quite fluent once she was in the country for a few days), sacked for a ten-yard loss a contentious woman reporter with a thin face and long blond hair who would not abandon this theme.

"Herr O'Malley recognizes storm troopers very well, red or brown, right or left. He was beaten by some of them at Little Rock, an experience not unknown, I believe, to German artists."

Clancy had once again lowered the boom.

I was also haunted by deep ambivalence about Germany. Anyone who lived through the war and the discovery of the Holocaust cannot escape such mixed feelings. But I did not believe in collective guilt. I had come to see, I kept insisting, not to judge.

"Judge not," my agent/translator snapped, "that you be not judged."

"I see long before I judge," I would say, "and what I see is surely a function of what I am. You may not like what I see or what I am, but I cannot pretend to anything other. What was it a German religious leader said?"

"Hereon I stand, I can do no other," my translator quoted Luther before I could.

That's the trouble with a certain kind of translator, Irish Catholic woman translator, to be specific.

"And what are you, Herr O'Malley?" someone at the press conference asked.

"I'm an Irish Catholic Democrat from the West Side of Chicago with a camera," I held up my Leica. "A German camera, as a matter of fact."

Most did not comprehend my response, much as they liked my reference to the German camera.

"You will excuse my ignorance, Herr O'Malley," an infinitely polite, rotund gentleman with a beard and thick glasses said, "but what precisely"—a courtly bow—"iss dis Irish Catholic Democrat from the West Side of Chicago?"

"I'm not really a very good example. Let me see," I faked it, "how can I find an example . . . ? I know, her!"

I pointed at my translator, who blushed contentedly as the crowd applauded.

"More seriously, I can only say that you will have to discover that by looking at my pictures and comprehend that I come to see and to understand, not to judge."

"The West Side Irish"—Rosemarie could not be denied the last word, not ever—"are very empiricist, very pragmatic; they have universal ideas, maybe only once or twice in their lifetime, like dragonflies mate—and often with same result, death."

More laughter and applause.

Maybe I should have stayed home and let her do the whole tour.

The trip to Germany was a replay of our summer at Long Beach, which had been pure idyll. As instructed, I had relaxed, read, played with my children, swum, and even played golf and tennis, badly, with my wife and Peg and Vince. I'd worked on my impressionistic study of kids (which did nothing to decrease my reputation as a sentimentalist). I'd finished my dissertation, which had for a year lacked only a few extra footnotes. I'd also begun my work on "Beauty at Every Age," which would continue for years. I had started with Mom, much to her pleasure, and continued with various matrons of diverse ages in Long Beach and Grand Beach. These shots were not "foggy" (Rosemarie's word) Ektachrome efforts but available-light Tri-X black-and-white, a real challenge.

This study was also erotically disturbing because the challenge I had set for myself was to see not only beauty but eroticism in all the ages of the life of a woman. If that's what you want to see in your lens, then you'll find it eventually, and get yourself caught up in it.

You've seen the study, in its most recent revision, so you know that in those days I was emphasizing bare shoulders, an altogether alluring technique, even if I tried for more subtle effects in later years.

I'm proud of the fact that even today feminists bicker about this study, some arguing that it recognizes many different kinds of womanly allure and others arguing that I exploit women at every age. The latter group, as far as I can tell, think that women at all ages ought not to be attractive to men.

Maybe in some other cosmos.

It was fortunate that the energies stirred up while I worked on the study that summer could be released, if that's the right word, in my relationship with Rosemarie. Or maybe it was the fiery passion with my wife that sensitized me to the attractiveness of other women.

The best news of the whole summer was that Rosemarie's drinking problem seemed to have vanished completely. Everything was working again in our marriage. We had both learned from our mistakes and would not repeat them.

I was hopelessly in love with the woman, far more than on our honeymoon. She was mine and I was hers and all was right with the world.

I could not get enough of her. Or she of me. Swimming and golf had rounded her body back into its nuptial perfection. She was provocative, tantalizing, seductive. My hands were attracted to her body like filings to a magnet.

Freedom from the fear of immediate pregnancy had reignited my woman's sexual appeal and her sexual hunger. Rosemarie loved being a mother. She wanted a fifth child, so she hardly was a victim of the contraceptive mentality against which the leaders of our church would rail. A time of respite from childbearing and more responsibilities of child rearing had given her new life and new hope. She was a happy, satisfied, self-confident woman.

I talked to Father Raven, now a pastor in a Negro (as we called it then) parish, about it on the golf course one afternoon during his annual visit to Mom and Dad's place. He was at least ten strokes ahead of me when I raised the question.

"I don't see"—he paused for a backswing—"how most men and women living with the demands of our culture can be asked to sleep in separate bedrooms. Arguably it's an ideal, and that's what some of the moralists, even in Rome, are saying, but an ideal that is virtually impossible in practice."

"We Americans don't like to admit that we are deviating from an ideal. We'd like to think that what we're doing because of our decisions is good and virtuous." My drive carried fifty yards at the most.

"I'm merely offering you one way out. Can your marriage survive without sex?"

"With Rosemarie?"

"In separate bedrooms?"

"Not a chance."

"Well?"

I hit my second shot; with an image of Rosemarie in my head it carried close to a hundred yards.

"You have to preserve your marriage, don't you?"

"Lesser of two evils?"

"That's how you could explain it to the Vatican."

"I see."

As well as I ever would.

I do understand how in the next ten years the Church came to lose its once enormous credibility as a sexual teacher. It didn't listen to married people (even though it admitted that it should listen to them) and eventually married people didn't listen to the Church.

And I had to contend not only with a healthy and happy wife but an insatiable one.

"I began this summer," she murmured one unbearably hot evening, "determined that I had to please you if I wanted to win you back. Now I'm just a pleasure-hungry tart."

"Pleasure-hungry wife."

"Same difference."

"You never had to win me back, Rosemarie."

"You know what I've learned?" Her fingers traced a path from my face to my loins. "I've learned that a husband and a wife always have to win one another. It's a challenge and an amusement that just never stops. Once you think you've won him permanently, then you've lost."

"You're probably right."

Her fingers moved back up my body, light, teasing, frivolous. "Just as true for the man as for the woman. Courtship is not a time. It's—what word am I looking for?—it's a dimension of marriage."

"Absolutely."

It was that night, I think, that I began to see something about our marriage, something very important, that I did not want to see. I mean see it the way I "saw" Jim Clancy's great little practical joke.

The "vision" was obscure that hot summer evening, but it was there in my head as my wife mounted on top of my body, and it would remain in the obscure dark alleys of my brain, haunting and bedeviling me. Like the image of Jim Clancy's ice-cream bar.

Our renewed romance, courtship, passion continued on the trip to Europe, especially when we left behind the ceremonies and Frankfurt and

Bonn and Stuttgart and in Rosemarie's 300 SL roadster, bought in Stuttgart, traveled by ourselves through the German cities and countryside.

"You're going to sell the gull-wing when we get home?"

"Course not, it's certain to be a classic."

"It leaks and it's hard to get into the damn thing."

"That's why it will be a classic. This one probably will be too, and it cost only eighteen hundred dollars. A bargain like that you can't pass up."

We had opened the show in Stuttgart and would return at the end of the trip to receive some sort of prize. At first I anxiously watched the crowds who came into the gallery for a sign of Trudi or Magda or Erika.

Then I realized that my mixture of anxiety and hope was ridiculous. If they had not tried to get in touch with me in the last twelve years, why would they wander into a gallery exhibiting my pictures?

And would I recognize any of them?

Probably not.

We had dinner with Kurt and Brigitta, older now yet still handsome, and their four quiet and smiling kids. He was rector of the university and a member of parliament, she a Frau Professor. They told Rosemarie stories of my Bamberger exploits that went far beyond simple truth, just like the now legendary game with Mount Carmel.

We stayed at the reconditioned Bamberger Hoff and ate dinner at the Vinehaus Messerschmidt, as it was again called. Rosemarie insisted that the last night of our visit be spent in my old room at the Vinehaus.

She announced that the room was cute, even adorable, and seduced me with joyous determination.

Only much later did it occur to me that I had made love once with another woman in the same room.

"It's almost impossible to describe how the city has changed," I would tell her often in the next couple of days. "It's hardly the same place. I felt like kind of reverse deja vu; I feel like I was never here before."

In the decade that had passed, Bamberg had shed its drab and worn coat and clad itself once more in a sparkling set costume for a medieval film. Or maybe it was only the difference between winter and summer.

We walked through the Altstadt, visited the rose garden of the Residence, admired the Rider in the Dom, even retraced the path down the Judenstrasse from the Oberfarre to Kasernstrasse. Bamberg was a young and chic countess again. Those who had despoiled her had stayed to become her servants and admirers. Trudi's house on the Obersandstrasse still seemed shabby. It exuded no magic vibrations for me, no reminders that up there on that second floor I had been initiated into the mysteries of love.

"Was this street important to you?" Rosemarie asked me. "You seem kind of spooked."

"We tried to pick up some East German refugees here, turn them over to the Russians."

"Did you?"

"Blew it."

"Deliberately?"

"You bet."

She laughed in approval.

I said very little as we strolled back across the Rathaus bridge, except to say that Cunnegunda had reminded me of Mom when I was here before.

My wife nodded silently. Then she threw her arms around me. "Poor, dear Chuck. You must have been so homesick."

"I missed all the women in my life, I guess."

My Rosemarie wept in my arms, beneath the smile of Saint Cunnegunda, for pain that I had not understood and still couldn't quite acknowledge.

She would frown from time to time, trying to puzzle out, trying to understand, wanting to share in my teenage experience, but not able to grasp it.

"Sometimes I think I know what you mean," she said with a sigh as we drove out to the farmhouse in the Bohemian Alps. "Then it eludes me."

"Don't worry, I'm not sure I trust my memory. I'm concentrating on what I see today. Let the contrasts emerge from the work."

She nodded her agreement.

The farmhouse wasn't there anymore. It had been replaced by a big new home with an adjoining barn. In front of the house was a Mercedes 180. A tall, slender young man was working on a tractor in front of the barn, a boy about the age of Kevin assiduously trying to help him.

"That's the boy who was in the house when we raided it," I said, pointing at the young man.

"Doesn't look much like a werewolf."

A sturdy young woman emerged from the house to shout something to her husband. Two younger kids, a boy and a girl, trailed behind her.

Rosemarie explained in her colorfully inaccurate German that I was an American photographer interested in pictures of German farms. Would they mind if we took some shots?

At first they hesitated, then, won by my wife's dizzy charm, they laughed and agreed with great good nature. They even served us some strawberries and thick cream.

"They didn't recognize you, did they?" she asked as we left.

"I had a big old white helmet on. I was a pale, scrawny kid and scared silly of the SS, who we thought were lurking in the house. No reason that they should recognize me."

"Well you're not pale after the summer at Long Beach."

"I'm still scrawny?"

"In an attractive way. Hey"—she dodged my lascivious hands—"don't distract the driver."

"I'm not going to show the picture of the farm today in a companion shot with the farm twelve years ago. There's no point in that"—I continued to distract her, but with less insistence—"and it wouldn't be fair to them. Anyway, this is not to be a before-and-after project."

"It may be"—she frowned again—"that he doesn't even remember the incident, not really, anyway. Memory is a strange phenomenon."

I had the bad taste to remember the bridge just outside the town where Trudi and I had made love—if that was what it should be called. And then I had the good taste to dismiss the image of bringing Rosemarie there.

I would find another place.

"You are still distracting the driver, depriving the poor woman of her sanity, in fact."

"I know a mountain stream with a little meadow. We could eat lunch there."

"And?"

"Well, we could see what happens."

"I'm sure it will."

It did.

"Clever of you to bring a blanket, husband mine."

"I try to be prepared."

"I noticed."

Eventually we drove back to Stuttgart, happy with one another and pleased with ourselves.

I would receive the prize at the big concrete gallery, then we would drive into the Black Forest for the final five days of my planned shoot. When that was finished we would fly back to O'Hare in a jet, thank God.

I never did remark that this year the kids were able to get ready for school not only without my presence, but without their mother's presence.

Disaster struck the first full day in Stuttgart, the day before I was to receive the prize.

Late in the afternoon, while I was working on my acceptance speech, I heard Rosemarie stride into our suite and slam the door with more than her usual vigor.

Earthquake.

I didn't have to look around to know that she was furious with me.

"Well!"

I did look around. Her face was drawn, there was a tiny red spot on each cheek. Her lips were drawn in a thin, dangerous line. She was breathing heavily. I had never seen her so angry.

I could not avoid the quick thought that angry in a white two-piece dress Rosemarie was incredibly lovely.

"What's wrong?"

"I just had tea with Trudi."

"Who?"

"Trudi Weiss—that's her name now. And I saw your son, a very cute little redhead that looks just like you."

"My son?"

"His name as you may well imagine is Karl. That's German for Charles, as I'm sure you know."

30

"Why didn't you tell me?" She slapped a card with an address on it next to the manuscript of my talk. "That's where Frau Weiss lives. You ought to visit her, you know."

Her eyes said "murder"—the same rage I had captured twice when she was a child. I was afraid for myself and for our children.

The fear that had been teasing at the corner of my mind since her father's death had now become raw terror.

I passed my tongue over my dry lips, searching for words that I could not find. "I didn't know about the boy, I really didn't. I searched here often when I was in the service. They disappeared. How did you find them?"

"I was over at the gallery"—she collapsed into the big beige couch on the other side of our suite—"listening to what the *volk* were saying. They like the stuff, not that it matters anymore. And then I see an O'Malley, a junior version, but a real O'Malley, no doubt about him. He's with his mother, a blonde. I recognize her too. She's the girl in your picture, you know which one."

"Yes."

"Well"—Rosemarie was surging toward hysteria—"I follow them home, ring the doorbell of their nice little house, and say that I would like to take a close look at my husband's son."

"Dear God, Rosemarie, why?"

"Why not? Your Trudi doesn't try to bluff. She recognizes me instantly from all the pictures in the gallery. She invites me in for tea. Wasn't that sweet of her?"

Would I be able to explain? Ever? In terms that Rosemarie could understand? I wasn't sure.

"It's not what you think, Rosemarie."

"Oh"—she waved her hand contemptuously—"she told me a little of the glorious story. What a hero you were. Saved them all."

"I did not want to abandon them. I searched—"

"I don't care about that." She leaped off the couch. "What I want to know is why the fuck you didn't tell me?"

It was a fair question. I had thought about it often and prepared my answer. The only trouble was that now I couldn't remember it.

"Rosemarie"—my voice cracked on the word—"I thought about it and I decided that it would not . . . not help matters any."

"I told you about Dad."

"That was different."

"How the fuck was it different?"

"You said then that the reason to tell me was to explain why . . . why you would be under stress sometimes. I didn't think that my . . . my affair with Trudi made that much difference."

"Screw them and leave them, huh, O'Malley?"

Why didn't I yell at her to shut up and act her age?

It never occurred to me to do so. I felt too guilty to defend myself.

"It wasn't that way, Rosemarie. It really wasn't. We were both young and lonely and scared. I thought I loved her. I don't know, to tell you the truth, what she thought, whether in her situation she had any choice. She wasn't a whore, Rosemarie, nothing like that."

"That's patent. I'm not angry at her. I'm angry at you."

"We weren't engaged then, Rosemarie. I was not unfaithful to you. I've never been unfaithful to you."

"Was she better in bed than I am?" She was striding back and forth across the parlor. "Were her tits better than mine?"

"No to both questions, not that they're to the point. We were kids, Rosemarie, kids."

"You still love her, don't you? Do you want to divorce me?"

"Rosemarie, that's asinine. Calm down so we can talk about it reasonably. You're acting like a maniac."

"Do you think so? Funny, I don't, you miserable, lousy little son of a bitch. I asked you a question. I demand an answer. Now that I've found your mistress for you, do you want to get rid of me?"

"All right." I buried my face in my hands. "I'll answer if you insist, but I think our years together should make the answer clear before I say it."

"Goddamn it, you little motherfucker, answer me!"

I didn't mind the "motherfucker," although it was not part of Rosemarie's normal vocabulary. Or even her drunken vocabulary. I didn't like the "little" at all, but now was not the time to debate that.

"No." I sighed. "I don't want a divorce."

"Do you still love her?"

"Not the way I love you."

"That's not an answer."

"Yes, it is," I shouted back, "you've no right to cross-examine me this way!"

"Right! Will you look at who's talking about rights? Well, I have a right to know if you still love her. DO YOU STILL LOVE HER?"

"I haven't seen her"—I struggled out of my chair at the table, now angry myself—"in ten years."

"So?"

"Damn it to hell, Rosemarie, will you simmer down and listen? It was a teenage love affair, a long time ago. It has nothing to do with us now."

"Then why didn't you tell me?"

"I thought it would unnecessarily upset you—"

"And there I was"—she slammed the table—"thinking that you were very clever as a virgin lover. She taught you how to love."

"You taught me a lot more," I said heavily.

"Bullshit . . . you still haven't answered my question: DO YOU STILL LOVE HER?"

"I have fond memories"—I tried to choose my words carefully, knowing that I was guilty till I was proven innocent, and I couldn't prove myself innocent—"of those months. As anyone would of a teenage love affair. But I have no desire, not the slightest, to renew that affair. You're my wife and my lover and my agent and my friend. There isn't, there can't be, there never will be anyone else."

"Bullshit. You're a lousy lying little fucker," she screamed. "I'll never trust you again."

"Is there nothing that I can say"—I was filling up with tears now, my whole life disappearing before my eyes—"that will persuade you that . . . it's been over for ten years?"

"There's a red-haired little boy that suggests it hasn't."

"I didn't know about the boy."

"Are you proud that you have an illegitimate child?"

"Of course not. But I'm glad he's alive."

"I BET you are."

"I can't take this anymore, Rosemarie." I choked on the words. "I'm going out for a long walk. I hope you've calmed down when I come back."

"Don't bother coming back!" she shouted after me.

I walked for hours, all the way to the outskirts of the town, almost as far as the Mercedes works. I knew that I had bungled the confrontation. My decision not to tell her about Trudi, damn it, was the right one. Why couldn't she see that?

Because she was shocked and upset. Understandably. She had reason to vent her emotions. I should have vented my emotions back at her. The confrontation flickered out because I had run away from the fight. It would have been much wiser to stand up to her and clear the air. If I had continued to shout at her, she would have run out of steam eventually and we could have picked up the pieces.

I could not deal with an angry woman who shouted obscenities at me. I had run away from my wife's temper and foul tongue.

Mistake.

I was not at all sure that I could avoid the mistake again when I returned to the hotel.

I walked back to the Bahnhaus Platz with much less energy than had marked my hike to the edge of the city. Too much exercise, I told myself as I rode up the elevator to our suite that I absolutely had to stand up her.

I wasn't sure I could.

In fact I didn't have to.

There was a note waiting on the bed:

"Gone home."

31

"Your wife is even more beautiful in person than she is in the photographs." Trudi Weiss was stiff and formal as she poured tea. "She was so polite and kind with me. I was afraid that she would be angry. But she is quite sweet."

You bet.

"She will not be angry with you?" Trudi continued. "I imagine it was quite shocking for her to see a little boy who looked so much like you."

"My only red-haired child," I said ruefully as I balanced the teacup in my hand, "so far."

"Yes, that is what Frau O'Malley said."

Did she now?

There was no doubt that the cute redhead playing in the backyard was my son. He looked like me and was blessed with the O'Malley family zest in greater amounts, I dare say, than I ever was. He had bounced in from school, dropped his schoolbooks, shaken hands politely with me, and then vaulted into the yard with his soccer ball. His athletic talents had certainly not come from me.

"She is angry? She was, as I say very sweet, but she seemed under great tension."

"Rosemarie is high-strung." I sipped the tea. "She'll be all right in a day or two."

I spoke with a lot more confidence than I felt.

"It was foolish of me to come to the gallery. I had seen all your books. Including"—she smiled faintly—"my picture. I wanted to see the prints themselves."

"And perhaps see me?"

She considered her teacup. "Perhaps. I hope I did no harm."

"Why didn't you write me?"

"I found I was pregnant." She looked up and quickly averted her eyes again. "It was my fault. I did not want to be one of those women who seduced an American so they could go home with him. I thought that would be most improper. Magda and Erika—yes, we use our own first names again—agreed. You were so young and innocent and brave. Was that not correct behavior?"

"I think you were pretty brave too."

She shrugged indifferently. "I did not intend to use you, Karl. I told myself that then and I still say it. I was so confused and so frightened. I did love you. Or I thought I did"—she was crying now—"or I told myself that I did . . . the confusion all returns when I talk about it."

Herr Weiss was a former Luftwaffe pilot. Together they owned an import-export company. They were "quite successful," as she put it. Their detached house, spanking new, with a big garden in back and elegant Scandinavian furniture in every room, was sufficient proof of that. The house smelled of fresh varnish and was so polished and bright that I had the impression that it had just been unwrapped from clean brown packing paper. The German "economic miracle" writ small.

Herr Weiss was a very good husband, I was told, kind and gentle and hardworking—not at all authoritarian like so many German men are "even today." He loved little Karl like a child of his own and the love was returned. He knew who the boy's father was. He too "admires your work greatly."

Magda had remarried, a surgeon at the hospital. She too was happy in her new life. Erika was a student at the university in Tübingen.

Here were some recent snapshots.

Magda looked twenty years younger than she had in Bamberg—a handsome woman in her late forties with an equally distinguished-looking husband. Erika was quite a young beauty. Herr Weiss was a genial giant, a bit overweight, with an instantly attractive smile. Karl looked like Charles Cronin O'Malley in his First Communion picture. Especially since it was his First Communion picture.

They all lived happily ever after.

"I will always be grateful to you, Karl, for my new life. And for little Karl too."

Was there any sexual chemistry between us?

Not the slightest at first. I found it hard to believe that I had ever made love, at times wanton love, with this stilted, formal woman, the very model of upper-middle-class Teutonic propriety. I might not have even recognized her.

Not that time had been harsh to my first romance. She was a handsome, self-possessed woman approaching her thirties with a mature attractiveness which would be well preserved by the best clothes and the most expensive makeup. But voluptuous she was not. Indeed, she could hardly be said to be beautiful. Had she ever been beautiful?

The most that could have been said for the girl in the picture was that she was pretty.

"I learned a lot from you too, Trudi."

"You have no regrets then?" She offered me a piece of fruitcake. I declined politely. I must return for the presentation of the prize.

"No. You?"

"But of course not."

I rose to leave. "Should we stay in touch now that I have found you?"

She rose too, slim, fastidious, well groomed, polite. "What do you think, Karl?"

"I will send you copies of my new books. Perhaps we can exchange Christmas cards."

"I think that will be very proper."

"If you and your family should come to America . . ."

"We would have to think about that, wouldn't we?"

"I suppose so." We were standing together at the door. My cab was waiting in the road. The name of the game was anticlimax.

Then my emotions changed completely. I had loved this woman once, passionately if shallowly. She had loved me too. That was over, but the picture of us being in bed together again was still very attractive. In theory, not in practice.

All right, that was better. Somehow.

I kissed her, solidly but briefly. She replied in kind.

"It is good to see you again, Trudi."

"It was most kind"—she faltered, suddenly close to tears—"of you to visit us. I am sure"—she regained control—"that Herr Weiss will be happy to hear you were here."

I wanted to say something significant. So did she. I still love you. I shall be ever grateful to you. I am happy that you are happy.

None of the words came.

Trudi had the last words.

"God is good."

I wasn't so sure.

In the yard, little Karl was still kicking his soccer ball. Probably a little kraut with no wit or humor.

Then he grinned up at me as he missed a kick. Ah, there was a little Celt in him after all. I picked him up, spun him in the air, and kissed him.

The little brat loved it, just like his father had at the same age. And, unlike his father, he wasn't afraid to show it.

He took affection for granted. So I hugged him and kissed him again and waved goodbye to his mother, who had been watching us uncertainly from the door. He laughed and she smiled and for a moment she was the Trudi of old as she waved at me.

"*Auf Wiedersehen*, Herr O'Malley," my son said.

"Till we meet again," I replied in English.

For a couple of moments I felt happy. And then I remembered Rosemarie.

I had phoned home that morning, forgetting that Rosemarie would have been able to catch a plane out of Frankfurt only about the time I was calling. Why had I not gone up to Frankfurt, I demanded of myself, and brought her back?

Because I was afraid of her, that's why.

I went through the pompous formalities of the award and the endless toasts of the big, heavy dinner thereafter with my mind elsewhere. What should I do? Let it blow over and then go back, or cancel the rest of the trip and go home right away?

I was furious at my wife and became more furious every time one of the hosts expressed infinitely courteous dismay that the lovely Frau O'Malley had been called home because of an illness in the family.

She'd run out on me at a critical time, damn her. She had reason to be upset, granted, but no reason to act like a spoiled child.

Like her father.

And I felt very guilty about that comparison. As I should have.

Dear God, what might she do to the children?

Was she really a killer?

Maybe she had reasons before. What if she thought she had reasons now?

In my comedy of errors, coming back to Stuttgart was the worse mistake of all, the most unpleasant surprise.

I called her the next morning. She hung up as soon as she heard my voice. I thought about calling Peg and decided against it. She might be as furious at me as Rosemarie was.

So I called home.

"I'm so glad you called, darling," the good April murmured dimly. "Rosemarie flew home yesterday. She was quite upset. Had a wild story about your having a mistress in Germany all these years."

"Mom, have I been back in Germany since I was discharged from the Army?"

"That's what I said to her, darling. She didn't seem to comprehend, poor thing." Pause. "She'd had a little bit to drink."

I was sure that would happen. Damn the woman. "Probably more than a little."

"Poor child, she's had a hard life."

"I'm tired of hearing that, Mom."

"Yes, darling, I'm sure you are. She is too, I think."

I looked at the phone. Mom had never said anything quite like that before.

"I wonder if I should come back or stay here and finish my project. . . ."

Her answer was prompt and decisive, most unlike Mom. "I don't think you could be any help now. Why don't you finish your work, dear, and then come home. Peg and Dad and I will keep an eye on the children and make sure nothing serious happens." This couldn't be my mother, could it? "Darling?"

"Yes?"

"Are you still there?"

"Yes, Mom, I was thinking about what you said. I suppose you're right. I'll finish the work. Keep in touch, will you?"

"Certainly, darling."

"And Mom . . . take care of her if you can."

"Certainly, dear, until you come home."

What did she mean by those last four words?

I was supposed to do something when I came home?

What?

Again the vision of our marriage loomed, dark and ominous in the twilight corridors of my brain, back alleys like those in Bamberg. It faded away, more slowly this time.

I picked up the phone to call Trudi, laughed at myself, and put it back on the receiver.

What did Mom expect me to do?

I was afraid even then that I knew.

32

"He does look a little bit like you, dear, a very pretty little boy."

"That her husband?" Dad peered over my shoulder. "Nice-looking guy. My kind of man, I suspect."

"Probably," Mom agreed. "Have another sip of port, dear."

Port glasses in hand, my parents were calmly and dispassionately considering pictures of my sometime mistress and my illegitimate son. Doesn't one see pictures like that every day?

"I have to say, Chuck"—Dad refilled my glass—"that I really didn't think you had it in you."

"She really is quite an attractive young woman." Mom peered closely with her trifocals. "Perhaps not your type exactly, but still stunning."

I could not believe my ears. These were my straitlaced, West Side Irish Catholic parents.

"You guys seem proud of me."

"Well, we don't completely approve," Mom said as she put the pictures down, "but she is very attractive."

"And how could we not like that little boy?" Dad sipped his port, the best you could buy in Chicago now. "Even in your self-deprecating version of the events, you seemed to have acted, well ... with courage and resourcefulness."

"And as I say"—Mom finished her glass of port—"all's well that ends well. Isn't that true?"

In this best possible of all best possible worlds.

The redheaded punk may have been a bastard, but he was their grandchild.

They had met me outside of customs at O'Hare. Peg and the others had apparently been warned off. Things were not good on Euclid Avenue. Mrs. Anderson and the maid had been fired. Phone calls from Peg and Mom were not answered. The kids were crying. Mrs. Anderson wouldn't leave. Peg had crept in every day to make sure that nothing bad was happening. Rosemarie started drinking early in the morning and was drunk by noon. She spent the day locked in her office, drinking, smoking, and playing records. She wouldn't talk to anyone. Some nights she slept in the office.

However, there were some signs that the drinking was tapering off. Last night when Mom had called, she had spoken for the first time. "Leave me alone. I wish I were dead."

"But, dear, she sounded almost sober."

And poor Mrs. Anderson reported that she had gone up to her own room.

I was brought to the parental house on East Avenue with advice that I spend the night there. The place was as always awash in blueprints. How did anything ever get built?

"I must say"—Mom was plucking at the harp, adjusting the keys—"that I think Rosemarie has behaved very badly in this matter. Very badly, poor thing."

"What a man does before he is married," my father mused, "is his business."

My mother raised a delicate eyebrow. "And a woman too."

"Well"—my father laughed genially—"what's sauce for the gander . . ."

"The other way around, Vangie darling."

These two charming strangers were going to tell me exactly what they thought I should do. I'd better listen carefully.

"The child"—Mom tightened a harp string—"has always been a little, uh, delicate."

I had not told them about Rosemarie and her father. That was a secret to be revealed to no one.

"Small wonder"—Dad picked up a roll of blueprints, looked at them in surprise and then put them at the other side of his big worktable—"with those odd parents she had."

Mom plucked a string and frowned. "Mind you, there's nothing seriously wrong with her. She just needs a firm hand now and then, that's all."

"Firm hand?"

Dad nodded his agreement. "Firm hand."

"The poor thing would probably welcome it. She did behave very badly this time, didn't she?"

"What is the content of this firm hand?" I looked from one to the other of my parents. They had rehearsed the whole scene. How many other scenes . . . ?

"Content? Oh, you mean what should you tell her? Well, I think it's really very simple. Isn't it, Vangie dear?"

"Very simple indeed," Dad agreed.

"And it is?"

"Why, tell her, very gently but very firmly, that she has to see a doctor or you'll get a divorce and take the kids with you."

"I see. You mean a psychiatrist?"

"Well, yes, that's what they call them, isn't it? Like Ted?"

"Rosemarie isn't crazy, Mom."

My mother, who twenty years earlier would have talked in whispers about putting people away and about "Dunning" (the state mental hospital at the end of the Irving Park streetcar line), was now quite calmly prescribing psychiatric treatment for a daughter-in-law she loved almost as much as she loved her own daughters.

"Well, I know that, dear. She's probably not even an alcoholic, that's what they call them isn't it? She should really see a doctor, shouldn't she? I mean don't you think she ought to have a long time ago?"

"With parents like those two"—Dad nodded wisely—"it's a miracle she's survived as well as she has."

"Poor sweet thing." Mom began to play something pure and sweet.

I said that it was time for me to get some sleep. It looked like I had a long day tomorrow.

I woke up at three o'clock, as one usually does on the east-west jet lag, and tossed and turned for a couple of hours. Finally I got up, made breakfast for myself in the kitchen, read the papers, and made a few phone calls.

Promptly at ten o'clock, I asked my parents to wish me luck and walked down Greenwood to Euclid. It was a glorious Indian summer day, a promise that spring will come once again.

After a long hard winter.

A day just like the one on which I took her to dinner in the Chinese place on Fifty-fifth Street. Or like the day I had won my first tennis set from her.

I let myself into the house. April Rosemary, the complete oldest-child-fussbudget, embraced me and poured out the whole story.

In sum, "Mommy is real sick," and April Rosemary had to stay home from school to help Mrs. Anderson with the kids. And she had made Kevin go to school because he was no help at all.

"Fine," I said judiciously. "But now that I'm home you can go to school at lunchtime, can't you?"

"Yes, Daddy, if you write me a note for S'ter."

They were still S'ter, were they? "Sure I'll write a note. I better talk to Mommy first."

Actually, I went upstairs first to see Jimmy Mike and Sean, who were raising hell with Mrs. Anderson.

"She sure is sick, Mr. O'Malley, real sick."

"We'll take care of her, Mrs. Anderson, don't worry. And thank you for staying."

"She was so sick, I just couldn't leave."

Sick, huh? Drunk, that's what.

I knocked on the door of her study.

"Who's there?"

"Chuck."

"Go 'way, I never want to see you again."

"It's your house and your door. You're the one who will have to pay for it if I break it down."

Tough beginning, huh?

What if she says go ahead and try? You're in front of the house in the Bohemian Alps once again.

I was at least as scared as I had been in the hotel in Stuttgart. My throat was dry, my hands were wet, my chest hurt. The ugly vision of our marriage was now visible all the time, not focused yet, but looming there in grim and silent accusation, like the stone statue in *Don Giovanni*.

"Whatya want?"

I scarcely recognized my wife. Her face was bloated and puffy, her hair snarled, her blue bathrobe dirty, her makeup heavy and smudged, her eyes bloodshot—a chronic alcoholic who looked as if she had been in a mental institution for a month. The room smelled of cigarette smoke, urine, and vomit.

Elvis was singing on the phonograph; appropriately enough, the song was "Don't Be Cruel."

"I want to talk to you, Rosemarie." I turned off the power on the stereo system, causing poor Elvis to screech to a halt.

I never did like the so-and-so.

"I don't want to talk to you. Go 'way." She tried to push me out the door.

I refused to budge. "Nonetheless you are going to talk to me, understand?"

"Big fucking deal." Still, she backed off.

There was a lighted cigarette on one of her precious Ming dishes. She was aware of a foul aroma.

"Sit down, Rosemarie." I gestured toward the judge's chair behind her Sheraton desk.

"I don't have to."

"I said SIT DOWN."

Was that my voice? I wondered. What if she won't?

"Big fucking deal." She sat down.

Trying to maintain my appearance of calm, confident self-control, I walked to my appointed easy chair, removed an empty gin bottle from it, and deposited the bottle in the wastebasket.

"You have two choices, Rosemarie." I kept my voice firm and controlled as I recited my carefully prepared lines.

"Yeah?" she sneered at me. "I'm impressed."

She picked up the cigarette, inhaled, and blew smoke in my direction.

"The first choice"—I spoke very carefully—"is divorce. I spoke to Ed Murray this morning. He assures me that I will have little difficulty in obtaining custody of the children. I have every intention of doing so. I don't know what will happen to you after a divorce, but then you will be your problem and not mine."

Had I gone too far? Did I sound too harsh?

She drew on the cigarette again and then, impatiently, snuffed it out. "And?"

"And what?"

"The second choice, asshole."

"The second choice is that you phone a psychiatrist and make an appointment for treatment. Today."

She slumped back in her chair and bowed her head. Would there be an explosion? What would I do if she refused to choose?

"Which do you want?"

"The choice is yours, not mine."

She was silent for a few moments.

"Yeah, I understand, but I have to have some idea of which you prefer."

"The second, of course."

"Why?" she lifted her head and stared defiantly at me. Would there be more about whether I wanted to marry Trudi? "Wouldn't you be better off without me?"

"No."

"Why not?"

"Because I love you, as much as ever."

She looked down again.

I walked over to the window and opened the drapes so that the autumn sunlight could pour in. Such a beautiful day, not appropriate for ending a marriage.

Would she never speak?

And when she did, what would she say?

I turned around, impatient to end the scene. "Well?"

Her answer was one I could never have anticipated in all the scenarios that had run through my brain earlier in the morning. Yet the response was pure Rosemarie.

"I don't know any psychiatrists."

"What?"

"I said"—she glanced up at me and then looked away—"I don't know any psychiatrists. I mean, I can't talk to Ted, can I? My sister-in-law's husband and all . . ."

Such an easy surrender? Even at her worst the woman was a magical mystery. And the ugly vision in the back of my brain loomed larger, as temporarily the lights went up on the stage and then flickered out.

"Here are three names." I removed a sheet of paper from my notebook and put it on her desk.

"Ted's suggestions?"

"No."

She considered me suspiciously. "Whose?"

"Dr. Berman's."

"Oh. . . . He's a good man, isn't he?"

"The best."

"Fixed up that cute Kurt man, didn't he?"

"Yes."

She ran her finger down the list. "One's a woman. Martha Stone. She'll probably be best."

"Ted gave her the highest marks."

"All right, call her for me."

"No."

"No?"

If only I could stick it out for a few more seconds, I might just win for both of us. "You call her yourself."

"You want me"—she smiled crookedly—"to make it my commitment, not yours?"

"Precisely."

She reached for the phone, then hesitated.

Dear God, don't let her change her mind.

She ground out her cigarette (with a gesture that signaled the end), straightened her robe, flipped her hair off her shoulders, and sat up straight, like a seventh-grader right in front of S'ter's desk.

You look your best when you call a shrink for an appointment.

"Dr. Stone? May I talk to her please?" She turned away from me so I wouldn't see her face. "Yes, Doctor, I'm sorry to bother you. My name is Rosemarie O'Malley." Smooth as Irish linen, the president of an affluent parish women's society talking to Monsignor. "I'd like very much to talk to you. . . . That long a wait?" She turned to me, terror in her eyes. "Yes, I think you could say it's very definitely an emergency.

"Tomorrow? At two? Thank you very much, Doctor. I'll be looking forward to it."

Very softly she replaced the receiver.

Neither of us said anything for a long minute or two.

"Okay?" She raised an eyebrow.

"Okay," I said, and then realized that I still had to hang tough. "For the present."

"One step at a time."

I nodded. "One step at a time."

Too incredibly easy. Why had I been such a coward? What else could she possibly have said?

"Chuck, I think I'll go upstairs and sleep for the next twenty-four hours. I'll look bad enough when I meet the doctor. I don't want to look as bad as I do now."

"All right, I'll ask Mrs. Anderson to clean up in here."

"No, don't do that; poor thing has had to put up with too much of my shit this last week." She rose shakily. "I'll do it first thing in the morning."

She left the office on unsteady feet, but with a faint hint of determination in her shoulders.

I've done it, I thought with enormous relief. I've done it! I began to straighten up the room.

And, God help me, it was easy—the easiest thing in the world.

33

I woke up at four, fell back to sleep, and then didn't get out of bed till ten. The house was back to its routine order. Rosemarie's office was spotlessly clean and sweet-smelling.

"Missus went for a long walk," Mrs. Anderson told me. "Poor thing was up before me. She done cleaned up that whole mess by herself and threw out all them terrible cigarette boxes she bought."

I wondered what Rosemarie thought when she found her study neat and clean. She probably knew who had done it.

Poor thing? Mrs. Anderson had been around the Irish too much.

Rosemarie returned home at four, pale and haggard in a smartly tailored, light gray autumn suit. She went directly to her study, and, door open, scribbled furiously on a yellow legal-size notepad.

Progress, I supposed.

April Rosemary came to the darkroom, where I was preparing to develop my film from the trip to Germany. "Daddy . . ."

"Yes, dear?"

"Mommy is all pretty again."

"Thank you, dear, for telling me."

"You're wonderful, Daddy. You made her pretty again."

"Thank you very much, honey. I love you." Fine time to start crying.

"I love too, Daddy."

Rosemarie, a little less haggard, ate dinner with the rest of us. First, she asked the kids about what had happened in school the last week. Then, as though nothing had happened between us, she asked about the details of my last week in Germany.

"I arranged for shipment of the roadster."

"Oh, did you? That was very sweet."

What would happen next? There was no road map for this. I used my private darkroom line to tell Mom and Dad that it was so far, so good.

"Wonderful, darling, I knew you could do it. Now, excuse me, I must call Peg."

Everyone on the sidelines cheering.

I slept that night in the guest bedroom as I had the night before. I would not intrude back into the master bedroom unless I was asked.

Was that . . . proper?

Trudi's word.

I didn't want to fall back into old habits so quickly.

I figured that it was "proper" for the present, but not for the long run. Besides, my libido was dormant.

So it went to the end of the week, through the weekend (no discussion of a trip to Long Beach), and into the next week.

She was attending Mass again every morning. And certainly she was in daily contact with Mom and Peg. The old conspiracy of the three Irish goddesses was functioning again.

On Tuesday afternoon I abandoned the darkroom about four o'clock. My eyes were blurry from long hours of work. It was still too early to be certain, but it looked like the shoot in Germany had worked. There was, oddly enough, no discernible difference between pictures before our battle and afterwards.

As I opened the closet to find a light sweater, a very meek voice called from Rosemarie's study.

"Chuck, do you have a minute?"

I put the sweater back on its hanger. (You can guess who kept the closet neat.)

What would happen now? Another surprise, that much was certain.

Trim in a beige sweater and skirt, she was sitting at her desk. In front of her were a new legal-size notepad and a pen.

Resting against one of the legs of the desk was a green Marshall Field package.

"Sure you have a minute?" she asked anxiously.

"As many as you want."

"That's sweet. It may take less than a minute, even. . . . This is embarrassing. . . . My shrink wants me to ask . . . well, why you want to stay married to me. No"—she flushed—"she wants me to ask why you love me."

"It will take longer than a minute."

"As many as you want." She smiled wanly. My wild Irish Rosemarie was sneaking back, but slowly and cautiously.

"Let me figure it out." I tried to order my thoughts. "Now don't argue, let me finish."

"I promise." She picked up the pen and poised it over the yellow pad. "I have to write it all down."

"Like my idea notebook?"

"No, like your yellow pad!"

We both laughed, pleased that we were able to break the tension.

"These are not," I began unsteadily, "in their order of importance."

"I understand."

"You're a wonderful mother, except when you're compulsive and when the kids resist and you stop. You play the big-sister game with them to perfection. I've never seen anyone better at it."

She wrote rapidly.

"You've forced me"—my voice choked a little—"to do what I was afraid to admit to myself I wanted to do, and to be what I was afraid I couldn't possibly be. I don't think anyone else could have done that.

"You're smart, smarter than I am; shrewd, shrewder than I am; funny, funnier than I am. I couldn't find a better agent. You know everything. By next summer you will have passed me in the darkroom and God help me if you ever start looking through a viewfinder. And, oh yes, even when you're being hard as nails with clients, you still charm the birds out of the trees."

She hesitated, then continued to write.

"You're a marvelous lay, always were good, and you're getting better."

She was blushing furiously but still writing. "How do you spell 'lay'?"

"You're a magical mystery, always unpredictable, fascinating, hypnotic. I delight in your mystery. The more I know you, the more mysterious you become. Even if you weren't as beautiful as you are, you'd still drive me out of my mind by your marvelous surprises. Layer upon layer of mystery and surprise, even more fun to peel away than peeling away your clothes."

She looked up, pen still poised. "This is the first time I've heard a lot of these things."

"My fault for not saying them before and more clearly than I have."

She waved the pen, brushing aside my apology. "Regardless. I'm astonished. Finished?"

"No, put down that I think you have the most beautiful breasts in all the world."

"Chuck, I can't write that."

"Put it down. Otherwise your shrink will think I don't have any hormones. And add that the ass isn't bad either."

"All *right*."

"Finally, for the moment, I admire—no, adore—your guts, courage, determination, willpower, gallantry, whatever it should be called."

"Gall?"

"A lot more than that. Put all the words down."

"Yes, sir." She glanced over the list. "It's awfully hard to . . ."

"To believe?"

"No, Chuck, I believe you. You really have said most of this before. I just didn't hear it. It's hard to connect it with what I think of me."

"I'm right."

"I know you are," she answered promptly. "It will take a little while to absorb it, that's all."

She folded the paper and put it in her purse.

"I'm going to make it, Chuck." She sighed. "It'll be tough and it'll take time, but I'm going to make it."

"The shrink say that?"

"Certainly not." She waved her hand in dismissal of such an absurd thought. "Shrinks never commit themselves like that. She said that I had lots of resources, including a strong husband. Besides, I've survived this long, haven't I?"

"You have indeed, against long odds."

"And"—her voice cracked—"I'll be eternally grateful to you"—the tears begin to flow—"for insisting . . ."

She reached out across the desk to me.

I jumped up, grabbed her hand, kissed it, and then knelt on the floor next to her, the precious hand still pressed against my lips.

"My cute little redhead." She ruffled my hair and wept softly.

"One more thing," she said when it was time for the tears to stop. "Well, two more. I have to apologize."

"No, you don't."

"Yes, I *do*." Her hand slipped away from my lips. "And I have to do it without hating myself like I've done the other times."

I wrapped my arms around her knees and rested my head on her thighs—an appropriate enough position to receive an apology.

"You see . . . well, that's how it went all wrong in Stuttgart. I knew right after you left the hotel that I'd been terrible. I was astonished by Trudi and Karl and upset and angry and that was all right. But I should have listened to you and accepted your explanation, which was obviously the truth. Instead I was furious, mostly at myself. I tried to write out an apology, I wanted to say that it was really kind of a sweet story and that it shouldn't have hurt me at all and that I knew you loved me and that I'd been a little shit. Then I concentrated on me as shit instead of you as hurt. So I tore up the apology and ran away. I was mad at me, not you."

I tightened my grip on her knees.

"So I apologize twice, first, for being so angry at you when I had no reason to be, second, for punishing you because I was mad at me. I won't do it again. No, that's too much. I'll try not to do it again."

"You're not a shit."

Silence. Then, "The woman on this page isn't. She does shitty things sometimes, though."

"And who is she?"

More silence. "Me. I. Whatever."

We both laughed again, cautiously, hopefully.

Then we were silent again, each with our own thoughts.

"It's the business with Daddy, poor man. Not just the rape. He wanted a son. I've always felt second-best, like I'd let him down. And kind of soiled."

"You're *not* soiled."

Her fingers tightened in my hair. "That's what you say."

"I'm right."

"I know." She sighed. "I know . . . we never talked about it after that night."

"I didn't know what to say." I shifted uncomfortably. "I knew it was the problem, but . . ."

"You're not my therapist," she growled. "You don't have to say anything, unless I say something, okay?"

"Okay."

"Just so you understand that none of the shit has anything to do with you. When I drink it's me I'm mad at, not you. Ever. Okay?"

"Okay."

For the moment.

Again I waited for her to resume the conversation.

"And one more thing, Chuck." She hesitated. "I'm terribly sorry for laughing at you."

"When did you laugh at me that you shouldn't have laughed at me?"

"That day at Riverview . . . when you got sick on the Flying Turns."

"My God, Rosemarie, that was in 1945!"

"I know . . . and I've felt guilty about it ever since."

"I think I was rude when you tried to help me. I'm sorry about that too, but . . ."

"It's always bothered me, I was such a little bitch."

"I was scared stiff by your concern afterwards. Does that help?"

"A little." She slipped out of my grip. We both rose.

"Finally?"

"Finally . . . my, I'm as organized today as you are . . . well, finally . . . I mean, that Field's package."

Inside the package I found a white diaphanous gown and robe. They made them more transparent every year.

"If you want to do the lace and candlelight and claret"—soft laugh—"for you, that is, and steak thing tonight after I put the kids to bed . . . I mean, you don't have to . . ."

"I think"—I placed the package on her desk—"that I might want to."

"Great!" She snatched the gown up and beamed as she draped it around her body. "I figured you might. Now go back to your darkroom and let me get the family organized."

"I think I'll take a walk first."

"Whatever." She dismissed me with a wave of her hand.

I should have been overwhelmed with joy. My gamble had paid off. My Rosemarie had been reclaimed from the brink. It was the high tide and the turn, as the poem says. Yet as I walked very slowly through the autumn finery, I now knew what it was that I had been afraid to look at in the vision of our marriage. The ugliness of what I saw dismayed me.

The floodlights illumined the stage of my second big mistake in my marriage, just as they had the first mistake in the airport in Mexico City when we were returning from our honeymoon.

The candlelight dinner was all that was promised. Rosemarie was giddy and tense and embarrassed by the gown, which made imagination unnecessary. I ought to have been aroused to the edge of frenzy—my wife, even coming out of the depths, was incredibly lovely—but I felt dull, leaden, heavy.

"Something wrong, husband mine?" She passed the carrots to me. "The gown too much?"

"The gown is wonderful and the woman inside even more wonderful." I pushed back my chair and stood up. "It's me, not you."

"I don't understand, Chuck. If you'd rather wait till I am better . . ."

"That's not it." I started to pace restlessly. "This is all wrong, Rosemarie, all wrong."

"Wrong?" Worry lines spread across her face. "How?"

I slumped back into my chair. "I feel like I've been guilty of infidelity."

"I've given you enough reason." She reached across the table and took my hand.

"Not that kind of infidelity. Maybe something worse. Now I have to hunt for the right words, Rosemarie."

She continued to hold my hand, possessively, fiercely.

"Look"—I struggled to describe the "vision" I saw—"you've forced me to make my dreams of being a photographer come true, right?"

She nodded.

"Sometimes against the most dogged and stubborn opposition from me, right?"

She nodded again, a faint smile twitching at her lips.

"And last spring, when I was running on empty, you forced me to stop and refuel, right?"

"Not the best metaphor, but okay."

I grinned back at her, still feeling hollow and drained. "All right, you forced me to renew our marriage. Whenever you did push me, you took a great risk. You could never be sure how I'd react—"

"I was pretty sure."

"You drew the line. Clancy lowered the boom."

She tilted her head and stared at me intently, trying to understand. "If you want to put it that way."

"I grew up in a family where lines aren't drawn. And the booms aren't lowered. No, that's not true. They are lowered all the time, they're as subtle as the atmosphere. But because they're so subtle, I never learned how . . ."

"And you married a woman on whom subtlety of this sort would be completely lost?" She was smiling again, and clinging to my hand for dear life.

"I was astonished by your answer to my ultimatum."

"That I didn't know any psychiatrists? But I didn't?"

"That you would see one at all."

She frowned, puzzled. "What else could I say? You were right. I knew that as soon as you said it."

"Don't you see? I could have insisted that you see a psychiatrist anytime since our honeymoon and you would have done so, right?"

"Promptly. I'd even thought about it myself pretty often. I needed a little push."

"I wouldn't push. I was too frightened to give that little push. So I let you go through years of unnecessary hell. Isn't that infidelity?"

"You've been a good husband, Chuck." Her eyes were filling up. "Don't do this to yourself."

"Pretty good, maybe, some of the time, but I messed up on this. I'm the one who needs to be forgiven. Not you."

"I never thought of it that way." She still watched me, puzzling, searching. "I suppose you're right, kind of. Maybe this is the first time I'm really ready for it. . . . *Anyway*"—she grinned crookedly—"I *do* forgive you"—the tears flooded up again—"the way you forgave me, and . . ." Her crooked grin exorcised the tears. "Don't let it happen again!"

"I'll try."

"You'd *better*. Now, do you want ice cream or me?"

"The ice cream can wait."

"Good. Let's go to your room. I mean, we'll go back to *our* room tomorrow, but tonight I want to feel that I'm so attractive that my husband just dragged me off."

"I think I can manage that."

Our love was quiet and restrained, a subdued wedding night.

"Not as passionate as last summer," she murmured apologetically.

"What we begin now will be much better than the summer."

"It won't always be easy, Chuck."

"I know that."

It wasn't easy, not at all, especially not the next day, when I forced myself to work up the courage to ask Peg what had really happened the day Clarice Clancy had died.

34

"Why should you believe me"—Peg refilled my teacup—"if you don't believe your wife?"

We were sitting in the "sunroom" of the Antonelli house. Outside, the tender warmth of Indian summer continued to bathe the world in golden gloss. Johnny Antonelli, the newest of the babies (with bright red hair), slept peacefully in his crib. His mother's violin lay on an antique table next to the music stand. Dressed in a white blouse and dark blue slacks, brown hair falling to her shoulders, slim, slim waist enclosed in a cowboy belt, her pert breasts firm against the fabric of her blouse, my sister was a wondrously beautiful, self-possessed woman—her mother's daughter with none of April's vagueness.

"I believe that she believes what she told me." I barely tasted the tea. "But if I'm going to see her through this period in her life, I have to know the truth."

Peg sat on the couch against the wall of the sunroom and lifted her own teacup. "I suppose so." She nodded. "Maybe you should have seen me about this long ago."

"Maybe I should have done lots of things long ago."

"Is she going to make it, Chuck?" Peg sipped her tea slowly, thoughtfully.

"Yes."

She nodded again. "I think so too. . . . You should hear her talk about you. Poor child adores you. 'He's so authoritative that I just know he has enough strength for the two of us.' "

"Rosemarie has more than enough strength for herself."

"Sure she does." Peg grinned. "But let her think that you're the powerful one just now. Seriously, Chuck"—astonishingly, my sibling's eyes were shining with admiration—"you've been wonderful, just perfect with her this time. I *know* it will work out."

"I'm ashamed that I waited so long. And maybe I ought to be ashamed that I let this . . . this doubt torment me."

"Well . . . more tea? . . . it was never a problem till now. I mean, Rose is a great kid, but face it, Chuck, she's come from a strange family. She's worth the effort, but let's not fool ourselves about the effort."

Peg was a stranger to be discovered, just as my mother had been.

"I will believe you, Peg," I said simply.

"I'm sure of that." She uncurled her long legs, walked to the coffee table, refilled her cup, and passed a plate of cookies to me. I succumbed to the temptation, as I always do. "You know that her father was molesting her?"

"Raping her."

"I thought as much. She never said exactly what he was doing. I didn't know what incest was . . . exactly."

"She told me before we were married."

"Good for her. I hoped she would." Peg was frowning thoughtfully. "Her father was raping her, her mother was beating her. And somehow she still survived and is our wonderful . . ."

"Wild Irish Rosemarie!"

"Right." Peg grinned briefly and then became serious again. "What I have to do is figure out whether I should wait till her therapist sends her to me to find out what really happened that day or bring it up my-self."

"Do you have to choose?"

"Maybe not. Maybe it will come up indirectly. Anyway"—she blew on her tea—"I'll listen for the opportunity."

"She didn't kill her mother?"

"Certainly not." She sounded impatient with my stupidity. "I mean not only in the general sense that Clarice's problems were created by her own parents and by her husband, not by poor Rose, but in the more specific sense that she didn't push her down the stairs. The wonder is that Clarice didn't kill *her* before that day."

"The beatings were that bad?"

"Rosie tell you she came after us with an umbrella?"

"Yes."

Peg shook her head. "Poor kid can't admit to herself how bad it was. Chuck, it was a poker from the fireplace. If I hadn't been there, she would have killed Rose. You know the way Rosie is—all bark and no bite."

"Oh?"

"She'd try to ward off the blows when her mother hit her, but she'd never fight back. If I wasn't there, she would have tried to shield herself from the poker, but she wouldn't have done anything else."

"Really?"

"Sure, you know that Rosie's temper is all show, don't you? Hell, I figured that out in third grade."

"All show?"

"Sure. Has she ever hit you?"

"Well, no."

"See?"

"I've never hit her either."

"You don't have a temper. Anyway, count on it, like I say, there's no bite at all."

So now I learn that.

"What would have happened if you hadn't been there?"

"What would have happened?" Peg put down the cup and saucer with a bang. "Poor Rosie would have cowered at the door, hands over her head, and whimpered while Mama bashed her brains out."

The shadows were lengthening across Peg's vast garden of mums. Darkness and winter were approaching.

"Dear God!"

"Oh, He sent me all right."

"Rosemarie didn't push her down the stairs."

"Chuck, what's the matter with you?" Peg gestured at the pieces of my dossier next to her Belleek teapot. "Can't you draw the obvious conclusion from your evidence? Isn't it apparent who killed Clarice Clancy?"

"I'm afraid not."

But then I saw, just as she told me.

"I did." She rose from the chair and picked up her violin. "Who else? I'm glad I did. She would have killed Rose—that day or the next day or the day after. I saved Rosemarie's life. I'm not sorry about that at all."

"You pushed her down the basement stairs?"

"Not deliberately." She tucked the violin under her chin and began to tighten its strings. "She came at us with the poker and swung it at Rosie's skull. I pushed Rose out of the way and grabbed the poker. Poor dear woman, she was terribly strong when she was drunk. We wrestled all over the parlor for the poker. She pulled it out of my hands and ran back to the doorway where poor Rosie was bleating like a sheep at the stockyards."

"Peg—"

"I leaped on her back and pulled her away, so she missed, by maybe a few inches. Then she turned on me. I don't think she knew the difference between the two of us. We struggled for the poker again. Finally I pulled it out of her hands. She jumped on me and I pushed her back. Hard. Real hard. She tumbled over and . . . well, you can imagine the rest."

"But why does Rosemarie not remember the fight?"

"She can't permit herself to think"—Peg drew the bow across the strings—"that her best friend pushed her mother to her death. Better to imagine that it was pure accident or blame herself when she's worried and frightened. For all her strength, Rosie's pretty fragile sometimes. I don't have to tell you that, do I? By the way, Chucky Ducky," she tapped my head with the violin bow, "you're marvelously tender with her. Now that you draw the line or lower the boom or whatever, you're the perfect man for her. You know that—always did think you were perfect, didn't you, big brother?—but it doesn't hurt to hear it from someone else."

"Then what happened?"

She tested each of the strings, then rested the violin against the music stand. "I was scared. And terribly sad, because I knew Mrs. Clancy was dead. And I was excited—sky high—because I knew she would have killed us both. I had saved Rosie's life. She was hysterical, poor kid. So I knew I had to figure out what to do. I told her what we would have to say and made her promise to say exactly what I told her to say. I don't know"—she placed the violin under her chin again—"maybe we should have told the police the truth. Now I think they might have believed us. Still, Rosie has enough to carry through life as it is without a reputation as a killer."

She began to play something—Mozart, I think.

"Incredible."

She continued to play. Slowly, thoughtfully.

"Sometimes I can't believe myself that it really happened. The police were too dumb even to notice the gash on the door that the poker made. After it was all over I went back with your Brownie—remember you gave it to me when you went to Fort Benning—and took a picture of it. The gash I mean, with the poker next to it. I've got it around some place. I'll dig it up for you."

"In case you needed evidence?"

"I read mystery stories. It was probably silly. Anyway, I was as cool as the ice Mr. Walker used to bring up our back steps. Until the next night. Then I fell apart and cried myself to sleep. I still feel like crying, for poor Mrs. Clancy, I mean. I tell myself I did her a favor. Suppose that she had killed Rosie? How could she have lived with that?"

"You tell April?"

"MOM?" She suspended Mozart. "She would never have been able to cope! I told Daddy later. We went to see Father Raven. They both thought that maybe we ought to have called the police but that it was too late now. They both"—she shrugged indifferently—"thought I was a heroine."

"I agree. . . . No guilt?"

"A little. Not much. Like I said, she would have killed Rosie. Maybe me too. Naturally I told the guy." She tapped Vince's picture with her bow, "When we were married, I mean. He understood. Said"—she grinned— "he'd stay away from stairways when I was angry at him. . . . Do I sound indifferent to Mrs. Clancy's death? I'm not. I still weep for her. I pray for her every night. But I had to protect Rosie's head from the poker."

"No." I shut my eyes. "No, Peg, you don't sound indifferent at all."

Dear God in heaven, how much you must have loved my Rosemarie to send such a fierce and tender woman to protect her.

"We worried about you and Rosie. I mean all of us. Dad and I especially because I had to tell him most of what I knew. Mom is good on the little things, Dad on the big ones. We knew how much you had always loved her"—she laughed—"staring at her with your tongue hanging out. Well, almost. So we would have a hard time preventing the marriage. And she always loved you every bit as much as you loved her. But she had so many problems. . . ."

"You didn't want me to marry her?"

My whole world of explanations was coming apart.

She sat on the arm of my chair, put the violin on the coffee table, and put her arm around my shoulder.

"We wanted you to marry her. Wanted it in the worst way. But we worried, not about her, but about you. Finally Dad said, 'Hey, Chucky loves her. He'll take care of her and they'll both be happy. And we can't stop him anyway, even if we wanted to and I don't think we do.' So that was that. And it has all worked out, hasn't it?"

"I'm glad"—the words were true again in the saying—"that you didn't try to stop me."

"See!" She bounced off the arm of the chair and reached for her violin.

"This helps a lot, Peg." I stood up slowly, to make sure my legs were still capable of supporting me. "Together we can do it. Rosemarie and I. I'll yell if we need help."

"Damn well better," she said gruffly. "I'll walk you to the door."

She peered into the crib, as mothers do, to make absolutely certain that the child is still breathing. Johnny was very much alive. She smiled fondly at him, this ferocious woman warrior.

"I think"—I wrapped my arm around my beautiful sister—"I've lucked out with the women in my life—mother, sister, wife."

"You sure have." She was crying against my shoulder. "Don't ever forget it."

"If I do you'll remind me."

"Oh, Chucky." She was sobbing now and clinging to me. "What would have happened to all of us if we hadn't grown up with Rosemarie to love and treasure?"

That was one way of putting it.

Come to think of it, maybe the only way to put it.

For the O'Malley clan, poor, fragile Rosemarie had been and still was pure grace.

— 35 —

I pondered the statement I had written the day after my conversation with my sister. Clipped to the paper was Peg's blurry picture of the door and the poker, not legal evidence, but conclusive as far as I was concerned.

> I have concluded my ill-advised and faithless investigation of the deaths of Clarice and James Clancy. The county coroner's verdict was correct in both cases—accidental death and murder by person or persons unknown.
>
> If my sister had not been present to intervene the day Mrs. Clancy fell down the steps, the woman would have killed Rosemarie—second-degree murder or perhaps voluntary manslaughter.
>
> Peg saved Rosemarie's life and arguably mine too.
>
> For what would I have been without my Rosemarie?
>
> Did Jim Clancy know the truth about what happened? I doubt it, or he would have tailored his story to fit the actual facts. In his bitter, hate-filled, love-starved mind he may actually have believed his version of the events.
>
> I stand guilty as charged: guilty of not trusting my wife; guilty, Othello-like, of permitting a tiny doubt to become a deadly cancer of suspicion; guilty of seeing murder in eyes where there was only raw terror. I thought I saw the expression of a black widow. But it was only the face, in Peg's excellent metaphor, of a lamb going to the slaughter.
>
> I write this concluding note and will maintain the file to remind myself of the folly of which I am capable, even about someone I always loved. More than life itself.
>
> The only worry that remains, just as it did when I found the papers in the safe at Lake Geneva, is the chocolate ice-cream-bar factor. I still worry about Jim Clancy's last trick. Maybe it's not out there, a trap waiting to be sprung. But deep down I think it is. I haven't won the game yet.

36

Rosemarie's battle for survival was a lot more difficult than either of us had expected that night of our reconciliation after the trip to Germany.

I had lowered the boom once, but despite Peg's reassurance that Rosemarie's bark was without bite, her rages still frightened me. It is one thing to have determined irrevocably that you are going to be faithful to your obligation to challenge your spouse and quite another to know when and how to make that challenge.

I still don't know whether Rosemarie's insistence that winter that she wanted to have our fifth child and "get it over with" was foolishness. Her psychiatrist had argued vigorously against it. We did talk about it and I did make my points about waiting a little longer till her therapy had progressed. Before I knew it, Moira was on the way.

It was a difficult pregnancy, much worse than any of the others. And it coincided with the most acutely difficult phases of her therapy, about whose details she almost never talked.

Yet there were good times too, times when I felt I had been especially blessed in my choice of a wife.

In early January, the phone rang in my office, the listed phone anyone could call.

"O'Malley," I said firmly.

"Charles C., how come I don't see you at the Magic Tap anymore?"

"I don't hang around there these days," I said, reaching for the voice.

"I don't either. Where *do* you hang out?"

"Timmy . . ."

"Who else?"

"You've come home?"

"Dragged home, Charles C. . . . by women!"

"Which women?"

"Well this Jenny Collins broad who claims to love me and your good wife Rosemarie H. who put her up to it. I don't suppose she told you."

"Home to stay?"

"Yeah, I've been talking to your good friend Dr. Berman. He wasn't surprised when I ambled into his office. Said I'd missed my last appointment and he'd charge me for it!"

Ten long years.

"You're going to marry Jenny?"

"Don't have much choice, do I?"

"I guess not."

"So where do you hang out these days? We should talk."

"Come over for supper. Rosemarie would love to see you."

He hesitated. "Yeah, soon. Something more informal first. Catch up, know what I mean?"

"We usually hang out at Petersen's on Chicago Avenue and Harlem."

"Yeah, you always were an ice-cream guy, weren't you? I am too these days."

"Tomorrow night, seven-thirty?"

"Why not? Bring your bride?"

"Bring yours?"

"No choice," he chortled. "See you then."

"Rosemarie," I said to her the next afternoon, "I have an insatiable craving for a malted milk."

"I'm the one who's pregnant."

"Regardless."

"Why not?"

Promptly at seven-thirty we were seated at our table. It had been a long time. The teenage waitresses didn't recognize us. The manager did. He demanded that we sing. So we did "Younger Than Springtime," our theme song. Jenny and Tim wandered in while we were singing, and joined in. Then came the hugs and the kisses and the squeals of delight.

I hadn't known Tim very well before he went into the service, so I couldn't say that he was his old self. He was, however, a relaxed and very funny man. Jenny glowed with happiness. We talked about the old days and old friends. He and Rosemarie compared notes about shrinks like they were people from New York.

"So what are you going to do now?"

"The usual thing . . . buy a house, have kids, get married, a little later than most people, but what the hell."

"In the reverse order," Jenny clarified for him.

"Sure . . . lemme see, which comes first? Oh, yeah, get married."

He hugged Jenny gently and added, "That's why I came back. No choice in the matter."

"You're not planning on working?"

"Hell, no! My family is so happy that I'm back they bought me a seat down at the Exchange. That should be a lot of fun!"

For Timmy Boylan it would be.

"You guys will come to the wedding."

"We wouldn't miss it!" Rosemarie said.

"You'll kind of be friends?" he said tentatively, for a moment so very fragile.

"Couldn't drive us away."

"Great! Let's have some more singing!"

So we went through our usual repertory of songs, much to the delight of the waitresses, who begged us to come back often. Rosemarie promised that we would—and we'd bring the kids.

As we were leaving, Tim hugged Rosemarie with one arm and shook my hand firmly with the other.

"Thanks, Rosie, Chuck, for never losing faith."

As we walked home, I said to Rosemarie, "Did we never lose faith?"

"I didn't. That's why I made Jenny go over to Ireland and bring him home."

"You didn't tell me about it."

"You had enough to worry about."

On a cold night in February of 1959, after we had returned from a trip to New York to arrange for my first exhibition at the Museum of Modern Art, Rosemarie glanced up from *The Last Chronicle of Barset* (finishing Trollope was her project for this pregnancy).

"Do you want to tell me about Trudi?"

"What about her?" I put aside my bills from the New York trip, still a careful accountant at heart.

"Nothing, if it makes you angry for me to ask," she replied mildly.

"I'll answer whatever I can," I said, knowing that I would never finish the proofs of my book about the Marshall Plan that night. "Or at least I'll try to answer."

"Well . . . I promise I won't lose my temper the silly way I did in Stuttgart last fall. I had no right to object to what happened before we were married. But I am kind of curious . . . I bet it's a good story . . . if you want to tell me."

"It's a good story all right, Rosemarie. And I guess I've wanted to tell you for a long time. You have to understand what it was like in Germany eleven years ago: most people were cold and hungry and scared. Some were especially scared because there were those who wanted to settle scores with them. It's hard to appreciate what it was like unless you were there."

"I'll try to imagine." She closed Trollope.

"You also have to realize that I was both very young and very lonely."

"I know."

"I did some things you wouldn't believe possible. I don't mean sex with Trudi . . . I mean their escape from the FBI."

"The FBI!" Her eyes widened in enthusiasm. She snuggled up in her chair, ready for a good yarn. "Trudi didn't tell me that. This will sure beat *Barset*."

"Jeeps instead of carriages."

So I told her the story, all of it that there was to tell. I'll admit that nothing of the love or the adventure was lost in the telling. I usually manage to rise to the occasion when I find an appreciative audience, and that night Rosemarie listened with rapt attention.

"My God!" she exclaimed when I told her about the French border guards who almost stopped me. "How did you ever get out of that one, Chucky?"

"I rode off on my great white horse Silver."

"Come on, the truth."

So I told her about my bluff.

"That's more fun than Silver," she exclaimed. "You always were gutsy. Remember the guy you hit with the beer mug at Jimmy's before we were married."

"That was crazy. There was nothing to be gained by it. A couple of lives were at stake on the autobahn."

"Anyway, get back to Stuttgart."

So I told her about the hasty farewell in the mists near the Bahnhoff with the big Mercedes sign, and the fog on the trip back to Bamberg, and near collisions on the autobahn. She jumped out of her chair when I described the tank truck looming a few feet ahead of me in the fog.

"Don't hit it!"

"It's not a TV film, Rosemarie."

"Sorry." She giggled. "Well, it should be."

"No, the ending is too vague. Anyway, I still had the FBI to worry about back in Bamberg."

So I ended the story with as much drama as possible, concluding with the General's words when we filed the case.

"And that was that."

"And you never heard from her again?"

"Not until you saw the kid in the gallery."

She nodded, now untroubled by the experience. "Well, thank God, for any number of reasons"—she grinned—"that I recognized him. Not that there was any doubt. A boy just like him kissed me once at Lake Geneva, right after he vomited a chocolate ice-cream bar."

"Karl."

"Karl indeed. Why didn't she get in touch with you ever? Did she say?"

"More or less. I'd say a mixture of fear and pride and wisdom. She didn't want to take advantage of me. She knew I was too young to marry. She sensed it would never work—all points that I was too inexperienced to understand."

"Did you know about Karl when you left them in Stuttgart?"

"No. I suppose"—I counted up months—"she might have had her suspicions. She certainly wouldn't have told me, for the same reasons she disappeared. Later I had sense enough to wonder occasionally. I guess I never took the possibility seriously."

"No wonder you were reluctant to make the trip to Germany."

"I wanted to know, and yet I didn't want to know."

"Now?"

"I'm glad I know."

She paused, considering the whole story carefully.

"I think it's a beautiful story, Chuck. Light opera maybe. Could I play the role? No, not Nordic enough." She burst into laughter. "Seriously, it's a story of young love and honor and bravery and wisdom and sacrifice. There is nothing in it of which you should be ashamed or about which I should have been upset."

"Sin?"

"Such as it was"—she waved her hand—"long since forgiven by God. . . . And you never told me because you were afraid I would react . . . well, the way I did?"

"I don't know. I mean I never really thought of telling anyone because I was ashamed of what had happened. I didn't think you'd understand."

"And I didn't."

"You do now."

"Regardless." She waved her hand again, not ready to plead mitigating circumstances. "A beautiful story and a beautiful little boy as the fruit of love. I'm ashamed of myself all over again."

"Don't be. You were caught off-guard."

She opened her mouth, probably to attack herself again. "Well, to give me full credit, which is what the shrink says I should do, *now* I understand and appreciate your story."

"I'm not sure I ever will."

"Funny thing is"—she bit her lip—"one part of me always knew. On our wedding night"—she grinned wickedly—"I mean our wedding morning, you were so gentle I knew that you had made love before. I even thought it might be the blonde in the picture. And in that same little corner in the attic of my head where I knew all those things, I said it's all right. It's over now. And it's none of your business anyway."

"She lived in that house in Bamberg."

"In the Obersandstrasse? Maybe I even guessed that. So I really was terrible, wasn't I, Chucky? I knew and I didn't mind and then when it turned out to be all true I turned into a bitch."

I held her close. "It was a turning point, Rosemarie, a blessing in disguise."

"Better late than never." She leaned against me, drained of strength.

"Not all that late."

She regarded me carefully. "Right, Chuck, late, but not all that late and not, as it turns out, *too* late. . . . You would have been happy with her, wouldn't you?"

What do you say to that? Think quickly. Come up with a good answer. "Yes."

"But"—she glanced up at my face, pondering the data judiciously—"not as happy as with me. With Clancy you get a lot more lows, but a lot more highs, and you really dig the highs, don't you?"

"You said it for me."

"Can I write her?"

"Trudi? Why?"

"To apologize. I really should, you know."

A kooky idea, maybe; but perhaps good therapy. I had learned a couple of months before never to suggest that she talk about something with her therapist.

"If you want to write, by all means do so. I can't object and even if I could I wouldn't."

"Great." She picked up *The Last Chronicle of Barset* again. "Did you really cuss out that Frenchman the way you said?"

"Cross my heart."

She embraced me enthusiastically. "Definitely you'll sing the tenor role." Her maroon robe fell open to reveal luscious breasts swelling in preparation for the coming child. We cuddled together. Then she bounced back to her chair. "I'll finish this chapter and then we'll make really sweet love. Me on top because of our friend here."

I stood up and removed the book from her hands. "Finish it tomorrow, woman."

Even though I had been married to her for almost nine years and ought to have known better, I did not think she would really write to Trudi.

She strode into my study on a bitter cold March day a few weeks later, and threw a letter on my desk, "Well, there it is. I hope you like it."

"It" was a letter.

> My Dear Frau Weiss,
>
> I am writing to you, long after I should have, to apologize for my coldness when we met in Stuttgart last year. I was surprised to see you and Karl at the gallery, but surprise is no excuse for being rude.
>
> I also want to tell you that things are fine again with me and Charles. Our crisis in Stuttgart was a turning point.
>
> I am expecting our fifth (and last!) child in August. She will seal our reconciliation.
>
> I know that your love for Charles is not a barrier to my love for him. I also hope that my love for him is not a barrier to your happy memories of what he did for you and who he was for you.
>
> I don't suppose that it is possible, but I would like it very much if we could all three of us be friends.
>
> I trust that you and Herr Weiss and your children are all well.
>
> Rosemarie Clancy O'Malley

"That's very lovely, Rosemarie." I gave the letter back to her. "It hits just the right note. I don't think it's absolutely necessary."

"The hell it isn't." She stormed out of the room.

A week later Trudi's reply arrived.

> Lieb Rosemarie,
>
> My most sincere congratulations on your pregnancy. I hope you and your daughter will be healthy and happy.
>
> What name will you give to her?
>
> I find that I too am expecting another child. Herr Weiss and I are both very happy. We have waited so long. Karl is exulting too. He thinks it will be a little sister, but I am not sure.

I am prepared to believe that your child will be a daughter if you say so.

I am also most happy that it is well again with you and Charles. He is a most wonderful man, as we both know.

I do not know whether it is possible for all three of us to be friends, but I should think it would be possible for you and me to be friends. We have much in common.

We were, after all, saved by the same man, were we not?

Herr Weiss joins me in greeting you and all your family.

With affection,

Trudi

" 'Leib Rosemarie.' How about that for putting me in my place!"

"Will you write back?"

"Certainly!"

I fingered the letter gingerly. "I'm not sure I'd feel at ease if you and she joined forces.

"The monster battalion again?"

"Monstrous regiment."

"Whatever."

There were occasional airmail letters from Germany after that. I was no more informed of their contents than I was of the contents of the phone conversations with the good April and with Peg.

I was informed, however, that Trudi's second child was a daughter and that her name was Maria.

One afternoon, a few weeks before the coming of Moira the Red, I found a photo of Karl, black-and-white in a silver frame, on my bookcase.

"Thank you for the picture of Karl," I said after supper when we were watching Sid Caesar on TV.

"I know he's on your mind a lot," she looked up from *Phineas Finn*. "In black-and-white he doesn't look much like you, so no curious daughter will notice. It's the red hair."

Indeed this son of mine that I would never know well and whose destiny was, as I thought then, out of my control, was on my mind a lot. I loved him and worried about him and wondered about him.

"You don't miss much, good wife."

"Naturally, husband mine"—she continued to read Trollope—"what else?"

Most of the incidents during and after the coming of Moira were not that simple. Rosemarie's delivery was complicated and painful. And Moira—unlike James, whose survival was never really in doubt—almost didn't make it.

Rosemarie came home from the hospital severely depressed. Nor did the depression ease after a couple of weeks. She was morose, grim, and not interested, for the first time, in recovering her figure.

"What difference does it make?"

How hard does a husband push when his wife seems to be a victim of postpartum melancholy.

I telephoned Dr. Stone.

"I am responsible for the treatment of her problems, Mr. O'Malley. You are responsible for insisting on the realities of your marriage and family life. Is that not so?"

"I don't want to aggravate her condition."

"Rarely do we aggravate conditions with those we love when we insist on reality, Mr. O'Malley. If this were one of those rare situations, I would surely tell you."

"What should I say to her?"

"Really, Mr. O'Malley, wouldn't you know that better than I?"

"Just a little hint?"

"And you call her a Maxwell Street merchant? Very well. One hint. You say to her, kindly but firmly, 'Rosemarie, cut it out.' "

"I've said it many times before."

"Does it work?"

"Always."

"Well?"

There were benefits to that fifth child.

Moira the Red was a special prize.

"Well," April Rosemary said, sighing just like her mother when she looked at the tiny, tiny girl-child with the bright red hair, "she is *so* beautiful that I *suppose* we'll have to spoil her."

"Love her a lot," I corrected.

"That's what I mean, DADDY."

The transformation in our firstborn was remarkable. With another little girl in the house, *finally*, she dropped her fussbudget persona and became the serene child that we had known early in her life. And a little mother modeled in the image of her own mother.

I was holding Moira up in the air one day and she was making happy "ga-ga" sounds at me.

"Daddy loves Moira," April Rosemary told her wide-eyed brothers, "because she has red hair just like he does."

"Daddy," I said, trying to sweep them all into a single embrace, "loves all his children."

"But," my eldest insisted, "he has to love us all differently because we're all different. Mommy said so."

That was that. I was outnumbered again.

At long last I worked up enough nerve to say, "Rosemarie, cut it out."

"What did you say?" She threw away the volume of Toynbee's *A Study of History* she was reading and rose from her chair, eyes dilated, face white, lips a thin angry line.

She missed, just as Peg had predicted she would.

I remembered the ten-year-old tyke about to have another one of her frequent tantrums. That image melted me into tenderness, not the emotion I needed.

"Well," she thundered, "are you going to answer my question?"

She hadn't thrown the book at me. The rage was in her eyes, however. What I had once thought was killing rage. It was not, I now tried to persuade myself, dangerous.

Rather it was a sign of fear—a fragile and terrified woman trying to defend herself.

"You heard me."

"Cut out WHAT?"

"You know very well what I mean."

"A hell of a husband you are." She stormed out of the room. I heard doors slamming in the distance.

My stomach turned over slowly a number of times. I had been less frightened in the Bohemian Alps and when hiding in her father's home at Lake Geneva.

I drew a deep breath and forced myself to walk, with infinite slowness, up the steps to our room.

She wasn't there.

I pondered for a moment and walked back down to the first floor and then to the basement.

The Second Brandenburg was blaring with loud enough trumpets to serve on judgment day.

In maroon sweat suit she was pumping away on her exercycle.

"Don't overdo it the first time," I said, sounding like a bored confessor with an uninteresting penitent.

"Fuck you!" Her face was still twisted with rage.

"Don't blame your sore muscles on me." I walked to the machine and pushed hard on her thigh.

She stopped pedaling. "Asshole," she muttered, the fight going out of her.

"Are you angry because I stopped you or because it took me so long to try to stop you?"

"Both." The ends of her lips flicked up and down as though she might just smile sometime soon.

"I'm sorry for the second, not for the first."

"*Well*, you should be." The thigh muscles became docile under my hand and the blessed crazy imp expression appeared on her face. "Besides, if my muscles are sore, maybe someone will massage them with ointment."

"That could be arranged anyway."

"Sure?"—her voice choked—"even when they're still so flabby?"

"Sure." I began to knead the muscle under my control. Then its partner on her other leg.

Sobbing, she threw her arms around me. "I'm so sorry, Chuck, so very, very sorry."

We must have clung to each other for an hour.

"You probably need a nice hot bath before the anointing with oils."

"That"—her eyes widened in surrender—"sounds like a very wise idea. A long leisurely bath, huh?"

"You bet." Then I said the word that first came to my lips at the airport in Mexico City. "You're a very gallant woman, Rosemarie."

"Gallant?" Her tears were replaced by laughter. "Me?"

"You. Now, about that hot bath." I unzipped her jacket.

We progressed in the next several months, though there were terrible set-backs too.

For Rosemarie every new day was an occasion to begin again at the starting blocks. She was skilled at the race now, but the need to run it would never leave her life.

And I had to run it with her, with less skill and less courage than she, truth to tell.

I continued to worry, not every day but at least once a week, about the ice-cream bar.

~ ⤳ 37 ⤳ ~

Rosemarie was waiting for me in our marriage bed when I came up from the darkroom. She was bathed, anointed, perfumed, and serene, her long black hair artfully arrayed on a pillow, her arms on top of the sheet, her bare shoulders cream on cream.

An invitation to sex?

Well, that prospect was not excluded, but the invitation was to a dialogue, one of those rare interludes in which my wife summed up for me her progress in therapy—without ever once quoting her psychiatrist.

It was late January of 1961. Moira was not only adorable, she was blessedly quiet. My wife and I had returned to Mexico for a second honeymoon on the tenth anniversary of the first. She had been distracted, preoccupied, no longer the dynamic bride I had married at the first wedding in the new St. Ursula's. The vacation, low-key and subdued, had been both pleasant and pleasurable. A husband and a lover had nothing about which to complain, only a lot about which to worry.

John Kennedy was inaugurated after we returned to Oak Park; the short years of Camelot had begun. We did not know then either that it was Camelot or that the years would be short.

"How's the project coming?" Rosemarie called after me as I went into the shower.

I was catching up on my "Parochial School" show, long delayed by a last desperate push to publish my book before January 1, 1961.

"Now that he's a doctor, even if he isn't a real doctor like Uncle Ted," April Rosemary had asked her mother in a stage whisper, "is Daddy going to stop being a crab?"

"Hush, dear," said her mother. "Daddy's a nice man most of the time."

Brat. No, two brats.

Turning on the shower I yelled, "Still way behind."

I thought I heard her say, "Maybe I can start helping again."

Therapy and Moira the Red had removed Rosemarie once again from the darkroom. If she returned, I thought nervously as the shower's warmth caressed my skin, it might be a critical turning point.

It seemed like a good time for a turnaround. Kennedy was about to set up the Peace Corps. Khrushchev was reforming Soviet agriculture. A South African black had won the Nobel Peace Prize. John Updike had begun his "Rabbit" series. Young people (that did not include me because I was now thirty-two) were dancing the Twist. At Mom's songfest we were singing the songs from *Camelot* and "Michael Rowed the Boat Ashore"—with my older daughter shouting down everyone else in the room as she urged Michael to row. A new and better era had begun with the new decade.

Or so, alas, we thought. That era somehow seems more distant today than the late forties and the early fifties.

However, I remember with precise details the chain of events that began when, wrapped in a long terry robe, I sat at the edge of our marriage bed and began to stroke Rosemarie's wondrous black hair.

"I'm probably not an addict," Rosemarie began, as she always began such reports with a startling statement that seemed to assume months of previous discussions.

"I didn't think you were."

"Yes, you did," she said firmly. "An alcoholic."

"Not like most alcoholics."

"Actually it took the longest time for me to persuade Dr. Stone that I wasn't promiscuous—with men, I mean. I guess lots of women who are abused by their fathers go that route. I told her that when it comes to self-destruction the Irish would choose the bottle over sex any day."

I gulped.

"Do you understand?" Her hand touched mine.

"I guess. Go on."

"Well, anyway, I'm not your typical alcoholic. Don't worry, I'm not going to experiment or anything like that. I'm too afraid of the stuff. But the problem is that if I don't drink I'll think I have everything under control again and find some other way to destroy myself."

"Not if I can help it." I drew both our hands down to the side of her face.

"Dear, sweet Chucky." She kissed my hand. "And sometimes it's hard to separate what I'm doing because it's a good idea and what I'm doing because I want to punish myself for what happened with Daddy."

"Like Moira?" I could have bit off my tongue as soon as I said the words.

"Maybe you ought to be a shrink too." She was not upset by my comment. "Economist, photographer, psychiatrist. Chucky Ducky the Renaissance man."

"With a Renaissance wife." I kissed her forehead.

"Really? No, I think I'm actually early medieval. Anyway, getting pregnant when I did was terrible. Only it was a good idea to finish the family. And I so love our poor little redhead tyke. So it's all mixed up. I guess maybe I've learned something about tricks I play on myself, but I don't know whether I can stop them."

"Sure you can." I slipped my hand under the sheet and rested it on her smooth, moist belly. Rosemarie was in perfect shape again, slender, strong, agile: the lithe woman athlete.

"Hey, don't tickle me, not yet anyway."

"I hadn't started."

"You were thinking of it. Not that I mind when you do it." She grinned lasciviously and then became serious, even gloomy. "I'm never going to be all right, Chuck. What happened will always be part of me." Her eyes filled with tears.

"For better rather than worse."

"Maybe. The thing is, well . . . I've lived so far by isolating that from all the rest of my life, walling myself into two separate compartments. Now I'm trying to put them together, take down the walls, know what I mean?"

"I think so."

"I always thought that energy and determination were all I needed. Now I see that I need some wisdom, a lot of insight, and even more of the courage to accept what is. I have to learn to be good to myself, which is the hardest of all. I have to treat me like you do."

She looked so unspeakably fragile that I wanted to take her in my arms and hold her close till Judgment Day. And after. It wasn't time for my hand to start moving yet.

I looked into her deep blue eyes, was absorbed by them and then drawn into my wife's soul.

Her soul—I can think of no other term.

I was immersed in a wild, beautiful, haunting, exotic landscape—vast deserts, deep, rich valleys, towering snowcapped mountains, multicolored gardens, clashing cymbals, soft violins. I knew her better than any human should know any other human. I was captured by her more than any human should be captured by another human.

When the interlude was over, a few seconds or the many hours it seemed, I bent over her face and kissed her gently and with all the love in me.

"Hmm. Nice. A little tickle now and then won't hurt. . . . You can't just take down the walls and leave the bricks on the ground. The next morning they're back up again. I'll be doing that for the rest of my life."

"Easter Sunday is not achieved easily."

She smiled. "I knew you'd understand."

I wasn't sure that I did, but at least I had said the right thing.

"See, the problem is that I intended this conversation to be a big success; I'd tell you all my progress and my insights and we'd have a big celebration. I wouldn't let myself do that. I turn it into a wake."

"Most vital corpse I've ever seen." This time I did tickle her.

"Chucky, cut it out!" She didn't mean it.

She twisted in feigned attempt to escape; the sheet fell away from her breasts; I claimed both of them. She grabbed my hands. "There's one more thing I have to tell you. It's not part of the celebration and I wasn't going to mention it tonight, but you're so gentle I have to get it off my mind."

I returned my hand to her belly, this time taking the sheet down with it.

"Cover me up, please," she whispered. "Let me talk just a little bit more. You can hold my breasts. Please, I want you to."

I did as I was asked. My heart pounded anxiously.

"Did Daddy ever show you the pictures?" She closed her eyes.

"Pictures?"

"When I was in first year at Trinity, he hid a camera before . . . before we had sex. There were maybe half a dozen pictures. I didn't know about them. He showed them to me at Christmas the year before we were married. Remember? The day you gave me the tennis dress?"

"A day I'll never forget." My voice had become a hoarse rasp.

"He said he'd show them to you if I ever dated you. He threatened it again when we became engaged. I didn't know whether he would or not. I told myself I didn't care. I should have warned you about them the day I told you about everything else. You were so upset I lost my nerve."

"He never tried that. And it wouldn't have made any difference."

The stage lights had gone up again and I saw a terrifying scene on the stage in my mind.

"There's nothing more, Chuck." She opened her eyes and looked at my grief-stricken face. "I'm sorry to cause you so much pain."

"It's your pain that hurts me, Rosemarie. . . . Did it . . . ?"

"Have any effect on my posing for you? I don't think so. It was such a different, uh, context, I guess. Maybe there was a little wall there, but you always make my body feel good and innocent. It's not the same thing."

Every trace of sexual desire had deserted me, not because I felt that Rosemarie's beautiful body had been tainted by those pictures, but because she had been hurt, violated, degraded, abused by an evil monster.

A sad and pathetic man, maybe, but an evil monster too.

"In fact"—she brightened—"Dr. Stone thinks that book helped my self-esteem a lot."

"You don't quote her very often."

"Oh, damn." She pounded the bed. "What I SHOULD say, if I were being good to myself, is that the book DID restore a lot of my self-esteem." She put on her mock-serious expression. "You know, for an Irish matriarch, I am not completely unattractive."

"Not completely." I bent down and kissed her lips. Enough sexual desire returned so that my lips wandered down to her breast, still partially covered by the sheet.

Then the celebration of resurrection began. As was fitting for our two roles, it was a celebration filled with comedy.

When it was over and she slept peacefully in my arms, I found that I had another question and an answer to an old question.

I knew at last what was Jim Clancy's final ice-cream bar.

38

Should I talk to Vince or to Ed Murray? Vince knew his way around the law profession as well as anyone. He didn't have the political contacts that Ed had. This wasn't, however, a political game. And Vince was family. I might need a man with family loyalties before this was over. Especially a man with Southern Italian family loyalties.

For that matter Ed Murray was almost family. Cordelia had become the foster sister's foster sister, as thick as the proverbial thieves with Peg and Rosemarie. They lived two blocks away from us and three blocks from Vince and Peg—in a home that, according to Rosemarie, had been a "nice compromise between Lake Forest and Beverly."

Rosemarie had surely found them the house.

"Love is expansive, it seeks to embrace the whole world," she had told me piously when I wondered if there was room in her friendship with Peg for a third person.

It turned out she was right. The "monstrous regiment" grew by one.

Still, near-family was not quite the same as family. I would consult with Vince.

I rode downtown on the Lake Street El and found Vince working on a brief in his office in what was then called the Field Building (now the LaSalle National Bank Building) on LaSalle Street.

It was a prestigious office, in an important law firm, for a very successful young lawyer.

"Not bad for an Italian kid from Division Street."

"Cut it out." He grinned as he shook hands. "The guy married well, that's all."

"That he did, that he did."

"Assistant concert master for her symphony." He beamed proudly. "In musical circles I'm becoming famous because I'm her husband."

We talked about our wives and kids for a few moments. Then I told him what I wanted.

"I suspect that Jim Clancy has left some dirt with his papers, nothing criminal, but something that would hurt Rosemarie terribly. The only reason it hasn't come out is that old Joe O'Laughlin, who was Jim's lawyer, died a few months after Jim. It's probably sitting somewhere in the office of whoever took over O'Laughlin's practice."

"He was one of the great, all-time scumbags of the Chicago Bar. Crooked, corrupt, incompetent. No one ever did figure out where he put all his money. He was apparently not planning on dying, ever."

"I figure that the only reason this dirt hasn't surfaced is that whoever has it probably doesn't know he has it."

Vince drummed his fingers on his big mahogany desk. "Jim Clancy leaves the papers—or whatever—with Joe O'Laughlin. Gives him instructions to go public with them after a few months maybe. Joe dies and leaves no instructions with whoever took over that part of the Clancy files. So the stuff sits there for all these years, like a ticking bomb."

"Precisely. We have a lot of Jim's papers in our own files. No income tax returns from the forties and fifties, however. So someone else has them."

"The sleaze vultures picked his corpse pretty clean. I'd say that if you haven't heard from anyone, the guy that has them is as inefficient as O'Laughlin. The stuff is gathering dust in some scumbag's office."

"That's the way I figure it too."

Vince nodded. Not once had he asked or even hinted at asking what the dirt was.

"You want me to poke around very gently and find out who might have those tax returns?"

"Very gently. And not a word to anyone. Not even to Peg."

He rolled his soulful brown eyes. "Especially not to Peg."

That afternoon, the smell of the hunt in my nostrils, I turned to the new question.

"Do you mind," I asked Rosemarie, who I found in the darkroom working on the "Parochial School" pictures, "if I have a visit with Dr. Stone?"

She hesitated. "Is something wrong?"

"Not with you. I want to make sure that I'm responding properly."

Not the whole truth, but only a little lie.

"You are . . . still, I don't mind if you talk to her. Maybe it would be a good idea. Don't expect any answers."

I did indeed expect an answer, but that was not the point.

"Good, I'll call her later on this afternoon. Now let's see about these playground pictures."

Moira, blissfully sleeping, let us work for a whole hour before she woke up and demanded (if Rosemarie was to be believed) that her Daddy hold her and sing to her.

Irish songs at that.

Afterwards I phoned Dr. Stone.

39

I was angry at my wife. Why had she not told me that Dr. Stone was absolutely gorgeous?

With a wedding band and a large ruby on the third finger of her left hand.

And fully aware of the impact of her tall, blond, Scandinavian beauty on me.

Shrinks weren't supposed to be beautiful, not that beautiful. On the other hand, maybe she understood from the inside what it was like to be a woman desired by most men and envied by most women.

I must buy Rosemarie a big jewel. Why had I not thought of that before?

"As I'm sure you understand, Mr. O'Malley, I cannot discuss the nature or progress of a patient's therapy with anyone, not even a spouse."

"I quite understand, Doctor."

"I cannot provide you with any prognosis, other than the unnecessary observation that she is an intelligent and determined woman."

"I quite understand, Doctor."

"I cannot tell you that the effect of the traumas she has experienced will ever be eliminated from her life."

"I quite understand, Doctor."

"I cannot offer you any advice on whether you should consider ending your relationship with her." Dr. Stone raised an eyebrow, obviously expecting a reaction to that observation.

"I quite understand, Doctor."

"I cannot promise you that your children will be unaffected either by her past experiences or by her present struggles in treatment."

"I quite understand, Doctor."

"In short, Mr. O'Malley"—she frowned, bemused by the little redhead who had found himself such a beautiful wife—"while I am happy to meet you with Mrs. O'Malley's permission, I'm afraid that as in most other such interviews, I cannot say much that would reassure you."

"I quite understand, Doctor."

"If you understand all of these factors, Mr. O'Malley"—she considered the ends of her fingers, trying to remain patient—"then why have you come to see me?"

"I had a different question."

"And that is?" Both eyebrows went up this time.

"Why has she survived?"

"I beg pardon?"

"Given what she's been through, I am astonished that she is as healthy and as normal a woman as she is. Sure, she has some serious problems, and, sure, they'll be with her for the rest of her life in one way or another. But why is she still alive?"

"That *is* a very interesting question." Dr. Stone relaxed. "Intellectually and personally too, I would imagine."

"Baffles you too?" I turned on all my Irish charm.

She actually smiled. "At first, very much so. You always want to distinguish between your patient's real strengths and her neurotic mechanisms. Actually, there is no great mystery about Rosemarie's survival."

"Indeed?"

"The literature on the subject leads us to look for a number of factors, all of which seem to be present in her history—genetically determined strength; a powerful person with whom to identify in early years, in this case her grandmother; deep insights—Rosemarie, as I'm certain you know, has certain mystical traits and experiences."

So that's what they were.

"I see."

"And, perhaps most important, as a result of these other factors, a propensity to seek out and ally with those who can most effectively help one maintain some sort of basic personal integration."

"In Rosemarie's case, who would that be?"

She now smiled broadly. "Surely that is evident?"

" 'Fraid not."

"To use her term"—the smile became a grin—"the crazy O'Malleys."

"Us?"

"At a very young age, Rosemarie intuited where her salvation could be found and clung to it with remarkable tenacity."

I remember the overheard conversation between Mom and Dad in the apartment on Menard in 1940. They knew even then what was happening.

"I'll be damned."

"I rather doubt it, Mr. O'Malley."

"But she's saved all of us!" I exploded from my chair and began to pace around the doctor's office. "All of us!"

"Oh. How interesting. Why don't you explain what you mean."

"I wouldn't be a photographer if she had not edged me into it. Both my sisters' marriages would have fallen apart if she hadn't intervened, rather dramatically in fact. My brother wouldn't be a priest, much less the effective priest he is if Rosemarie had not installed herself as his confidante. My parents would not be as happy as they are today if Rosemarie hadn't mandated that they be happy. God only knows how much she has helped our nieces and nephews and our friends."

"Really?" It was hard to tell whether she was actually surprised or only professionally surprised. "And you have told her this often?"

"No . . . hardly ever."

"May I ask why not?"

"You know why not."

"You'd be an interesting patient, Mr. O'Malley. You'd drive me back to my training analyst almost every day. Yes, I know why not, but I want *you* to say it."

"Because she doesn't want to hear it. She'd be furious."

"You're afraid of her fury?"

"Sure."

"With good reason?"

"No. She's a pushover when I tell her to cut it out."

"And why doesn't she want to hear that it's been a two-way street, that in fact the balance of payments, if we may use a term from one of your professions, is rather more on her side than on the opposite side?

"I should get on the couch?"

"That won't be necessary. I repeat, why would your wife not want to hear that she's been a blessing to all the crazy O'Malleys?"

" 'Grace' is the word Mom uses."

"An excellent word. Now, why doesn't she want to hear it?

"Because that would make her more lovable than she wants to admit she is."

"Marvelous." Dr. Stone rose from her desk. "Now let me say this to you, Mr. O'Malley: It is of the utmost importance that your wife hear this truth as often and with as much variety and persistence as possible. She will react negatively at first. You must not permit that to deter you."

She shook hands with me.

"I thought you had a rule against giving direct advice to family."

Her grin was almost like Rosemarie's imp grin.

"I just broke that rule, Mr. O'Malley."

40

"The news is not good, I'm afraid." Vince sounded discouraged.

"Okay. Let's have it."

"The relevant part of O'Laughlin's practice seems to have gone to a guy named Bob Roache, in his early forties, who makes Old Joe look like a paragon of integrity. Drinks, gambles, mixes with the Outfit. Lots of women. Doesn't work hard. Seems to have lots of money. Almost debarred a couple of years ago. An Adlai Stevenson idealist gone sour."

"He won't let me look at the stuff."

"Worse than that. If he finds out you're looking for something, he'll search for it too and then sell it to you, for as much as he can get."

"Should I call him for an appointment?"

"No, don't do that. It will alert him. Stop in at his office after lunch, about three o'clock, given his hours. He'll be a little tuned, maybe a lot tuned, and mellow. Offer him some money. Do it discreetly . . . I know you can do that. Then don't leave his office until you find what you want. Take it with you."

"How much money?"

"Two thousand. And in cash."

"Naturally."

I hung up and went back to the darkroom. Under Rosemarie's efficient management the "Parochial School" project was back on schedule.

"Vince," I said before she could ask. "Minor business."

"Is he all right?"

"Never sounded happier. He's got a good wife. Almost as good as mine."

"Blarney, but I love it. . . . Now what about this sweet old nun? Bride of Christ?"

We went back to work.

"What did you think of Dr. Stone?" She asked with elaborate casualness.

"You didn't tell me she was gorgeous."

"You didn't ask. Some dish, isn't she."

"You bet."

"Would you like to sleep with her?"

"Who wouldn't?"

"Well, that's an honest answer anyway."

"Impressively competent."

"I bet she thought you were cute."

"You ask her."

Rosemarie giggled. "There'll be enough material in that question to keep us going for months."

End of conversation.

I was no more going to tell her about my session with her shrink than she would tell me about hers.

And I was going to approach very carefully my fulfillment of Dr. Stone's instructions.

The next day I visited Robert Roache's expensive office suite in the Conway Building. The pretty blond secretary said, with considerable indifference, that he was not expected back that afternoon. Would I care to leave my name?

No I would not. I'd be back again some other day.

~ 41 ~

Rosemarie's lips were drawn in a tight angry line—a thin jagged pencil mark scratched across her pale face.

"I won't listen to that crap, Chuck, it's simply not true."

"Rosemarie," I pleaded. "It is true. If you had not prodded me, I never would have become a photographer. Or finished my doctorate either."

"I'm not a prodder," she shouted. "Nor a meddling matriarch. I'm not responsible for anyone else's mistakes besides my own."

We were sitting in her office, sipping soda water at the end of a February day on which moist snow had piled up on the streets and walks. The kids, all but Moira, were building a snowman on the lawn, one that looked suspiciously like me.

For all my care and preparation I had bungled badly my attempt to tell Rosemarie that she had been grace for me and all the crazy O'Malleys.

She heard me say that a) she had meddled in our lives, and b) she was responsible for our mistakes.

That was not what I said at all, but she would not abandon her interpretation. Routed, I had to find a way to get off the field of battle to return again with another plan of attack.

"Rosemarie, would you please listen to me carefully?"

"I have listened, damn it, and I'm saying you're wrong and I don't want to hear anymore of it."

"You have *not* listened. I did not say you were responsible for anyone else's mistakes and I did not say you were a meddling matriarch."

"You said I was a matriarch!" she scowled at me.

"Not today."

"Well, you've said it before and you're thinking it now."

"I said you were a matriarch like my mother is."

"That's silly. I'm as different from her as night is from day."

You see what happened? The subject became my words instead of her grace. A neurotic response indeed, but a remarkably ingenious one. Today I was not going to win.

"What I'm trying to say is—"

"I KNOW what you're trying to say and I don't want to hear it. Now don't bother me with it anymore. I have to call the kids in and get supper ready."

"Rosemarie—"

"You invade my privacy"—she jumped out of her chair—"by talking to my shrink. Then you come back and try to play shrink for me yourself. Well, you're no damn good at it. Don't ever try it again."

She sailed triumphantly out of the room.

I had fallen flat on my face.

Or perhaps on another part of my anatomy.

Bayonets fixed, the redcoats marched across the broad green field under a clear sky. Their cannons boomed behind them, producing puffs of white smoke. My ragtag peasant battle line had only spades and pikes and an occasional rusty musket. And my 50 caliber machine gun. Tim and Jenny were there, Cordelia and Ed, Peg and Vince, all dressed in Irish peasant clothes. When the advancing battle line was only fifty feet away, I opened fire. They kept coming. My bullets were blanks! They stormed into us! Somehow I changed the scene, reloaded my weapon and opened fire again. The redcoats turned and ran. I continued to mow them down. Then I saw Rosemarie on the ground, a lance protruding from her chest.

"Rosemarie!" I shouted.

I sat up in bed, uncertain as to what was real and what was not.

"Chucky," she said sleepily, "are you having another one of your nightmares?"

"Are you all right?"

"Sure," she raised her right hand feebly to wave me away. "Just sleepy. It was only a dream."

"Sorry," I said, now wide awake.

"It's okay. Try to get some sleep. Tomorrow is a big day."

It sure is, I thought.

Bob Roache did not intend to permit me to search the Clancy files un-
watched.

Why hadn't I expected that?

I finally found him in his office on the Friday afternoon before the
family and a few guests were coming to dinner, allegedly to see the final
shots for the "Parochial School" exhibit.

A man in his early forties with thinning brown hair, bloodshot eyes, and
an expanding belly, Roache looked far too seedy for his tailor-made gray suit
and his plush office. He did not seem particularly happy to see me, but was
not antagonistic either. He may have had three or four drinks at lunch, but he
was also watching me shrewdly, searching hungrily for the main chance.

A crook, but a clever crook.

"I suppose the boxes are around here someplace." Bob Roache affected
to be bored. "I don't know that we have time to hunt for them right now."

"It's just some income tax returns that we need to settle a few questions
about inheritance taxes. Old Jim Clancy had his fingers in a lot of pies."

"So I hear," Roache murmured. "So I hear. Why didn't Ed Murray call
me?"

"I thought it would be easier this way. You can phone Ed and verify
who I am and the nature of the problem."

"Oh, I'm sure that won't be necessary, Charley." He grinned crookedly.
"Your face is familiar enough."

It was essential that I get at those papers now. If I left his offices without
them, he'd search in them all night and find what I thought was there.

"I can't understand how there was so much confusion after O'Laughlin's
death."

"Mostly because there was a lot of confusion all during his life," Roache
said, yawning. "He liked it that way. Easier to cover his tracks. When they
were closing up his firm, they practically gave the stuff away. I only glanced
through it."

"I see."

I wanted to break the cheap shanty Irish bastard's neck.

"I don't mind turning the whole packet over to you, but I think I should probably have a court order." He fiddled with the big sapphire on his right hand. "Just to be on the safe side."

"I'm sure we could get it and we will, but if I could glance through the files to make sure that what we're looking for is in them. Then we can ask the court to expedite the matter."

I was reciting almost verbatim the careful scenario in which Vince had rehearsed me.

"Well, there's the matter of our expenses in storing and protecting these materials for several years." He yawned again. "Office space in this part of the Loop has gone through the roof the last couple of years."

"I can understand that."

"You'd be willing to pay for our services in storing your father-in-law's records?" His eyes glinted.

"Within reason, surely."

"Would five thousand be reasonable?"

Just like that.

"That's a lot of money, Bob."

He shrugged indifferently. "I'm sure there's a lot of money involved in Jim Clancy's estate. Otherwise you wouldn't be so eager for his records."

"That's true," I admitted. "I could go a thousand dollars."

"Two and it's done. You can search them today and we'll deliver the whole stack as soon as you get the court order."

"Fair enough." I reached for my checkbook.

"In cash."

"Cash?"

"Only way."

I opened my wallet and counted out the twenty one-hundred dollar bills that I had place there before boarding the El that morning.

"I see you came prepared." He began counting the money. "Pleasure to do business with a man like you."

I was ushered into an empty office and the blond secretary, with obvious distaste for the effort required, brought in, one by one, six legal-size card-board file boxes and piled them on the desk. Bob Roache settled comfortably into a chair in the corner of the room.

"I got nothing to do this afternoon, so I may as well keep you company. That way I can assure the court that nothing has been removed."

"Okay by me. Suit yourself."

It wasn't okay at all.

I started with the oldest box—late thirties. Tax returns, commodity sales receipts, canceled notes, copies of deeds: the dry records of pirate's bloody life.

Nothing that looked like an envelope of pictures that might be addressed to the police or to one of the papers.

"Nothing in it?" Roache cocked a curious eye.

"I suppose enough material for a couple of novels, if someone knew what it all meant, but no tax returns that seem pertinent."

"What years are you looking for?"

"Forties, early fifties. This box is earlier, but I want to be systematic."

I went through the second box more carefully. There were many envelopes, bits of paper, notes on yellow sheets. I looked carefully at each one, fearful of rushing and missing something important.

"Nothing here either."

He glanced at his watch. "Want to call it a day and come back tomorrow?"

"Not if I can continue now."

"I'm not going anywhere."

The third box, mostly records from the forties and the fifties, was the one in which I expected to hit pay dirt.

I would, that is, if my theory was correct. On that gray February afternoon with the world thawing outside and a crucial family gathering that night, I began to doubt my theory.

When I had finished a minutely careful examination of box number three, I had even more doubts about it.

Roache had been called out of the office to take a phone call. He didn't seem particularly upset, reasoning perhaps that what I was looking for was too big to be stuffed into a pocket.

"Not here either."

"You'd make a good lawyer." Roache laughed. "You didn't miss a thing in that box."

I resolved that if I find something I must hide all reaction to it and hope there was some way I'd get a second chance if Roache's phone rang again.

"I kind of thought it would be in that box. Right year."

"Godawful mess, isn't it?"

The fourth box was the worst mess of all. Papers, folders, notes, bills had been crammed into it, as if someone was rushing to finish a task.

Now I was sure I was wrong. No ice-cream bar today.

Halfway through the box I found the 1950 tax return. Automatically I opened it. Inside was a yellowed letter-size envelope. On it was printed in large block letters: TO BE DELIVERED TO THE EDITOR OF THE CHICAGO AMERICAN SIX MONTHS AFTER MY DEATH.

Cautiously I felt the sides of the envelope. There were thin objects inside. They might well have been photographs.

Struggling to maintain an appearance of indifference and calm, I put the return back in the box, its corner sticking out, and continued my search.

I ached to look up to see if Roache was watching me with special care. If I did I would give the game away.

"Nothing here," I shoved the box aside. "Maybe our hunches were wrong."

"No refunds," he joked.

"None expected."

I started on the fifth box, forcing myself to be as careful as I had been with the previous boxes. Roache now looked bored out of his mind.

Would the phone never ring? What would I do if he was not distracted? Try to slip the envelope into my jacket pocket while he was sitting in the room with me?

Pretty risky.

"Well"—I moved the fifth box to the edge of the desk—"last one."

"Good hunting." He was examining his fingernails.

Then the blonde appeared again.

"What is it now, Denise?" he snapped.

"The Senator, Mr. Roache."

"Oh damn it. Excuse me, Charley. Don't steal anything while I'm out."

"Fat chance," I murmured.

At last free to tremble, my fingers shook uncontrollably as I jumped up and began to search frantically in the fourth box, the one with the tax return and the envelope.

I couldn't find the corner of the return that I had left sticking out.

It wasn't there. Was I in the wrong box?

Quickly I looked through the others. No turned-up corner in any of them either.

I was badly confused now. Which box had it been? It could have been any of them. I was blowing it.

I took a deep breath, thought of how much I loved my wife, and plunged back into the third box.

I heard Roache's voice in the corridor.

Then I remembered that the 1952 return had been in the middle of the file in the fourth box. I jammed my hand into it and pulled out a return.

Sure enough. 1952!

He was talking to someone at the door.

I pulled the envelope out, stuffed it into my inside jacket pocket, and then shoved the return into the fifth box, the one I was examining when Roache left the room.

At that very moment he returned.

I commanded my heart to slow down, my nerves to stop.

"No luck yet," I said easily.

"Hope you didn't steal anything?"

"Want to search me?"

He laughed. "Don't be ridiculous."

If I had not suggested it, he might have insisted.

I continued to work my way through the box. A few minutes later, I pulled out the return.

"I'll be damned! Wouldn't you know it would be in the last place you look."

"It's always the way. Is it the right one?"

I sat down at the desk and made a pretense of studying the form.

"Sure looks that way. . . . would you put it in a separate envelop so we can find it quickly when we get the court order."

"Why not?" He took the return. "I'll have Denise take care of it and bring the boxes back to our storage room. We'll make a copy of this return first thing Monday morning." He leered at me. "No extra charge."

He'd spend the weekend trying to figure out what was in the return that was so important. Well, good luck to him in that.

"I'll give her a hand."

Denise and I moved the boxes into a musty, windowless room in which files and folders were crammed in total chaos. She thanked me. With elaborate show, Roache took the envelope in which she had placed the allegedly precious return and locked it in a safe in his office.

"A pleasure to do business with you," I said cheerfully.

"Same here."

We would seek the court order and have a clerk at Vince's office go through the documents carefully to see if there were any more time bombs. I was sure I had the ice-cream bar.

I walked across the street to City Hall, found the men's room, and inside a toilet stall opened the envelope. I felt the contents to make sure they were photographic paper and then closed the envelope.

Someday, maybe, I would tell Rosemarie the whole story.

I tore the envelope and its contents into tiny pieces and flushed them down the toilet.

Outside on Washington Boulevard, despite the somber February day and the deep slush, I felt like a man reborn.

So long, Jim Clancy, it's been good to know you.

43

My family watched me anxiously as I poured the dessert wine (Neirsteiner Glocke *Eiswein*), passing Rosemarie's upturned glass as I always did.

They knew something was up.

We had admired the prints for the new show, devoured Rosemarie's beef bourguignonne and savored the chocolate cream pie with chocolate sauce.

There remained only the *Eiswein* and the usual songfest.

I guess my tension gave the game away. Rosemarie was watching me suspiciously.

One more toss of the dice. Hell, I was on a roll.

I raised a Waterford goblet. "I propose a toast to my good wife, who put this show back on the track, despite the fact that, as her daughter . . . her elder daughter, that is . . . will tell you, I've been crabby because of my work in becoming a doctor. And she will add that I'm not a real doctor like Ted, either. Anyway, to Rosemarie!"

"To Rosie!" they all shouted.

She blushed, pleased and flattered. And temporarily off-guard.

"And to the new engagement ring, not quite on the tenth anniversary of the first one, but still one she's deserved for the last ten years."

Rosemarie bashfully held up her right hand, on which the new ruby glittered.

"The Depression must be over at last," Dad observed with a cheerful wink.

"No interruptions," I begged.

"Whose charge account is it on?" Jane lifted her glass.

"I'm not sure." Rosemarie shrugged her shoulders. "I haven't had the nerve to ask."

I had bought it for her after leaving Bob Roache's office with the extra two thousand I had in my hip pocket, just in case.

I confessed to Rosemarie, because she would have figured it out anyway, that I'd thought of the new ring when I saw Dr. Stone's.

"If you don't mind"—she kissed me again—"I won't wear it to her office. It might distract both of us."

"If you're all finished with your cheap cracks"—I held the goblet in the air—"to Rosemarie's new ring and all it represents."

"Hear! Hear!" Ed Murray shouted.

"Hear! Hear!" Timmy Boylan echoed.

I took a deep breath and glanced at each of the members of my family around the dinner table. Well, here goes. . . .

"Rosemarie"—I turned the crystal stem carefully in my fingers—"without whom none of the crazy O'Malleys would be as happy as they are!"

"Hear! Hear!" Ted raised his glass.

"Hear! Hear!" they all responded.

"I don't have to listen to his crap," she screamed. She bolted from her chair and charged toward the dining room door.

Around the table, everyone stared in astonishment.

The fat was in the fire. I had better think quickly.

"Don't you dare leave this room, Rosemarie," I barked at her.

She stopped in the doorway.

"Come back here."

You win one, you push your luck.

She came back.

"Sit down."

Sullenly she sat, and prepared to assail us.

"And be quiet."

She closed her mouth.

"Now listen to us."

She scowled, a caged leopard being tormented by trainers.

I wondered if anyone would understand what was happening. If they knew what was happening, who would take the lead?

Astonishingly, it was Michael.

"How many times a week do I phone you, Rosie?"

"Two or three," she grumbled.

"At least."

"All right, at least."

"Have you ever given me bad advice?"

"I don't think so." She was staring at her hands, white and clenched on the table in front of her.

"Would I be a priest if it were not for you?"

"How do I know?"

"Rosie?"

"Well, maybe not."

Then the brothers-in-law joined in.

"I'd be a very junior partner in Doctor's surgery," Ted said, "if it was not for you. And I remind you that's an exact quote from your warning."

"And I'd be a bitter bachelor," Vince added. "That's a quote too."

"Hey," Timmy joined in, "I'd still be in Ireland if you hadn't sent this beautiful woman to drag me home."

We were doing nicely.

Ed grinned cheerfully, the South Side joker even in times of stress. "Hell, Rosie, you found me a wife; maybe she is too refined for the South Side, but I couldn't have done much better myself."

"You didn't save our marriage, Rosie." Dad was smiling broadly. "You just made it better than we ever thought it could be."

Peg and Jane were both crying.

Jane tried to speak and broke down completely

"Making you part of the family," Peg sobbed, "was the best thing that ever happened to us. Oh, Rosie, you dear, sweet goof, why try to deny what is so obvious. We all needed you. We still do."

"I'd be dead." Cordelia Murray was dry-eyed, but so sad that her face would break your heart. "I mean that, Rosie, dead."

"Mom?" I asked. "We haven't heard the final word yet."

"Well, dear"—she sighed—"I don't know what all the fuss is about. We loved you, Rosemarie, from the very beginning because you were so sweet and good and lovable. And then you loved us back. And it's worked out wonderfully."

The only dry eyes at the table were my wife's.

She glared around the room, humiliated and enraged.

Christopher, I prayed, if your good spirit is near, help her.

Then my Rosemarie's lips began to twitch and her eyes began to sparkle. In the end she would be saved by her inability to resist the temptation to a comic line.

"Well, regardless"—she waved her hand in a zany slice at the air— "who else would take care of the crazy O'Malleys?"

Epilogue

"Chuck? Jack Kennedy. We met at the McCarthy hearings, if you remember."

"I remember, Mr. President."

It wasn't someone imitating the President, though he did sound like one of the comedians who imitated him. I had told very few people that I'd met him seven years before.

"Good. The reason I'm calling is that we're having a dinner at the White House in honor of some of the country's scholars and artists and I wonder if you'd—"

"Take some pictures? I'd be glad to."

He laughed. "No, that wasn't what I had in mind, though that would be fine. I want you to be one of the guests."

"Thank you, Mr. President." I felt very foolish. "I'd be delighted."

Typically, I had tried to think of excuses for not going.

"And Mrs. O'Malley too."

"I'll ask her, Mr. President."

"Good, good. I've enjoyed your books very much, particularly the ones on Germany."

"Thank you, Mr. President."

"Is Mrs. O'Malley as beautiful as she is in the books?"

"Even more beautiful, Mr. President."

"Great. I'll be looking forward to seeing you again and meeting her."

"I'll ask her to come, Mr. President."

Would she come if I told her she was invited?

Is the Pope Catholic?

Jack Kennedy was reputed to be a womanizer. But the invitation for Rosemarie did not sound like womanizing was on the President's mind. Admiration, rather.

I walked back down the stairs to the darkroom where Rosemarie was experimenting with color prints.

She still saw Dr. Stone, though now only once a week or so.

"Who was on the phone, husband mine?"

"The President."

"The president of what?" She pulled off the protective gloves she wore when working with chemicals.

"Of the United States."

She laughed, "We sound like one of those comedy acts. Who was it *really*?"

"It really was Jack Kennedy. He wanted to invite you to dinner. He said I could come too."

"I can't!" she wailed.

"Why not?" So maybe the Pope wasn't Catholic.

"I have nothing to wear."

No worry about the papacy. "I imagine you can find something simple and inexpensive in time. White, please."

"What else!"

Some of the distinguished artists and writers and scholars had handsome wives (only a few women were invited in those days on their own credentials). Some did not. My Rosemarie, in the fullness of her glory as she approached thirty with serenity, was easily the most beautiful woman in the White House that night.

When she was asked what she "did," she invariably replied "Mother" and held up five fingers.

I would add, "She's my assistant and agent and boss and she sings with a chamber group."

She would throw back her head and laugh.

Later on in our marriage this act would not do at all.

A tall black-haired Irishman took us aside as we came into the East Room.

"Pat Moynihan, Labor Department. The President would like to talk to you briefly afterwards, if you don't mind," he bowed with infinite Edwardian courtesy to Rosemarie, "Mrs. O'Malley."

I would learn later that he too was married to a dark-haired, pale-skinned Irish wife and understood the protocols.

"Certainly." Rosemarie bowed back, playing the Queen/Empress role to the hilt.

I decided that I wasn't really needed at the dinner.

"You're the most beautiful woman here," I told her.

"Shush," she whispered back, flushed with pleasure, I would add.

"Best breasts."

"Charles, *please!*" The marine band began to play again. "Now stop ogling and dance with me. That's 'The Tennessee Waltz.' "

"I know what it is."

Not true.

The glitter and the glamour of the night reminded me of Handel or Johann Strauss: music, laughter, clinking glasses, handsome men, beautiful women, sparkling conversation, bright gowns, glowing china and silver—surely an imperial capital.

Then I decided that certainly not in the London of the early Georges and probably not in the Vienna of Franz Joseph had there been so much style and elegance. This was *the* empire.

"What thinking, husband mine?"

"That the little redheaded kid should be on the outside with his nose pressed up against the windowpane."

"Don't be silly." She frowned disapprovingly. "How many times do I have to tell you that you're a genius? You belong here more than most of these people."

I wasn't so sure, but if my Rosemarie believed it, that was probably enough.

It was the night the President, God be good to him, delivered his famous line: "The only time in the history of the White House when there was more talent in this room was on nights when Thomas Jefferson dined by himself."

Pat Moynihan never would admit it, but surely it was his line.

Afterwards we were ushered into the Oval Office for brandy—only the President, Pat, and the two of us.

Rosemarie declined the brandy with a regal smile and a slight wave of her hand.

The President and my wild Irish Rosemarie knew who they were at once. Two splendid Irish monarchs on a state visit to one another. The little red-haired runt was a harmless court jester invited along because he was occasionally amusing.

"I've read your new book on Germany with great interest." The President lit his cigar. "I like the balance and objectivity. It's hard to keep your head screwed on properly when you're talking about our enemies turned allies, isn't it?"

"Yes, Mr. President." I stumbled over the words, "I don't believe in collective guilt, however."

"Neither do I. Well, I suppose you wonder what I want from you? As you know, I've tried to broaden the base of our ambassadorial appointments. There's no reason why we should be limited to business and professional diplomats when there's a lot of other talent in our society, is there?"

I still didn't see what was coming. "Certainly not, Mr. President."

"I've consulted with a number of knowledgeable people"—he riffled a stack of papers on his desk—"and they agree that you are a remarkably gifted and multifaceted man. In addition to what you've accomplished in photography, you've written a brilliant book on the success of the Marshall Plan. So I'm asking you if you would be willing to serve as our ambassador to the Federal Republic of Germany."

Two trains of thought ran through my head, like a dual-track tape playing in a hi-fi system. The first track listed all the reasons to say no: I was too young. I had no experience. I lacked the skills of a diplomat. I was afraid of facing Trudi and Karl again. I was afraid to separate Rosemarie from the help of Dr. Stone. I had five children. I did not want to be an ambassador.

The second track told me that I had already made another serious error in my ongoing comedy.

Do I have to tell you what it was? Of course not.

I was about to politely decline. But before I could speak, Rosemarie intervened, cutting short the words her husband would regret saying for the rest of his life.

"Surely, Mr. President, we'll be honored and delighted to represent you in the BRD." Clancy lowered the boom. Again. With the proper technical name for West Germany. "When do we leave?"

Chicago, Grand Beach, Tucson
1986–1999